"Red Alert!" shouted Lieutenant Sulu's voice over the ship's comm system. "This is not a drill! Repeat: This is not a drill!"

Kirk keyed the intercom. "Kirk here. What is it, Lieutenant?"

The three-sided viewer situated at the center of the table activated, and Sulu's image appeared on all three screens. Kirk could see the agitation on the helm officer's expression, despite the younger man's best efforts to mind his bearing.

"*Sir, some kind of energy beam has locked onto us. Origin point unknown, but it's definitely not the Certoss ship.*"

"All hands to battle stations," Kirk ordered. "Deflector shields to full strength. Stand by all weapons."

"*Shields and weapons are ready, sir, but we have no target. Whatever's generating the beam, it's nowhere in our sensor range. It looks to be a very powerful scanning beam, and its intensity is continuing to increase.*"

The hiss of the briefing room's doors sliding open made Kirk look up, and his eyes widened as he saw not the gray bulkheads of the corridor beyond the entrance, but instead a bright, roiling cloud of blue-black plasma, coalescing as if from the air itself. A high-pitched whine flooded the room, but the cloud seemed to contain itself within the frame of the doorway as it grew larger and brighter.

STAR TREK®

THE ORIGINAL SERIES

FROM HISTORY'S SHADOW

Dayton Ward

Based upon *Star Trek*
created by Gene Roddenberry

POCKET BOOKS
New York London Toronto Sydney New Delhi Certoss Ajahlan

Pocket Books
A Division of Simon & Schuster, Inc.
1230 Avenue of the Americas
New York, NY 10020

This book is a work of fiction. Any references to historical events, real people, or real places are used fictitiously. Other names, characters, places, and events are products of the author's imagination, and any resemblance to actual events or places or persons, living or dead, is entirely coincidental.

This book is published by Pocket Books, a division of Simon & Schuster, Inc., under exclusive license from CBS Studios Inc.

First Pocket Books paperback edition August 2013

POCKET and colophon are registered trademarks of Simon & Schuster, Inc.

Manufactured in the United States of America

10 9 8 7 6 5 4 3 2 1

ISBN 978-1-4767-1900-9
ISBN 978-1-4767-1901-6 (ebook)

For Ira, Robert, Toni, and Jack:
Thanks for making us believe in the "Little Green Men."

Historian's Note

This story begins approximately one week after the return of the *U.S.S. Enterprise* from its time travel mission to 1968 Earth and its encounter with Gary Seven and Roberta Lincoln in the original *Star Trek* episode "Assignment: Earth."

AFTEREFFECTS

ONE

U.S.S. Enterprise
Earth Year 2268 (ACE)

"*General quarters! Intruder alert, Deck 8!*"

James Kirk emerged from the turbolift to find Spock waiting for him. Standing behind the first officer was a four-person security team—three junior officers led by the *Enterprise*'s veteran chief of security, Lieutenant Commander Barry Giotto. Beyond the small group, two more security officers with phasers drawn stood outside the doors at the end of the short corridor.

"They're still in there?" Kirk asked, nodding toward the doors leading to the cargo bay on this deck.

Spock nodded. "Affirmative. Two life-forms. Our internal sensors detected an attempt to access our communications systems."

"We've secured all access points, sir," Giotto added, offering a formal nod that was fitting for his stern expression, which in turn seemed to complement his gray hair, itself a rarity among security officers. "Nobody's getting in or out of there without our knowing about it."

"They managed to sneak in there, well enough," Kirk said. "Any idea how they got aboard in the first place? Have they been here since we left Starbase 9?" The *Enterprise* had been on course for its next assignment since departing the starbase nearly a week earlier. There had been no stops or contacts with other vessels during that time, and—to the best of Kirk's knowledge—the only incoming or outgoing communications were of the usual authorized and expected variety.

Though his expression remained fixed, Spock's eyes narrowed. "Lieutenant Uhura has already dispatched a message to Starbase 9 with a request to inquire into that possibility. A reply should be forthcoming."

"Then I guess we're on our own for the time being." Any discussion about a possible security breach, and whether the intruders hiding within the cargo bay were the only results of that infringement, would have to wait until their uninvited guests were in custody. "What do we know about them?" Kirk asked, gesturing toward the door.

Spock held up his tricorder. "According to my scans, one of the life-forms appears to be female; a native of Certoss Ajahlan."

His brow furrowing, Kirk asked, "That name rings a bell. The Taurus Reach?"

"Correct, sir," replied the first officer. "According to our data banks, the *U.S.S. Endeavour* visited the system during their surveys of the region last year. Prior to that, contact was limited to unmanned probes and a first-contact team when Federation colonization and exploration efforts moved into the Taurus Reach. By all accounts, the Certoss people are peaceful, bordering on pacifistic, and their culture revolves around an ardent devotion to the arts."

"So how does a peaceful Certoss native turn up uninvited in one of our cargo bays?" the captain asked.

Spock's right eyebrow rose. "I am at a loss to answer that, just as I cannot explain why the other intruder is a Vulcan."

That caught Kirk by surprise. "You're sure? Any chance it could be a Romulan?"

"A thorough examination by Doctor McCoy should remove any doubts," Spock said, "but my tricorder readings indicate Vulcan physiology." As though anticipating Kirk's next remark, he added, "The fact that both intruders represent pacifist civilizations is not lost on me, Captain."

"I never thought it was," Kirk said, suppressing a smile before returning his full attention to the very serious matter at hand. "What about their trying to get into the comm system? Do we know who they might be trying to contact?"

Shaking his head, Spock replied, "No, sir. I submit that such questions might best be answered by our guests."

"Agreed. Did you scan any weapons in there?"

"Affirmative." Spock looked at his tricorder again before adding, "It appears to be a rudimentary particle beam weapon."

Pointing to one of Giotto's junior security officers, Kirk indicated for the young crewman to hand over his weapon. He took the Type II phaser and verified its power setting. "Phasers on stun, Mister Giotto. I'll lead the way."

To his credit, the security chief maintained his professional bearing. "Captain, with all due respect, my team and I can secure the room first."

With a small grin, Kirk reached out and clapped the older man on his left shoulder. "You never stop trying to keep me out of trouble, do you, Barry?"

"Mister Spock keeps telling me it's a lost cause, sir," Giotto replied, his expression never wavering.

"Probably true," Kirk said as he began moving toward the cargo bay. He nodded to the pair of security guards still standing watch near the door. Ensigns Nick Minecci and Pasqua Hawthorne both nodded at his approach. Eyeing both junior officers with what he hoped was a look of confidence, Kirk said, "Ready to say hello?"

Minecci nodded, holding up his phaser. "Yes, sir."

"Right behind you, Captain," Hawthorne added.

To Kirk's right, Spock stepped to the nearby comm panel and pressed its activation control. "Spock to bridge. Deactivate the security lock on Cargo Bay 1."

A moment later, Lieutenant Hikaru Sulu's voice replied, "*Aye, aye, Mister Spock. Lock deactivated.*"

Kirk moved to stand to the left of the door, with Giotto mimicking him on the entrance's opposite side. "Alternate entry," he said to the security team. "If you detect a threat, don't hesitate to fire."

The doors parted with their characteristic high-pitched pneumatic hiss, and Kirk got his first look at the chamber beyond. Containers of varying size and shape occupied the space along the far bulkhead, either stacked atop one another on the deck or else stored on shelving units rising three stories to the ceiling. A large expanse of floor right inside the entrance was empty. He scanned the shelves, seeing nothing out of the ordinary, and nothing appeared to be moving among the crates. Once past the doorway, he sidestepped to his left and saw Giotto mirroring his movements as the security chief stepped to his right. At the door, Spock activated his tricorder, and the device's warbling tone echoed through the cavernous bay as the science officer conducted his scans.

"Ten meters in front of us," the Vulcan said, pointing toward the center of the room. "Both life-forms are stationary."

"Whoever you are," Kirk called out, raising his voice, "there's nowhere for you to go. I'm Captain James Kirk, in command of this vessel. If you surrender peacefully, I promise you will not be harmed." When no answer came, Kirk frowned. "Okay," he said, looking to Giotto, "let's go."

Following Spock's direction, Kirk moved toward the center of the room, his phaser leading the way. As he approached the set of stacked cargo containers separating him from their still-unidentified guests, he motioned for Giotto to make his way around the far side of the storage units. Even without Spock's tricorder, Kirk now was able to sense the intruder's presence. He heard breathing and the rustling of clothing. Muscles tensing in anticipation of a confrontation if not a full-blown firefight, Kirk stepped around the stacked containers and leveled his phaser at the figure standing in the open. It was the Vulcan, who appeared flushed and disheveled. At his feet lay what could only be the particle weapon detected by Spock's tricorder.

"That is my only weapon," he said, standing in place and holding his hands away from his body. "I am not a threat. It is my counterpart who should concern you."

Before Kirk could ask what that meant, Spock called out, "Captain, the Certoss life sign has disappeared."

What?

"Captain!" shouted a voice, Giotto's, from the stack of crates to his right.

The call was followed by the sounds of scuffling and fighting. Kirk began moving in that direction, catching sight of Ensigns Minecci and Hawthorne. "Watch him!" Kirk ordered before darting between a pair of cargo containers, following the sounds of struggle until he saw Giotto flung backward into one of the larger crates. The security chief grunted in pain as he struck the oversized, unyielding box, and it was only then that Kirk realized Giotto no longer held his phaser.

"He's got Giotto's weapon!" Kirk warned the rest of his people as he lunged forward, stepping around another stack of containers and catching sight of the dark figure trying to hide among another freight consignment. Kirk's eyes registered the phaser in the intruder's hand even before the weapon's emitter moved to aim at him.

Kirk fired first.

His phaser's harsh blue-white beam sliced the air, catching the stowaway in his chest and sending him tumbling backward to the deck. "He's down!" Kirk called, stepping toward the stunned intruder while keeping his phaser trained on him.

You mean her.

Though humanoid, the Certoss's skin possessed a pigmentation that resembled copper. There was no hair on her head, and Kirk noted the three long fingers and what appeared to be two opposing thumbs on each hand. She was dressed from neck to toe in a dark gray skin-tight bodysuit. As Giotto moved into view, one hand rubbing the back of his neck as he retrieved his phaser from the Certoss, Kirk asked, "Are you all right?"

"My pride hurts worse than anything else, sir," replied the security chief. "I don't know where she came from. One second I was alone, the next she was in my face."

"Spock said something about her life signs disappearing from his tricorder scan," Kirk said. "Maybe she's got some kind of personal cloak or shield."

Pointing to the odd device the Certoss intruder wore strapped to her chest, Giotto said, "Could be this thing. I've never seen anything like it."

"We'll have Spock and Scotty give it the once-over." Hearing footsteps behind him, Kirk turned to see Spock with Minecci and Hawthorne, escorting the Vulcan intruder.

"I regret trespassing aboard your vessel, Captain," the Vulcan said, indicating the motionless Certoss. "It was unintentional, I assure you; a consequence of my pursuing this individual."

It took Kirk an extra moment to realize that the trespasser's clothing was not typical Vulcan civilian attire. Instead, it consisted of black trousers and a matching jacket worn over a white shirt with a length of black ribbon hanging from his neck. Kirk recognized it as a business suit, of the sort he had seen less than a week ago.

On Earth. Three hundred years ago?

Kirk looked to Ensign Minecci, who had moved to cover the fallen Certoss. "Minecci, alert sickbay. Tell Doctor McCoy he may need to provide medical treatment for a female Certoss native."

"Aye, sir," the ensign replied before stepping back from the Certoss and disappearing between the stacks of crates.

For the first time, Kirk lowered his phaser as he regarded the Vulcan. "Who are you, and how'd you get aboard my ship? And while you're at it, perhaps you'll tell me why you're wearing clothing that's three centuries out of date and from my planet instead of yours."

"Three centuries," the Vulcan repeated. "Interesting. It is your contention that you traveled through time to Earth, and that we are now in what would be my future?"

Kirk nodded. "That's right." Then, it occurred to him that until this very moment, he had failed to consider one very obvious possibility. "Did you somehow get aboard while we were back in Earth's past?" Of course, even as he spoke the words, he realized he was prompting more questions than answers. "What were you even *doing* on Earth, anyway?"

"My name is Mestral," the Vulcan replied, "and though

I did not board your ship while you were visiting Earth, that is where I came from. As measured on your planet, I had been there for more than a decade." He gestured to the unconscious Certoss. "My unlikely travel companion has been living there even longer, though her motives were quite different than mine. Whereas I was content to live in peace among your people, she and others of her kind were working to bring about your world's destruction." Then, as he was about to say something else, he paused, and Kirk saw the slight change in his expression as the Vulcan's gaze shifted. Kirk turned to see Spock standing behind him.

"Fascinating," said the science officer before he stepped forward. "Were you acting against her?"

Mestral's eyes narrowed. "In a manner of speaking. I was . . . assisting in a clandestine effort to locate and neutralize the Certoss agents before they could put their plans into motion."

"You mean Gary Seven?" Kirk asked, his recent encounter with the mysterious, genetically advanced human operating on twentieth-century Earth still fresh in his mind.

"I only recently became familiar with that name, Captain, though I have never interacted with that person. I suspect that any explanation I provide regarding my time on your planet will perhaps be difficult to accept." Was it Kirk's imagination, or did he detect the hint of a smile on the Vulcan's face? "I imagine it also will take considerable time."

"Then I suggest we get started," Kirk said, "because I for one can't wait to hear what you have to say."

But I'm betting I'm not going to like it.

TWO

Holding the piece of unfamiliar technology so that he could examine it with his own eyes, Montgomery Scott saw nothing that his tricorder and other diagnostic instruments had not already told him.

"It's a transmitter of some kind, Mister Spock," he said after a moment, setting the article down on the worktable in his office. "So far as I can tell, it's not even capable of receiving any sort of signal; only sending one, and even then it couldn't broadcast very far on its own." He pointed to a small protrusion on the device's face. "This is what passes for an antenna. Very small, but fairly powerful, and likely capable of linking with any larger communications network within its broadcast range, so long as the interface protocols can be worked out."

"The Certoss intruder was working to connect to a communications terminal in the Cargo Bay 1 operations office," Spock said. "It was this tampering and the device's own energy source that Lieutenant Uhura detected from the bridge."

"This thing would need a larger communications array to work, but even then, its capabilities look pretty limited." Scott shrugged. "To me, it looks like it might be a distress beacon of some kind."

Spock, standing next to him at the table with his hands clasped behind his back, asked, "But most of its components are not of Certoss origin?"

Scott frowned as he shook his head. "That's what's bugging me about this, sir. This thing has been cobbled together with parts from several different pieces of twentieth-century technology, plus a few bits that couldn't have come from that time period, but neither are they exactly consistent with what we know of Certoss technology." Shrugging, he added, "Of course, I've only had time for a quick review of the data we have on Certoss Ajahlan, but so far, what I'm finding here doesn't line up." The discrepancies had bothered him throughout his examination of the odd items taken from the Certoss intruder, who now resided in the *Enterprise* brig.

"I shall conduct a more thorough review of the relevant library computer entries," Spock said, before gesturing to the other item on the table. "And what of this device?"

"Definitely not a product of twentieth-century Earth technology, though it does contain some components that fit the time frame. From the looks of it, those parts were used to effect repairs of one sort or another."

During the *Enterprise*'s recent time travel mission to observe Earth's people and events taking place three hundred years ago, Scott had taken advantage of the opportunity to conduct sensor scans in an attempt to learn more about the technology of the era. Of course, much of that research had been set aside when the *Enterprise* crew became entangled in the activities of Gary Seven. He was one of a small group of genetically enhanced humans placed on Earth throughout the twentieth and twenty-first centuries by a still-unknown alien cooperative with a mission, as Seven had explained it, "to prevent Earth's civilization from destroying itself before it can mature into a peaceful society." Still, the ship's computer had collected and stored the data, of which Scott so far had accomplished only a cursory review.

"Interesting," Spock said, inspecting the odd device for himself. Activating his tricorder, he waved it over the unidentified item. "Its internal power source and transmission array are not intended for any sort of long-range broadcast."

"From what I can tell," Scott replied, crossing his arms, "it's not meant to emit anything much farther than the body of the person wearing it. This has to be what that Certoss lass used to mask her life signs, but beats me how the bloody thing works. I tried to activate it, but it's not having any of that. The same goes for the transmitter, if that's what it is. I guess we'll have to ask their owner about them."

Spock nodded. "Indeed." A beep from his tricorder as he continued to scan the alien devices seemed to catch his attention, and Scott noted the barest change in the Vulcan's expression as he consulted the unit. "My scan appears to have found something unusual with the transmitter." He adjusted a control on the tricorder and repeated the scan. "It is emanating a multi-phasic power reading."

"What?" Scott asked. How had he missed something like that? "Are you sure?"

"Affirmative," replied the first officer. "I am not surprised that your instruments failed to register it. My tricorder is programmed to detect a much broader spectrum of readings than your diagnostic tools." Then, as though realizing he may have said something a human might find inappropriate, he looked up from his tricorder. "It was not my intention to impugn your skills, Mister Scott."

The chief engineer smiled. "Worry not, sir. However, I wouldn't mind you having a look at my scanners. Maybe you can give them the same bit of adjusting you've obviously given your tricorder." He nodded to the Certoss transmitter. "After we figure out this wee beastie, though."

Handing Scott his tricorder, Spock said, "If you'd please monitor these readings while I attempt an adjustment." He reached across the table and retrieved the multi-phasic transducer from Scott's diagnostic kit, adjusting the compact unit's power setting before aiming it at the Certoss device. The chief engineer studied the tricorder's display screen as Spock worked, noting the fluctuations as the transducer went about its work. Then, the tricorder beeped at the same time Spock nodded in apparent approval.

"That should prove sufficient," the Vulcan said. "If we can activate it, we should be able to gain a better understanding of its functionality before we risk allowing it to transmit."

The device, with no assistance from Spock or Scott, chose that moment to activate of its own accord.

"What the devil?" Scott asked, flinching in response to the shrill beeps the device emitted.

Retrieving his tricorder, Spock said, "The unit has acquired a connection with our communications system and is transmitting some form of encrypted burst data packet."

Scott grabbed the device and pressed each of the buttons on its recessed control pad, and a moment later the electronic litany ceased. "Irritating little bugger."

"*Bridge to engineering!*" called the voice of Ensign Chekov, filtered through the intercom system. "*Mister Spock, our sensors have just detected a subspace burst transmission originating from your location!*"

Stunned by the report, Scott almost felt his jaw go slack. "Subspace? That whole array is under constant security lockout. How in the name of William Wallace was this thing able to do that? It couldn't possibly be that sophisticated."

"I don't believe it is," Spock said, taking the device from Scott and eyeing it with his hard, dark eyes. "All that would be required was the interface protocol. As intriguing as this unit's capabilities may be, however, I'm afraid we face a more pressing question."

"Aye," Scott said, nodding in comprehension. "We need to find out who's on the receiving end of that message."

Kirk took a seat at the briefing room's table across from Mestral. A pair of security guards, Ensigns Minecci and Hawthorne, stood to either side of the doorway leading from the room, but the Vulcan wore no restraints. A glass of water sat untouched on the table. Doctor McCoy had given Mestral a physical and found him to be in good health, and the mysterious guest even had accepted the physician's offer of a meal prior to being brought here.

"I trust you're being treated well," Kirk said by way of greeting.

Nodding, Mestral replied, "Yes, Captain. Thank you." He sat with his hands clasped and resting on the table before him, ramrod straight in his chair. His expression, of course, betrayed nothing, though his eyes tracked Kirk's every movement.

Kirk glanced to the guards at the door. "I apologize for the security, but until we can corroborate your story, I hope you'll appreciate the need for caution."

"Given the circumstances," Mestral said, "anything less would be imprudent and illogical. Rest assured, Captain, that despite the years I have spent living among humans and after acquiring several of your people's habits, I have not yet learned to take offense even when none is intended."

The chuckle Kirk almost released was interrupted by the door opening to admit Spock, who settled himself in the seat closest to the computer interface terminal at the head of the table. Kirk watched as the science officer, who had been carrying a pair of computer data cards, inserted one of the cards into the terminal's reader slot.

"I have run a check against Vulcan Science Academy computer records," Spock said, turning his chair to face the group, "and there was a Vulcan crewmember named Mestral assigned to a survey ship that conducted a reconnaissance mission of Earth during the twentieth century. That ship crash-landed in 1957 in a sparsely populated area of North America, which at the time was referred to as 'Pennsylvania.' According to Academy records, two of the four crewmembers were later rescued, but Mestral was reported as having died along with the ship's commander in the crash."

Mestral nodded as he listened to Spock's report. "T'Mir agreed to file that report on my behalf. As I never again encountered anyone from my home planet, I assumed that her explanation was accepted without incident, and the matter closed."

"Other Vulcan ships did visit Earth in the years following your landing," Spock said, "though a review of survey records filed by those vessels' commanders reveals no further mention of your name." Turning to Kirk, he added, "Captain, it's worth noting that I did not offer any information from my review to Mestral prior to this meeting, though he correctly named the female Vulcan who was rescued from Earth in 1958."

"The other surviving member of our crew was named Stron," Mestral offered.

Kirk asked, "What made you decide to stay on Earth?"

For the first time, Mestral reached for the nearby glass of water and took a sip before answering. "During the three months that transpired between our crash and the rescue ship arriving at Earth to retrieve us and what remained of our vessel, I had become . . . accustomed to living among humans." His expression seemed to soften. "I had always been intrigued by your planet and its people, Captain. Our study of humans to that point led us to believe that your species was on the verge of numerous societal and technological advancements. The development of nuclear energy in particular was something of interest and concern to us, as we did not yet know if such progress might herald a new age of discovery and exploration or the utter destruction of your world."

"A bit of both, actually," Kirk said. "We know that Vulcans were observing Earth for decades before—" He stopped himself, his expression growing sheepish. "I'm sorry, Mestral, but I almost revealed information pertaining to events that for you haven't yet taken place."

"I understand, Captain," the Vulcan replied. Looking to Spock, he added, "It is good to see that relations between our two peoples appear to have grown and strengthened in the time you say has passed. As for time travel, in my century, researchers and other subject matter experts at the Vulcan Science Academy maintained that was impossible. My encounters with Gejalik and her fellow Certoss have shown me a very different perspective."

"The Academy was forced to reevaluate its stance in light of certain incidents and other occurrences that have taken place since your time," Spock said. "Though not at all common, time travel has been achieved using various methods, none of which are easily duplicated."

Leaning forward, Kirk rested his elbows on the conference table. "What about this Gejalik and the other Certoss agents operating on Earth in your time?" he asked, realizing as he did so how strange the question sounded, directed as it was to Mestral. "How did they come to be there?"

"Some form of temporal displacement technology on their homeworld, Captain," the Vulcan replied, "though I never did ascertain much in the way of relevant data regarding any such mechanism."

Kirk asked, "How were they able to blend in with the human population? Vulcans, at least superficially, can pass for human well enough. That is, so long as no one takes a serious interest in you, but the Certoss? Did they use harnesses like the one she was wearing to appear human?"

Mestral nodded. "It essentially is a form of holographic projection system, allowing the wearer to present whatever outward appearance is desired, or even render themselves invisible. From what I have observed, the most common use for the device is to simulate the appearance of other living beings. It includes within its framework a universal translation device that enables the wearer to further blend in with another species, provided it has been programmed with the necessary languages."

Spock said, "Mestral, when you were captured, you said that the Certoss agents were working to effect humanity's destruction. This behavior, along with the technology they appeared to employ, is very much at odds with what we know of the Certoss people."

His brow furrowing, Mestral shook his head. "I am unable to explain that discrepancy, Commander. I can offer only my testimony based on what I witnessed, and the actions I took to prevent them from achieving their goal. Once the Certoss agents realized we might well defeat them, they worked to summon assistance."

"The signal sent by the transmitter was aimed at the Certoss system, Captain," Spock said. "It used our subspace array to dispatch its burst packet."

Mestral replied, "That was always a goal of the Certoss agents. Though they have proven quite resourceful at adapting to the limitations of technology available to them, those restrictions prevented any such realistic attempt at contacting their homeworld. At least, not until they discovered the presence of your ship in orbit."

"How were they able to accomplish this?" Spock asked.

"As I said, Commander," Mestral replied, "they were restricted; not powerless. They were able to construct a device that allowed them to scan Earth orbit for the presence of space vessels, perhaps with the goal of exploiting any ship or opportunity that made itself available. I was pursuing Gejalik when I discovered she had learned of this ship. I cannot be sure, but I believe her original plan was to come aboard prior to your departure, but when that proved impossible, she . . . devised another course of action. I caught up to her, but was unable to apprehend her before we both were transported here."

Kirk asked, "What about the equipment used to bring you here?"

"I am unable to speak to its capabilities," Mestral replied. "When I found Gejalik, she had infiltrated an office building in New York City that contained a collection of advanced computer and other equipment, very much out of place with respect to the human technology of the time."

"Mister Seven's office," Spock said.

Mestral turned his attention to the first officer. "As I said before, I am not familiar with that individual, nor do I have any idea how any of the equipment operated, but I would have welcomed the opportunity to study it in detail."

"You mentioned others with whom you were working," Spock said. "After your arrival, you presumably elected to keep your identity a secret, but later partnered with what you described as a 'clandestine organization' with the goal of preventing Earth's destruction?"

Mestral paused for another drink of water before saying, "I do not believe the organization with which I found myself began with that particular goal, but it became one of its paramount concerns as years passed." Eyeing the two *Enterprise* officers, he added, "Perhaps it would be helpful if I recounted the entire story of my activities on your world."

Kirk grunted. "I imagine it's quite the eye-opener."

"An apt description, as I understand the term, Captain," Mestral said. "What you may well find even more startling to know is that the relevant events begin several years before my arrival on your planet."

BEGINNINGS

THREE

Wright Field, Dayton, Ohio
September 23, 1947 (ACE)

Another day, another office in the backyard of nowhere.

Sitting in the steel chair with its cracked cushion behind a worn wooden desk that was lacking the bottom file drawer on its right side, Captain James Wainwright took a long drag on his cigarette and wondered who he might have angered. He watched the smoke trailing from his cigarette to the ceiling, noting the visible water damage staining a few of the tiles. The rest of the room was an unimpressive affair; the cinder-block walls were painted a light gray and featured an assortment of nails which once had held pictures or art or whatever else the office's prior occupant had chosen for the workspace. A black phone, a dull metal ashtray, and nothing else adorned the desktop. Along the wall opposite Wainwright's desk was a set of five metal cabinets, which to him looked as though they might have been rescued from disposal mere moments before his arrival. Three of the cabinets were black, the others gray like his chair and walls, and all of them scuffed, scratched, and dented. Morning sunlight filtered through dusty blinds that were hanging before the pair of single-pane windows, which were the most interesting feature of the office's rear wall. Wainwright glanced through the windows, which faced west, and noted the looming line of storm clouds darkening the horizon beyond the other buildings and hangars within view.

"There's an omen," he said to no one, switching the cigarette to his left hand before reaching for the mug of steaming coffee sitting on the desk. It was the only breakfast he had managed to acquire since being directed to this office by the hapless sergeant on duty in the building's main lobby. It would have to do until such time as somebody told him why he was here, who had summoned him, and why everything surrounding his presence at Wright was, apparently, a big damned secret. He sighed as he drank his coffee, looking once more to his reflection in the full-length mirror mounted on the wall to his right. His blond hair, which he kept closely trimmed because he felt it looked better with his balding dome, was looking a little long. He had not had time for a haircut; in accordance with the orders given to him the previous day, Wainwright had caught the first available flight from Roswell Air Force Base—Roswell Army Air Field until its renaming less than a week ago. A bumpy ride aboard a C-47 Skytrain transport from Roswell had seen to it that he arrived at Wright Field just in time to catch a fitful few hours' sleep in the visiting officers' quarters, with instructions waiting for him in his room to report to this particular nondescript office building at 0700 hours.

Glancing first at his wristwatch and then the clock on the wall above the office door, Wainwright verified that it was, in fact, 0748 hours. Less than a minute later there was a knock on the door, and he rose to his feet as a man dressed in a dark suit entered the room. Wainwright recognized him at once.

"Professor Carlson?" he asked, his eyes narrowing in confusion. "What the hell are *you* doing here?" As Wainwright recalled, Jeffrey Carlson was in his late thirties, though he seemed to have aged several years since their last meeting following a mysterious event the military was striving to keep secret, but which already was being referred to in some public circles as "the Roswell Incident." Carlson looked tired, with bags under his blue eyes, though the eyes themselves still harbored that spark of intelligence and awareness Wainwright remembered.

"Good to see you, too, Captain," Carlson said, smiling as he extended his hand.

Wainwright nodded, taking the proffered hand. "I have to say, Professor, that you're the last person I expected to see here, of all places."

"I know you've got a lot of questions," the professor replied, "and I'm sorry about how you were sent out here. I trust the flight wasn't too bad?"

"So, you've got something to do with bringing me here?"

Carlson smiled again. "I'm afraid so." He gestured for Wainwright to retake his seat behind the desk before retrieving one of the straight-backed chairs from the table by the windows. "When I was briefed into my own assignment here, you were one of the first people I thought would make a good addition to the group." Turning the chair so it faced away from Wainwright's desk, he straddled it and laid his forearms along the top of its backrest. "We didn't get to talk too much about what happened at Roswell, did we? Then everything was classified top secret, and nobody was talking about it at all. Let me ask you something, Jim: What do you think the United States should be doing now that we know, without any doubts, that there are beings from other worlds with an apparent interest in Earth?"

As far as Wainwright could remember, Carlson never had referred to him by anything other than his rank and last name. In truth, they had never had much interaction at all, until that fateful day back in early July when an honest-to-goodness spacecraft from another planet crash-landed near Roswell, New Mexico. The craft and its occupants, three odd beings who identified themselves as "Ferengi," had at first attempted to negotiate opening some kind of new trade market here on Earth. The alien in charge, who called himself Quark, had offered to Wainwright's superior, Lieutenant General Rex Denning, the chance for humanity to acquire all manner of advanced scientific and other technological knowledge. Denning, to his credit, had remained suspicious of the aliens from the beginning, skeptical of their intentions right up until the moment they escaped custody, retrieved their spacecraft, and disappeared back to the stars from whence they had come.

Reclining in his chair, Wainwright fished the pack of cigarettes from his shirt pocket and offered a smoke to Carlson before taking a fresh one for himself. "To be honest, Professor, I'm torn on the whole thing. On the one hand, I thought we had a chance to learn from the Ferengi. Remember what the one, Quark, was telling General Denning? Our own spaceships, machines that create food out of thin air, weapons? It all sounded too good to be true." He paused, flipping open the stainless steel lighter he had pulled from his trouser pocket and lighting his cigarette before passing the lighter to Carlson. "How much of that was just lies to cover up their invasion plans? You remember what that other Ferengi, Nog, said, right? That we're 'ripe for conquest'? Well, if that's the case, then I figure we need to be doing everything we can to make sure we're ready when that invasion fleet of theirs decides to come for us."

Carlson took a long pull of his cigarette and blew a stream of smoke into the air above his head. "I still think that story of theirs about an invasion fleet is crap, but I can't rule it out. Besides, even if that Ferengi might've been screwing with us, some other bunch of aliens from a whole other planet might well be gunning for us. In fact, there are people in Washington who think this kind of thing has been going on for years. Remember the brouhaha back in thirty-eight, when that radio show ran a fake broadcast pretending to be an invasion from Mars?"

"You mean *The War of the Worlds*?" Wainwright had not heard the broadcast, but he had read about the national reaction in the following day's newspaper. "I remember. It was a dumb stunt."

Shaking his head, Carlson smiled. "There are those who think the fake radio-show story was just a cover-up for someone finding a real alien ship."

"Come on." Wainwright shook his head in disbelief. "That's crazy."

Carlson shrugged. "Granted, there's never been any proof. Then again, nobody's got any proof about what happened at Roswell, either. Still, plans for what to do if Martians or somebody else comes calling have been in motion for some time, but they really started heating up after Roswell. That's why I'm here, and why you're here."

Wainwright stopped himself from taking another drag of his cigarette as he regarded the professor. "What are you talking about?"

"The National Security Act signed by President Truman last week?" Carlson asked. "The one creating the National Military Establishment and making the Air Force its own branch of the military? Well, buried deep in all of that red tape is another project with a simple, twofold mission: seek out any and all evidence of extraterrestrial activity on Earth, and develop strategies to combat any aliens who are proven to pose a threat. The group's code name is Majestic 12, or MJ-12 for short. Officially, it doesn't exist, but as of 0700 hours this morning, you're a part of it." Sticking his cigarette in his mouth, he extended his hand to Wainwright. "Welcome aboard."

Caught off guard by this revelation as he shook Carlson's hand for a second time, Wainwright was unsure what to say. During their joint time at Roswell, particularly during the incident involving the three aliens, he figured the professor believed him to be little more than a typical brainwashed military robot, incapable of exercising any thoughts not already programmed into him by his superiors. In truth, Wainwright had not been very impressed with Carlson's behavior during the Ferengi affair. Part of him still believed the civilian and his fiancée, a nurse with the Air Corps—now the Air Force—named Faith Garland, had helped the aliens to escape. Despite Carlson's insistence that they had been manipulated by the Ferengi's so-called "insidious mind-control powers," Wainwright still harbored suspicions that the professor and his fiancée had acted of their own free will. Both Carlson and Garland had struck him as naïve in their hopes and beliefs that the aliens had come in peace rather than with conquest in mind.

"I know what you're thinking," Carlson said, as though he indeed possessed the ability to read Wainwright's thoughts. "You're still wondering what might really have happened with me and Faith back at Roswell. The truth is I really don't know what to think about the Ferengi, whether they were yanking our chains or if they were a scouting party for some kind of invasion fleet. My gut tells me those three weren't a threat to anybody, but this project is bigger than that. Much bigger."

Wainwright leaned forward, reaching to stub out his cigarette in the ashtray sitting on the desk between them. "So, what is it I'm supposed to be doing?"

"Initially, you'll be working with me," Carlson replied. "Our primary job at this point is to investigate reports of any unidentified craft. Since Roswell, there's been a surge in reports of people seeing flying saucers all over the place. We'll conduct interviews, gather any evidence that might present itself, and go from there."

"Evidence?" Wainwright asked, frowning. Though originally a skeptic so far as the existence of beings from other worlds was concerned, Roswell had made him a believer. That did not mean he would accept without strict scrutiny anything presented to him as proof of extraterrestrials.

Carlson nodded. "A few of the reports we've received have included photographs of strange flying objects, or figures the witness purports to be aliens. Most of the pictures I've seen are terrible—out of focus, bad exposure, double exposure, whatever—but a few of them will definitely get your attention, Jim. There may be other evidence, too, of a sort similar to what our Ferengi friends had."

That indeed got Wainwright's undivided attention. "What? You mean ships, or other technology?"

Shrugging, Carlson stood up from his chair. "I don't know for sure, yet. The top brass is being very tight-lipped until we get our team together and organized. You probably already know that everything we do here, every last thing we see, hear, read, or talk about, is classified top secret, Jim. Not a breath about anything to anyone."

"What about my wife?" Wainwright asked. "I wasn't able to tell her a damned thing before I left Roswell yesterday. What's my cover story?"

"All of that will be given to you," the professor replied. "Everything will be handled. Arrangements are already being made for your family here. You'll move them just like any other change of assignment. So far as anyone not affiliated with the project is concerned, you'll just be another officer with duties requiring frequent travel. The Air Force is chock-full of men and women just like that. You'll blend in fine."

The decree that he would, in essence, be forced to lie to his wife, Deborah, as part of the normal consequences of his job at first troubled Wainwright, but he comforted himself with the knowledge that it would not be the first time duty had made such demands on him. During the war, the months leading up to Operation Overlord had been fraught with secrecy, with the success of the entire campaign hinging on the allies' ability to keep even the slightest hint of its planning and preparation from making its way to the Germans. Likewise, the American development of atomic weapons also had been conceived and carried out in near-total isolation, with no one suspecting the mammoth, even horrifying results of that endeavor until one fateful August morning in 1945 in the sky above the now-devastated Japanese city of Hiroshima. Keeping secrets, Wainwright knew, even from his own wife, was just part of the job.

The idea of refusing this assignment—if indeed that even was an option—was laughable. For Wainwright, this was the job of a career, or a lifetime, even if everything he did or saw while attached to this new project—Majestic 12—never was revealed to the public. This was important; it was historic, and here he was, James Wainwright, at the beginning of it all.

"Tell me something, Professor," he said after a moment. "What do you think we'll really find? I mean, once we start digging, what are you hoping for?"

Pursing his lips, Carlson pondered the question for several seconds before answering. "You mean do I hope we find friends out there, with all manner of advanced technology they're willing to share with us? Absolutely." Sighing, he took one last puff on his cigarette, watching the smoke swirling above him before crushing the butt in the ashtray. "But if there are enemies out there looking to kick our asses? Then, yeah, I want to be ready for that, too."

FOUR

Muroc, California
October 15, 1947

With his back to the wall in the corner booth of Jack's Roadside Diner, Adlar divided his attention among the other patrons, the door, and the two-lane highway beyond the restaurant's gravel parking lot. Only the occasional passing car disrupted the otherwise tranquil scene of the arid, barren terrain bordering the western edge of Muroc Army Air Field. Dust from a car leaving the diner was carried on the slight breeze, adding new layers of grime to the other vehicles scattered across the lot. Inside the restaurant was a mix of men and women, many of them dressed in military uniforms. There were a few examples of men dressed in clothing denoting some form of social or financial stature, but to Adlar, most of the diner's other patrons appeared to represent various forms of labor-intensive if not outright servile endeavor. Listening to several of the conversations taking place at other tables, Adlar heard more than one person complaining about the heat. He found the warm temperatures here rather comfortable, given the similarity to the climate on his home planet.

The various, competing odors of fried, boiled, and grilled foodstuffs filled the air inside the diner. It had taken some time for him and his companions to acclimate themselves to the numerous forms of human sustenance. Even now, three years after their arrival, Adlar and the others still relied upon the nutritional supplements that were part of the equipment and supplies brought with them to Earth. Still, Adlar had acquired a taste for a broad spectrum of Earth-centric cuisines. Careful scans of some of the meals he had prepared using native ingredients had yielded an interesting, often humorous and sometimes frightening array of information regarding the different foods' dietary usefulness. To his occasional amusement, Adlar was forced to admit to the odd contrast between a particular item's taste and its worth with respect to his health. One food in particular, bacon, had become a personal indulgence during his time on Earth, yet appeared to contain no discernible nutritional value.

As his waitress—a middle-aged, bored-looking female with the name "Maxine" stitched on her blue shirt—delivered a plate containing eggs, toast, and bacon, Adlar's attention was drawn to the diner's front door. He looked over to see his companion, Gejalik, entering the diner. Like him, and thanks to her own mobile camouflage emitter, she was able to effect an outward human appearance. In keeping with her current cover identity, Gejalik presented herself as a human female. Her long brunette hair was pulled back and secured in a ponytail, and she wore a conservative gray skirt and white silk blouse. The heels of her shoes clicked on the diner's tile floor as she approached, before she slid into the booth to sit across from him.

"You're late," Adlar said by way of greeting, the subcutaneous translator inserted beneath the skin of his throat rendering his speech in flawless human English.

Gejalik nodded. "I know. I wasn't able to leave the office until the colonel returned from his staff briefing. Things are very busy on the base."

"I can imagine," Adlar replied as he picked up one of his utensils and began partaking of his breakfast. The simple act of holding and using the implement had required practice in order for him to appear natural while eating in public, but after this much time spent among humans, such things now were second nature. "What are they saying?"

The previous day had brought with it an impressive feat, at least so far as measured by the current level of human technological advancement. An experimental aircraft guided by a human pilot had accelerated to heretofore unattainable speeds, traveling faster than sound itself. Though pre-mission briefings regarding Earth's supposed "normal" timeline provided him with historical facts surrounding the prior day's events, Adlar still wished he could have witnessed it for himself.

"Despite the inconsequential nature of the accomplishment, the military leaders are very proud of themselves," Gejalik said, keeping her voice low so as to avoid being overheard by other diner patrons.

Adlar frowned. "It's not inconsequential when viewed in the proper context. You're forgetting where these people are, technologically. They've barely taken their first steps toward the future you and I take for granted."

For the first time since her arrival, Gejalik smiled, an expression Adlar found appealing on her human façade. "You always seem to be defending them."

Shaking his head, Adlar countered, "I don't defend them. I prefer to view such things with the correct perspective. Think of our home planet, and where our people are, technologically and socially, at this precise point in time. One could argue that Earth in many ways is currently on par with if not superior to Certoss Ajahlan as it exists in this era."

He could see that his remarks, as often happened when he spoke in this fashion, were beginning to irritate his companion. Perhaps she wondered or worried that expressing such views suggested he might not be up to the task they had been given. Even with the obstacles that had arisen since their arrival on Earth, Adlar never had wavered from their mission. One could still admire a civilization, he felt, even while working to bring about its eventual destruction.

It was not the primary mission to which he and Gejalik along with their two companions, Jaecz and Etlun, had been assigned by their military superiors on Certoss Ajahlan. Instead, they originally were to have been part of a larger effort to disrupt the efforts here on Earth of the Na'khul, a rival race that had become an enemy of the Certoss people as a consequence of the Temporal Cold War. That conflict, waged across time itself and all but consuming numerous civilizations, was being fought on multiple fronts spanning centuries. Earth at this point in its nascent history had been one of those fronts, though not of its people's own design. According to the briefings provided to Adlar and his companions prior to setting out on their mission, the Na'khul had inserted themselves into a global conflict that had been raging here. Working in secret, Na'khul operatives undertook several actions to alter key events in the war's earliest days, along with providing advanced technology in order to favor one of the smaller, more militaristic nation-states.

Though the Certoss had fought a largely defensive action during the temporal campaigns, there were occasions where more aggressive tactics had been required. Earth presented one such example in the eyes of Certoss government and military leaders who had come to know that—either because of or in spite of Na'khul interference in its history—humanity would develop to a point of technological advancement that ultimately presented a direct threat to the Certoss people. War between the two civilizations would result in the fall of Certoss Ajahlan. For obvious reasons, that could not be allowed to happen. Thwarting the Na'khul's efforts here on Earth was a logical first step toward preventing any future conflicts between humans and the Certoss.

Fate, it seemed, had other ideas.

Waiting until the waitress took her order and moved on to assist diners at another table, Gejalik asked in a low voice, "Has there been any new contact from Jaecz?"

"No," Adlar replied, "not since his letter." He retrieved an envelope from his jacket's interior pocket. Inside were two sheets of folded paper filled with handwritten script in Jaecz's home language. Though he understood most of the passages, a few words or phrases still required additional scrutiny. Adlar, like Gejalik, had grown up speaking, reading, and writing a different language, only later learning his friend's native tongue. "I've found nothing in any of the avenues we established for exchanging communication. Jaecz has not attempted contact in more than three months."

"I wonder if he found anything at that base in New Mexico."

"Whatever was there," Adlar said, pausing to verify that no eavesdroppers might be lurking within hearing range, "the Air Force has since taken to denying everything."

In his own capacity, using one of his human personas in order to pose as an intelligence officer in the United States Army, Adlar had determined that an unidentified craft had crashed three months earlier in the desert near Roswell, New Mexico. The events that had transpired in the immediate aftermath were the focus of much speculation, given the military's initial reporting of the crash and the subsequent retraction of their statements to that effect. Rumors abounded about the recovery of an extraterrestrial vessel along with other artifacts of technology and even the bodies of the ship's dead occupants. As to the craft's present location, Adlar's surreptitious investigation had determined that if it did exist, it no longer was at Roswell but instead had been transported to some other, undisclosed location.

"Perhaps Jaecz was captured or killed," Gejalik said. The waitress had deposited a cup of coffee for her, but it sat untouched. Unlike Adlar, she was far more discerning with respect to human cuisine, instead preferring organic foods eaten without much in the way of preparation.

Adlar nodded. "I considered that possibility and even attempted to investigate it. I found nothing to indicate he's been taken into human custody." Such a report, like the Roswell Incident, would without doubt attract all manner of attention throughout the ranks of the American government's intelligence community. "Wherever he is, it's more probable that he's simply gone into hiding. Maybe he's even trying to make his way to us. I've left messages, letting him know we'll be staying here, at least for now."

Eyeing the coffee before pushing it away from her, Gejalik released a small sigh. "It's a pity we couldn't confirm the existence of the spacecraft. Accessing its communications systems alone could have proven worthwhile."

"Indeed," Adlar replied, nodding in agreement.

It had been his hope that such a vessel might provide them with a means of contacting their homeworld. There had been no interaction with their superiors or any other member of their race since arriving on Earth three years earlier and after having traveled across time more than five hundred years. The communications equipment they had brought with them for that purpose, modified to interface with the temporal displacement apparatus that had transported them here, had failed to make contact across the centuries. No malfunction or other fault had been found in the device itself, leading Adlar and the others to believe something must be amiss either with the other apparatus, or else some other, larger, and as yet unknown issue had manifested itself. Adlar's main concern with any situation on Certoss Ajahlan was similar to what he and the others faced here, as the mission for which they had trained seemed at odds with the current reality.

Arriving on Earth in what on the humans' calendar was the year 1944, Adlar and his fellow operatives had found no sign either of the Na'khul agents or their influence on the massive conflict that had been dubbed "the Second World War." Rather than being dominated by the nation-states of Germany and Japan, the United States and its allies instead were on the offensive against both enemy powers, in keeping with the planet's allegedly "correct" timeline.

A massive invasion of the European continent had forced the German military toward ultimate defeat, followed mere months later by Japan's unconditional surrender. The latter victory had come at a tremendous cost, with the Americans being the first in their world's history to unleash the overwhelming fury of nuclear weapons on an enemy target.

In the wake of the war, an unprecedented era of prosperity was taking hold, particularly here in the United States. Still, new enemies and tensions were making themselves known, with another powerful nation, the Union of Soviet Socialist Republics, asserting itself as the primary contender against American interests throughout the world. Scarcely three years after the end of the war, and already it was apparent that tensions between the two factions likely would dominate the political discourse for years, or even decades, driving the military-industrial complex of both nations along with smaller powers across the planet to push for ever more advanced weapons and other technology.

"The longer we remain here," Gejalik said, "the more obvious it becomes that Earth's proper timeline—or, most of it, at least—appears to have been restored. And, the longer we go without contact from our people, the more I think that events there are not the same as they once were, either. Is the war over?"

Adlar shook his head as he bit into a piece of bacon from his plate. "We have no way of knowing," he replied after swallowing.

It was even possible that in this timeline, Earth no longer posed a threat to his people. With no means of contacting anyone off-world, it was not possible to learn whether the temporal conflict had ended, let alone what might have brought about its conclusion or its lasting impacts on the many affected planets and civilizations. Returning to Certoss Ajahlan without external assistance was not an option, at least so far as utilizing the time-displacement mechanisms that had engineered their transport to Earth. Faced with being marooned here for the foreseeable future, the operatives by consensus had decided that their first duty aside from avoiding discovery was to carry out their mission's other objective: preventing humans from gaining the technology required to one day pose a threat to the Certoss people.

From the information on Earth's future history he and the others had been given, Adlar knew that the aviation advances currently being made—including yesterday's first successful supersonic flight—soon would give way to the aerospace age as the United States and its most formidable competitor, the U.S.S.R., fought for supremacy beyond the confines of their small planet.

It was this push for space that, if Adlar's grasp of human history was correct, would provide the Certoss agents their best opportunity to accomplish their mission. It was the realization of that goal that was proving difficult, owing in large part to the fact that much of the technology that their group might purloin from humanity for their own uses had not yet been invented.

"We cannot wait too long to regain contact with Jaecz," Gejalik said. "Etlun will be here within the week, and after that we'll be forced to make a decision."

Adlar nodded in agreement. He looked forward to Etlun's return, as he had missed her presence during the past weeks. During their time on Earth, they had forged a personal bond on which he had come to depend for emotional comfort. Though such bonds had been exchanged between all four of them at one point or another, he had come to rely upon Etlun's companionship more than the others', and his feelings for her seemed to increase the longer she was away.

Like Jaecz, it had been weeks since her last contact, for understandable reasons. For some time, she had been working to infiltrate yet another military installation, attempting to gather new information regarding the ongoing development of nuclear weapons technology. Such work was carried out under the strictest safeguards, and even with the proper forged documentation and a human alias crafted with meticulous detail, penetrating the multiple layers of security surrounding these continuing projects required care and persistence.

"If we do not hear from Jaecz by the time Etlun returns," Adlar said, "then we will dispatch another message and alert him that we are moving. Once we reach our agreed destination, we will apprise him accordingly."

With their own equipment carrying the risk of discovery if used to any great extent, the agents had adapted to various forms of Earth-based communication in order to keep one another informed of their individual progress. The practice of corresponding via hardcopy transcription and sending it for delivery to predetermined locations was perhaps the most secure avenue, its major drawback being the significant delays incurred while waiting for the receiving party to respond in kind. Radio communication was unreliable and subject to monitoring, as was the use of telephones. The operatives even had developed a system of sending messages via short missives printed in prominent newspapers that could be obtained in most major cities, but this method, like the mail, involved waiting for one's query to be read and answered.

"Patience?" Gejalik asked, smiling.

Adlar nodded. "You know me too well."

Patience was not merely a watchword for him, or even a "virtue," as he had heard it described by some humans. Instead, it had become a way of life, particularly given the time he and his companions had spent here, trapped on Earth. It was a protection against the humans, who must never know that aliens lived among them. At least, not yet; not while there was still so much to do, and not just by the Certoss agents, but by humanity itself. After all, the coming technological advancements would play a major role in the tumultuous history to come. Left to their own devices, the people of Earth might well bring about their own destruction if certain events or circumstances unfolded in a manner unlike what history supposedly had recorded. The slightest deviations here or there would be all that was necessary to effect a much different outcome.

The key, Adlar knew, was finding where and how to introduce those deviations, without being discovered, and perhaps doing so without ever receiving help from their homeworld.

Patience.

FIVE

U.S.S. Enterprise
Earth Year 2268

Spock studied the female Certoss prisoner as she knelt on the floor in the middle of the brig cell. Her legs were tucked beneath her, and her hands rested on her thighs. She maintained a straight posture, facing directly ahead with her eyes closed. With the exception of raised cheekbones and a slim, angular jaw, her features were almost flat. A pair of small holes above her mouth indicated nasal passages, with no cartilage or other bone structure forming a nose. The same was true of her ears, also represented by a pair of openings on either side of her head. According to the medical data banks, what at first could be mistaken for secondary auditory canals instead were part of larger organs within the skull that assisted in maintaining balance, much like Andorian antennae.

Her skin's copper tinge complemented the light blue coveralls she had been given to wear in lieu of her bodysuit, and the small room's overhead lighting reflected off her hairless head's smooth surface. She appeared to be meditating, and for a moment Spock listened for any signs of humming or any other sounds she could be making to enhance whatever ritual she might be observing. Instead, he heard only the low hum of the force field that was the barrier containing the prisoner within her cell. She had not moved or offered any other indication that she was aware of his presence.

Precisely eighty-seven point four seconds after stepping in front of the brig's entrance, Spock saw her wide yellow eyes open and focus on him.

"Commander Spock," Gejalik said. "Are you ready to resume our conversation?"

The first officer nodded. "I have briefed Captain Kirk on what you've told me. He's asked me to convey to you his thanks for your cooperation."

"I see little point in offering any resistance to your queries," Gejalik replied. "The fact that we stand aboard a vessel of such sophistication and built by humans tells me that our mission was a failure."

"From our perspective, the obvious evidence would support your conclusion. However, an alternate reality may very well exist in which your efforts proved successful."

Pushing herself to her feet, the Certoss smoothed wrinkles from her coveralls before stepping closer to the force field. "Do you believe in the theory of parallel, alternate, or branching timelines? Even when we were taught such things during our mission briefings, I found it hard to accept."

"I have studied several theories and other data supporting the existence of such branching," Spock said. "Prior to that, I was skeptical about such hypotheses. However, I recently was reminded that there was a time, not that long ago, when my people believed time travel to be impossible."

Gejalik smiled. "So, you believe what I've been telling you?"

"Mestral has corroborated several aspects of your account. Other portions are supported by information we already possessed. For example, your statements pertaining to the Temporal Cold War in which your planet was embroiled."

Though most aspects of this conflict remained unknown to the populace at large, Spock and Captain Kirk had learned of the time-spanning campaign after the bizarre accident that had resulted in the *Enterprise* traveling back to Earth of the year 1969. Following that incident and the chaotic sequence of events that had ensued as Kirk and his crew worked to return to their proper place in time without disrupting history, the captain and Spock had been debriefed by Commodore Antonio Delgado at Starbase 9. The flag officer had provided Kirk and Spock's first insights into the secret war that had waged across centuries and involved a still-unknown number of planets and civilizations. The revelations had been surprising, coming as they did in the wake of the *Enterprise*'s accidental detour to twentieth-century Earth.

"Upon learning of the conflict," Spock said, "I conducted my own research, comparing the sensor readings collected during our time in the past against available historical records. I was unable to find anything that might indicate influence by your people, or any of the other 'factions' known or believed to have been involved."

According to Delgado, the Temporal Cold War—from Earth's perspective—had been resolved earlier in the century, prior to the conclusion of the Earth's Second World War.

Gejalik nodded. "We suspected the same. Our theory was that whatever happened to end the war took place while we were in transit from Certoss Ajahlan, and that we somehow were insulated from changes in the timeline. We believed that our planet was affected by whatever happened to bring about the end of the war, preventing us from contacting it."

"And despite this obvious disruption to your mission parameters," Spock said, "you chose to continue pursuing your goal of interfering with human history."

"We are soldiers, Commander," the Certoss replied. "Without instructions to the contrary, our orders were to proceed with our mission until informed otherwise."

Not for the first time, Spock wondered if Commodore Delgado, himself in apparent command of a cache of information pertaining to the Temporal Cold War and its impacts, was aware of the Certoss agents' time on Earth and the goals they had pursued. The commodore had made no mention of this during his debriefing after the *Enterprise*'s return from 1969. That might well have been for security reasons, given the classified nature of the conflict and everything connected to it. Might there still have been Certoss operatives on Earth at that point, working in secret even as Kirk and his crew were forced to interact with several people and events of the time? Indeed, the *Enterprise*'s encounter with a pilot of the United States Air Force, Captain John Christopher, almost had ended in a massive alteration of history that might well have aided the Certoss's efforts.

In the moments following the *Enterprise*'s abrupt appearance in low-earth orbit, Christopher had been sent to intercept and investigate what had been an "unidentified flying object," much like the numerous sightings reported all over the world throughout that period. The threat presented by Christopher's aircraft and its arsenal of weapons—primitive though they may have been by twenty-third-century standards—had forced Kirk to order the pilot brought aboard after the ship's tractor beams destroyed his plane.

Christopher's learning of the *Enterprise* and its crew and how they had traveled from the future had put Kirk in the unfortunate position of decreeing that the pilot could not be returned home, for fear that his knowledge might contaminate and somehow alter history. Things only grew more complicated when Spock learned that Christopher's future son, Sean Geoffrey Christopher, would in years to come command Earth's first manned space exploration mission to Saturn. This necessitated leaving the Air Force pilot in his proper place and time, and only added to the challenges faced by Kirk and his crew in their own quest to return home. So far as Spock had been able to determine in the aftermath of those events and after a careful review of historical records, the *Enterprise*'s visit to the twentieth century and its subsequent interaction with Christopher had left no lasting effects on the timeline.

We cannot always expect to be so fortunate, Spock reminded himself. Despite the misgivings Kirk had communicated to Delgado regarding the hazardous potential of attempting to engage in any method of controlled time travel, the commodore was very interested in the techniques Spock and Scott had employed to bring about their return from the twentieth century, and it was that fascination with the process that had brought about the *Enterprise*'s recent, sanctioned time-travel mission to 1968 Earth. Spock was certain that the relative success of the mission would only further motivate Delgado to continue his impassioned research into the possibilities such knowledge presented. Was it this sort of obsession, harbored either by Delgado or others like him—whether part of the Federation or some as yet unknown species—that ultimately brought about the Temporal Cold War in the first place?

An interesting hypothesis.

And what of Gary Seven, the mysterious human living on Earth in the twentieth century, himself an agent from an unknown alien organization possessing advanced technology and at least some knowledge of future history? What role, if any, had he and his benefactors played in the conflict? Delgado seemed to have no knowledge of Seven prior to their most recent debriefing, but that did not mean the commodore was being truthful in that instance, either.

"You seem preoccupied, Commander," Gejalik said, and the first officer realized he had been engrossed in his silent contemplation for longer than would be considered a polite pause in any conversation.

"I apologize," he said, opting against offering any further explanation. "You earlier said that you were one of four operatives dispatched by your military to Earth. Were similar teams deployed to other locations or time periods?"

Again, the Certoss seemed at ease with providing what Spock might consider privileged information. "There were other teams receiving the same training, though the information they were given was specific to their mission and target destination and time period. So far as I am aware, ours was the only team assigned to Earth, and we were the first group to be transported through our time-displacement generator. I do not know what happened to the others."

Spock nodded. "If, as you suspect, the changes brought about by the end of the temporal conflict came about while you were in transit, this may have had the effect of altering your planet's history to the point where the reality in which your mission was launched no longer exists in any recognizable form."

"It's a possibility to which I've given much consideration since arriving here," Gejalik replied, and Spock noted the change in her demeanor. Though her facial features did not seem to lend themselves to a broad spectrum of expressions, he still believed he was seeing what his human colleagues might describe as "melancholy." He had encountered such reactions while in the company of his human shipmates through the years, but he often was uncertain how best to act in such situations.

"Even if I'm able to return to my homeworld," she continued after a moment, "I'm still generations out of time. I won't be born for more than a century." She paused again, and the smile returned. "I long ago fell into the habit of measuring time as humans do. It was necessary to adapt to their world in every conceivable way, no matter how seemingly insignificant. Even when we were alone, we continued to display human mannerisms and speak in the relevant language, going so far as to adopt slang or other colloquialisms. It became second nature to act like our human counterparts and even to think like them. There were times when I thought I might be more human than a member of my own people. I certainly will be an alien to them should I return now."

Spock considered her plight, knowing that in a very real sense, the predicament she faced was quite similar to that posed by the *Enterprise* crew when they had thought themselves marooned in Earth's past. Faced with three centuries of foreknowledge, every single member of the ship's complement represented a danger to the timeline, and it was a dilemma Captain Kirk—and Spock himself—had contemplated as they considered the choices available to them.

What options, if any, were available to Gejalik? While there were those parties who almost certainly would deem her an enemy of the Federation for her actions, there was the intriguing matter of her being from a timeline quite different from the one she now occupied. Could a soldier, operating under orders as in Gejalik's case, be held responsible for the decisions and decrees of an authority that no longer existed? It was a question Spock suspected would occupy the attention of Federation science and legal experts for some time, assuming the issue even was brought to their attention. Would other parties—Commodore Antonio Delgado, for example—move to quell this matter and see to it that it never received that sort of scrutiny? If so, what would become of Gejalik herself?

That line of thought was interrupted by the whistle of the ship's intercom followed by the voice of Lieutenant Nyota Uhura.

"*Yellow Alert. The ship is now on Yellow Alert. Captain Kirk and Mister Spock, please report to the bridge. Captain Kirk and Mister Spock to the bridge, please.*"

Displayed upon the bridge's oversized main viewer was the image of a spacecraft of unfamiliar design, moving at what Kirk guessed to be a very high rate of speed. Unlike most vessels with which he was familiar, he found the unidentified craft as much a work of art as it was a functional construct. Possessing no angles or straight lines, it featured long, gentle curves, as if the entire hull was created as a single piece rather than being assembled from components. It suggested grace as well as speed, something Kirk found appealing.

It's beautiful.

"Report," he commanded, refocusing his attention on more important matters.

From where he sat at the bridge's helm station, Lieutenant Hikaru Sulu looked over his shoulder. "Sensors detected its approach a few moments ago, sir, traveling at high warp on an intercept course. It'll be within our weapons range in less than two minutes. Our shields are up and weapons are on standby, but they don't appear to have any weapons at all."

"You're sure?" Kirk asked, looking to where Chekov manned the science station in Mister Spock's stead.

The young ensign nodded. "Aye, sir. They have shields, but they're not raised. I've been able to identify the ship configuration, Captain. It's a Certoss vessel."

"Certoss?" Kirk repeated, frowning. "They're a long way from home."

So far as he knew—which, admittedly, was not much—the Certoss people, though capable of interstellar travel, in general preferred not to stray too far from the worlds of their own star system. It was one of the few data points that had stood out to him during his recent review of the survey reports filed by the *U.S.S. Endeavour*'s captain following her initial contact with the race.

There was, of course, a very valid reason for the ship to be here, sitting at this moment in his brig, but to arrive here and now?

Curiouser and curiouser.

"The vessel is about the size of a small scout craft," Chekov said, "with a length roughly three times that of a standard Starfleet shuttlecraft, and about twice the width. Sensors are picking up nine life-forms aboard, all Certoss."

Kirk nodded at the report. "Thank you, Ensign."

Behind him, the turbolift doors parted and Spock emerged onto the bridge, pausing as he got his first look at the vessel displayed upon the viewscreen. His right eyebrow rose.

"Fascinating."

"That's what I was thinking," Kirk said, before looking to where Uhura was sitting at the communications station. "Try hailing them again, Lieutenant."

"Yes, sir," Uhura replied, reaching for the Feinberg

receiver inserted into her left ear as her right hand moved across her console's array of controls. "They're not responding, but I can confirm that they are receiving our hails."

"Keep at it," Kirk said, leaning forward in his chair. "And just to see what happens, advise them that we think we know why they're here, and we'd like to discuss it with them. Maintain Yellow Alert for now, until we see what this is about. Spock, I don't suppose our guest mentioned anything about this?"

The Vulcan shook his head. "No, Captain, but we did activate her communications device. It's possible that the Certoss vessel intercepted whatever message was sent, but I am at a loss to explain how they could have responded so quickly."

Kirk had been thinking along similar lines. From what he remembered, the Certoss system was nearly two weeks distant even at maximum warp. Given its people's penchant for staying close to home, the odds of encountering a Certoss vessel were slim enough already. What was a Certoss vessel doing in this area of space in the first place?

"Captain," Uhura called out from the communications station, "we're now receiving a response to our hails. They seem most eager to speak with us."

Smiling, Kirk nodded. "I thought that might get their attention. On-screen, Lieutenant."

The main viewscreen shifted from an image of the alien vessel to that of a Certoss. She wore a flowing, wine-colored gown highlighted by streaks of light blue, and a large oval pendant hung around her thin neck. Appearing older than Gejalik, this person stood before what Kirk at first thought might be a piece of abstract art. A closer look told him that it was some form of a wall-mounted control panel, a pattern of multicolored swirls not merely decorative but instead looking to be the layout of controls and monitoring devices. As with the ship itself, its internal components seemed constructed with aesthetic form as well as function in mind.

I'll bet Scotty'd have a field day poking around over there.

"Greetings," he said, rising from the command chair and making his way around Sulu to stand before the viewscreen. "I'm Captain James Kirk of the *Starship Enterprise*. Are you in need of assistance?"

On the screen, the Certoss female replied, "*Greetings, Captain Kirk. I am Minister Ocherab, of the Unified Envoy Vessel* Balatir. *I apologize for this rather unexpected meeting, but your sensing devices hopefully have determined that my ship carries no weapons, and that we intend no aggressive action toward you.*"

From the science station, Spock said, "Captain, the library computer verifies that a vessel matching that name and description is in service to the Certoss planetary government. In fact, since formal first contact by the *U.S.S. Endeavour*, it has been used to ferry Certoss representatives to meet with Federation diplomats."

"Stand down from Yellow Alert," Kirk said, satisfied with the report before returning his attention to Ocherab. "Minister, may I ask what brings you this way, and why you were on a course to intercept us?" It may have been his imagination, but he thought he detected what might pass for uncertainty or even embarrassment on the Certoss leader's face as she looked down for a moment.

"*Captain, I must confess that I do not understand all the aspects of my current mission, but the simple answer to your question is that my government directed my vessel to this region of space.*" She appeared to falter, as though unsure of her own words, before continuing. "*Our original instructions were to rendezvous with your vessel and to seek out a meeting with you, Captain. At that time, no specific time or location was given, and this information was only relayed to me upon our arrival in this sector. However, it is my original orders that raise the most questions.*"

Intrigued even though he was sure he understood at least part of Ocherab's confusion, Kirk asked, "In what way, Minister?"

As though deciding there was nothing to be gained by delaying any more, the Certoss straightened her posture as she gazed out from the viewscreen. "*Captain, I know this will sound odd, but the reason we are here is because we were directed to this location, at this point in time, in order to pick up a passenger reportedly in your custody. This individual is of great interest to our science ministry, owing to the fact she dispatched a message to Certoss Ajahlan.*" She paused, looking to someone or something offscreen before nodding. "*As you measure it, her message was sent three centuries ago.*"

"Three centuries?" Kirk repeated, forcing his expression to remain neutral.

It seemed the day was not yet done being odd.

SIX

Wright-Patterson Air Force Base, Dayton, Ohio
April 21, 1952

Staring at the handwritten letter for the third time, his eyes tracing each character's curves rendered in a style as familiar to him as his own hand, James Wainwright felt his teeth clenching as sadness welled up within him.

I know your work is important to you, and you're driven by your duty. It's one of the many things I've always loved and admired about you, but I'm tired of being the second most important thing in your life. I know this wasn't always true, and I don't know what's changed, but I know that I just can't tolerate it anymore.

"Sir?" a voice called out, soft and tentative. "Are you all right?"

Wainwright cleared his throat, looking across to where Airman First Class Allison Marshall sat behind her desk, staring at him over stacks of files, books, and other papers. The piles of paperwork, along with still more material crammed into desk drawers, filing cabinets, and even the adjacent office, had all but come to define her existence—and his. She was dressed in the female variant of the Air Force enlisted member's service uniform, with a dark blue skirt and jacket over a light blue dress shirt, and a dark blue neck tab rather than the tie worn by her male counterparts. Her dark brown hair was pulled back and secured in a small bun at the base of her neck.

Drawing a deep breath, he shook his head. "It's . . . nothing. Just some personal business."

"It's Deborah, isn't it, sir?" Marshall asked without batting an eye.

You don't talk to me, about anything. Is it because you can't, or you just don't want to?

In most other circumstances, Marshall's question would have been inappropriate, given their professional working relationship and Wainwright's position as her superior officer. Still, the nature of their duty assignment and the conditions under which they often were forced to operate—long hours, traveling, and maintaining secrecy from family and friends—had seen to it that they had become close friends and even confidants. Until Marshall was assigned as his clerical assistant early the previous year, Wainwright had not had anyone with whom he could discuss his work except for other case officers, and they all had their own assignments and security directives to follow. Though his wife, Deborah, at first was put off by the notion of her husband traveling across the country with another woman, she never once raised any questions or suspicions that anything untoward might be occurring between him and Marshall.

Please know that I love you, Jim, and I always will.

Wainwright nodded. "I suppose I knew it was coming." He folded the letter and returned it to the matching envelope he had found the previous evening on the kitchen table. Deborah and their son, Michael, had not been there when he came home after yet another trip to some other city for still another in a seemingly unending series of investigations. Earlier in the week, Deborah had broached the idea for her and Michael to go back to California to visit her parents for a while. Given Jim's workload and the schedule he had been keeping in recent months—along with wishing to avoid an argument—he had raised no objections. Time apart would do them good, she had told him, which Wainwright had almost found humorous considering the long periods of time he was forced to be away from home, and Deborah's letter had confirmed the California trip.

The rest of her message, on the other hand, had hit him like a hammer.

And it's your own damned fault, he reminded himself.

"If you don't mind my saying so, sir," Marshall offered, "I don't think you're being very fair to yourself."

Wainwright slid the envelope into his top desk drawer. "Military life's hard on families, Marshall, and that's before the military adds on a lot of extra baggage to carry around." His wife, both before and after Michael's birth, had endured her share of service-induced separations, beginning with the war. She had married him in a quiet, rushed ceremony just two nights before he shipped out for England in early 1944, and he had communicated with her only via letters for nearly a year afterward. Deborah had weathered his time away in superb fashion, occupying her days working in a factory near her family's home in Sacramento. They enjoyed a delayed, extended honeymoon after his return before he settled into his postwar duties. In the fall of 1946, Michael entered their lives, and Wainwright now brought along his family to new assignments. Life continued in routine, even boring fashion as he worked at the base in Roswell, but everything changed on that fateful day in 1947.

"Oh, I can imagine, sir," Marshall said, averting her gaze as she returned to moving various papers and files around her desk. "I can only seem to keep a boyfriend as long as I stay here, but the minute I'm sent somewhere? Kiss him good-bye."

Despite his mood, Wainwright smiled at her comment. At twenty-six, Allison Marshall was smart and unafraid to speak her mind, a trait he admired. Though military discipline prevented her from straying too far from traditional courtesies and demeanor, she had no problem voicing her opinions to him if she felt she needed to be heard. Their working relationship was such that he long ago had encouraged her to dispense with protocol when they were alone.

"Well, it's their loss, then," Wainwright said. Clearing his throat, he tried—with only marginal success—to put the letter out of his mind. Though he knew saying as much reinforced everything Deborah had been trying to tell him, there really were more pressing matters demanding his attention just now. "Do you have the report on the Kansas City sighting? Captain Ruppelt's been asking about it."

Marshall held up a file folder. "Finishing it up now, sir. I'm waiting on the photos we took to come back from the lab."

"Good." The photographs he and Marshall had collected were nothing spectacular; just supporting documentation of the people who had reported seeing an "unidentified flying object" or "UFO," as the Air Force now called such unknown craft, as well as the area where the alleged sighting had taken place. As one of the senior members of the project here at Wright-Patterson, Wainwright was sent to Kansas City, Missouri, to investigate the report as filed by their liaison officer at Whiteman Air Force Base, the closest installation to the city. Marshall had gone with him. "Thanks for turning that around so quickly. I know we just got back last night, and it was a Sunday night to boot, but you know how Ruppelt can be."

"Not a problem, sir," Marshall replied, ever the consummate professional so far as their actual work was concerned. She paused, and Wainwright watched her eyes take in the stacks of paperwork cluttering her desk. "I'm not saying a vacation to San Diego or Miami wouldn't go unappreciated, though."

For the first time that morning, Wainwright chuckled. "I'll see what I can do, but I wouldn't count on anything more than a weekend pass anytime soon. If anything, I think we're going to be getting busier."

From its humble beginnings here five years earlier, the original Majestic 12 project had evolved far beyond the investigation of the original spacecraft landing at Roswell along with any possible aftereffects of that incident. Within months of the project's inception, the Air Force launched another initiative, Project Sign, with a primary mission of investigating the increasing number of UFO sightings.

As this mandate was separate from MJ-12 operations, Professor Carlson—still a central figure in the original group's leadership committee—had requested of the new project's commander, Captain Robert Sneider, that Wainwright be designated as a liaison officer between the two groups. For nearly a year, Wainwright and other Air Force officers investigated reports submitted by military personnel as well as civilians. Though no hard evidence had been collected during this time, details as relayed from individuals claiming to have seen strange aircraft bore enough similarities that senior government and military officials were becoming convinced that some form of extraterrestrial activity was taking place in the skies above America and, indeed, the entire world.

Skeptics also put forth theories that some of these sightings might well be top-secret aircraft from the Soviet Union. Such notions had been bandied about even before the launch of Project Sign, and Wainwright had heard rumors that investigations such as those currently being conducted were taking place as much as a year before the Roswell Incident. Wainwright and other project officers had been able to debunk such theories, though their investigations did not always lead to evidence of alien activity. Doubts in the higher echelons of government and the military soon began to take their toll. Despite credible witnesses, compelling photographic evidence, and other collected findings, a lack of tangible, actionable proof had begun to chip away at the support Project Sign had enjoyed at its inception. A report submitted by Captain Sneider to the Air Force chief of staff, General Hoyt Vandenberg, containing a comprehensive assessment that many of the reported sightings could be attributed to extraterrestrial activity, was rejected. When the project became public, this invited more skepticism and even ridicule, resulting in Sign's deactivation and subsequent replacement by a new initiative, Project Grudge.

Straightening a stack of papers before putting them inside a brown file folder stamped "TOP SECRET," Marshall placed the completed file in a cardboard box containing several more folders of identical design.

"While I'm waiting on the photos from the Kansas City trip, I thought I might catch up on some filing, sir. We've got several older case logs here that need to go into storage next door."

"Probably a good idea," Wainwright said, eyeing the other file boxes and folders littering the office. Captain Ruppelt had been keeping him and Marshall busy during these past few months, leaving little time for the mundane yet necessary paperwork that accompanied each investigation. "Double check with the master list, and make sure we keep anything from an active file here, even if it's just for something small. Until we get used to the new system, I don't want anything to get lost."

Marshall nodded as she picked up the file box and headed for the door. "Yes, sir. It's nice to have people actually being interested in what we're doing, for a change."

"You can say that again."

Following the debacle that Project Grudge turned into, a new attitude now gripped Wainwright, his fellow officers, and everyone connected to the secret work with which they had been charged.

Prior to this new shift, Project Grudge's former primary directive—at least so far as the Air Force and the Pentagon were concerned—had been to find plausible explanations for any "UFO sightings" that did not point to extraterrestrial causes. It was a definite shift in mindset when compared to the attitudes that had driven Project Sign. The prior effort, which worked outward from the truth of what really had happened at Roswell, was motivated by a need to understand the larger ramifications of the aliens' presence on Earth, and what it might mean for humanity in the years to come.

Now Project Grudge's aim was to ignore or debunk any claims of extraterrestrial activity, engaging in a more organized public relations effort with the aim of presenting the results of its investigations to the citizenry, rather than pursuing the truth. Wainwright had come close to resigning his commission on two separate occasions, but Professor Carlson had talked him out of it, convinced that soon, something would happen to change the minds of skeptical leaders.

It did happen, on September 10, 1951, when both civilian

and military pilots reported sightings and near collisions with varying numbers of unidentified disk-like craft in the skies over New Jersey. The mass sighting and sheer number of corroborating reports demanded an investigation, during which Project Grudge was called to answer for its seemingly apathetic approach to UFO sightings. In the aftermath of that investigation, Grudge was deactivated and a new project put into motion; one that would treat sightings and reports seriously, but with no bias for or against any extraterrestrial explanation. Indeed, the project's primary mandate for all personnel was to vigorously pursue whatever evidence or other information presented itself, regardless of where it might lead. In short, the directive was simple: Keep an open mind.

And so it was in early 1952 that James Wainwright, with great enthusiasm and renewed hope, found himself once again transferred from Majestic 12 and assigned as an investigating officer for the newly christened Project Blue Book. Liaison officers for the project were assigned to every Air Force installation, acting as a starting point for reports submitted from those regions, with all such accounts sent up the chain of command to the project's commander, Captain Edward Ruppelt, and the main task group at Wright-Patterson.

Wainwright, by virtue of seniority and his tenure with the previous projects, was a principal case officer, dispatched by Ruppelt himself to investigate any reports or sightings with a high probability of obtaining incontrovertible proof of extraterrestrial activity. The new initiative, grounded as it was by Ruppelt's directive to carry out every investigation with all due rigor and attention to every detail, demanded even more from the officers in his charge. More research, more time spent traveling, and more long nights spent in this office, filing reports detailing the results of those efforts.

I know your work is important to you, and you're driven by your duty. It's one of the many things I've always loved and admired about you, but I'm tired of being the second most important thing in your life.

Deborah's words, as though she stood before him speaking them aloud, rang in Wainwright's ears. Balancing his work against his home life had been difficult during the eras of Sign and Grudge, but Blue Book had only increased that strain. While the new project was still in its earliest days, he had tried to prepare her for the increased requirements it would place upon him. Of course, many of her questions touched on those aspects of his assignment that he was not allowed to share.

You don't talk to me, about anything. Is it because you can't, or you just don't want to?

Wainwright hoped one day to be able to tell Deborah everything, to show her what had so consumed him these past five years, and what it meant for the very safety of the human race. Since his arrival here and from the beginnings of the Air Force's investigation, hundreds of UFO sightings had been reported. While the majority of these had proven either to be false or else explained by conventional causes, and many of these were reported as part of Project Grudge's public relations endeavors, there were still dozens of reports requiring increased scrutiny. Some of these cases remained open because alien activity had not yet been ruled out. Then there was the even smaller number of files that pointed without doubt to vessels of extraterrestrial origin. According to the initial top-secret assessment provided to the Pentagon by Captain Ruppelt, there could be no denying that Earth was under almost constant surveillance.

It was a claim questioned by the highest tiers of government and military leadership, despite being supported by thousands of pages of information and photographs as collected by the Air Force during the past five years. Though Wainwright had not seen anything conclusive pointing to the existence of aliens on Earth since that day at Roswell in 1947, he had heard rumors of other case officers stumbling across spacecraft or advanced technology. There even were reports of bodies being recovered from crash sites, with all of the evidence spirited away to high-security storehouses around the country. There was an area of Wright-Patterson with several buildings operating under a tight security cordon, with access by visitors restricted to those authorized by the base commanding general. Even with the security clearance Wainwright held, he had never been granted access to that section.

Maybe one day, he thought, but he would not be holding his breath.

A knock from outside the office interrupted his thoughts, and Wainwright looked up to see a shadowy figure standing just beyond the door's glazed, translucent window. "Come in."

The door opened to reveal Lieutenant Darren Benjamin, one of Captain Ruppelt's aides. Like Wainwright, he was dressed in the standard blue officer's service dress uniform, with blue trousers and jacket over a light blue shirt with a dark blue tie. A lock of his dark brown hair dropped down across his forehead, and Wainwright suspected the younger man used some sort of hair tonic to achieve that look.

"Good morning, sir," Benjamin said, closing the door behind him and moving to stand before Wainwright's desk. He was carrying a green file folder; on the cover Wainwright could see the stamped words "TOP SECRET." Stopping in front of the desk, Benjamin held out the folder. "Captain Ruppelt asked me to deliver this to you pronto."

"Another sighting?" Wainwright asked, taking the folder and laying it on his desk. As he opened the file and began perusing its contents, his eyes locked on one particular piece of information on the report's top sheet. "Yuma?"

"Yes, sir," Benjamin replied. "Last Thursday, the seventeenth. At least a half dozen witnesses reported seeing a flat, white disk traveling in a straight line across the sky over the mountains of the testing ranges. Two more people reported seeing it again the next day. All of the observers were military personnel. We got the call that day, with the follow-up report arriving Saturday afternoon. Given the nature of the incident, and the witnesses involved, Captain Ruppelt wants you to head out there and have a look."

Wainwright sighed, chastising himself for the breach in military bearing in the presence of a junior officer. "Sorry, Lieutenant. I guess I'm still tired from the last trip. We just got home last night."

Never mind the empty house.

"Understood, sir," Benjamin said. "For what it's worth, the captain mentioned that very thing when he handed me the file. He told me to tell you he apologizes for sending you out again so soon, but . . ." The younger man's expression turned sheepish. "You know how it is, sir."

Nodding, Wainwright forced a small smile. "Yep. That's how it is, all right." He spent a brief moment scanning the report's top sheet before flipping to the supplemental pages, looking for certain key phrases that Blue Book liaison officers at other bases had been instructed to use when taking statements from witnesses. So far as he could tell, the accounts as provided by the Yuma base personnel were detailed, lacking the sort of embellishment he long ago had come to associate with reports submitted by less-credible observers. For a moment, his inner cynic—cultivated after years of taking reports of alleged sightings from people just looking for attention or validation from the government or society at large—wondered if the witnesses had worked together to arrive at a consistent story to tell the Yuma liaison officer. The questionnaire developed by Captain Ruppelt for use when interviewing those making such reports was designed to detect such collusion, but experience had taught Wainwright that the process was not foolproof. He knew he would not be able to judge the veracity of this report until he had a chance to question the observers for himself.

Guess I should start packing. Again.

SEVEN

Yuma Test Station, Yuma, Arizona
April 22, 1952

"Well, considering this is my first time here," Wainwright said, guiding the Jeep down the narrow, dusty service road, "it's definitely everything I hoped it'd be."

As she held on to the dashboard from where she sat in the passenger seat, Marshall's laugh carried over the sound of the vehicle's engine. "Just once, why can't they send us to Florida, or Paris?"

Wainwright did not reply, opting instead to swerve the Jeep so as to avoid a large rut in the unpaved road, which had appeared after the vehicle he was following also dodged to miss it. He still managed to catch the furrow with the Jeep's rear tire, sending him and Marshall bouncing in their seats and Wainwright's head brushing against the Jeep's canvas top.

"I think I just broke my tailbone," Marshall said, recovering her grip on the dashboard. "Are we sure this road isn't part of the actual bombing range?"

"Might be," Wainwright said, both hands on the wheel in what he hoped was not a vain attempt to keep the vehicle from swerving into the ditch on either side of the road. The sun was dropping lower on the horizon, and he wanted to be back at the base's main garrison area, rather than driving out here in what promised to be near-total darkness with nothing but the Jeep's dim headlights to guide the way.

Located in southwestern Arizona near the borders of California and Mexico, most of the land designated to the Yuma Test Station was uninhabited; nearly two thousand square miles of harsh, desolate desert landscape. Wainwright knew that the army had first established a presence at Fort Yuma before the Civil War and that the testing range now accounting for the immense size of the current base made it one of the largest military installations in the country if not the world. It had been used during World War II for testing various weapons and mechanized infantry equipment, and similar work had continued after the war's end and even now as the current conflict raged in Korea.

"I hope we can get back without blowing a tire," Marshall said after Wainwright failed to miss another bump in the road, "or one of my kidneys. Didn't you hit that one on the way out?"

Chuckling, Wainwright replied, "This is nothing. In France, I actually broke the axle off a Jeep when I ran it into a crater made by one of our bombers. I thought the colonel I was driving back to his command post was going to kill me right there on the road."

"That bad, huh?" Marshall asked, around what Wainwright thought might be a suppressed giggle.

"Yep. I couldn't wait to get back to my unit. At least then, the only ones to be scared of were the Germans."

A flickering light from somewhere behind him reflected off the Jeep's metal dashboard and Wainwright glanced over his right shoulder to look for the source. "I think you left the Geiger counter on," he said, returning his attention to the road.

Shifting in her seat, Marshall attempted to reach for the unit, which they had brought with them from Wright-Patterson. The device, along with their jackets and other items, lay just beyond her fingers. When the Jeep hit another rut, she turned back around in her seat. "Sorry about that, sir. I thought I'd turned it off."

"The way we're bouncing around here, the switch could've hit the side or something," Wainwright said. "Wasn't worth bringing along, anyway."

Upon their arrival at the testing station, Wainwright and Marshall, accompanied by Lieutenant Brian Pearce, the Blue Book liaison officer from Luke Air Force Base near Glendale, Arizona, had visited with each of the witnesses to the previous week's sighting. Each witness's report was consistent with the others, without sounding as though the accounts had been rehearsed or coordinated. Further, their statements along with his own gut feelings told Wainwright the witnesses were being straight with him, and he believed they had seen an unidentified craft in the skies above the testing range where they had been carrying out a series of weapons-fire exercises.

A visit to the area where the sightings had taken place had proven to be a near-total waste of time through no fault of the witnesses, owing to the fact that there simply was nothing remarkable about the terrain making up ninety-eight percent of the Yuma Test Station. Still, he preferred to study the area with his own eyes, to get a sense of what the witnesses had seen. The vast expanses of undeveloped land and the surrounding mountains would seem the ideal place for a craft to fly in near seclusion, whether a product of top-secret military research or otherworldly origin. An examination of the ground over which the unknown object had been seen had yielded nothing in the way of physical evidence, and the sweeps Marshall had conducted with the Geiger counter also turned up nothing.

The Jeep ahead of his, which was carrying Lieutenant Pearce and driven by the on-duty range safety officer, slowed as both vehicles rounded a bend in the road and approached a quartet of small buildings. They had passed the buildings on their way out to the area where the sightings had been reported, and there had been no sign of occupancy. Now, however, a five-ton cargo truck sat before the largest of the structures.

"Wonder what's going on?" Wainwright asked, guiding the Jeep to follow the lead vehicle off the road and onto the patch of gravel that served as a parking lot in front of the buildings. On the other side of the truck was another Jeep, which, unlike theirs, had no top. "They weren't here before, right?"

Marshall shook her head. "No, sir."

"Maybe they're dropping off supplies for an upcoming exercise."

Three of the buildings were Quonset huts; long, single-story structures fashioned from sheets of corrugated steel bent over a curved metal frame with a plywood façade covering each end of the resulting shelter. The fourth building was a larger, two-story warehouse. According to the safety officer—an army captain named David Cardillo—the buildings were staging areas for equipment and personnel assigned to training exercises in this area of the installation, and similar arrangements were scattered across the base. In and of itself, the outpost was unremarkable, as was the cargo truck and the trio of soldiers standing near its back end at the warehouse's entrance.

Shutting off the Jeep's engine, Wainwright watched Captain Cardillo and Lieutenant Pearce emerge from the passenger side of their vehicle. Cardillo, though of average height, possessed the brawny frame of a boxer or wrestler, his tan uniform tailored to his muscular frame almost like a second skin. Pearce, dressed in an Air Force blue duty uniform, was of slighter build, looking almost boyish standing next to the more imposing Cardillo. The enlisted soldier acting as their driver remained behind the wheel, though he was not visible through the rear window due to the fading sunlight. As the safety officer walked toward the soldiers and their truck, the threesome all came to positions of attention and rendered salutes.

The safety officer returned the salutes, and Wainwright heard him ask, "What are you boys doing out here?"

"Guard duty, sir," one of the soldiers, a corporal, replied. They were dressed in typical field gear, including helmets and sidearms in black leather holsters suspended from the green cartridge belts around their waists. One of the troopers carried an M1 carbine rifle slung from his left shoulder. "The rest of our unit's due here tomorrow at sunup."

"Due here for what, Corporal?" Cardillo asked.

"Weapons training, sir," the soldier replied. "We're getting ready for our annual requalifications."

From his seat in the Jeep, Wainwright was able to see the frown on Cardillo's face as the captain asked, "Really? I don't know anything about that."

Behind Wainwright, the Geiger counter squawked.

"What the hell?" he asked, frowning as he looked over his shoulder. The illuminated gauge on the unit's face allowed him to see the indicator needle twitching. It was just a few ticks away from the gauge's zero mark, but the reading was steady.

What the hell is right.

"Where's it coming from?" Marshall asked, and they both looked to the warehouse before which Wainwright had parked the Jeep. "They wouldn't store nuclear weapons out here, would they?"

Shaking his head, Wainwright replied, "Not likely, and not without a damned sight more than three guards. Wait here." He pushed himself from the driver's seat, making his way to where Cardillo was still talking to the soldier while Pearce stood nearby. The safety officer's voice now had taken on an edge of irritation.

"Well, nobody informed the safety office of any exercise," Cardillo was saying. "I'll need to check this out." Then, his voice softened a bit as he regarded the soldier. "Probably just a screwup. You boys grab a smoke while I call back to garrison and get it straightened out."

Wainwright was the first to see one of the soldiers reach for his sidearm.

"Gun!" he shouted, his right hand already moving for the holstered .45 caliber pistol on his hip. With no time to brandish his own weapon, Cardillo charged the other man, throwing his body at the corporal and sending both men slamming into the side of the truck. Pearce, though unarmed, still moved forward to help but then he turned and dove for cover as the soldier with the M1 rifle brought that weapon to bear.

"Look out!"

Wainwright heard Marshall's warning from inside the Jeep an instant before sharp cracks split the air, the rifle's reports echoing off the nearby buildings as bullets tore into the side of the cargo truck. Ignoring his flight cap as it fell from his head, Wainwright ducked behind the side of the Jeep, hearing Marshall yell something he did not understand.

He ignored her, pulling back on the .45's slide and chambering the first round from its magazine before rising up from behind the Jeep. Eyes widening in shock, he saw Lieutenant Pearce lying facedown on the gravel lot. Cardillo still was scuffling with one soldier, whereas a second one was no longer in his field of vision. That left the third trooper, the one with the M1, and Wainwright looked up in time to see that soldier leveling the rifle at him. Ducking back down, he heard the snap of the weapon just before a round slammed through the Jeep's windshield. He saw that a spiderweb had appeared across the glass, radiating outward from the single hole on the driver's side of the window. He started to rise from his crouch, hoping to locate the remaining soldier.

"I said to stay down, damn it!" Marshall yelled, scrambling from the Jeep and throwing herself down to the ground. Wainwright noted that she had discarded her black service shoes—impractical as the heels might be for a firefight—before the sound of more weapons fire made him flinch.

Peering over the Jeep's hood, he caught sight of Cardillo's driver emerging from his vehicle, .45 in hand. He moved to his left, aiming the pistol at the trooper with the rifle. He fired twice and struck the side of the cargo truck near the other soldier, who ducked but did not move for cover. Instead he turned and aimed his rifle at the driver, firing a single shot that struck the soldier in the chest. He pitched forward, falling against the hood of his Jeep and sliding to the ground.

Wainwright ducked again as the trooper swung the rifle in his direction, hearing the sound of another shot. The encroaching darkness was making it more difficult to see their adversaries. Already the shadows were starting to blend together, the weak illumination offered by single bulbs above the doors to the buildings only exacerbating the worsening visibility problem. Leaning around the front of his Jeep, Wainwright fired one frantic shot, hoping to force the other shooter to seek cover. From his vantage point he saw Cardillo delivering a roundhouse punch to the corporal, sending the other man tumbling to the ground. The soldier started pulling himself to his feet but Cardillo had retrieved the other man's fallen pistol, backpedaling to give himself room and cover as the trooper with the rifle stepped around the truck and gave chase. Wainwright aimed his .45 at the soldier and fired two quick shots. Both rounds found their mark, striking the soldier in the chest and sending him stumbling into the side of the truck. Despite the pair of direct hits, Wainwright was stunned when the man moved, rolling onto his side.

Huh?

Another pistol fired from his left, and Wainwright felt something whip past his cheek. Recoiling away from the near miss, he dropped to one knee as he caught sight of the third soldier. He was near the front of the cargo truck, using it for cover. Cardillo, his attention focused on the trooper with the rifle, did not see the new threat behind him.

"Captain!" Wainwright shouted, rising to his feet and holding his .45 with both hands as he pulled the trigger. The pistol bucked with each of the three shots he fired, two of the rounds catching the other man in the chest and the third striking him in the neck. The soldier staggered, dropping his weapon before sagging to his knees on the gravel. Cardillo, seeing that the man was down, returned his attention to the other two soldiers, but both of them now were scrambling away, running around the back end of the cargo truck. No sooner did Wainwright lunge from behind the Jeep than the soldier with the rifle reappeared, holding the M1 against his right hip and firing multiple shots in rapid succession.

Wainwright threw himself forward, gritting in pain as his elbows, knees, and palms slid across the lot's unforgiving gravel. Behind him, he heard bullets ripping once more into the Jeep and even the sound of a tire being punctured. The firing continued, with the soldier now turning his weapon on Cardillo's Jeep. Rolling to one side, Wainwright extended his right arm and fired again, getting off only one shot before the .45's slide locked to the rear. He had emptied his magazine. Cursing himself for not keeping better track of his ammunition, he fumbled for the pouch on his cartridge belt. Across the lot, Cardillo was on one knee, aiming his pistol at the soldier. The captain fired two shots and the trooper jumped back behind the truck.

Then more gunfire pierced the air and Wainwright turned to see Marshall, propped against the Jeep's hood and brandishing a .45. The pistol looked enormous in her smallish hands but she handled the weapon with confidence, gripping it with both hands and controlling its recoil as she fired.

"Nice shooting," he said. Though it was not typical for female Air Force personnel to carry weapons, it was Blue Book policy for field investigators to be armed while on assignment. Wainwright congratulated himself for opting to interpret the regulation to include Marshall, despite her "official" designation as his secretary.

She snapped off another shot. "Thank my father."

Retrieving a fresh magazine from the pouch on his belt, Wainwright snuck a look over the hood and saw the trooper pulling back, darting out of sight behind the cargo truck.

"They're making a run for it!" Wainwright shouted as he exchanged his pistol's empty magazine for a new one. Hearing the sound of a Jeep's engine, he pushed himself to his feet and ran for the front of the truck. The other Jeep was pulling away, with two figures in the vehicle's front seats. The soldier in the passenger seat was aiming the rifle behind them, and Wainwright leapt behind the truck as still more bullets tore into its side.

Son of a bitch!

Hearing the Jeep's tires leave the gravel and spin on the dirt of the service road, Wainwright lunged from behind the truck and fired his pistol. Plumes of dust and dirt filled the air, concealing the fleeing vehicle's escape as he emptied the .45's magazine. The Jeep was gone, the sound of its whining engine already fading in the growing darkness.

"Captain Wainwright!"

He jerked his head at the sound of the summons to see Marshall and Cardillo standing over the body of the fallen soldier, with Marshall frantically waving for him to join them. With one last look down the road where the Jeep was now out of sight, he grunted in frustration before jogging across the lot. Cardillo was training his pistol on the unmoving form of the downed soldier.

But, it was not the soldier.

"What in the name of . . . ?" The rest of his sentence trailed away as Wainwright stepped closer, his gaze fixing on the figure lying on the ground. The first words his brain seemed capable of forming in order to describe what he was seeing were "not human."

"What is it?" Cardillo asked, his expression a mix of shock and disbelief. "One of those Martians you guys are always supposed to be chasing?"

While possessing at least the general shape and form of a human, the thing had no hair, and its skin was of a ruddy red-brown complexion. Its hands were smaller than a typical adult human's, with three long, thin fingers flanked by what looked to be a pair of thumbs. There were no ears or nose to speak of, and its cheeks and jawline gave the thing an almost childlike appearance belying what Wainwright instinctively regarded as an obvious adult musculature. Gone was the army soldier's uniform, with the creature instead wearing a black single-piece form-fitting garment. Strapped across its chest was some kind of harness, supporting a device or gadget that Wainwright did not recognize, but it did draw his attention to one other detail.

"A female?" he asked, moving closer for a better look. The thing's body suit conformed to its wearer's physique, and beneath the harness were unmistakable female attributes, at least so far as humans were concerned.

"Looks that way," Marshall said, her voice containing more than a hint of incredulity. Wainwright had to remind himself that this was her first time seeing an actual extraterrestrial. This creature, which still seemed to possess several *humanlike* physical characteristics, reminded him of the Ferengi from Roswell, whose bodies also had as many apparent similarities to humans as they did differences.

"It was able to make itself look human somehow," Marshall said. "How?"

"No idea," Wainwright replied. His eyes moved from the creature's face to the liquid, too dark and thick to be human blood, pooling beneath the supine figure from the wound in its neck. "Damn." His bullet had killed the alien. He shook his head, angry with himself at the wasted opportunity to question the thing despite knowing he had fired in self-defense. Were the other two soldiers aliens like it? What did they know, and how many more of them were out there? "Are there phones in any of those buildings?"

Cardillo nodded. "Yeah. They all have offices with working phones, wired to the garrison switchboard."

"Good. We need to report this." Wainwright already could hear what Professor Carlson might say upon learning of their discovery. Then, remembering what had prompted this mess, he looked to Marshall. "Get the Geiger counter." Inserting his second—and last—spare magazine into his pistol, he said, "We're going to check the warehouse."

Everything about the building's interior was unremarkable, with the notable exception of the object in the middle of the floor. So far as Wainwright could tell, it was a spaceship.

"Oh, my God," Marshall said, dividing her attention between the Geiger counter and what sat before them.

"Holy Christ," Cardillo said, his voice wavering. When Wainwright looked over at him, he saw that the safety officer's complexion had gone pale, his eyes wide with astonishment. "It's a flying saucer, isn't it? A real, honest-to-God flying saucer?"

That was Wainwright's first thought. Flanked by tables, tools, and work lights that only served to highlight just how out of place the damned thing appeared to be, it was not saucer shaped. Instead, it was triangular in shape, long and thin and to Wainwright resembling a pie wedge or arrowhead. Perhaps twice the length of a station wagon, the thing certainly looked like some form of vehicle or craft. Its hull or outer skin was a dark gray, though he was unable to make out anything resembling rivets or weld lines. The skin was not reflective, almost absorbing the light cast down upon it from the work lamps, and it looked rough in texture, akin to sandpaper or roofing shingles. Scattered on the floor and the tables situated around the craft were pieces of equipment Wainwright could not begin to identify.

"What's the Geiger counter saying?"

Waving the device in the craft's direction, Marshall replied, "This is the radiation source, all right, but the meter's not doing much more than it was outside. We're not in any danger, so far as I can tell."

"Radiation?" Cardillo asked, now looking even more nervous.

"We'll be okay," Wainwright said, trying to sound reassuring. "That said, I'm not planning on standing too close to it for very long." Unable to resist the temptation to get a better look, he stepped forward, the muzzle of his pistol centered on the open compartment taking up almost a third of the craft and set back perhaps three feet from the thing's forward edge. It resembled a cockpit, or the extraterrestrial equivalent, with a canopy raised to expose a single seat encompassed by a horseshoe-shaped control panel or dashboard. The console was festooned with all manner of buttons and indicators, some bearing labels in a script Wainwright did not recognize.

"Does it have power?" The craft's streamlined, angular shape conveyed speed, and Wainwright had to wonder what might drive such a machine? He heard no discernible sound of an engine, but there was something, a sensation that seemed to play across his exposed skin, telling him that the thing was generating or putting off some kind of energy.

Marshall said, "Only way to know would be to climb in and try firing it up."

"I think we'll let the experts do that," Wainwright said, again imagining Jeffrey Carlson's reaction once he got his first look at this baby. He hoped he could be present when the professor and his team got their hands on the craft and began taking it apart in a quest to understand whatever secrets it might contain. His eyes lingering on the cockpit, he realized something odd about its interior. "The seat," he blurted.

Looking over his shoulder, he saw Marshall's and Cardillo's confused expressions and pointed to the cockpit. "This is from a bomber; a B-29 or something." The canvas upholstery and lap belt now was recognizable. How had he missed that? Peering closer, he saw that the seat had been fastened to the deck inside the cockpit with conventional bolts. Of note also were additional seams in the deck, indicating where something else had once been attached. He also noted the presence of what looked to be contemporary materials holding something in place beneath the consoles. A maze of wires, hoses, and contraptions he did not recognize filled nearly every inch of available space.

"I think this thing used to have more seats," he said. Then, casting a glance at the unidentified components and other parts on the floor and tables, he frowned. "No, wait. This other stuff, maybe it was crammed in here." Studying the lines on the cockpit floor, he nodded at his own statement. "Yeah, that might be it. They may have taken out some of this stuff to make room for the seat."

Cardillo frowned. "But, why?"

Before Wainwright could answer, Marshall interrupted him. "Sir, you need to see this. You both do."

Turning to where she was standing near a stack of packing crates, her .45 once more in her hand, Wainwright saw that she was aiming the pistol at something he could not see. He drew his own weapon as he crossed the floor to where she stood, and it was not until he came abreast of her that he saw what she meant.

"Oh, my God," he whispered, feeling his jaw slacken as he beheld the bodies of six soldiers. All male, the ones lying faceup had their eyes open, wide and fixed. One of those was an officer, his lieutenant's bars visible on his shirt collar.

Wainwright saw no bullet wounds or other visible signs of violence on the bodies, but their ashen color told him what he needed to know. "All dead."

"Yes, sir," Marshall said, her voice low. "Looks that way."

Coming up behind them, Cardillo got his first look at the bodies, and Wainwright heard him gasp. "Jesus." Without hesitation, he stepped around the two Air Force officers and knelt beside the deceased lieutenant. "I know this man," he said after a moment, reaching out as if to touch the body before stopping himself. "Lieutenant Matthew Graham. He's involved with some super-secret testing group here on the base. All hush-hush and whatnot." Rising to his feet, he turned and gestured past Wainwright and Marshall toward the ship. "Stuff like that, I guess." His expression changed, becoming harder, and when he spoke again it was with a tinge of anger in his voice. "This is your sort of business, right? Want to explain to me why one group of soldiers would kill another over something like this?"

Wainwright shook his head. "I don't know, Captain." He looked back to the mysterious craft. Then, he realized what was bothering him. "Oh, *damn*." Before he realized what he was doing, he ran out of the warehouse and back to where the form of the dead alien still lay on the gravel lot. Behind him, he heard Marshall and Cardillo running to catch up.

"You thinking what I'm thinking?" he asked Marshall, who nodded.

"Yes, sir," she answered. "That ship in there doesn't belong to *this* thing, whoever or whatever he—or she—is. At least, it didn't before."

"Was the ship in there retrieved from another landing or crash site, or is it something they've built based on what we know about alien ships?" It was very possible that some extensive research-and-development effort was taking place, of which he had not been informed. Maybe Professor Carlson knew something.

I'll just have to ask him, the next time I see him.

Marshall said, "Neither of those answers tells us about the people that thing *does* belong to."

Wainwright shook his head, trying once again to process from the beginning everything that had happened over the past several minutes. Two different alien species? From where? Why, and why here and now? What did it all mean, and what was he—and the rest of Earth, for that matter—supposed to do about it?

His eyes locked on the dead alien, Wainwright sighed. "I'm thinking the real next question is: Just how much trouble are we in, anyway?"

EIGHT

Yuma, Arizona
April 23, 1952

Leaving the lights off, Gejalik peered through the curtains at the dusty, mostly empty parking lot. The same three cars that had occupied spaces in front of other rooms remained the only signs of life at the roadside motel. A fourth car, the one she and Adlar had used to make their escape from the army base, was parked outside their own room. Gejalik already had changed the vehicle's license plates, after first making sure that her actions were not being observed by any of the motel's staff or other guests. It was perhaps an unnecessary precaution, given that their departure from the base while still driving the Jeep had raised no suspicions. After leaving the installation, they exchanged the military vehicle for the nondescript black sedan. They also had changed their appearances from that of army soldiers to civilians. Only then had they made their way to this motel, which had been their base of operations since arriving in Yuma.

Hearing movement, Gejalik turned to see Adlar emerging from the room's cramped bathroom. Like her, he had removed his mobile camouflage emitter and resumed his normal appearance. He was unclothed from the waist up, and Gejalik noted the patch of lighter skin on his upper arm from the wound he had just finished treating. "You have addressed your injury?"

His expression fixed, Adlar nodded, glancing at his arm. "Yes. The bullet passed through without causing severe damage, and there was little blood loss. I was able to heal it without complications."

"Do you require a pain suppressant?" Gejalik asked. Though several of the oft-used compounds in their medical kit had long ago been exhausted, she and her companions had been able to fashion acceptable substitutes using ingredients found in ample supply here on Earth.

"The pain is negligible," Adlar replied, flexing his arm as though to test the treatment he had performed on his wound. "I expect that I shall be fully recovered within a day." When he spoke, his voice lacked much of the authority and confidence he normally exhibited. That was understandable, given recent events.

"Excellent," Gejalik said, nodding in approval, and relief. With the loss they already had suffered, she was grateful Adlar had not been more seriously injured. "I know you and Etlun were intimate. I am saddened by her passing."

Saying nothing for a moment, Adlar merely stood in the middle of the room, looking at the dingy, stained carpet. When he returned his gaze to hers, Gejalik saw the sadness in his eyes.

"It was not our intention to bond," he said after a moment, his voice quiet. "Not in the beginning, and not even after we had been here for some time. We both knew it was improper and that it violated conduct protocols, but . . ." His words faded, though Gejalik suspected she knew what he might say next.

"Such things rarely are bound by rules and protocol. It was the same with Jaecz and I, and even Etlun, for a time."

Separated not only by distance but also by time from

everything and everyone for which they cared, it was natural that the four of them turned to each other in order to satisfy such needs. Even Adlar, the group's leader, was not immune to such failings, if indeed one considered compassion and love as a weakness. Gejalik did not, though she recognized the detriment such distractions could have during any covert or dangerous mission.

Adlar, his mood still somber, seemed intent on compartmentalizing his personal feelings for Etlun, at least until a less pressing moment presented itself. Ever the dependable leader, he drew a deep breath, his expression of sorrow seeming to vanish as he moved to sit on the edge of the room's lone bed.

"Etlun's loss is tragic, of course," he said, but despite the straightforward observation, Gejalik still perceived a trace of grief in his voice. "Equally unfortunate, however, is the loss of the ship. That, coupled with the certainty that they will study Etlun's body, means they now know of our presence here on Earth, and they will be taking steps to address that."

"They have suspected the existence of beings from other worlds for some time," Gejalik countered. "Such beliefs have informed their culture, particularly their various entertainment mediums." She had studied several examples of this fascination with life from other planets, finding particular amusement in the bizarre human obsession of extraterrestrials using their superior technology to invade Earth. In a manner typical of this species, they assumed with no small amount of arrogance that a truly advanced civilization would find anything of interest here. While history—assuming it played out in accordance with what she and the others had been told prior to undertaking their mission—ultimately would record this planet's impact on interstellar affairs in the centuries to come, its current technological and sociological status rendered it rather insignificant. Fate and circumstance had seen to it that the Earth of this time frame had been made part of a larger conflict about which it knew nothing, and perhaps even was responsible for the threat the planet one day would represent.

So, perhaps the childish fiction stories are not so wrong, after all? This, to Gejalik, also was amusing.

"While they may be aware of aliens among their kind," she continued, "they know nothing about us or our mission, and they will learn little from Etlun." She disliked the callousness of her statement, but it was a prudent observation.

Nodding, Adlar said, "I know. At least if we had managed to make use of the ship, her death might have more meaning."

They had been surprised to discover that a small cadre of human military and civilian scientists had been working with the craft in the first place, which Etlun determined was reconstructed from the remains of a vessel that—through no small feat of skill and good fortune—had been brought down by Air Force fighter planes. Despite their best efforts, Etlun and Adlar had been unable to decipher any clues as to the ship's point of origin, though they had rationalized that it must have been dispatched from a larger vessel. That much was evident from its propulsion system as well as its relative lack of consumables and other long-term subsistence equipment.

Adlar had first detected its presence on Earth using the limited scanning devices at their disposal, and he activated a communications signal he believed the ship capable of receiving while being well beyond the ability of current human technology to detect. As he had hoped, the vessel intercepted the signal and even dispatched a response, which had allowed Adlar to pinpoint its location in Yuma, Arizona. The region's relatively isolated terrain coupled with the restricted nature of a military installation had allowed the humans in possession of the craft the freedom to conduct experiments on the ship while reducing the chance of any unwanted attention.

Upon arriving in Yuma, the Certoss agents had wasted little time disposing of the humans guarding the craft in the secluded storage facility, after which they came to understand at least some of what the humans were attempting. It was obvious that a reverse engineering effort had taken place, with the Earth scientists working toward an experimental flight with a human at the ship's controls. Accessing the vessel's compact onboard computer, Adlar had learned that the ship was an unmanned survey vessel tasked with simple passive reconnaissance, and upon the completion of its automated mission would follow its programming and signal for further instructions. Another, larger ship was waiting somewhere in deep space to receive that signal, all while continuing with its own survey tasks at another, unknown destination.

It was Adlar's idea to use the craft to somehow make direct contact with its owner, a plan requiring modifications to the ship in order for it to carry a passenger including the installation of a life support system; something the humans had not yet done. Much of the computerized survey and recording equipment taking up space in the cockpit area had been removed and a seat installed for a pilot—a human pilot. Adlar and Etlun had planned to fashion a serviceable environmental control system to support a lone occupant, using whatever materials they could find on the army base without attracting attention. After a short test flight to verify the operational status of the new and modified onboard systems, it had been their intention to once more try contacting their fellow operative, Jaecz, before deciding which of them would make the attempt at a rendezvous with the other alien vessel, after which it was hoped their benefactors might help them make contact with Certoss Ajahlan. All of that careful planning had come undone at the hands of the human soldiers who found them at the military base.

"The humans now have proof of what they have always suspected," Gejalik said, "that they are not alone in the universe, and that representatives of several different civilizations have visited their world. Their anxiety over this revelation surely will motivate their desire to learn more, and this may well prove advantageous to us."

Adlar said nothing for a moment, rising from the bed and moving to the small sink at the back of the room, positioned against the rear wall next to the bathroom door. Gejalik watched him run water from the faucet, wetting his hands before pressing them to his face, then repeating the action to the top of his head.

"We know that the American military has pursued investigations of extraterrestrial activity, and Jaecz has reported that similar efforts are under way in other countries around the world. If we could infiltrate that program, it would give us insight into their progress." He turned from the sink and leaned against the vanity. "I doubt that anything they currently know could possibly lead them to us, and neither can they comprehend why we are here. Still, it would be wise to confirm my suspicions."

"Agreed," Gejalik replied. They already had been infiltrating the American military establishment almost since their arrival, taking on numerous guises and identities in their ongoing quest to acquire ever more information. "It's even possible that more thought and effort will be channeled toward responding to a perceived extraterrestrial threat by using nuclear weapons."

In the wake of the Second World War, a new emphasis now was on the proliferation of such weapons even as other global powers worked toward the same goals. Maintaining close ties to the military and the immense industrial infrastructure that had been created to support it was the best means of keeping apprised of rapid technological advancement. In just the handful of years since the United States's deployment of two atomic devices against its lone remaining enemy, Japan, to bring about the end of that conflict, the Soviet Union and Great Britain also had conducted successful tests of such weapons. Meanwhile, the political strain between the United States and Russia had only increased now that America's principal rival had become a "nuclear power." It was this heightening tension, Gejalik knew, that likely would provide their most promising leads toward accomplishing their mission.

"Any weapons the humans might bring to bear would be of little use," Adlar said, his gaze not on her but instead on the dingy linoleum tile covering the floor space near the sink. "They likely would do more harm to their own planet, rather than having any detrimental effect on an attacking force from space. Such a foolhardy tactic would only help the aggressors."

Gejalik considered this. "It would render large portions of the planet uninhabitable. Hardly a satisfactory conclusion, for either side. Then again, isn't this not at all dissimilar to the result we're trying to bring about?"

"In a manner of speaking," Adlar said. "While I would like to think we might find a means of accomplishing our mission that did not involve genocide, manipulating events so that Earth's major factions unleash their own destruction upon themselves is still the course of action with the greatest chance of success."

It was not the first time he had expressed such thoughts, of course. Though Gejalik knew him to be a steadfast soldier, Adlar did possess a contemplative side that often had put him at odds with his superiors who tended to see things in much more stark, easily discernible lines of thought. Gejalik often had wondered if their extended exile here on Earth might be affecting Adlar's perspective with respect to their goals, and whether he could be persuaded to abandon the mission. There was a time when she believed such a notion to be ludicrous, but now? She found it difficult to remain so confident, and she even wondered if Etlun's death could somehow be playing into whatever doubts he might be harboring.

"You disapprove of our mission?" she asked, deciding a forthright query was warranted.

Sighing, Adlar shook his head. "Such actions do not require my approval in order to proceed; merely my obedience."

"That does not answer my question," Gejalik pressed.

Adlar pushed himself from the vanity, stepping back into the main part of the room. "Are you doubting my loyalty?"

"No," Gejalik replied. "Merely your resolve." Before Adlar could respond, she held up her hand. "It's not an unreasonable concern, given everything we have experienced during our time here. After all, our experiences have shown us that this planet and its people have much to offer. Perhaps, if history had unfolded in different fashion, our two worlds might be allies."

"And that is precisely what has consumed my thoughts," Adlar said. "The question was always there, but the longer we remain here, the more I deliberate it. Perhaps the wise course of action is to do nothing, and allow history to unfold without our interference?" When Gejalik said nothing, he paused, scowling as though he was studying her expression. "Surely you must have considered this?"

"Of course, I have," Gejalik snapped, turning from him and returning her attention to the slight opening between the curtains. "But our situation has not changed. Our orders are clear: Proceed as previously directed."

Releasing an audible grunt of irritation, Adlar once more sat on the bed, pounding his fist into the mattress.

"I would never willfully disobey an order I thought to be just, but I find it impossible to dismiss the idea that our previous orders might no longer be valid. We could be working to stop a threat that no longer exists, or never existed, or never will exist." He stopped, and Gejalik watched his expression soften. "I think I should have paid greater attention during those temporal theory classes they forced upon us as part of our training."

His unexpected change in tone made her laugh, something she could not remember doing for some time.

"I have contemplated similar questions," she said after a moment, "and I agree that the issue might well be far more complicated than either you or I can even imagine. However, until we know the answers, you and I both know we have one course of action."

Nodding, Adlar reached up to rub the small indentation between his eyes and above his nasal passages.

"I find myself hoping that the humans will simply find a way to do our work for us."

"That is not an outlandish possibility," Gejalik replied, "particularly when considering current events."

The conflict being waged in Korea was the first real test of the political strain between the United States and the Soviet Union, with the former's government having already committed to the use of atomic weapons if the president felt such measures were warranted. Despite the looming specter of unleashing such devastating weaponry, a growing segment of the population seemed to have grown tired of war. It was a sentiment Gejalik could appreciate, even though she knew that Earth would endure its share of armed conflict for many years to come. Weapons would continue to be developed and built, armies would train, and governments would posture, each looking for some advantage or leverage to use over the others.

It was here, she knew, that their greatest opportunity to further their own goals was to be found.

Releasing another tired sigh, Adlar reclined on the bed. His hands clasped atop his chest, he stared up at the room's low ceiling. When he said nothing for several moments, Gejalik moved from the window to stand next to him.

"Are you unwell?" she asked.

Adlar's gaze did not move from the ceiling. "I am thinking of Etlun."

"I understand," Gejalik said, also feeling the loss of their friend and comrade. Though a lifetime of service had taught her the harsh realities of death and sacrifice, she could not help feeling as though the world around her and Adlar had just become larger and more foreboding. Anxiety, itself an uncommon sensation, gripped her. "Do you wish to be left to your solitude?"

Though it took him a moment to answer, when Adlar did reply his voice was low and quiet as he extended one hand to her. "No."

It was with great relief that Gejalik moved to lie next to him, feeling his warmth against hers and the comfort and security—real or imagined—their closeness offered.

NINE

U.S.S. Enterprise
Earth Year 2268

The coffee was terrible.

Frowning, Kirk examined the dark brown liquid in his cup, eyeing it with suspicion and contempt. "I think I need to have a word with Mister Scott," he said, placing the cup on the briefing room table and pushing it out of reach.

"Trouble, Jim?" McCoy asked from where he sat across the table from Kirk. A telltale hint of amusement played at the corners of the doctor's mouth.

"I'm pretty sure I've been poisoned with stuff that tasted better." Kirk glanced to the bank of food slots installed in the briefing room's rear bulkhead, not recalling any notes about the food processors in the daily status and maintenance reports he reviewed at the beginning of his duty shift. Sighing, he leaned back in his chair and crossed his arms. "You know, it'd be nice if the food processors were the most difficult thing we had to deal with today."

"And when do we ever have that kind of luck?" McCoy asked, making a point to pick up his own cup of coffee and drink from it. "Besides, this isn't that bad. Maybe you've just had too much today."

Kirk nodded. "I won't argue that, but it's the only thing that makes writing those reports bearable."

Since the abrupt arrival of the *Enterprise*'s pair of unexpected guests along with the Certoss vessel, he had spent a good deal of time composing his official statements for Starfleet Command, all while Spock, McCoy, and Scott endeavored to provide him with information to supplement his official detailing of the odd events as they had transpired.

"I can't wait to hear what they say about this report," McCoy said, taking another sip of his coffee. "It's always fun to see their reactions whenever we run into something like this."

Kirk chuckled. "Do you have any idea how hard it is to describe some of the things we've encountered? Not just the details of the events themselves, but also what I was thinking and feeling at the time. When I go back and look at some of those reports, even I have a hard time believing some of those things really happened."

There were occasions where the details of previous missions still sounded ridiculous, and he worried that others, while reading his reports and log entries back at headquarters or even in some Academy class decades from now, would consider certain accounts to be far-fetched if not outright fabrications. Therefore, he time and again found himself struggling to compose his official logs and reports in a manner he hoped would convey with absolute conviction and with all seriousness that the events as recounted did indeed happen.

McCoy offered him one of his sly, sideways grins. "Look at it this way, Jim: If commanding a starship doesn't work out, you've got plenty of material to write a book or three." He paused, and the smile widened. "Though, you may have to work on the whole believability thing."

"You're right," Kirk said, returning the grin before

retrieving his coffee cup and rising from his chair. As he crossed the room toward the row of food slots, he glanced over his shoulder. "Nobody would believe any self-respecting captain of a starship would ever put up with a chief medical officer like you."

Shrugging, McCoy replied, "Well, I am quite unbelievable."

As Kirk retrieved what he hoped was a fresher, better-tasting cup of coffee from the food slot, the briefing room's doors opened to admit Spock. The first officer was followed by Ensign Minecci, who led a security detail escorting Mestral and Gejalik.

"Captain," Spock said in greeting as Minecci directed his charges to chairs at the table. Neither Mestral nor Gejalik wore restraints, and whereas the Certoss still was dressed in the blue coveralls she had been given, her Vulcan companion had been provided with a red variant of the work uniform. Once the pair was seated, Minecci and his team moved to stand a discreet distance behind them, out of easy reach but close enough to intervene should circumstances require such action.

Nodding at the new arrivals as he resumed his place at the table, Kirk said, "I'd like to think that the need for security is temporary, but that's really up to you."

"Understood, Captain," Mestral replied.

To his right, separated from him by an empty chair, Gejalik added, "You have nothing to fear from me, Captain. I have no desire to cause any further disruptions for your ship or its crew."

"I appreciate that," Kirk said. His gut, along with the observations Spock had shared, already had convinced him that Gejalik posed no real threat, appearing resigned to her current situation. "As Mister Spock has no doubt made you aware, we've been met by a vessel supposedly dispatched from Certoss Ajahlan for the express purpose of locating my ship." He already had ordered Lieutenant Uhura to follow up on that score in the hopes of validating the peculiar claim, and he had done his best to placate Minister Ocherab while at the same time withholding the more outlandish aspects of the situation. "That vessel is currently sitting off our starboard bow, and its commander is waiting patiently while we try to figure out just what, exactly, is going on. You can imagine she has a number of questions of her own. According to her, Certoss Ajahlan received a message nearly three hundred years ago, presumably sent by you."

The Certoss agent nodded. "That is correct, Captain."

Kirk already had given careful consideration to his line of questioning prior to their guests' arrival. Things were complicated enough with Certoss Ajahlan having received the mysterious message three centuries ago, with a follow-up provided in the present. If Spock was correct about what he had told Kirk of his interview with Gejalik, there would seem to be additional temporal considerations, given that the agent currently in his custody appeared to be from a path through history not traveled by her home planet. Had the time stream changed for her, or for the rest of her people, and what did that mean for everyone and everything else?

I'm going to need more coffee.

Resting his elbows on the table, he asked, "Mestral, you said earlier that you were working with military officers to track Gejalik and her companions. Do you know what happened to them?"

"My human colleagues were pursuing an investigative lead that required us to separate," the Vulcan replied. "As for the other Certoss operatives, it is my understanding that one was killed in 1952, prior to my arrival on Earth. Another actually visited me soon after my companions were rescued and returned to our homeworld. There was a confrontation, after which he disappeared. When I began working with agents of the American military, we attempted to track the movements of Gejalik and her remaining companions. Our investigations took us in different directions. I traveled to New Jersey and New York, whereas my human partners went to Florida."

McCoy, sitting with his arms folded across his chest as he observed the proceedings, released a small grunt. "And I guess we all know what happened after that."

"We operated with extreme stealth, Captain, living in disguise for months at a time and with no contact amongst ourselves," Gejalik replied. "It was the only way to safely infiltrate secure installations or private firms and acquire the information, materials, and access we required to carry out our mission. During one of his own operations, Jaecz became aware of what he at first believed to be evidence of agents from another advanced race, working in secret on Earth. He discovered them through their own technology, which was far more advanced than anything humans could have developed on their own by that point in time. According to him and the notes he kept, it took him a span of years to successfully penetrate the layers of security surrounding these other agents so that he could covertly gather intelligence. I only just discovered before arriving here that while they were humans, they were not from Earth."

"Gary Seven." The name escaped Kirk's lips before he even realized he was speaking it aloud. Some of the puzzle pieces now were beginning to fall into place.

"You obviously have had previous contact with this person, Captain," Mestral said.

"That's one way to put it," Kirk replied. Before he could say anything else, the briefing room's relatively calm atmosphere was shattered as the ship shuddered around them. Kirk reached for the table to prevent being thrown from his chair as the bulkheads and deck groaned under the strain of what felt like something striking the hull. The ship's alert klaxon began wailing as the alarm indicator above the door flashed deep crimson, its pulsing in sync to the piercing emergency signal.

"*Red Alert!*" shouted Lieutenant Sulu's voice over the ship's comm system. "*This is not a drill! Repeat: This is not a drill!*"

Kirk keyed the intercom. "Kirk here. What is it, Lieutenant?"

The three-sided viewer situated at the center of the table activated, and Sulu's image appeared on all three screens. Kirk could see the agitation on the helm officer's expression, despite the younger man's best efforts to mind his bearing.

"*Sir, some kind of energy beam has locked onto us. Origin point unknown, but it's definitely not the Certoss ship.*"

"All hands to battle stations," Kirk ordered. "Deflector shields to full strength. Stand by all weapons."

"*Shields and weapons are ready, sir, but we have no target. Whatever's generating the beam, it's nowhere in our sensor range. It looks to be a very powerful scanning beam, and its intensity is continuing to increase.*"

The hiss of the briefing room's doors sliding open made Kirk look up, and his eyes widened as he saw not the gray bulkheads of the corridor beyond the entrance, but instead a bright, roiling cloud of blue-black plasma, coalescing as if from the air itself. A high-pitched whine flooded the room, but the cloud seemed to contain itself within the frame of the doorway as it grew larger and brighter.

"What the devil . . . ?" McCoy exclaimed, his voice hoarse as he rose from his chair and backed away from the conference table.

Gejalik and Mestral were standing now as well, and Kirk saw that the three security officers had drawn their phasers to cover their prisoners. Ensign Minecci was dividing his attention between them and what was happening at the door, his weapon moving back and forth.

"Captain," Mestral said, holding out a hand. "Wait. We have seen this before."

"*It's a transporter beam!*" shouted the voice of Montgomery Scott from the tabletop viewer, and Kirk glanced over to see that the chief engineer's anxious face had replaced Sulu on the screen.

More puzzle pieces?

"Scotty," Kirk snapped. "Is it the same one we . . . ?" The rest of his question caught in his throat as a figure appeared from within the blue fog. It was a human female, dressed in dark gray pants and a matching jacket over a white blouse. Her bright blond hair was long enough to fall just past her shoulders. Though he had last seen her only a week ago, there was a noticeable difference in the way she now carried herself. She was still quite young, but there was a confidence in her blue eyes that only was just beginning to assert itself on that earlier occasion. As she stepped into the room, the blue cloud behind her faded, leaving only the corridor outside the doorway.

"Hello, Captain," said Roberta Lincoln. "Long time, no see." Then, as though considering her statement, she smiled. "Well, for me, anyway."

"Miss Lincoln," Kirk said, studying her face and trying to make sense of what he was seeing. "Something told me you and Mister Seven would be showing up here eventually."

Lincoln nodded. "I would've come sooner, Captain, but as it happens, I only just became aware of this situation."

Listening to her speak, Kirk noted that her voice and movements carried with them a maturity he did not recall from their previous encounter. Her demeanor even seemed reinforced by her wardrobe. Gone were the bright, flamboyant colors and form-fitting attire he remembered, replaced with the far more reserved and professional ensemble she now wore.

Eyeing Mestral and Gejalik with interest, Lincoln said, "One thing I've recently learned is that Certoss field operatives are pretty good at covering their tracks."

"So, you know these people?" Kirk asked, gesturing toward his invited guests.

"I do now," Lincoln replied, stepping farther into the room. "As I'm sure you've already figured out, we have a lot to talk about."

Kirk sighed. "I can only imagine."

Behind him, McCoy grunted. "I guess you'll be writing another report."

TEN

Los Angeles, California
January 14, 1955

Ignoring the growing ache in his hands, Cal Sutherland urged his swollen fingers to continue punching at the typewriter keys in rapid-fire fashion. After struggling with the angle he had wanted for this article, he had found his rhythm and the words now were coming fast. His fingers moved almost at a blur, working to keep pace with the thoughts coursing from his brain down into his hands. The ceaseless ticking of the keys impacting the paper was interrupted by the regular—and very frequent—sound of the typewriter's bell announcing that he had reached the page's right margin. As his left hand moved for the carriage return lever to push the machine's platen back so that it realigned the page with its left margin, Sutherland's right hand retrieved the cigarette stub from his mouth. Without looking, he reached for the ashtray on his desk, intending to snuff out the depleted cigarette, when he realized he was simply pushing it down into the mound of smoked butts that had accumulated there.

"Damn," Sutherland said, picking up the ashtray and dumping its contents into the wastebasket on the floor behind him. Then, he lifted the basket and brushed into it the dozen or so butts that had fallen from the ashtray to litter the papers on his desk. How had he not managed to start a fire in here? And where the hell was Glenda? Then, glancing through the open shades of his office's dirty window, he saw how low the sun had dropped toward the horizon.

What time was it, anyway?

He looked to the clock over his office door and saw that it was nearly six o'clock. Glenda usually left for the day around five. Even though it was a Friday night with deadlines looming—there likely were a few other people working in other offices, or down the hall in the bullpen—most of the secretaries would already be gone unless their bosses needed something urgent.

Coffee, for example, Sutherland thought as he examined the inside of the mug he did not remember draining. Grunting, he set the cup back down on the desk and picked up the cigarette pack, only to see that it, too, was empty. *Or some smokes.* Given the lateness of the hour, he considered the bottle of Scotch in his desk's bottom drawer, but decided for the moment to resist imbibing. Once the article was finished, he would celebrate in proper fashion.

A knock on his door made him look up, and through the door's frosted glass window he saw a burly figure waiting outside. "Yeah?" he called out, and the door opened to admit the robust form of Tom Larkin, his friend and colleague. He was wearing his suit jacket and hat, telling Sutherland that the other man was on his way out of the building.

"I'm hungry," Larkin announced. "You?"

Sutherland nodded. "Yeah, now that you mention it." So engrossed was he in the new article that he had skipped lunch. That happened a lot these days, particularly around deadline time. He knew he was running late with the article, and his layout editor had called him four times that afternoon to remind him.

Larkin hooked a thumb over his shoulder. "I'm going down to Mabel's to grab a quick bite. They got meat loaf and pork chops on special tonight. Interested?"

"Sounds like a plan," Sutherland replied. Mabel's, a corner diner a few blocks down the street, was a favored lunch and dinner hangout for several of the people in the office. The coffee was always hot, and the waitresses always did commendable jobs filling out their uniforms. "I need a break, anyway." Flexing his tired fingers, he leaned back in his chair and blew out an exasperated sigh. Then his gaze fell upon the page still in his typewriter and he smiled.

"What's that about?" Larkin asked. "You finally done with that piece?"

"Almost, yeah," Sutherland replied. Just a few more paragraphs to close it out and the new article would be finished, and with a little polish it would be the centerpiece of his magazine's latest issue.

Stepping into the office, Larkin said, "When are you going to quit writing about flying saucers and get back to where the real action is?"

"This is the real action," Sutherland retorted, pointing at the typewriter. "Just wait until you read this baby." As editor in chief and the lone staff writer for *Watch the Skies*, one of six magazines written and published from the offices of Schlitz Periodicals, Sutherland strove to bring the magazine's small yet loyal and growing readership actual, hard evidence proving the existence of beings from other worlds and the incredible craft in which they had traveled to Earth from some far-flung planet. "Sooner or later, more and more people are going to pay attention to all these pictures, and reports, and denials by the government. You'll see."

His current project, writing about sightings of unexplained

lights in the desert skies near Las Vegas, had taken him weeks to assemble. The interviews he had conducted, and even the road trip he had taken in order to take pictures of the witnesses as well as the area where the sightings had occurred, should really make the piece sing, he decided.

Larkin chuckled. "You really do believe that stuff, don't you?"

Unlike Sutherland, the other man had long ago settled into his role as writer and photographer for one of the other Schlitz titles, *Tinseltown Tattler*, a Hollywood tabloid rag that had the distinction of having given Cal Sutherland his first writing job after his time in Korea.

"You've seen the same pictures I have," Sutherland said, "and read the same reports and witness statements. Are you telling me you still don't believe *any* of it?" Rising from his chair, he crossed to the coat tree in the back corner of his office. He pulled on his suit jacket before retrieving his favorite brown fedora from the tree's top. He moved to straighten his tie, but then decided to leave it loose and his shirt collar unbuttoned. Mabel had seen him dressed in much sloppier fashion over the years, after all.

She's also seen you dressed in a lot less, he reminded himself, fond memories eliciting a small, knowing smile.

"How many times have we had this discussion?" Larkin asked, punctuating his question with a belch. "Nope, I really don't think little green Martians are coming to suck out our brains." Digging a finger in his left ear, he added, "Besides, after five years chasing stories and idiots around this town, I can't figure out what any aliens would want with us."

Watching his friend examine whatever it was he had extracted from his ear, Sutherland said, "Yeah, me neither."

No matter their motivations for being here, he had

become convinced that such beings *were* here or, at least, had been here and might well be coming again. Bringing that truth to the public was not an easy task, what with every movie studio in Hollywood doing their level best to outdo each other and push the latest alien invasion and monster film into theaters. Martians bent on subjugating humans—the women, at least—seemed to be everywhere thanks to movies, comic books, and magazines sold on every corner and with stories written by anybody who could put their fingers to a typewriter.

Larkin wiped his finger on his trouser leg. "So, why keep doing this? Not for nothing, but downstairs was a lot more fun before you left."

"I got tired of peeking through windows and rummaging around trash cans and sleeping in alleys or in the bushes, hoping for one decent picture," Sutherland replied, noting his now steadily grumbling stomach as he moved for the door and opened it.

Chuckling, Larkin flashed him a wide grin. "Okay, I'll admit the pot busts are getting old, but some of those crazy parties?" He whistled. "I never get tired of those. You should see some of the pictures I've been getting. Too many to use! That's okay, though, because I've got me a little side business thing going, selling my extra stuff to a couple of those girlie rags. You know, like . . ."

Sutherland held up a hand. "I really don't want to know. And don't let Garner catch you doing that," he said, referring to Larkin's editor on the *Tinseltown Tattler,* an irritable, unpleasant man named Harold Garner. "He'll toss your sorry butt down the garbage chute." Sutherland had known Garner when both were working as staff writers on the *Tattler* and even then he had been an insufferable bastard. It only stood to reason that he would be promoted when the magazine's former editor, Chuck Elliot, retired the previous year.

"That's okay," Larkin replied, shrugging. "I think he knows already, but he also knows he can't pay me what one of those other places would if I went to work over there full time. I'm still his best writer, so he cuts me a lot of slack."

"Just watch your back," Sutherland said, waiting for Larkin to follow him into the hallway before closing and locking his office door. "Garner's probably just biding his time, waiting for the right moment to drop the hammer on you."

The man's elevation to management in the wake of Elliot's leaving was just one of the reasons Sutherland had opted to change jobs when the opportunity presented itself.

That, and the job really was crap on a cracker.

A combat correspondent for the United States Army in Korea after serving as an infantryman in Europe during World War II, Sutherland had seen and reported on the best—and worst—aspects of the latter conflict. Ready for a definite change once his time in uniform had concluded, he found his first real writing job thanks to Chuck Elliot at the *Tattler*. It had taken him a while to get used to the very different approach to "journalism" the magazine practiced. Still the best selling of all the Schlitz publications, the *Tinseltown Tattler* delighted in filling its pages with lurid pictures and gossip about the actors and actresses flitting about Hollywood. After a year spent toiling away for that magazine's editor, during which he had photographed and written about all manner of drug busts, sex parties, shady business deals, tragic romances, and even a few unfortunate deaths, Sutherland came to realize that while he liked working for Elliot, the *Tattler* was eating at his soul.

Then, *Watch the Skies* came along.

A skeptic from the outset, Sutherland at first had accepted the offer from his publisher to write for the newest title in the Schlitz arsenal with the idea—and challenge—of approaching the work from a pure investigative journalism standpoint. He treated the subject with the same objectivity he believed to be practiced by another writer with whom he had become acquainted, Donald Keyhoe. Sutherland had read the other man's books, including the notable *Flying Saucers from Outer Space,* which Keyhoe, who originally had professed doubts as to the possibility of UFOs being actual alien craft, had written using interviews and official Air Force reports as source material. Though appearing to possess at least as many critics as he did supporters, Keyhoe's reputation was hard to impugn, standing as it did on the foundation he had built as a writer with an eye for detail and accuracy. Many of his more vocal detractors, including some from inside the Air Force, tended to point to his career as a writer of outlandish fiction stories featuring characters with superhuman or even supernatural powers as evidence of his overactive imagination and propensity for embellishment.

After digesting the book and spending untold months corresponding with Keyhoe via mail about the effort invested to write it, Sutherland became convinced the other man firmly believed every word he had written. With that in mind, he vowed he would hold himself to the same standards Keyhoe had exhibited when researching his books. Unlike the nonsense that fueled gossip rags around town like the *National Register*, *Hush-Hush,* and even the *Tattler,* Sutherland wanted *Watch the Skies* to be different; a lone voice of truth amid a mob of people content to be fed a diet of derivative fantasy and even outright lies, some of which were printed in yet another of the magazines bearing the Schlitz Periodicals banner.

Down the hall from the *Watch the Skies* offices were those of sibling publication *Startling Universe,* which specialized in science fiction stories of the sort Sutherland had come to see as a hindrance to his own job. His irritation at the two magazines' seemingly contradictory goals was only furthered by his publisher's decision to use the same in-house artist to provide illustrations for both titles. In some instances, the same picture of a bizarre creature from outer space had graced pages in issues of each magazine, done solely as a cost-saving measure. Sutherland routinely fought this practice, but was overruled every time.

Remembering that he wanted to check to see if anything had come for him in the afternoon mail, Sutherland pointed toward the office mail room as they started down the hallway. "I'm expecting a package," he said by way of explanation.

"Another top-secret delivery from your mole inside the Air Force?" Larkin asked, grinning again.

Sutherland scowled, glancing over his shoulder and then toward the lobby to see if anyone may have overheard the other man's remark. "Why not just run downstairs and yell up at me from the sidewalk," he said. "Not everybody needs to know who or where I get my leads." Satisfied that no one was eavesdropping, he added in a lower voice, "But, yeah. I'm hoping for some new stuff."

His passion for wanting truth, professionalism, and objectivity for *Watch the Skies* and the work he was doing only deepened when he began receiving help from a most unexpected source. One day, the afternoon mail had brought with it a large brown envelope with no return address but a postmark indicating it had been sent or at least dropped into a mailbox from Dayton, Ohio. The envelope contained dozens of pages of mimeographed documents that Sutherland recognized as being military in nature, with each of them carrying the same single code name designation: PROJECT BLUE BOOK.

The package also contained a letter with no signature or other clues as to the sender's identity, who purported to be someone placed within the Blue Book hierarchy and wanting to ensure that the truth continued to flow out from beyond the cloak of secrecy enveloping the project. Sutherland's unknown benefactor—assuming he was not lying for some reason—seemed to share the same concerns harbored by those who denounced the military's efforts as either insufficient, apathetic, or deceitful. To that end, he was providing the enclosed documents, and would continue to pass on other information if and when he was able.

Struggling to contain his excitement, Sutherland spent the rest of that night poring over the documents contained in that initial package. He read with disbelief the accounts of what really had happened in Roswell, New Mexico, in 1947 as well as other sightings in the following years about which little more than rumor was generally known, particularly the controversial light sightings in Lubbock, Texas, in 1951 and the odd craft reports from Yuma in 1952. From the copious notes he assembled from his research as well as other information he obtained from interviews he conducted with witnesses to back up the supposed official reports, Sutherland produced what would be the first in a series of stories detailing the Air Force's ongoing investigation of UFO sightings as well as the results of those efforts. Driving the meat of his feature were the details of the reports he had received from his anonymous sponsor, which often differed to a great extent from the information disseminated to the public.

After the publication of the issue containing that piece, *Watch the Skies* began to see an increase in newsstand sales as well as subscription requests. Reader responses came in all forms, from telegrams to letters mailed here to the office, and most of the reaction seemed positive. Sutherland also learned that the military was reading the magazine when two officers from Edwards Air Force Base arrived at the Schlitz Periodicals offices for a visit. Their demeanor was cordial, no doubt designed to put him at ease, and they never accused him of possessing unauthorized information, but Sutherland's journalism and interview training told him they were snooping and hoping to learn about his sources.

Expecting some form of military response to his writing, he had taken steps to ensure that the prized Blue Book information provided by his nameless source was protected, hidden away in one of a dozen safe deposit boxes at different banks around town, each held under a false identity he had created for preserving such valuable materials. Now aware that the government might have someone monitoring his activities, he remained vigilant, working to make sure the Air Force never learned of his enigmatic inside man or the information he provided.

Sorry, flyboys.

The only thing waiting for Sutherland in his mail room inbox were a few interoffice memos he likely would never read, along with two pieces that—judging by their handwritten return addresses—he took to be fan mail or other reader correspondence. Those he enjoyed reading, and he tucked the envelopes into his jacket pocket. He frowned at the lack of any package for him.

"Guess your secret admirer forgot about you again," Larkin said, smiling. "Think he found someone better? You know, someone who takes him to *dinner* once in a while?"

Laughing at the none-too-subtle hint, Sutherland held up his hands in mock surrender. "Okay, okay. Sorry. Let's get some grub." Turning to leave the mail room, he reached for his back pocket and did not feel the expected bulge there. "Hang on. I forgot my wallet."

"Mabel's going to run out of cherry pie if you keep stalling," Larkin said.

Sutherland snorted. "Trust me, Mabel's cherry pie *isn't going anywhere*." As he expected, Larkin chuckled at the crude joke, shaking his head. "I'll just be a minute."

Jogging back up the hallway, Sutherland fumbled for his keys as he reached his office door and let himself in. His wallet was waiting for him on his desk, and he was crossing the room toward it when he detected movement out of the corner of his eye. Looking up, he fixed his gaze on the frosted glass window of the door leading to his office's second, adjoining room.

Beyond the glass and the single word—"Private"—painted in black letters upon it, someone moved past the door.

ELEVEN

What the hell?

Someone had broken into his office? Sutherland used the other room as meeting and storage space once he had come to understand that writing for *Watch the Skies* required voluminous research. It also was something of a personal study area, and usually was where he inspected any files or other information he acquired and which he preferred to treat with caution and secrecy. While he had long ago turned to concealing the most sensitive materials away from the office, he did keep some of the juicy bits here in his files, just in case the government or someone else came snooping. He figured that if they found something of interest here, they might be thrown off the scent of the really eye-opening stuff he had elected to store elsewhere. Was that happening now?

Looks like somebody's curious.

In addition to the door leading from his main office, the room had a second point of entry from the hallway, but like this door it featured a lock for which he possessed the only key. The only way someone could be in there is if they had picked a lock on one of the doors, or climbed through the sixth-story window. Standing next to his desk, Sutherland listened for telltale signs of movement from the other room, but heard nothing. Had he imagined the movement?

No, he decided. Whatever caught his attention had for

the briefest of moments blocked the light of the desktop lamp he could still see through the glass. His imagination was not playing tricks on him. Keeping his eyes on the door, he moved so that he could open his desk's upper right drawer, from which he extracted the pistol he kept there.

The Colt M1911 .45 caliber semiautomatic pistol felt even heavier than usual in his hand. Though he maintained it in good working order and made a point of taking it to a nearby firing range at least a few times a year, it had been a long time since he had even considered aiming such a weapon at another person. He even had questioned the wisdom of keeping the gun here in his office, but left it there after the aggrieved husband of the woman he had been dating showed up one evening to "discuss" the relationship. Though other, smaller pistols might seem a more prudent choice, the simple truth was that the .45 was the one weapon aside from the M1 Garand rifle that Sutherland still could break down and reassemble while blindfolded. He trusted its reliability and stopping power. What he had to wonder about was himself. Though he lifted weights to stay in shape, he still was several years removed from the young, lean man who had waded ashore in Normandy against the hellish onslaught of German machine guns. During his tour in Korea, he had never so much as drawn his pistol from its holster except to clean it. Would the old training and instincts come back?

Hell of a time to start doubting yourself.

Ignoring the slight tremor in his hands, Sutherland pulled back the pistol's slide to verify that the first of the magazine's seven rounds had been chambered. He tightened his grip on the weapon as he stepped around his desk and toward the door. For the first time, he was seized by the nagging sensation that the party in the other room—whoever they might be—now knew that their presence had been detected. He was wondering when a bullet with his name on it might come screaming through the glass when he heard the sound of another door opening, and Sutherland realized that the intruder was exiting into the hallway. Lunging forward, he grabbed the doorknob and turned it, only to curse upon realizing it was locked. He could hear running footsteps echoing beyond the wall, heading toward the rear of the building, and he sprinted for his main office door. By the time he emerged into the hallway it was to see a man dressed all in black, rounding the corner at the end of the corridor. The stairwell lay at the end of that short passage, which meant escape for the interloper.

"Hey!" Sutherland shouted, running toward the intersection. Upon reaching the corner he slowed, leading with the .45 as he turned into the shorter hall and leveled the pistol at the door leading to the stairs. The door was swinging shut, and he heard the sounds of shoes on stairs, heading downward.

"Cal!" a voice shouted from behind him, and he looked back to see Larkin lumbering into the hallway from the mail room, an expression of confusion clouding his round features.

Holding up his free hand, Sutherland called out, "Stay there!" before running to the stairwell door and yanking it open. Footsteps were clapping on the stairs below him, and he went to the railing in an attempt to spot the escaping stranger. Seeing the figure two flights below him, he stuck his pistol over the rail and yelled again.

"Stop right there or I'll shoot!"

The intruder did halt his descent, but Sutherland's eyes

went wide as he saw the man, who wore some kind of ski mask to cover his face, raise his arm and point a pistol of his own. The gun's muzzle seemed massive even from this distance, aimed as it was at his face. Sutherland jumped back from the railing, anticipating a shot and even flinching in expectation. It took him an extra moment to realize that the other man had not fired. Instead, Sutherland heard the renewed sounds of the intruder making his escape down the stairwell.

Clever. Very clever, asshole.

Switching the pistol to his left hand, he took the steps two and three at a time, keeping his hand on the railing and using the heavy wooden anchor post at the bottom of each landing to swing him around to the next flight of stairs. His quarry was damned fast, though, having already made it to the first floor and through the door leading out of the stairwell. By the time Sutherland reached the bottom landing and burst through the door into the building's foyer, he appeared to be alone. He kept his pistol ready, but a quick check of the room confirmed his suspicions. Inspecting the building's front and rear street-level exits, he saw no clue as to which direction the other man may have gone. Outside the building's front entrance, he noted that street lamps had come on as dusk approached.

"Damn it," he grunted, realizing for the first time that he was breathing hard. He reached up to remove his fedora before using his jacket cuff to wipe dampness from his forehead. It would do no good to attempt giving chase, even if he knew which route the intruder had taken to make his getaway. Whoever he was, he doubtless had made it to a nearby alley or a waiting car, and now was gone.

The only question now is: What did the bastard take?

Sutherland opted for the elevator to return him to the sixth floor, and when the doors opened he saw Tom Larkin waiting in the lobby, his worried expression only deepening when he noted the pistol in his friend's hand.

"What in the name of holy hell was that all about?" Larkin asked.

Blowing out his breath, Sutherland shook his head. "Damned if I know. Somebody broke into my office." Ignoring the confused stares of those few coworkers who had not yet left for the day, he moved from the lobby and through the bullpen that served as a common workspace for the staffs of *Watch the Skies* and the other magazines with offices on this floor. He was walking toward the hall leading to his office when a new thought—something that should have occurred to him well before now—came to mind. "What I don't understand is how he got in there in the first place, and how he managed to do it so fast. You and I weren't out of there but for a couple of minutes."

He was waiting for an opening.

"Son of a bitch," Sutherland said, feeling his jaw tighten as realization dawned. "He had to be casing the place, just hoping for a chance to get in here, which means he was after something specific." Quickening his pace with Larkin on his heels, he ran up the hallway until he came to the open door leading into his office's second room. With his pistol still in his hand, he took an extra moment to clear the interior before stepping through the doorway.

"Anything missing?" Larkin asked from where he stood at the entrance.

Moving around the room, Sutherland eyed the filing cabinets lining the walls. Each was secured with a padlock and a metal bar running through the drawer handles. Without a key like the one on the ring in Sutherland's pocket, there was no easy, fast way to access the cabinets' contents. None of the file boxes stacked on top of the cabinets or even under the small, square table occupying the room's center appeared to have been disturbed.

Then, Sutherland's eyes fell on the large brown envelope sitting on the table, positioned before the chair in which he almost always sat when working in this room, and he realized that his unknown visitor had not come to take anything.

"I'll be damned," he breathed. Engaging the .45's safety, he placed the weapon on the table as he moved to get a better look at the envelope. With only the dim illumination from the small corner lamp, he had almost missed the package.

Behind him, he heard Larkin stepping into the room. "Damn it, Cal. What's going on?" When Sutherland looked up, it was to see his friend's attention focused on the envelope. "Is that what I think it is?" he asked.

"Only one way to find out," Sutherland replied. The envelope bore no mailing information. There was no clue as to who had delivered it, and indeed only two words were handwritten on the envelope's front: "Cal Sutherland." He opened the envelope and slid its contents onto the table. As had been the case on previous occasions when he had received packages of this sort, it was a collection of official-looking documents—mimeographed copies—and a typed cover letter bearing no clue as to its writer's identity. Like the other such letters he had been given, this one also was short and to the point.

Mr. Sutherland,

It is becoming more difficult to obtain reports so that I can send them to you. I believe that my superiors suspect that someone connected to the project is providing you information. If they find me, I will go to prison, so I must be careful.

I still believe what you are doing is right, and I want to help, but I hope you will understand that my attempts to contact you will be less frequent from now on. Until then, I hope the information I am providing will help you.

Good luck.

As usual, the writer had chosen not to sign the letter. Likewise, there was no pithy attempt at a nickname or alias as part of some clever sign-off, asking him to "keep watching the skies!" as was the case with much of the reader mail he received.

"So, what is it?" Larkin asked. Stepping closer for a better look, he reached out to spread the papers across the table. "They're all stamped 'Top Secret.' Are you even supposed to have these?"

"Not really," Sutherland replied, though he knew of no laws preventing him from reading any government documents—even those intended for a very restricted audience—that might come to him. On the other hand, his unknown benefactor faced the very real threat of prosecution, thanks to a regulation enacted by the military that made it illegal for service personnel to discuss any classified reports or other documentation pertaining to UFO sightings or witness interviews. Anyone found to be in violation of that regulation could be sent to prison and fined up to ten thousand dollars per offense. Whoever was assisting him did so at great risk to himself.

Setting aside the cover letter, Sutherland examined the

documents, each of which bore some kind of stamp or label marking them as classified along with the Blue Book designation. "They're reports," he said for Larkin's benefit. "Investigations of recent sightings." The locations, he noted, were scattered across the country. He was familiar with some of the incidents, while others were new to him.

"I don't get it," Larkin said, taking off his fedora and scratching his balding head. "I thought you said this guy always mailed you the stuff. Why would he break in here and risk getting caught if all he wanted was to give you that?"

"I don't know," Sutherland said after a moment, when whatever seemed to be bothering him refused to come together and form a cohesive line of thinking. "Something about this is just off." Why *would* his unknown ally risk the danger of coming here and exposing himself if he truly was offering more of the same assistance he had provided? And if he was a friend, why the hell had he pointed a gun at Sutherland?

Well, you did say you were going to shoot him.

"Yeah," Sutherland said, nodding to himself as he began gathering the papers in order to return them to their envelope. "Something's definitely up here." Figuring out what that might be would take time.

And coffee. And cigs. And Scotch. At present, he had only one of those three vital ingredients.

"Well," Larkin said, "I don't know about you, but I tend to think better when I'm not starving."

And food.

Though Sutherland rather would read over the papers than eat, he knew he was going to be in for another long night, and maybe Larkin was on to something. Dinner first, he decided.

"Let's go see if Mabel's got any of that pie left," he said, retrieving the .45 so that he could return it to his desk. He also grabbed the envelope. There was no way he was leaving it here. Besides, it would make for good dinner conversation. Eyeing his friend, Sutherland smiled. "So, you think this is the real action yet?"

"Definitely looking up," Larkin replied. "Still not as much fun as those crazy parties, though."

Approaching the mouth of the alley, James Wainwright paused to remove the ski mask covering his head and face and stuck it into his jacket pocket. After all, it would not do to alarm any pedestrians he might encounter at this early evening hour. He took several deep breaths in an attempt to bring his elevated respiration back under control, reaching up to smooth his hair and wipe sweat from his face. The dash from the office building had been risky, but far less worrisome than being caught—or even shot—by the magazine reporter. The man's disheveled appearance was deceiving; given his service training and experience, Sutherland might well have succeeded in wounding or even killing Wainwright had the opportunity presented itself.

The dark sedan was waiting for him with its engine running and lights off when Wainwright emerged from the alley and opened the unlocked passenger door before plunging inside. As planned, Allison Marshall had taken the precaution of covering the interior light with dark tape so that it would not illuminate either of them when he opened the door. She was sitting in the driver's seat with both hands on the steering wheel and greeted him with an expression of concern.

"Go," he said, by way of return greeting.

Marshall put the car into gear and stepped on the

accelerator, guiding the sedan into the early evening city traffic. Settling into his seat, Wainwright glanced first in the rearview mirror before looking over his shoulder. Though he did not expect to see any signs of pursuit, he was not ruling out the possibility. Cal Sutherland, from the information Wainwright had been able to gather, was rather resourceful as a journalist, even if he chose to devote his talent and skills to tabloid magazines.

"Sir?" Marshall prompted after driving in silence for a couple of blocks. "Did you do it?"

Turning back to face forward in his seat, Wainwright nodded. "I delivered the package, but I didn't get a chance to do anything else." Sighing in frustration, he removed the small .38 caliber revolver from his waistband and placed the weapon in the glove compartment, exchanging it for the pack of cigarettes and his lighter. "He almost caught me when he came back to the office for something." What truly irritated him was that he had waited most of the afternoon, hiding in an unused office down the hall from Sutherland's and biding his time until the reporter left for the day. He should have held his position long enough to ensure the other man was out of the building before entering his office, and he had nearly been shot for his lack of patience.

Idiot.

Dividing her attention between the traffic and him, Marshall asked, "So, you didn't find anything?"

Wainwright extracted a cigarette from the pack and lit it, savoring that first draw as he inhaled the smoke into his lungs. "I only had a couple of minutes, but I didn't see anything useful." The material visible on Sutherland's desk was interesting though not damaging, and a quick perusal of the desk drawers had yielded nothing. On the other hand, the filing cabinets in the adjacent office had enticed him, requiring far more time to unlock each of them in order to examine their contents than was available to him. "Something tells me the stuff we'd be looking for isn't even there."

"What makes you say that?"

He pondered Marshall's question as he took another long draw from his cigarette. After blowing smoke out the open passenger window, Wainwright shook his head. "Just a gut feeling, I guess. Sutherland strikes me as smart and sneaky enough to cover his tracks. If there's anything really incriminating, I'm betting he's got it squirreled away somewhere else."

As part of his regular Blue Book duties, Wainwright tried to keep himself updated on how various segments of the civilian population treated the notion of UFOs and possible alien activity on Earth. This research took many forms, including the review of any printed materials that prominently featured anything pertaining to the subject. News reports of sightings, newspaper interviews with alleged witnesses, and even books and magazines, from which there seemed to be a steady, increasing focus. *Watch the Skies* was just one periodical that regularly crossed his desk. While it had started out as little more than sensationalist tripe not far removed from the gossip columns infesting many Hollywood-based publications, in the past year the stories it contained had taken on an air of heightened legitimacy, setting it apart from other such efforts. This seemed to resonate with its readership, which was reported to be growing with each new biweekly issue, but it also had attracted the Air Force's attention.

After carefully reviewing a stack of the magazine's back issues, Wainwright had come to the conclusion that its coverage of UFO sightings, witness accounts, and even the military's official responses to the reports was just a bit too good. In particular, this level of quality seemed to stand out when *Watch the Skies*, usually in the form of an article written by Calvin Sutherland, called on the Air Force to be more forthcoming with details regarding a particular investigation. There was nothing in the magazine's content that suggested a direct connection to a military source; certainly no classified photographs or report excerpts. Still, Sutherland almost certainly was receiving information and assistance from someone connected to Blue Book. His occasional oblique references to having read top-secret documents only supported that assertion.

Wainwright had communicated his concerns to Captain Charles Hardin, the officer currently overseeing the project. The possibility of an information leak to a civilian print publication, even one so fringe and low-impact as *Watch the Skies*, warranted attention, and to that end Hardin had ordered Wainwright and Marshall to investigate.

"I know what you're thinking, sir," Marshall said in the midst of making a left turn. "You want to go back there anyway, right? Just to get a better look?"

"Yeah," Wainwright replied, reaching to snuff out his half-smoked cigarette. "Even though I think anything really damning won't be there, that doesn't mean we won't find some clue about whoever he's talking to. Mailing address, a postmarked envelope, something."

Given the presence of Blue Book liaison officers on most major Air Force bases around the country, finding the source of the leak could be problematic. The only thing Wainwright had to go on was a gut instinct, based on what he had read in various *Watch the Skies* articles, which told him Sutherland's contact likely was someone based at

Wright-Patterson. To that end, Wainwright had devised a plan calling for him to offer up information that was a mixture of factual data and documents he had created for the sole purpose of throwing Sutherland off the scent. It was Wainwright's hope that the reporter would attempt to contact his real source to corroborate or refute details from the fictional investigations he and Marshall had worked together to develop, and that Sutherland's contact in turn would reveal him- or herself in the course of attempting to gather more information on those counterfeit reports. Wainwright knew it was a risky gambit, depending on how Sutherland reacted to the apparent treasure trove of documents left in his office. The plan might well backfire and cause the reporter to become even more wary when it came to protecting his benefactor's identity.

Sensing the car slowing, Wainwright looked up to see that they had arrived at the motel that was their impromptu base of operations during this trip. A gravel parking lot was bordered on three sides by single-story structures each containing six rooms, with only a few cars occupying parking spaces in front of the rooms. How many nights had he and Marshall spent in places like this just in the last three years? Wainwright had lost count.

"Hungry?" Marshall asked as she maneuvered the sedan into the parking space in front of the pair of doors leading to their adjoining rooms. "There's that café down the block. I think it's open all night."

"More tired than anything else," Wainwright replied, not enamored with yet another meal in yet another roadside restaurant. "Tired of a lot of things." He waited until Marshall turned off the car's engine before shifting in his seat so that he could face her. "Do you ever get the feeling we're just wasting our time with all of this? That we're not getting through to anyone just how important this is?"

Marshall tapped her fingernails on the steering wheel for a moment before replying, "All we can do is our duty, sir, and work to convince the brass that they're wrong not to be treating this more seriously." Though she mentioned no one by name, Wainwright was certain she meant Captain Hardin along with some of his cronies higher up the chain of command who did not seem at all interested in any of the very real evidence Blue Book and its predecessor projects had collected over the years. "Sooner or later, they'll have to acknowledge what we already know."

"Let's hope so," Wainwright said. It had been nearly eight years since the Roswell Incident; eight years since the Ferengi spy had warned of the coming of an invasion fleet. With the passage of so much time, Wainwright had chalked up the alien's threat as little more than bluster, designed to throw off his human interrogators while he bided time for the escape he eventually had made. Even if that had been true, it did not discount the possibility of the Ferengi choosing to attack at some later time, perhaps after waiting for humans to grow complacent. The same could be said for any other extraterrestrial civilization that might target Earth. Perhaps Project Blue Book was becoming nothing more than a tool of misdirection, if indeed it had not already achieved that pitiable goal. So far as he was concerned—and he was all but certain that Marshall felt the same way—he had not been relieved of his duties, and therefore would continue to carry them out until such time as he was ordered otherwise.

What else could he do?

TWELVE

U.S.S. Enterprise
Earth Year 2268

This is just so totally weird.

Standing here, knowing that to James Kirk and Mister Spock, mere days had passed since her first meeting with them more than a year ago—or *three hundred* years, if one wished to engage in temporal pedantry—was more than a little disconcerting for Roberta Lincoln. She had traveled through time with Gary Seven only on rare occasions, and in a few of those instances they had encountered someone with whom there had been prior contact. During those meetings, the objective as well as the subjective passage of time, not just for her but also the other party, always added a layer of confusion for her. It also never failed to give Roberta a tremendous headache.

After assuring his chief engineer and the rest of his command crew on the bridge as to the stability of the current situation, Kirk severed the communications link on the tabletop viewer. "Where's Mister Seven?" he asked, gesturing for her and his officers to take seats at the conference table.

"He's tied up elsewhere, Captain," Roberta replied, opting against going into too much detail. "We've been pretty busy lately."

From where she still stood to one side alongside Mestral

and under guard by a trio of the captain's security officers, Gejalik asked, "Who are you? You said you know us. How?"

Hesitating as she moved toward one of the chairs at the table, Roberta studied the Certoss agent and her Vulcan companion, sympathetic to the numerous questions each of them surely wanted to ask. There would be time for that later, she knew. For now, there were more pressing concerns. "Captain, I'm afraid what I've got to tell you is pretty sensitive."

Kirk regarded her in silence for several seconds, no doubt weighing her request against his desire to acquire as much information from all available sources as quickly as possible. His eyes shifted to look at Mestral and Gejalik for a moment before he asked, "Answer one question for me first: Is Gejalik a threat? Or Mestral, for that matter?"

"No," Roberta replied. "They pose no danger to your ship or crew."

Nodding in approval at her response, Kirk looked to his security officers. "Ensign Minecci, please see to it that our guests are provided appropriate billeting. Post security details outside their quarters, but I think we can dispense with the brig for now."

"Aye, sir," Minecci replied before gesturing to the other security officers.

"Captain," Mestral said, "Miss Lincoln, I trust we will have an opportunity to speak with you further at some point?"

Kirk answered, "As soon as possible, Mestral." He glanced at Roberta again before adding, "You have my word." Waiting until Minecci and the security detail had escorted their charges from the room and the doors closed behind them, he placed his hands on his hips. "I trust I wasn't just lying to them, Miss Lincoln?"

"Not if I can help it," Roberta said, opting now to take a seat at the table. For a brief moment, she closed her eyes and took in the soothing, omnipresent hum of the *Enterprise*'s massive engines. Their reverberations—faint yet still noticeable if proper attention was paid—traveled through the deck plates beneath her feet and even into the soles of her shoes. The starship exuded power and confidence, much like the man who commanded her.

"I know you've got a lot of questions, and I promise I'll do my best to answer them." Waiting until the captain and his officers returned to their own seats, she offered what she hoped was a disarming smile. "First, to answer the obvious question: While, from your perspective, it's only been a week since your last meeting with me and Gary Seven on Earth in the year 1968, I've just traveled to you from over a year later."

"You are still working with Mister Seven," Spock said.

Roberta nodded. "What can I say? Saving the human race from destroying itself before it has a chance to grow up provides a lot of job security, and it sure ain't boring." If Gary Seven was correct, there would be plenty for the both of them to do in the coming decades, during which they would—he promised—either witness or directly influence a number of pivotal events in human history, though most of their contributions and even their mistakes would forever remain shrouded by secrecy. Despite the promise of no public recognition for their efforts, Roberta already had seen the first hints of the tangible effects of the work they did from the shadows of human history. Thanks to Gary Seven's mentorship and support, she had accepted that the future that one day would come to the people of Earth was worth toiling in obscurity.

Shifting in his seat, McCoy said, "Given everything that

we know was going on during that period, I'm guessing it had to be something pretty important to make you travel across space and time to find us." The doctor eyed Kirk with suspicion, but when he spoke again Roberta heard the gentle mocking in his tone. "What did you do now?"

"Me?" Kirk asked. "I've been behaving myself."

Roberta laughed, happy for the momentary distraction. She had forgotten about McCoy's penchant for irreverence. Then, she reminded herself that from the doctor's perspective, he had not yet met her.

Time travel makes my brain bleed.

"As you've probably guessed," she said, "I'm here because of your two unexpected guests. Though we were aware of Mestral's living on Earth, we never considered him a threat. Gejalik, on the other hand, is a different matter. Until recently, we didn't have a whole lot of knowledge about the Certoss, or their whereabouts or activities."

Frowning, Kirk asked, "Even though they'd been on Earth since the 1940s?"

"Imagine our surprise," Roberta said, shaking her head in momentary embarrassment. "They were very, *very* good at covering their tracks. They were on Earth even before the arrival of the first Aegis teams, and their mission depended on their long-term blending into human society while they carried out their work."

"Aegis?" McCoy asked.

Roberta nodded. "The group overseeing our activities on Earth." She shrugged. "Now you know as much about them as I do." Clearing her throat, she continued. "Remember, these Certoss operatives were trained even to elude agents from other, rival advanced alien civilizations sent to Earth to counter their objectives."

"But we're still talking about things that happened on Earth three hundred years ago," McCoy said, not quite scowling but instead regarding her in what Roberta recognized as his normal, skeptical demeanor. "What does any of that have to do with why you're here now?" She remembered that of all the *Enterprise* senior officers, Leonard McCoy—even more so than Captain Kirk himself—harbored no compunctions about speaking his mind regardless of the topic or audience. His Starfleet rank and position within its hierarchy seemed of little consequence to him, and at first she had wondered what compelled him to remain within such a rigid, protocol-driven organization. Based on what she had learned of the doctor's background, Roberta had concluded that McCoy's motivations had little to do with anything beyond his desire to be a superb and compassionate provider of medical care, and the friendship he shared with his *Enterprise* colleagues, in particular James Kirk and Spock.

"For what it's worth," she said, "it's got nothing to do with you, other than that your ship was the one that went to 1968 Earth as part of that time travel experiment. Luck of the draw, I guess."

"We get that a lot," McCoy said.

Kirk glanced to Spock. "Remind me to thank Commodore Delgado for the headache I'm sure I'm about to get."

"I will make a note of it in the ship's log," the first officer replied, batting not one Vulcan eyelash at his captain's remark, and Roberta found herself forced to stifle another laugh.

"Gejalik and her companions were sent to Earth from the future as agents acting on behalf of Certoss Ajahlan, a planet that had aligned itself with one of the anti-Federation factions during the Temporal Cold War. With the ending of the war and the timeline being restored, the reality in which the Certoss were an enemy of the Federation—and Earth—no longer exists. Obviously, Earth is not a threat to Certoss Ajahlan, and in this timeline there never was such a threat, but Gejalik and her fellow agents represent something of an anomaly, in that they're from the future in which that was the case."

Scowling once more, McCoy said, "I don't understand. If this Temporal Cold War business was resolved, and everything put back where it belongs, then how is it they were . . . left out . . . for lack of a better term? For that matter, how is it that you, or any of us, even know about it in the first place?"

"Great questions, Doctor," Roberta replied, "and not easy for me to answer. From what Gary's told me, the Aegis along with several other groups scattered across the galaxy have means by which they're able to maintain records showing the diverging paths in their people's history; a protected archive, I guess."

Kirk asked, "So, it's true that they came from our future?"

Nodding, Roberta said, "Yes, Captain; another two hundred or so years into your future. That was the era in which they entered the war. Even during Earth's twentieth century, their level of technology surpassed ours, though only by a few generations. Coming as they did from the future, they obviously held an advantage in any number of technological areas. Add to that their apparent knowledge of Earth's future history and how and where to influence it, and you start to see the problem."

Even as she spoke, she knew she was treading a very thin line so far as revealing information with respect to the Certoss. There was a risk that came with Kirk and his crew possessing knowledge of events from their own future as well as that of the Certoss, whether in this timeline or another that may or may not ever come to pass. As for the Certoss, the full truth behind their machinations and blatant interference in the affairs of Earth's past still were closely protected secrets, and with good reason. Despite all that was known about the Temporal Cold War, what remained a mystery was how the conflict began in the first place. For all she knew, inadvertent meddling by Starfleet with time travel might well be responsible.

"The other problem stems from Gejalik being in the here and now," she continued. "In addition to being from the future of the Certoss people, she also comes from a different timeline. In this reality, Certoss Ajahlan is not a military power of any sort, and hasn't been for centuries."

"From my review of their planetary history," Spock said, "the Certoss long ago abandoned their martial ideologies. Much like my own people, they emerged from generations of conflict in favor of scientific and cultural advances benefiting all segments of their civilization."

"Exactly," Roberta said. "They've never been a threat to anyone. Their history was altered as a result of the Temporal Cold War so that they never achieved that cultural 'enlightenment.' When the war ended, their proper timeline was restored."

McCoy snorted. "Are we sure this is the proper timeline? For any of us?"

"Would you prefer the alternate reality where Earth's only contribution to interstellar affairs was war," Roberta countered, "before humanity ultimately gets the collective spanking it would so richly deserve by that point? Remember, the Temporal Cold War wasn't all that kind to Earth, either. Gejalik and her people were on a mission to make sure humanity never made it to space, even if that meant destroying our entire civilization. All that was avoided, of course, once everything was put back on the right track." Eyeing the physician, she could not resist adding, "But 'right' is a somewhat relative term. You of all people should know that, Doctor."

"Point taken," McCoy said, settling back into his chair, his expression conveying discomfort at memories reluctantly revisited.

Now regretting what she had said, Roberta cleared her throat. "That wasn't fair, Doctor. I was trying to convey the seriousness of the situation, but I got carried away, and for that I'm sorry." She sighed. "This last year, working with Mister Seven, has been pretty intense. I've had crash courses in just about every subject you can think of. Sometimes I think it's a bit much for a simple secretary to take."

"Don't worry about it," McCoy replied. Though his expression remained dour, he nodded in apparent satisfaction.

Aware that she had transgressed, Roberta took an extra moment to compose her thoughts before continuing. "The biggest problem with Gejalik contacting Certoss Ajahlan in this timeline is that her people, in addition to being largely a civilization of pacifists, also have no knowledge—*none*—of their involvement in the Temporal Cold War. When the time stream was restored, it wiped away all evidence of their previous reality. Their people don't have access to the same . . . information . . . with respect to the war and its various temporal incursions that the Aegis possesses. Introducing knowledge of the conflict, as well as their role in it, could be unsettling to say the least."

"That is the second time you've mentioned the Aegis harboring information on the war," Spock said. "You also implied that they were not the only holders of such records. How is ownership of such data even possible, unless the party in question is able to monitor events outside a specific timeline?"

"You just answered your own question," Roberta said, knowing her attempt at clever evasion would not appease the Vulcan's curiosity, to say nothing of his formidable intellect and deductive reasoning skills. Before Spock could pursue that line of questioning any further, Roberta held up a hand. "I'm really not at liberty to discuss that with you. I've probably already said too much, as it is. I know it's a lot to ask, but I'm counting on you to trust me on this." For a moment, Roberta wondered how Spock might react if she were to tell him that there one day would be an organization within the Federation whose primary mission was to carry out the very tasks he had suggested?

I need to write myself a reminder to be around when he finds out about that.

"Right now, though," she said, "we have to deal with this issue, because it goes way beyond just whatever confusion or other difficulties Gejalik and her message might mean for Certoss Ajahlan."

"I don't understand," McCoy said, the lines in his forehead appearing to deepen as his brow wrinkled.

Kirk said, "I do." When Roberta turned to look at him, the captain had cast his gaze down upon the conference table. He was tapping the fingers of his right hand in absent fashion, and she imagined she could see his mind working. "Someone else could've picked up Gejalik's message. Someone who might know what it means."

"Exactly," Roberta replied. "And it's not just a possibility. It's happened." She released a sigh. "This is probably a good place to insert a joke about genies and bottles, but I don't feel like making it."

"What do we do?" Kirk asked.

Not liking the answer that was all she had to offer, Roberta said, "I honestly don't know for sure. This is . . . all pretty new to me."

Spock, sitting with his hands clasped before him and with the index fingers of each hand extended so that they joined at their tips, said, "And yet, you have come to assist us in remedying this situation?"

"Sort of," Roberta said. "At least, that's what I hope to do." Once more, she felt the pang of uncertainty. It seemed that the current state of affairs was getting more complicated with every passing moment. The time for reflection and casting about while trying to figure out how best to proceed was coming to an end.

There also was a joke to be made about a time traveler running out of time, she knew, but Roberta Lincoln had no overwhelming urge to make that attempt, either.

THIRTEEN

Carbon Creek, Pennsylvania
November 10, 1957

"Almost there," said their guide, Hugh Roberts, calling over his shoulder to Major James Wainwright and Staff Sergeant Allison Marshall as he led them through the forest. Though Wainwright had guessed him to be around sixty years old, he moved with the speed and agility of a man half his age, doing so without the aid of a flashlight and while following no discernible path. Dressed in denim coveralls with a red flannel shirt and an olive-drab military-issue field jacket, the only thing Roberts had with him was the hunting rifle slung over his right shoulder, and the large knife held in a belt sheath along his left hip.

"And you're sure we're heading in the right direction?" Wainwright asked, the air cold enough that he could see his breath.

The older man chuckled. "Sonny, I've been stomping around out here since before you were born. I could walk this whole mountain range with my eyes closed and never once run into a tree."

Walking alongside Wainwright and sporting a similar style of civilian cold-weather coat, Marshall said, "The trees are pretty thick here, sir. How were you able to see the . . . what you say you saw?"

Waving one hand ahead of him, Roberts replied, "There's

a few small clearings up yonder. Once we get there, you'll see what I mean."

His sighting, if that's what it had been, was one of dozens reported in the days following the astonishing news of the Soviet Union's successful launching into orbit of the first-ever artificial satellite. *Sputnik 1,* twice the size of a basketball, was at this moment circling the Earth at a speed of more than eighteen thousand miles per hour, completing a circuit of the globe once every ninety minutes or so. According to the classified reports Wainwright had read back at Wright-Patterson, the satellite had stopped transmitting its communications and gone inert a couple of weeks previously, its batteries now drained. Despite being operational for less than a month, the very existence of *Sputnik* had spawned a rash of new UFO sightings around the world. Many of the reports could be explained by the satellite itself, which was visible to the naked eye on a clear night and with favorable weather conditions. Others that could not be so rationalized—such as the mass sighting reported a week earlier by more than a dozen people in the small town of Levelland, Texas—were categorized for further investigation. The report submitted by Hugh Roberts also fell into the latter group, and was one of several new case files that had drawn Wainwright's attention.

Beyond the trees ahead of them, the moonlight seemed somewhat brighter, and Wainwright saw that they were approaching what might be a clearing. Even from here he was able to see rock outcroppings and a dark area that suggested some kind of ditch or other depression. Ahead of him, Roberts slipped his rifle from his shoulder and cycled its bolt-action to chamber a round. Wainwright stopped and held up a hand for Marshall to do the same.

"Mister Roberts?" he prompted, resisting the urge to

place his hand on his holstered .45 pistol. When the older man turned, Wainwright saw the worry in his face.

"You'll see," Roberts replied, before resuming his advance toward the clearing.

Wainwright exchanged looks with Marshall, who regarded him with the same apparent confusion he was feeling. "What's the matter with him?" he asked, keeping his voice low.

"I don't know, sir," Marshall replied. "He looks scared."

Yeah, but of what?

Opting for caution, Wainwright drew his pistol before again setting off after Roberts, who by now had reached the edge of the clearing and was standing in the moonlight, waiting for him and Marshall to catch up. Wainwright could see that the depression was larger than he first thought, and deeper. The moon's illumination also revealed how the trough extended to the clearing's far edge and into the trees, and that it was bordered by bare soil. Leaves had fallen to cover some of the dirt, but what was visible was still easy to identify as having been overturned.

"Oh, my God," he said, his eyes locked on the furrow. "This is recent, isn't it?"

Roberts nodded. "Yep. Three weeks to a month, I reckon."

"Wait," Marshall said. Crouching down, she removed her knapsack and set it on the ground. Extracting the Geiger counter, she activated the unit and aimed it toward the depression. It began ticking and the needle on its illuminated dial fluctuated, coming to rest two ticks above the zero mark.

"Are we okay?" Wainwright asked, feeling his own unease growing.

Marshall nodded. "I think so, sir. Whatever this thing's picking up, it's pretty faint." Looking up at Roberts, she asked, "You know what's causing this, don't you?"

Instead of replying, the older man gestured with the

barrel of his rifle. "Come on. Once you see it, you'll understand why I didn't want to say nothing." He led the way toward the trench and as they drew closer, Wainwright saw that a recent rain had somewhat compacted the churned dirt and grass. He traced its path across the clearing, his pace increasing with every step until he was jogging the length of the small glade. The beam of his flashlight played across the damp grass, dirt, and leaves as well as the occasional rock sticking up from the ground, but Wainwright brought himself up short when the light glinted off something metallic.

Son of a bitch.

It was, without doubt, some kind of craft, and though he had no proof, he knew with utmost certainty that it was a ship designed for travel in space.

"You saw it crash, didn't you?" Wainwright asked, hearing footsteps approaching from behind him and turning to see Roberts and Marshall running to catch up. He spared them only a glance before his attention was pulled back to the ship.

Clearing his throat, Roberts replied, "No, I didn't."

The odd reply earned him a quizzical look from Marshall, who asked, "What? Your report said you saw it on the ground."

"I did," the older man said. "I just never saw it flying. I came across it one night while I was hunting. Found it pretty much just like it is now. Wasn't even sure at first what it might be. You know, maybe it's one of them top-secret planes you folks are always working on. Then I remembered what other people had been saying about seeing something in the sky a few weeks back, and I realized this might be it."

"Why didn't you just say that from the beginning?" Wainwright asked.

Roberts shrugged. "Because it sounds crazy, that's why. You folks get reports about people seeing flying saucers all the time, and maybe sometimes you can figure out it's just a plane or something else. How many people do you get calling to tell you they found a spaceship in the woods? Hell, my wife would throw me in the loony bin for saying something like that." He gestured toward the craft. "I figured it best to get you out here to see for yourselves."

Wainwright continued inspecting the ship, which lay at the forward end of the scar it had carved into the hillside, and he now saw that a significant portion of the vessel in fact was buried beneath the soil it had displaced. It was difficult to gauge its true dimensions, though Wainwright guessed it was similar in size to . . .

. . . to the ship at Roswell?

Moving his flashlight beam over the ship's exterior, Wainwright saw that it was somewhat angular in shape, with enough curves and sweeping angles. The remnants of what might once have been stabilizer fins were positioned near the vessel's rear section, and Wainwright let his flashlight linger over what looked to be an engine exhaust port at the stern. Enough of the ship was visible that he was able to study features like seams between hull plates as well as ports and other openings. The metal was almost rust in color, and the configuration of the individual plates was unlike anything else he had ever seen. Shining his light across the craft's smooth surface, he noted what looked to be an access hatch. Embedded in the hull plating to one side was a small, recessed pocket with a series of backlit controls. Several small panels across the ship's surface bore what might be labels, their markings unlike any language with which Wainwright might be familiar.

"This is incredible," Marshall said, adding her own flashlight to aid in illuminating the ship. "Sir, do you think this could be a Ferengi ship?"

"A what?" Roberts asked.

Concentrating on the ship's exterior, Wainwright said, "Hard to say. There are some similarities." If this were a Ferengi vessel, it would be the first solid connection to the events in Roswell. Might the threat of eventual invasion conveyed ten years ago by one of the aliens finally be coming to pass?

He turned to Roberts. "Was the hatch open when you found it?"

Roberts shook his head. "It's been this way the whole time, so far as I know."

"So," Marshall said, "you didn't see anyone come out of it, or walking around it or anywhere nearby?"

"Never saw nobody anywhere near it," Roberts replied. "I don't know too many people who come out this way, even to hunt. It's too far from the road, and they don't like all the hills and gullies." He smiled. "That's one of the reasons I like it out here."

Wainwright shook his head. "Hard to believe no one else has found this thing or, if they had, that they've kept it a secret." He envisioned treasure hunters and glory seekers descending on the crash site. "We need to get our own people out here. Maybe even take this thing back so they can really study it."

"I hope Professor Carlson gets to see this," Marshall said. "The look on his face would be priceless."

Wainwright nodded in agreement. "You mean if they let him out of whatever hole they buried him in?" As years had passed and the Air Force's efforts to locate, verify, and study alien technology increased, the mysterious Majestic 12 committee, including Professor Jeffrey Carlson, had become ever more secretive. Its members had been scattered to various top-secret installations across the country, and a few were working abroad with American allies to track reports of alien activity around the world. Carlson, as one of the committee's senior and most respected members representing the project's scientific interests, was in great demand. Wainwright had only spoken with him a handful of times in the past three years, during which the professor had spent much of his time at the Air Force's high-security installation in the mountainous Nevada desert north of Las Vegas—it was so secret it did not even appear to have an official name. There also were rumors of Carlson's involvement in another clandestine project, an extensive, long-term research and development effort taking place somewhere in the Pacific Northwest and employing hundreds of military and civilian science and engineering specialists. Wainwright's discreet inquiries on that front had yielded nothing but quiet warnings for him to quell any such further curiosity.

Stepping closer to what he now presumed was some form of access hatch, Wainwright examined the recessed control pad. Tempted as he was to try opening what he hoped might be an entry into the craft, prudence won out over curiosity. Could its occupants still be in there? Aside from the dim illumination behind the keypad, the vessel emanated no sounds, lights, or other signs of power or habitation, but that did not stop Wainwright from considering the possibility of someone monitoring them from inside the ship.

Well, there's a comforting thought.

The sound of snapping wood—a branch or twig on the ground—from behind them made Wainwright turn in that direction, swinging his flashlight so that its beam played across the trees at the edge of the clearing. The light reflected on something metallic before whatever it was vanished behind the trunk of a large oak.

"Who's there?" he shouted, bringing up his pistol and

aiming it toward the forest, all while trying not to dwell on just how exposed they were here in the clearing. "Allison," he prompted, gesturing with his .45 toward the tree line and stepping to his right in an attempt to get a better look at whatever it was he had seen. To his left, he saw Marshall mirroring his movements toward the other side of the tree. Though they had not faced down extraterrestrials since that night in Yuma five years earlier, Wainwright knew that she was more than capable of handling herself if the situation called for it.

Roberts was a different matter, and the first clue Wainwright had that their guide might complicate things came when the older man chose that moment to fire his rifle. The crack of the high-velocity round echoed through the surrounding trees, the flash from the rifle's muzzle making Wainwright flinch. "Damn it!" he shouted, jerking his head in Roberts's direction only to see the man working the rifle's bolt to chamber another round. "Hold your fire!"

"Sir!"

Turning toward Marshall, he saw her jogging toward the trees, her pistol and flashlight held before her. "They're running!"

"Wait for me!" Wainwright warned, already moving to where he could see someone darting between trees, using the forest for cover. It took him an extra moment to realize that their visitor was not retreating. "He's over this way!" Despite his best efforts to catch the other person with his flashlight beam, his quarry eluded him.

But he can still see your light, idiot!

Wainwright doused the flashlight and halted his advance to the trees, looking and listening for signs of movement. The prowler likely had stopped as well and perhaps was figuring out his or her next move, but there was no way he could have run very far in just that handful of seconds. He had to be close, Wainwright knew; very close.

"See anything?" Roberts asked from behind him, and Wainwright nearly jumped out of his skin. The man had appeared as if from the very air, the barrel of his hunting rifle aimed toward the trees. "He went this way."

"I know," Wainwright replied, keeping his eyes trained on the forest; to their left, Marshall was moving closer, and he saw her body go rigid as though something in front of her had caught her attention.

"Freeze!" she yelled, setting her feet and aiming her pistol at something Wainwright could not see. "Put your hands up!"

Still not seeing who she had found, Wainwright ran toward her, aiming his own weapon at the trees and with Roberts right on his heels. As he moved past a large oak, he saw a figure standing alone and bathed in the beam of Marshall's flashlight, with both hands raised. It took Wainwright an extra moment to realize it was a woman, dressed in heavy civilian clothes similar to theirs. She appeared unarmed, but he did not discount the possibility of a weapon concealed beneath her jacket.

"Who are you?" Wainwright asked, switching on his own flashlight, and the beam caught the reflection of something in the woman's right hand. It was silver, and far too small and thin to be a firearm, and she was not holding it as one might wield a knife.

A pen?

Then, an odd buzzing sound filled the air, and everything went dark.

FOURTEEN

Carbon Creek, Pennsylvania
November 11, 1957

Wainwright's eyes opened and he jerked himself upright, his ears ringing with the unholy clatter of the alarm clock's bell. Reaching for the nightstand, he slammed his hand down on the clock's stopper and ended the assault on his hearing. The room's near-silence returned, broken only by the sound of the clock continuing to tick. He turned on the bedside lamp and saw that it was 6 a.m., his normal waking time, but he did not even remember setting the alarm.

Swinging his body so that he could rest his feet on the floor, Wainwright stretched his muscles, forcing away the lingering tendrils of sleep. There were none of the usual aches and pains that greeted him on most mornings, and now with greater frequency than in previous years. In fact, he could not remember the last time he had awakened feeling this well rested.

It was just as well, he decided as he stood and reached for the robe cast across the end of the bed. He and Marshall were in for a long day of travel, first driving back to Olmsted Air Force Base where they would—with luck—catch a passenger or cargo flight heading for Wright-Patterson that day. Their orders specified a return date of tomorrow, but Wainwright was hoping to convince the officer in charge there of getting him and Marshall moved to an earlier flight. After all, he had been doing this long enough now to have learned a few tricks for getting where he needed to be.

As long as there's coffee, I'll get by.

Pulling on his robe as he made his way to the window, Wainwright pushed aside the heavy curtain. It was still dark, but the first hints of pink were visible over the trees beyond the roadside motel's other set of buildings. Parked outside his room was the dark blue sedan he and Marshall had checked out of the motor pool at Olmsted. At the building that housed the motel's main office and reception desk, the owner was posting a short wooden pole into a mounting bracket affixed to the wall outside the front door. He then proceeded to unfurl the American flag wrapped around the pole, which now extended at a forty-five-degree angle from its holder. Other businesses across the street that were visible from his window also had flags displayed, and it took Wainwright an extra moment to remember that today was Veterans Day. He wondered how the federal holiday might interfere with travel.

He turned at the knock on his door and he angled his head to see Marshall standing outside his room. Already dressed in her uniform, she held what looked to be a coffee cup in each hand. Seeing him looking at her through the window, she smiled. After pausing to make sure his robe was secured about his waist, Wainwright unlocked and opened the door.

"Good morning, sir," Marshall said, offering him one of the coffee mugs.

"Morning," Wainwright replied, accepting the cup. He held it in both hands, enjoying its warmth as he smelled the coffee's aroma. "Where did you get this?" he asked, stepping back from the door and gesturing for her to enter the room.

"Front office," Marshall said, walking to the small table

set before the window and taking a seat in one of its two straight-backed chairs. "I went looking for a diner that might be open this early, but the manager insisted on making it for us. It's Veterans Day today, you know."

Wainwright nodded. "I know. You're up early." He figured she had to have been awake at least an hour, given her forthright, professional appearance.

"I had a good night's sleep, sir," Marshall said as she settled into one of the chairs. "Best one I've had in I don't know how long."

Wainwright grunted in agreement. "Funny. I was thinking the same thing when I woke up. I slept like a baby." Pausing, he frowned at his own statement. "Why do people say that? I don't think I slept more than two hours a night for the first six months after my son was born." That made him stop again. How long had it been since he last had spoken with Michael? The boy had recently celebrated his eleventh birthday, for which Wainwright had called to congratulate him. There was much to talk about, of course; school, sports, friends, and other important activities which so consumed boys of Michael's age. Wainwright had opted to refrain from asking about Deborah or her new husband, not wanting to put his son in the position of thinking he might be betraying his mother's confidence. Though the divorce had been amicable and both he and Deborah had pledged to remain friends for Michael's sake, Wainwright knew she eventually would find someone else with whom to share her life. She had done so, becoming involved with a civilian engineer in California. Wainwright had met the man and his gut instinct told him he was good for Deborah, someone who would be home most nights and would treat her and Michael with the respect and love they both deserved.

"Sir? Are you all right?" Marshall asked, and Wainwright realized he had been quiet for several moments. His coffee, now somewhat cooled, remained undisturbed in his cup.

Wainwright cleared his throat and shook his head. "Sorry. I guess I drifted away there for a minute." After tasting the coffee and deciding it would have been better if he had tried it when it was still hot, he set the cup on the table and moved to where his suitcase sat in a small nook near the bathroom. "I should probably get it into gear. No sense making you wait around on me. We can get some breakfast before we head back to Olmsted."

"We have an extra day on our travel orders," Marshall offered, taking a sip from her coffee.

Tossing the suitcase on the bed and flipping it open, Wainwright smiled. "Sure, but the sooner we get back, the sooner we can get started on our incident reports."

"I can hardly wait," Marshall replied, holding her cup between her hands. "I think I'm finally starting to run out of ways to describe how a witness didn't really see what they thought they saw."

"Just do what I do," Wainwright said, removing assorted clothing articles from a bureau drawer. "Go back to the older reports and copy from them."

"I've been doing that for years, now," Marshall countered without hesitation, eliciting a chuckle from Wainwright. After a moment, she added, "So, what do we call this one? Reflected moonlight? Weather balloon? Fighter jet?"

Shrugging as he placed his clothes in the suitcase, Wainwright said, "The jet, once we get final confirmation from Olmsted." They already had obtained a report from the base commander that Air Force jets had been flying training missions on the night of the sighting reported by Hugh Roberts, a local hardware store owner and avid outdoorsman. Though sightings also had been reported by other people in the vicinity of Carbon Creek, this sleepy rural town, nothing of any substance had come from any of those accounts.

"I really wanted to believe him, sir," Marshall said. "He sounded so sure of what he'd seen. His descriptions were so specific compared to what we usually get."

Wainwright nodded. "I know." Roberts's report, with its unusual details with respect to the alleged craft's movements and possible size, had looked promising. However, an interview with the older gentleman had convinced Wainwright that he, like his fellow witnesses, had seen nothing more spectacular than an F-102 interceptor on routine maneuvers over the Pennsylvania mountains. An excursion led by Roberts into the cold, damp forest where his sighting had taken place had yielded no additional evidence or anything else of value. His report, like so many others, would be yet another unsubstantiated and refuted entry in the Project Blue Book case files.

And yet, something about the whole thing still bothered Wainwright.

"What are you thinking?" Marshall asked, and when he turned to look at her he saw that she was studying him with one eyebrow raised.

"I'm thinking I want to go back out there and have another look around," Wainwright replied, pausing in his emptying a second bureau drawer and tapping his fingers along its top. "Maybe we'll see something in the daylight that we missed last night." Even as Wainright spoke the words, he heard the lack of conviction in them, and he sighed. "No," he said, shaking his head. "There's nothing out there." He offered a dismissive wave. "Let's just get our reports done, and put this one to bed, and move on to the next case." There was always a next case, he knew. That was one of the constants of this job. Somewhere, out there, the truth waited. It had not and would not be easy to find, but they had to keep looking. To stop searching was to invite disaster. "All we can do is just keep plugging along."

"Yes, sir," Marshall said, "but you know what I'm thinking right now?"

The odd question made Wainwright turn, and he saw that she had settled into her chair and once more was studying him. Now feeling self-conscious, he cleared his throat. "I think I've more than proven over the years that I never know what you're thinking."

"I'm thinking we've been doing this together for six years," Marshall said, "and I don't remember the last time you took a vacation, or even a long weekend. I'm thinking we've been doing this for six years, and you've never made a pass at me, or said anything that might even remotely be considered inappropriate or ungentlemanly."

Frowning as he sensed a knot of anxiety forming in his stomach, Wainwright said nothing for a moment, the ticking of his alarm clock the only sound in the room. Then, shifting his feet in a sudden bout of nervousness, he replied, "Allison, don't think I haven't considered it, but I'm your superior officer. It wouldn't be right." As years passed and the group working for Majestic 12 and Project Blue Book grew more insulated, Marshall long ago had evolved from her role as a simple clerical assistant. By necessity as well as her own skills, she was his trusted partner, regardless of the rank on her sleeves and despite the Air Force choosing not to recognize her contributions or those of other female personnel as being on par with their male counterparts. More than once, and with greater frequency as their professional and personal relationship continued to strengthen, he had given serious thought to throwing caution to the wind but had held back, not wanting to risk jeopardizing the trust and friendship they had built during their years working together.

Marshall smiled, rising from her chair and stepping toward him. "I'm thinking I don't care about that right now. I'm also thinking we have an extra day on our travel orders, and the next case will still be there tomorrow."

As she pressed her body against him and her lips met his, Wainwright decided he liked the way she thought.

Cal Sutherland glanced at his watch. It was coming up on six thirty, and he had not slept at all the previous night, but he was still firing on all cylinders.

"So, faithful readers," he said, dictating his thoughts as fast as he could relay them into his tape recorder's microphone, "the question that should be foremost on our minds is why the government isn't telling us the truth about the aliens. UFOs are crash-landing right here, in the very heart of our great nation!" Pacing the width of his small motel room, he reached the wall and turned to walk in the other direction. "Not only is the military concealing that information from the public, but they're also willing to kill innocent civilians who happen to see them as they carry out their cover-up!"

Sutherland's next thought was interrupted as the cord connecting his microphone to the tape recorder went taut and he realized he once more had to turn and pace back the other way. Grunting in irritation, he held up the mic and continued. "That's right, knowledge seekers! Even this intrepid reporter who risked life and limb in pursuit of the truth. While investigating reports of a sighting in the small, sleepy little town of Carbon Creek, Pennsylvania, I certainly got more than I bargained for. I followed two Air Force officials into the forest, having no idea what might be waiting for us out there, but I think they were as surprised as I was when they made what could be the discovery of a lifetime. Proof, readers! Actual proof that the aliens are among us!"

It had taken him no small amount of effort to track the Project Blue Book investigators Major James Wainwright and Staff Sergeant Allison Marshall from their headquarters at Wright-Patterson Air Force Base in Ohio here to Pennsylvania. Trickier still was doing so without tipping off the military to his own skulking and digging about in search of information. His connection inside the project, a person whose identity remained a mystery to Sutherland even after more than five years, had warned him that Wainwright and Marshall were aware of an information leak. They, in turn, had on a few occasions provided Sutherland with false reports and other data in a bid not just to hamper his own investigations but also in the hopes of luring out his source.

To his own irritation, Sutherland had fallen for the ruse the first two or three times, acting on the information supporting alleged UFO sightings in various locations around the country. After traveling to the remote town of Hermann, Missouri, the scene of a sighting as recounted in the report left for him by the mysterious visitor to his office nearly three years earlier, Sutherland began to suspect he had been set up. He had been unable to find the witness cited in the report, and neither had he been able to get any of the town's other residents to corroborate the story. At first, he thought the small, tight-knit community simply was protecting itself from exploitation by an "outsider," but then his anonymous though trusted source at Wright-Patterson had alerted him to the ruse. It was then that Sutherland knew that not only was the alien threat real, but also that his own government was taking an active role in keeping that information sequestered from an unknowing public.

"That's right, my friends," Sutherland said into the microphone, his other hand gesturing wildly in the air before him, "despite the military's best efforts to throw me off the scent, I'm still on the case, and not only did I see it with my own eyes, but I've got lots of nice, juicy pictures to share with you. It's like I've been telling you for years, boys and girls. The aliens are here. They've *been* here, and they've landed right in our own backyards, hiding under the cloak of darkness and the veil of secrecy thrown over them by our own government."

Sutherland smiled, pleased with how smoothly his oratory sounded to his ears. He had labored on the writing all night, working as fast as his fingers could fly over the keys of his Royal typewriter. Unable to keep his thoughts at bay long enough to transcribe them onto paper, Sutherland had abandoned the typewriter and had taken to rattling off entire passages into his tape recorder, supplementing that effort with hastily scrawled notes on the back of the typewritten pages. Wadded-up balls of paper littered the bedspread and the floor, and the place smelled of cigarette smoke, old coffee, bourbon, and his own sweat and wet clothes, but he ignored all of it. He was certain his pulse had not slowed since the first moment he had laid eyes on the crashed ship.

Pausing just long enough to drain the last of the cold coffee in the chipped mug that had been in the cabinet of the room's small kitchenette, Sutherland grimaced at its foul taste. "Just wait until you see this beauty, friends. It's big, it's sleek, and there's just no telling what sort of crazy alien doodads it holds. You and I don't know anything, but you can bet the Air Force will know. Mark my words, friends: They're tearing that bad boy apart as we speak, making that ship give up its secrets. And don't even get me started on what might happen if they've managed to put the bag on whoever—or *whatever*—was flying the thing."

In truth, Sutherland had no idea what would show up on the pictures he had taken. For obvious reasons, he had been unable to use a camera with a flash. Film for use in low- or no-light conditions was something he always included in his kit, but he still had been forced to shoot his pictures at some distance away from the ship. His vantage point had given him a clear view of the alien craft, more than enough to show off its smooth, curved, and angular lines standing in contrast to the surrounding trees and rocks. He tapped his left trouser pocket where he carried the small cylindrical canister. Only after he was able to develop the film it contained would he know if his efforts were successful.

"I know what you're thinking," Sutherland said, continuing his half-rehearsed recital. "This sounds too good to be true, and maybe it is! Only time and evidence will tell, but I can say one thing, faithful readers: The Air Force means serious business when it comes to keeping their secrets. It was only by the wildest stroke of luck that I avoided capture or even being shot!"

He never had been in any direct danger, either of discovery or injury, having concealed his movements while practicing good, sound discipline, just as his infantry training instructors had taught him a lifetime ago before he was sent to France. Wainwright and Marshall had never suspected his presence as they and their guide, Roberts, examined the crash site before something or someone else found their way to the remote clearing. More military people? A curious onlooker from town, or perhaps even other UFO enthusiasts who had figured out there was something to see here? Sutherland had no idea, and he had ceased caring when Roberts fired the first shot into the forest. Whatever had spooked the older man had drawn his attention, along with Wainwright and Marshall, toward the trees on the clearing's opposite side, giving Sutherland the opportunity he needed to get the hell out of there and back to his car.

Of course, his readers did not need those details. Technically, he was not lying, so for the purposes of style and entertainment, he could live with the slight aggrandizement.

Sutherland turned off the recorder, setting the spools of tape to rewind so that he could listen to his first attempt. With the bulk of his thoughts now saved, he could revisit them for transcription—and further embellishment—once he got back to Los Angeles. And after he married up his punchy prose with the photographs he had taken? Pure gold, he decided. He would be able to write his own ticket.

But first? I want breakfast.

He had been working all night, subsisting on lousy coffee and bourbon, and he was long since past needing some decent food, or whatever passed for that in this backwater town. There had to be one person capable of rustling up a steak and some eggs, right?

As if in response to his unspoken question, there was a knock at the door.

"Huh?" Sutherland grunted, frowning in confusion. Who would be calling on him at this early hour? Then, a knot of anxiety formed in his gut, as he wondered if Wainwright and Marshall somehow had learned that he was here in Carbon Creek. For a moment, he considered the .45 tucked under his pillow, but brandishing the pistol now might create more problems than it solved. "Who is it?" he called out.

"The manager, sir," replied a female voice, which was muffled by the thick wooden door. "You have a phone call at the front desk. They say they're from Los Angeles, and that it's important."

Throwing the bolt and unhooking the small chain lock, Sutherland opened the door, expecting to see the middle-aged yet still attractive blond wife of the motel's manager. Instead, a young woman stood on the porch, illuminated by the dim bulb mounted on the wall outside his room. Its feeble light reflected against something in the woman's right hand, and he saw the pen just before a strange metallic snap echoed in the early morning air.

FIFTEEN

Washington, D.C.
November 11, 1957

Swirling blue-black fog parted for her, and with the high-pitched, almost musical hum of the energy field ringing in her ears, Cynthia Foster stepped forward and emerged into the office. She released a small sigh of relief as she took in the familiar surroundings. It was good to be home.

Or something close to it. I'll take what I can get.

Cynthia turned back to the open closet, the interior of which contained all that remained of the dissipating haze of energy as generated by the translocator device installed behind the concrete wall. The last of the fog disappeared, leaving only the shelves and racks lining the inside of the walk-in closet. Stacks of office supplies as well as rows of clothing were all that were visible, concealing all traces of the otherworldly technology that had just allowed her to travel hundreds of miles in little more than a handful of heartbeats.

"Good morning, Agent 6," a voice called out as she closed and locked the closet door, and she looked over her shoulder to see her fellow agent, Ian Pendleton, smiling at her from where he sat at his desk. "Welcome back." Consisting of a black suit with matching tie and a white shirt, Ian's ensemble was for all intents and purposes the male counterpart to her own outfit. As always, his short blond hair was groomed with almost mathematical precision, the light application of Brylcreem he used reflecting the office's overhead lighting. He was reclining in his high-backed leather chair, resting his feet atop his desk, and holding what Cynthia presumed to be that morning's edition of *The Washington Post* or the *Times-Herald*. A cup sat in a saucer on the desk, and she caught the scent of Ian's preferred blend of hot tea.

"And a good morning to you, Agent 42," she said, smiling at the use of their code designations. Like Ian, her own moniker had been as much her identity as her given name for so long that she scarcely remembered a time without it. Indeed, the designations were more comfortable and familiar than the surnames provided by her supervisor just a few short weeks ago at the start of their assignment here on Earth.

She unbuttoned her jacket as she moved across the open, carpeted area at the office's center. Behind her desk, a pair of windows offered a view to the north, which was dominated by the western half of the National Mall. To her left, the Washington Monument stood above the trees, its dark silhouette catching the first rays of the morning sun. Lights were on in a few of the windows of the neighboring buildings, but at this early hour most of the offices and other businesses in this part of town were dormant, their occupants not due to arrive for another two or three hours. A special composite on the glass of this suite of offices presented the outward appearance of the lights being off during nighttime hours, affording her and her partner a measure of privacy as they went about their various tasks, many of which would be nothing short of shocking to average, everyday humans. Because of that, they operated behind the façade of the Pearson-Thorne Corporation, a private company specializing in military defense contracting. With the resources at their command, Cynthia and Ian were able to present to the smallest details the appearance of being a legitimate firm. One part of the illusion that amused Cynthia was that contemporary sociological realities required her to pose as a secretary, an administrative subordinate to Ian's authoritative senior executive officer.

That could change, she reminded herself, *in a decade or four.*

"You're here early," she said, eyeing him with suspicion. Though he was clean shaven and groomed, and his suit was fresh, there still were dark circles beneath his eyes. "Or, did you sleep here again last night?"

Ian turned the page of his newspaper. "I know you said it would be a routine mission, but I wanted to be here, just in case you needed anything."

Shaking her head, Cynthia frowned at him. "That's the third night in a row you've slept on that couch. You need to go home and get some real rest. Even you can't keep up that kind of pace forever."

"I know," Ian replied, sighing. "But this situation with the Vulcan ship is exhausting. This is what? The fifth time we've had to go there to keep someone from letting the entire world know that a spaceship from another planet has crash-landed in the middle of nowhere? How much longer will we have to keep doing this?"

Cynthia moved to the chair behind her desk. "Until the ship is retrieved, or our orders change." Unfortunately, their superiors were being frustratingly tight-lipped with regard to details about this, Cynthia and Ian's first major assignment since their arrival on Earth. It was not unexpected; indeed, their instructors had driven the point home throughout their training. The Aegis's interest in this planet was motivated by a desire to protect it from annihilation at the hands of its own people, and in doing so ensure that humanity received the opportunity to evolve into a technologically and sociologically advanced civilization. Rather than taking an active, public role in Earth's affairs, the Aegis instead preferred a more benign approach, for reasons known only to them. Like her fellow students, Cynthia had pondered those motives, weighing them against the knowledge that her sponsors—already possessing wondrous technology that would make them appear almost as gods to the people of this world—also harbored at least some insight into Earth's future history. As explained to Cynthia and her fellow students during their training, such knowledge must be used with caution, wisdom, and restraint, in order to help the human race find the path leading to what her instructors called "its proper destiny." To that end, when faced with taking actions that might affect humanity's future, field agents were given only enough information required to complete a particular task. This, their instructors had repeated over and over, was to prevent any agent from taking matters too much into his own hands, whether for righteous purpose or while pursuing his own ignominious agenda.

At first, Cynthia had wondered if that might just be coded speech for the Aegis manipulating humanity for its own purposes, but time and her own experiences, as a student and later an apprentice observer working with an experienced field agent on her first foray to Earth, had shown her the organization's true intentions. Humanity was fast approaching a volatile turning point in its history, and soon would face a number of challenges, issues, and crises. A wrong decision for any one of those situations, no matter how well-intentioned, could spell disaster for a civilization that still was centuries away from realizing its true potential. However, guiding the people of Earth through the hazards to safety and prosperity was not the answer; instead, they would have to find the path for themselves, and in many cases learn harsh lessons along the way. The Aegis, Cynthia had come to realize, was acting as something of an unseen mentor to the human race, taking quiet, measured action behind the scenes in certain situations, but otherwise allowing events on Earth to unfold without interference.

And then, there were situations like the Vulcan ship, which seemed designed to test the Aegis's "appropriate intervention" philosophy.

Closing his newspaper and folding it in half before laying it down upon his desk, Ian rose from his seat and moved to where Cynthia now was reclining in her own chair, facing the windows overlooking the Mall. "So, how did it go this time?"

"To be honest?" Cynthia sighed as she shifted to a more comfortable position. "It ended up being more complicated than we anticipated." Upon learning of the Vulcan ship's unexpected arrival on Earth, the agents had traveled to Carbon Creek to investigate witnesses to its crash-landing. The number of people who had seen the scout vessel descend from the night sky into that remote region of the Pennsylvania mountains was small, and suppressing their memories of the incident had proven straightforward if time consuming. That accomplished, they had installed a sensing device that would transmit a signal to their office here in Washington if anyone came close enough to the craft to see it for what it was. With the aid of the translocator, Cynthia and Ian had traveled back to Carbon Creek in order to similarly "handle" those interlopers. Having done this on four previous occasions, Cynthia had opted to take care of this incursion herself, advising Ian to get some much-needed rest. "It turns out we missed one of the original witnesses. A hunter. He led the Blue Book officers out to the crash site. And it gets better."

"There was somebody else?" Ian prompted.

Cynthia replied, "Exactly, including a reporter for one of those tabloid magazines." He had been an unanticipated complication of her plans to deal with the two Air Force investigators and their civilian guide, but she was able to handle him with relative ease. "It's a shame I had to destroy his film. He managed to get some pretty good pictures."

"So, we're in the clear again?" Ian asked, pausing to kiss her forehead before leaning against the edge of her desk. He reached up to cover his mouth in a vain attempt to stifle a yawn.

"For now, anyway." Per their instructions, she and Ian were to continue monitoring the site and preserve it from any outside contamination. The revelation of a Vulcan spacecraft on Earth in this time period would prove problematic, to say the least. Likewise, Cynthia and Ian also had been directed only to observe the crashed ship's surviving crewmembers, with no permitted assistance or other interaction. The Vulcan scientists, as the Aegis described them, had been sent to Earth to monitor what human history one day would call "the dawn of the Space Age," brought about by the Soviet Union's launching of the *Sputnik 1* satellite. It had been the latest in a series of clandestine reconnaissance missions to study Earth as humanity's knowledge progressed to the point of harnessing atomic energy. Even after the formal first contact between humans and Vulcans took place more than a century from now, it would be some time before the truth of Vulcan's prolonged interest in Earth was revealed to humanity.

As for *Sputnik*, the planet's major powers still were

coming to grips with the reality of space as a possible new realm for expansion and perhaps even conquest. Even now, the United States military was laboring to replicate what the Soviets already had done, with Project Vanguard on a track for launching its own satellite within the next ninety days. Once the Americans were able to show the world that they could go head to head against their Russian counterparts, the race for space supremacy would only accelerate.

Knowing this as well as what the future held, the Aegis had begun sending agents to Earth with a new, larger mission requiring more than simple observation. Cynthia and Ian were the first agents dispatched to the planet for this purpose, with their long-term assignment being the monitoring of technological, political, and sociological developments and undertaking whatever surreptitious action was deemed necessary in order to assist humanity through the turbulent times they soon would face.

"I've had the computer working on a better sensor we can install," Ian said, crossing his arms. "It'll have a greater range, and also will alert us of any aerial reconnaissance that might find the ship." Shrugging, he added, "I doubt that'll be a problem, but it doesn't hurt to be careful. More importantly, it'll let us know if the Vulcans return to the site."

Cynthia nodded in agreement. "Good thinking, though I'm guessing the Vulcans will continue taking all necessary steps to conceal their presence. We know they have a communications device, and they're sticking close to the crash site just in case their distress signal was picked up by someone."

"What if no one *did* hear it?" Ian asked. "What if it ends up that they're on their own so far as any drawn-out survival plans? The longer they stay here, the greater their risk of being discovered. If that happens, we might not be in a position where we can do anything to contain the situation."

"Let's not get ahead of ourselves." Cynthia reached over to pat Ian's knee. "For now, we've got enough to worry about, just protecting the ship and crew from discovery."

Still, Ian's was not an unreasonable notion. She had considered the same possibility more than once, and even had furthered that concern on to her superiors, but so far had received no response. If no directions were forthcoming, and she and Ian were left to their own devices and judgment so far as how to deal with the Vulcans, would that help or hinder Earth's future? Such scenarios, in the abstract, had been a significant part of her training, given the likelihood of field agents having to make momentous decisions without support. Whereas words like "discretion," "restraint," and "proportional" were bandied about the classroom with great frequency, theoretical discussions often lacked the nuance encountered in real-world application of such hypotheses.

Ian reached down to place his hand atop hers, which still rested on his knee. "You've been up all night, too. It's Veterans Day, and all government offices are closed. There's nothing on the schedule so far as Pearson-Thorne is concerned, so why not take the day and get some rest?"

"I thought I told you to do that?" Cynthia asked, twisting her hand so that her fingers could interlace with his.

Shrugging, Ian smiled. "I will if you will." He leaned forward and she stretched so that her lips met his.

The idea of a quiet, recuperative day had definite appeal, Cynthia decided. She and Ian had been lovers for nearly a year prior, during the last phases of their training, and it was a contributing factor toward their pairing for assignment on Earth in this time period. That was fortunate, considering how long they might be here, hiding in plain sight among those who always had called this world home. An intimate relationship with a contemporary human was out of the question, given the need for strict secrecy with respect to their true identities and mission.

Her thoughts of leisure—and other things—were interrupted by a muted, almost musical string of tones sounding from the other side of the office. Breaking their kiss and pulling back from Ian, Cynthia swung her chair around to see a section of the room's opposite wall swinging open toward her, revealing the master control console for their computer, the Beta 4.

"That thing's timing is impeccable," Ian said.

Unlike the office's other fixtures and appointments, there was nothing at all contemporary about the machine's appearance, design, or functionality. The console, molded from a black glass deca-polymer composite, housed an array of keyboards and other controls as well as six small display screens, all of which were dominated by a larger rectangular screen comprising the console's upper portion. As the wall finished swinging open, the console was already flaring to life, all of its screens activating to depict a selection of images from local morning news broadcasts as well as scrolling readouts of information captured from the teletype transmissions of numerous prominent news organizations located around the world.

"*Computer on*," said the computer, speaking in a clipped, masculine tone that reminded Cynthia of the awkward, clunky robots from low-budget science fiction movies. "*Recognize Agent 6. Recognize Agent 42*." A self-sufficient computing system possessing what its creators called "artificial intellect," the Beta 4 was the cornerstone of the agents' activities here on Earth. Capable of interfacing with all of the world's communications mediums, the computer had constant access to almost anything transpiring anywhere across the globe, so long as it was being documented or reported in some fashion. Interfaced with the translocator, it could send the agents anywhere in the world at a moment's notice, and it also was the agents' primary connections to their superiors more than one thousand light-years across the galaxy. In the event an abandoning of their assignment was necessary, the Beta 4 would be their lifeline back to the Aegis homeworld, after which the machine would destroy itself to prevent discovery and possible exploitation by anyone here on Earth.

"Hello," Cynthia answered. "What have you got for us?"

"*Since launch of the second* Sputnik *satellite,*" the Beta 4 replied, "*I have continued to monitor American and Russian military communications networks. I have detected considerable message traffic in response to a report submitted last week to President Eisenhower.*"

"Gaither's report?" Ian asked, and when Cynthia looked at him he had his arms folded once more across his chest, frowning as he rubbed his chin with his left hand.

The computer said, "*Correct, Agent 42. Analysis of classified communiques dispatched from Pentagon to high-ranking government and military officials indicates that plans are already in development to conform to several of the report's recommendations.*"

"We knew this was coming," Cynthia said. She had spent the previous Thursday evening reviewing the same report read by President Eisenhower earlier that same day. *Deterrence & Survival in the Nuclear Age*, authored by Horace Rowan Gaither, a civilian attorney and founder of a policy institute providing strategic research and analysis for the

Department of Defense, recommended a significant increase in military spending with an aim toward solidifying the United States's ability to employ and defend against nuclear weapons.

Ian nodded. "*Sputnik* isn't to blame, not by itself, but when you combine nuclear arms proliferation with the Russians' perceived advantage so far as exploiting space goes, it makes sense that the United States is going to be taking their own measures."

The Beta 4 replied, "*Based on report's recommendations and other orders disseminated through the highest echelons of American military leadership, primary focus will lie in the area of deterrence through means of amassing superior weaponry to deploy against the Soviets. Similar reports and directives from Russian government indicate their armed forces will mount a similar initiative.*"

"According to Gaither's reported projections," Ian said, "the total Soviet arms proliferation effort is already on par with America's, and it will only increase in the coming years. They may not have all of the financial resources of the United States, but they're pumping a larger chunk of what they *do* have into their military. The world could be facing nuclear annihilation in as little as five years."

"That's consistent with what we've been told," Cynthia replied, recalling the limited information they had been given regarding future human history. The Cold War that already had gripped the United States and the Soviet Union for a decade was heating up, and it would have direct as well as subtle effects on people, nations, and events around the world for years to come. What did that mean for her and Ian?

It means we're going to be busy.

SIXTEEN

U.S.S. Enterprise
Earth Year 2268

Kirk willed the turbolift to move faster.

"Red Alert. All hands to battle stations. This is not a drill."

Leaving Roberta Lincoln to conduct her own interviews with Gejalik and Mestral, he and Spock now were enduring what to Kirk seemed an eternity as the turbolift carried them to the bridge. Finally, the whine of the lift's transit slowed, and Kirk felt his muscles tensing in anticipation as the doors opened, flooding the car with the familiar, almost soothing background sounds of the *Enterprise* bridge.

"Report," he snapped, stepping out of the lift and getting his first look at the image on the main viewscreen. At the moment, only stars greeted him.

Though he had the conn while Kirk was off the bridge, Sulu still was seated at his helm console. "Sensors detected the approach of an unidentified vessel closing on our position at high warp speed. They're due to arrive in about fifty-seven minutes, sir. Our scans show the vessel is armed, and their weapons are active."

At the science station, Ensign Chekov turned from the console, a Feinberg communications receiver inserted into his left ear. "A single ship, sir. It has ignored all our hails to this point, and they're still on an intercept course. I have identified it as Tandaran in origin, and its configuration suggests it's a military vessel."

"Tandaran?" Kirk asked, frowning. "That doesn't ring any bells."

Spock, moving to relieve Chekov at the science station, said, "That is not surprising, as Starfleet's contact with them has been very sporadic since our first recorded contact more than a century ago. They are a humanoid race, and their homeworld is listed in the library computer as Tandar Prime, located in an area of non-aligned space adjacent to Gamma Ceti. The original first contact report, as well as subsequent survey missions, notes that the Tandarans are a somewhat militaristic race, though not so severe as the Klingons or even the Romulans. Reports indicate that while they do not avoid or reject contact or trade with other governments, they prefer to confine their activities to the region of space they control. So far as I am aware, there has never been any hostile action between our two peoples."

"What's their level of technology?" Kirk asked.

Clasping his hands behind his back, the first officer replied, "Comparable to ours. Sensors indicate their weapons could pose a threat. Their shields are capable of repelling any attack we might invoke, at least for a time. According to the records in our data banks, this type of vessel is designed for fast attack missions, with a crew complement of twenty-seven persons."

"And they're still coming full speed?"

Chekov nodded. "Affirmative, sir."

"Without further details and given their apparent reluctance to communicate with us," Spock added, "I am hard-pressed to classify their conduct as anything other than aggressive."

Stepping down into the bridge's command well as Chekov resumed his post at the navigator's station, Kirk said, "Let's have a look at them, Mister Sulu."

"Aye, sir," replied the helm officer, keying the necessary controls. At the center of the main viewscreen's computer-generated image now appeared a vessel. It was sleek and angular, presenting a compressed profile that to Kirk indicated the spacecraft might also be designed for travel within a planet's atmosphere. Dark hull plating covered the vessel from stem to stern, rendering it almost invisible against the backdrop of space save for the enhancement provided by the viewscreen's imaging processor. Kirk saw nothing indicating running lights or even exposed portholes.

It's a combat ship.

Continuing to study the Tandaran vessel as he leaned against the helm and navigation console, Kirk already was considering various tactical scenarios should the situation call for him to take action. "Any indications they have scanners of their own? Can they see that our shields are up and our weapons are active?"

"They do possess sensor technology roughly equivalent to our own," the Vulcan answered. "It is all but certain they have scanned us and have verified our current operational status."

And yet, they're being tight-lipped while bearing down on us. There could be no mistaking its posturing, Kirk decided, with its weapons and defenses already active even at this distance. "Well, something's got their hackles up," he said. "What are the odds it has something to do with the Certoss ship?"

"It is as likely a possibility as any other," Spock said. "However, I have consulted the library computer, and I find no record of any hostile action between the Tandarans and the Certoss, which is understandable given the Certoss people's pacifist nature. That said, there is the matter of our guests, and the unusual reasons for their being here."

Already thinking along similar lines, Kirk sighed. "Right." He shifted his position so he could see Lieutenant Uhura. "Open a channel, Lieutenant."

At her station, the communications officer nodded, her fingers moving across her console. Like Spock, she also wore a Feinberg receiver in her left ear, and she reached up to touch the device as she worked. "Frequency open, sir."

Turning back to the viewscreen, Kirk drew a deep breath before calling out, "Tandaran vessel, this is Captain James T. Kirk, commanding the Federation *Starship Enterprise*. You are in Federation space, approaching a Starfleet vessel and a civilian craft with your weapons active. What are your intentions?" When there was no immediate response to his greeting, he glanced over his shoulder to Chekov. "Plot a targeting vector, and make sure they know our targeting sensors are scanning them. Keep weapons on standby."

The ensign replied, "Aye, sir."

Looking over to where Spock stood at the railing, Kirk offered a small smile. "Assertive, I know, but I'm hoping it might stimulate conversation."

Spock's right eyebrow lifted. "Indeed."

Behind him, Uhura called out, "Captain, they've received and acknowledged our hail, and they're requesting to speak with you."

"Well," Kirk said, his smile widening. "How about that?" He schooled his features as he straightened his posture. "On-screen."

The image on the viewscreen shifted from the Tandaran ship to a humanoid male, dressed in a dark gray uniform jacket worn over a black turtleneck. He was bald, and deep lines creased his face. His eyes, narrow and deep green, moved from side to side, and Kirk got the impression that he was taking in every detail of the *Enterprise* bridge.

"Greetings," Kirk said, keeping his voice neutral. "I'm Captain Kirk. May we be of assistance?" The Tandaran's eyes fixed on him.

"*I am Colonel Abrenn of the Tandaran Defense Directorate, in command of this vessel,*" he said, his tone one of confidence, even arrogance. "*I have been dispatched by my government to investigate a message sent from this area to Certoss Ajahlan. We see that a Certoss vessel is present at your current location. My orders are to determine whether a threat to Tandaran interests exists.*"

Despite himself, Kirk could not help his expression of confusion in response to the Tandaran's statements. "I assure you, Colonel, that my ship poses no threat, either to your vessel or your people. As for the Certoss, theirs is a peaceful planet, and your scanners should have told you that their ship carries no weapons." Stepping forward, he crossed his arms. "On the other hand, your ship seems to be quite well armed."

"*As does yours, Captain.*"

Kirk nodded. "Yes, it does, though we prefer to use our weapons only in a defensive capacity. I'd prefer not to use them today, if it's all the same to you."

"*I agree with your sentiment, Captain,*" Abrenn replied, "*but I'm afraid that will hinge on what happens next, and where you stand should a conflict arise.*"

"As I already said," Kirk countered, "we have no hostile intentions toward you, and to be honest, I have no idea why you're even posturing this way." He took another step toward the viewscreen. "What I *do* know is that you're in Federation space, brandishing weapons and acting in a provocative manner, and now you've just threatened the safety of a Starfleet vessel. So, I'm done being polite. Explain your presence here, now, or I'll consider your approach an aggressive action and respond accordingly."

On the screen, Abrenn bristled. "*We are not here for you, Captain, but rather the Certoss ship. Our concerns are with the message it sent to its homeworld. If the content of the communique is accurate, then it and the Certoss people do pose a very real threat to our security.*"

Kirk already had opted not to correct the Tandaran as to the origin of the unusual Certoss message, deciding the presence of the Certoss operative aboard the *Enterprise* was not a detail Abrenn needed at this juncture. What bothered him more was the little alert going off in his head, warning him that the current situation, already replete with enough twists, turns, and mysteries, was about to get even more complicated by the addition of this new element.

"Colonel," Kirk said, trying to choose his words with care, "the Certoss people are pacifists. Are you trying to say that there's a reason to believe otherwise?"

"*More than you can possibly imagine, Captain.*"

Sighing, Kirk replied, "Oh, I doubt that, sir." He turned from the viewscreen, looking to Spock. "I think it's time we brought Miss Lincoln into this." He wondered what his enigmatic visitor would think of this latest development. "Something tells me she's going to find this *interesting*."

SEVENTEEN

Carbon Creek, Pennsylvania
January 22, 1958

The sounds from the television in the front room filtered through the open door leading from his bedroom as Mestral worked. From the kitchen, the aroma of the soup warming on the stove was a pleasant mix of vegetables and seasonings he had purchased earlier in the day. There also was fresh bread baking in the oven, and by his calculations Mestral knew it would be ready in just under five minutes. With slow, methodical precision, he was in the process of determining the most efficient means of placing his possessions into his suitcase. It was a simple exercise, though one in which he found a degree of enjoyment; not for the task itself, but for what its completion signified.

Tomorrow, Mestral would be leaving the small town that had been his home for more than three months as time was measured here on Earth. The security and relative obscurity it offered had served its purpose, but for him to pursue his goal of learning more about this planet and the people inhabiting it, he needed to travel. He wanted to observe humans in all their myriad environments, living and working not only among the cities they had built and the technology they had created, but also within the society they had forged. Primitive as they might be, they possessed a potential unlike many comparable species Mestral had observed on previous covert surveillance to other worlds. Their drive to push forward, to learn what was not yet known and accomplish what had not yet been achieved, was matched almost by their emotions, which based on their history were every bit as volatile as anything faced by ancient Vulcans before the Time of Awakening. If humanity could learn to harness its passions, its ability to evolve into an advanced society was all but unlimited. That Mestral was here, now, and a possible witness to such growth was an unparalleled opportunity for any xenosociologist.

And it begins tomorrow.

The time he had spent living with his fellow Vulcans, T'Mir and Stron, and studying the humans around him had provided Mestral with a robust collection of anecdotal data, which he had recorded with painstaking care in his portable scanner as well as the handwritten notes he had produced. The scanner and three journals, now filled to capacity with his observations, opinions, and even suggestions on how best to continue monitoring this world and its promising denizens, already occupied precious space in his suitcase. If nothing else, they—along with those he would continue to write—would provide an historical record of his activities here; an explanation if not a justification for his decision to remain on Earth in order to conduct what he hoped would be a very long-term covert pre–first contact survey.

Perhaps, one day, Mestral even would get to share his findings with colleagues, or they might be read by someone at the Vulcan Science Academy. He had no way to know when—or even if—his people and those of Earth might come together to establish formal relations, something he hoped would come to pass. Until that day came, and regardless of whether he played any meaningful role in such an event, he wanted to ensure that the time he would spend here, living in secret among the humans while at the same time endeavoring to better appreciate them and their potential, was not squandered. If his work one day provided a bridge of understanding between Earth and Vulcan, then Mestral would take great satisfaction from that accomplishment.

He had elected to remain behind, rather than going with T'Mir and Stron, after the trio learned that the distress message they had sent prior to crashing on Earth had been intercepted by a Tellarite freighter. That vessel in turn had contacted Vulcan and relayed the relevant information, resulting in the dispatching of a rescue ship. Faced with this new information, Mestral had asked his companions to do the unthinkable: lie to their rescuers and tell them he had been killed in their ship's crash along with their captain. T'Mir and Stron had been reluctant to honor this request, but eventually agreed, and Mestral had hidden in the depths of the coal mine as the rescue ship removed or destroyed all remnants of his wrecked vessel before ferrying T'Mir and Stron back to Vulcan.

And what of Maggie?

It was a question Mestral had asked himself several times in the days that had passed since T'Mir and Stron were recovered by the Vulcan survey ship. The time he had spent in the company of the Earth woman, Maggie, and her young son, Jack, had been an enlightening experience, but he could not ask her to accompany him in his travels, and he knew that staying here in Carbon Creek only increased the likelihood of her or someone else learning his true identity and nature. Indeed, he found it intriguing that Maggie herself had not yet stumbled upon the truth. Their friendship had continued to grow since their first conversation in the tavern she owned, the Pine Tree, to the point that Mestral could sense her desire to explore more intimate aspects of their relationship. Doing so was impossible, he knew, if he was to avoid revealing his alien heritage, and he had hastened his decision to leave town at the earliest opportunity.

Perhaps one day, I can tell Maggie the truth.

Music from the television in the front room told Mestral that the program was ending, a cue that also served to remind him that it was time to take his baking bread out of the oven. Placing the shirt he had been folding on the bed next to the suitcase, he turned and made his way from the bedroom. The pleasing odor of the bread was a welcome complement to the soup, which he also calculated as being near ready for consumption. He crossed the main room toward the kitchen to turn off the stove and move the soup pot from the hot burner.

Behind him, one of the wooden floorboards creaked, but before Mestral could turn, something slammed into the back of his skull.

Though not unmanageable, the pain still was quite evident.

Releasing an involuntary grunt as consciousness returned, Mestral opened his eyes only to confront a hazy, multicolored blur. A steady pulsing at the rear of his head reminded him of the impact it had sustained, but he also felt a dull ache along his left temple. When he tried to blink, he realized that his left eyelid felt as though something had stuck to it. He moved to touch his face and discovered he could not move his arms, though he was able to flex his fingers. Testing his legs told him that those extremities also had been bound to the chair in which he was sitting. As his vision cleared, he was able to make out the apartment's familiar surroundings.

He was facing the kitchen, and the air was filled with the acrid stench of something burning. The baking pan from the oven lay atop one counter, upon which sat a scorched, oval-shaped mass.

The bread, he thought. *A pity.*

"You're awake," a voice said from behind him, and Mestral jerked his head around, trying to see the speaker. "Excellent. For a time, I was worried I might have injured you too severely."

Verifying that his arms were securely fastened to what he now understood to be one of the wooden dining chairs from the kitchen's small dining table, Mestral again turned his head toward the voice. "Who are you? What do you want?"

"I want to know who you are," the intruder replied, after which Mestral heard slow footsteps across the apartment's wooden floor, and he waited until a figure stepped into his field of view. Though his eyes still were blurry, he discerned that his captor was a human male—or, humanoid, at least. He was dressed in nondescript denim pants and a dark red shirt, over which he wore a brown leather jacket. An olive-drab satchel that Mestral recognized as being of a type used by military forces was slung across his body from his left shoulder. His dark hair was short, in a manner similar to styles Mestral had seen favored by human male military members. "Who you are, and why you're here. I suspect the answers to those queries will occupy us for quite some time."

His throat dry, Mestral tried to swallow but found the effort difficult. "I do not understand why you are interested in me." Blinking again seemed to help his vision, as the apartment furnishings now were coming into better focus. He looked down to see that he had been tied to the chair with what looked to be sections of the cotton rope T'Mir had used for stringing up clothes to dry behind the apartment. Though not possessing any real tensile strength, it still was enough to immobilize him. Given time, Mestral believed he could loosen the rope's knots enough to free himself. "Do I know you?"

"No," the man answered. "As for my interest in you, it begins with the fact that you're a Vulcan."

Despite a lifetime spent learning and improving upon how to control emotional responses of any sort, Mestral's reaction to that simple statement betrayed him as he stiffened in his chair, his eyes narrowing as they fixed on his captor. Seeing no logic or gain to be made by lying, he asked, "How do you know that?"

The man pointed to him. "Your ears, of course, but also that blood on your face. I apologize for that, as it was an unfortunate result of you hitting your head on the counter when you fell."

"After you struck me," Mestral added.

His captor nodded. "Yes. Again, my apologies, for that and also for your restraints. I hope you'll understand my need to mitigate unnecessary risks."

"The fact that you know I am a Vulcan suggests that you have encountered my people before," Mestral said. "How is that possible? How did you find me?"

"Let's just say I'm not from around here," the man replied. Crossing the kitchen to the dining table, he retrieved another of the chairs and pulled it across the floor until it was positioned nearly two meters in front of Mestral. "Which brings me back to one of my original questions: Why are you here? I assume it's for some sort of cultural observation."

Endeavoring to hide the fact that he was continuing to test the ropes holding him to the chair, Mestral replied,

"I was a member of a survey vessel. Our planet has been monitoring Earth for some time, studying your technological advances and their effects on the planet's society. You are just now making your first tentative forays into space, and we are interested in tracking your progress. We represent no threat to you."

The stranger laughed. After a moment, he said, "Sorry, but you've made an understandable yet still incorrect assumption. I'm not human. My name is Jaecz, and my world is called Certoss Ajahlan, a planet even more distant from Earth than your own."

"I am unfamiliar with that planet."

"That does not surprise me," Jaecz replied. "From what I know, humans are not yet aware of Vulcans at this time. Indeed, they have no real knowledge of any extraterrestrial species save for a handful of scattered encounters, the details of which largely are kept secret from the rest of the public. You being here, among them, presents a tremendous risk of discovery."

"Our ship crashed," Mestral said. "Our captain was killed, and the three of us who survived were forced to approach this settlement in order to find food and shelter. For a time, we were unsure if our distress signal had even been received. It had, but rescue did not arrive until after we already had been living here in secret for more than three months."

Frowning, Jaecz leaned forward in his chair, resting his forearms atop his thighs as he clasped his hands. "Three months? I detected a ship in this area just three days ago. That was the rescue ship?"

"Yes," Mestral replied. "How were you able to detect it?" He felt the rope around his left wrist slacken. It was not much, but it was a start.

"Never mind that," Jaecz said, rising from the chair. "Where is this ship now?"

"On its way back to Vulcan, I presume." The rope securing his right arm also had loosened. Though he was able to disguise these movements by appearing to adjust his position on the chair in search of greater comfort, he could do nothing to test the restraints around his ankles.

Jaecz frowned, his eyes narrowing. "You didn't go with your friends?"

"No," Mestral said. "I wished to remain here in order to continue my study of human culture."

"The humans will throw you in a cage if they find you," the Certoss countered. "They're not too keen on visitors from other worlds lurking among them. Trust me on this." He paused, studying his captive. "Do you have means of communicating with that ship of yours?"

Mestral shook his head. "I do not. My companions took our communications equipment with them, to ensure it was not discovered by the humans, just as the rescue team disposed of the remains of our own vessel."

"Are you expecting me to believe that you have no means of contacting that ship, or your home planet?"

"If you know my people as you claim to," Mestral replied, "then you know that we do not engage in deceit."

For the first time, the Certoss laughed. "Spare me that old myth. Your people are more than capable of lying when it suits you. It's probably a consequence of your exposure to humans, who lie without effort about even the most inane things. You certainly had no problem engaging in subterfuge with the Andorians, or even my people."

"As I told you," Mestral said, "I am unfamiliar with your civilization." He almost was able to free his right hand.

Jaecz now was pacing back and forth across Mestral's field of vision. "Yes, yes. I know." He released a small laugh, though his attention seemed more on the floor in front of him than on his prisoner. "The funny thing is that you're telling the truth, and yet you're still so completely wrong. Vulcans and humans are staunch allies, something they'll demonstrate all too well when they come after my people."

What did he mean? To Mestral, it seemed as though the Certoss was giving voice to delusion. "Vulcans are a peaceful society. We do not attack others, and we use violence and arms as last measures of defense."

"Again, so very wrong," Jaecz said, before stopping his pacing in abrupt fashion and crossing the floor toward Mestral. "I've grown tired of these useless pleasantries, Vulcan, just as I long ago grew weary of living on this worthless hunk of rock and tolerating the parasitic, primitive vermin who call it home. I want to leave this place, and you seem to be my best hope of doing that. Tell me how to contact your ship, or I *will* kill you."

Hoping to delay any such action against him for a few more seconds, Mestral looked up at his captor while keeping his expression passive. "If you kill me, you will only hamper your own efforts."

"So you can communicate off-world," Jaecz snapped, reaching forward to grasp Mestral's jaw in his left hand. "Tell me."

Jerking his right arm upward, Mestral felt the cloth rope give way and he followed through with the motion, throwing as much strength as possible into striking his captor's arm and breaking the grip on his jaw. Jaecz's eyes widened in surprise at the unexpected move and he stumbled back. Reaching across his body, Mestral freed his left hand just as the Certoss stepped forward. He grasped his opponent's arm as it came at him and pulled Jaecz off balance, sending him crashing to the floor behind and to Mestral's right. Already hearing his captor lumbering to his feet, the Vulcan pulled at the rope holding his ankles to the chair, managing to free only the left leg before footsteps behind him made him abandon the effort. Then Jaecz was swinging down at him and Mestral threw his body left, sending him and the chair tilting toward the floor.

He fell heavily, his left ankle caught beneath the chair as it struck the floorboards, and he winced in momentary pain from the shock. The rope on his right leg was loosening, but it was not enough to pull himself free. Instead, he rolled toward the kitchen before turning onto his stomach and used his hands to push himself from the floor. He just managed to get himself to an awkward standing position as Jaecz approached, the chair lying to one side while still tied to his right leg and pain shooting through his left ankle. With no other weapon available and hobbled by the chair, Mestral did the only thing allowed by his current predicament and kicked out with his right leg.

The chair jerked upward, its back catching Jaecz under his chin and snapping back his head. Spinning as he fell, the Certoss dropped face-first with a heavy thud to the wooden floor. He lay unmoving as Mestral freed his leg, but it only was when he redirected his full attention to the downed Certoss that he realized his assailant's appearance had changed.

Instead of the dark-haired human who had confronted him, Mestral now saw a humanoid alien wearing a black, form-fitting jumpsuit. All that remained of its human appearance was the canvas satchel. Its skin was a shade of copper rather than an ordinary human's pale complexion, and there was no visible hair on its head. Instead of ears, two small openings on either side of the alien's head suggested auditory canals. Mestral stepped closer and, after determining that the Certoss was not faking unconsciousness, rolled the alien onto its back. Its eyes were closed, and Mestral saw the pair of small holes in the center of its face, just above its slack, open mouth.

"Intriguing," Mestral said, to no one. He noted the strange harness the alien wore across its chest, and the sets of controls embedded into it. Was it this device that allowed the Certoss to assume human form? It seemed to Mestral a logical deduction. Jaecz had fallen forward during the brief struggle, so had his impact with the floor triggered whatever control oversaw the device's activation? There was no time to answer any of the numerous questions presented by this mysterious alien.

There is one way, he reminded himself.

How long had it been since his last mind meld? Since well before setting out on the expedition that had brought him to Earth. Even on Vulcan, such opportunities were rare. After discovering his natural telepathic aptitude at a young age, Mestral's mother had instructed him how to utilize the technique in order to avoid harming another meld participant. She also taught him the necessity of keeping private his abilities, owing to Vulcan societal mores with respect toward those who chose to merge thoughts. While his mother and others with whom Mestral had interacted from an early age had shown him the ritual was something to be respected rather than shunned, it was viewed as aberrant behavior by the majority of Vulcans. Mestral always had found such attitudes illogical, but no more so than after his time spent on Earth. Humans possessed their own variety of irrational prejudices and hatreds, to be sure, often stemming from a fear of things not yet understood, or otherwise perceived as some threat to their well-being. At least here, such behavior could be explained if not justified, owing to an emotional and cultural immaturity that Mestral believed would correct itself over time. His own people, given the struggles their ancestors had overcome and the measures they had taken to rescue themselves from oblivion, had no such defense.

It was because of his mother's teachings and his own experiences that Mestral now found himself conflicted as he considered the unconscious Certoss before him. The prospect of a nonconsensual mind meld might be an expedient method of obtaining at least some information, but it went against everything he had learned and come to respect.

Given the current circumstances, I see no other choice.

Kneeling next to Jaecz, he ignored his reluctance and personal distaste and placed his fingers in as close to the proper position as he was able, given Certoss physiology. After a moment, he sensed the first tendrils of connection as he made mental contact with the unconscious alien.

"My mind to your mind," he whispered. "My thoughts to your thoughts." He did not yet know if the Certoss possessed telepathic capabilities, or, if so, whether such abilities were superior to his own. It therefore was a delicate balance of melding with Jaecz while at the same time maintaining his own mental shields against possible assault. Then, full contact was made, and Mestral braced himself as a torrent of thoughts, memories, and emotions rushed at him.

Mission . . . Earth . . . humans . . . war. Gejalik . . . Adlar. History . . . Na'khul. Etlun dead. Humans know. Mission . . . hide . . . escape. Time . . . future . . . war. Ship . . . Pennsylvania. Contact . . . mission . . . need information . . . call for assistance. Destroy. Mission. War. Earth. Destroy. Mission.

Jaecz's eyes opened.

The jolt of his abrupt awakening was such that Mestral yanked back his hand, severing the mental connection just as the Certoss pushed himself from the floor. His clumsy movements were enough to demonstrate that he still was hampered by the previous skirmish, but that did not stop him from regaining his feet. He blinked several times in rapid succession as he moved away from Mestral, raising his hands as though wary of attack. He stumbled several steps before bumping into the dining table, almost losing his balance, all the while never taking his eyes from Mestral. It was obvious that being struck by the chair had hurt him, his apparent disorientation perhaps explained by a head injury. Would that make him easier to confront, or more dangerous? The question was answered when Jaecz charged forward.

Mestral readied himself for the attack as the Certoss crossed the floor between them, but his own unsteadiness was his undoing as he tripped, stumbling forward and crumpling back down to the floor. Jaecz struggled to push himself up one last time but finally succumbed, collapsing once more into unconsciousness.

Mestral, fearing he may have killed the alien, verified that Jaecz still was alive. After retrieving his small medical scanner from his suitcase, he was able to calibrate the instrument in a manner to determine the Certoss's condition was not life threatening, but that he likely would not wake again for several hours. Mestral administered a general-purpose pain medication that his scanner confirmed was compatible with Certoss physiology, then left the intruder alone.

It is time to leave, he had decided, spending the next several moments securing the rest of his belongings—including the particle weapon from its hiding place—in his suitcase.

Those articles were joined by new items: the contents of Jaecz's satchel. The devices were of unknown construction and purpose, but he would have time later to examine them. He wanted to be well away from here when Jaecz came around, as another confrontation would in all certainty require him to kill the Certoss in self-defense. Ending the alien's life now was out of the question, though it was with no small amount of shame that Mestral had considered the idea.

No, he rebuked himself. There could be no justification for such a heinous act. Besides, leaving Jaecz alive might be helpful in locating his companions. That was the logical course of action, he knew, already refocusing his thoughts on the future as it lay before him now that he possessed knowledge of the alien's purpose here on Earth. His own priorities had changed, and while he could not stand by and allow Jaecz and his fellow Certoss agents to carry out their mission, there was precious little Mestral could do on his own.

He would need assistance.

EIGHTEEN

Wright-Patterson Air Force Base, Dayton, Ohio
July 29, 1958

"They're calling it NASA, sir," said Staff Sergeant Allison Marshall, sitting at her desk and reading whatever memo was at the top of the stack of similar documents. "National Aeronautics and Space Administration."

Reclining in the chair behind his own desk, Major James Wainwright held his coffee cup in both hands as he looked across the dimly lit room at Marshall. Night had fallen, and the office's only illumination came from the lamps sitting on their desks for the simple reason that neither of them had bothered to walk to the wall switch to turn on the overhead lighting. That was fine with Wainwright, as he preferred it this way. "NASA. Has a nice enough ring to it, I suppose. Eisenhower's been going nuts about space since *Sputnik*. He wants us up there, fast, so you can bet these boys will be getting all the money they need to do it."

"You can say that again." Marshall held up the memo for emphasis. "If only they'd channeled that effort toward us, we might've been able to get something up there before the Russians. A satellite, something based off the X-2, anything. Now, it looks like the civilians will be getting all the money and having all the fun."

"The military still has all the rocket research, along with

the best group of test pilots around," Wainwright countered. "This might be an 'us and them' thing on paper, but there's no way Eisenhower's going to let that be an issue when it comes to getting something done." The still fledgling Advanced Research Projects Agency had been formed earlier in the year as a response to the Soviet Union's launch of the *Sputnik* satellites. A military project operating under the supervision of the Department of Defense, ARPA had but a single, broad-reaching mandate: ensure the United States did not fall behind in its ability to exploit for military purposes emerging technology in any of numerous fields including communications, transportation, nuclear energy, and, now, space.

Rising from her chair, Marshall laid the memo atop the pile before moving around her desk. "ARPA's official mission is to keep us ahead of the Russians." The heels of her shoes clicked along the floor's linoleum tiles. "What about *other* things?"

Force of habit made Wainwright look toward the door as she asked the question. One thing he had learned after more than ten years on this job was that "caution" was his watchword; one never knew when someone might be listening, even within the confines of an office operating within the security envelope of a classified military project.

"I'm sure that's been factored in somewhere," Wainwright replied. "Eisenhower's as big a supporter of what we're doing as anyone."

The current president was on record with his belief in the possibility of life existing on other worlds, and his administration had provided Majestic 12 and Blue Book with generous funding and support. There were rumors that Eisenhower had met with extraterrestrials on three separate occasions in 1954. Despite his best efforts, Wainwright had been unable to confirm the meetings, or with whom or what the president may have conferred. Even Professor Carlson had been tight-lipped on the subject, which Wainwright had taken as tacit authentication.

He set his coffee cup on his desk as Marshall stopped next to his desk. Glancing at the clock over the door, Wainwright noted that it was coming up on seven in the evening. The words and numbers on the various reports he had been reviewing were starting to blur together, and the ache in his stomach told him it was well past time for something to eat.

Marshall leaned against one corner of the desk, folding her arms. Even this late in the day, after being in the office since before sunrise that morning, her hair, makeup, and Air Force duty uniform remained impeccable. *How does she do it?* It seemed almost too much effort for Wainwright to keep his tie straight. "I wonder what Professor Carlson thinks about this?"

"Good question," Wainwright replied, reaching up to rub his chin and frowning at the beard stubble beneath his fingers. Had he shaved that morning?

Yeah, fourteen hours ago. Go home.

"When was the last time you even heard from the professor?" Marshall asked.

It took him a moment to think about that. "A couple of months, I think," he said as he opened his desk's center drawer and retrieved the pack of cigarettes and lighter he had stashed there. "Between Washington, here, and that base out in Nevada, they've been keeping him pretty busy." The professor's duties, many of which carried a security classification so strict that even Wainwright did not possess the required "need to know," along with the established curtains of secrecy separating Project Blue Book from the other missions and operations overseen by the Majestic 12 organization, saw to it that the different groups exchanged little information, despite

Wainwright and Marshall still receiving most of their direction and assignments from the MJ-12 command structure.

After offering Marshall a cigarette, which she declined, he lit one for himself and took the first drag from it before blowing a stream of smoke into the air above his head. "Carlson's never told me straight out what he's been up to these past few years, but he's dropped enough hints for me to figure that his group and this new NASA organization won't be strangers." It was the professor who, for example, had been given responsibility for studying the craft discovered six years ago in Yuma, Arizona, by Wainwright and Marshall. As a consequence of that incident, the professor had exerted whatever authority he possessed to keep Wainwright and Marshall under his indirect supervision and attached to Blue Book. Without that influence, both then and in the years to follow, Wainwright was certain that he and Marshall would long ago have been transferred away from the project, perhaps even banished to some remote location such as one of the early warning stations in Alaska, where they would be unable to cause much trouble.

He reached up to stifle an abrupt yawn and caught Marshall smiling at him. "What?" he asked, taking another pull from his cigarette.

"It's late, sir," she replied, "and we've been here since before the sun came up. You should go home."

Wainwright nodded, blowing out smoke and moving to crush the remainder of the cigarette in his ashtray. "Fine idea. I'm beat, anyway." He stood, stretching his back and rotating his arms to work a few kinks from his shoulders. Sitting at a desk day after day had been taking its toll on him, despite his best efforts to remain fit with regular running and boxing at the base gym. He had celebrated his forty-first birthday earlier in the year, itself a stark reminder of just how long he had been stationed here, committed to this one effort. It was irregular for a military officer to spend such an extended length of time at any duty station, but the special demands of Project Blue Book and the assignments given to him and Marshall by Professor Carlson required a certain continuity that could be served only by keeping the same people within the organization's security envelope. "Or, maybe I'm just getting old."

"Not *too* old, I hope," Marshall said, casting a suggestive look over her shoulder as she returned to her desk. What had begun between them that morning last fall in Carbon Creek, Pennsylvania, had continued unabated, though they both had taken steps to keep their personal relationship guarded from the attention of their colleagues and superiors. So far, there seemed to be no indications that anyone around them was aware of their romantic involvement, or if they did suspect, then they had seen fit to keep that information to themselves. Regardless, Wainwright and Marshall did their level best to maintain proper decorum at work, though that did not prevent the occasional comment or look from being exchanged whenever it was just the two of them in the office. Of course, there was that one time they had pushed the limits of that façade right here, on . . .

Wainwright's reverie was broken by a knock on the office door. "Come in," he called out. The door opened and a male staff sergeant entered the room, wearing the duty uniform variant Wainwright recognized as one worn by personnel assigned to Wright-Patterson's military police contingent. Behind him was a tall, lean man Wainwright did not recognize, dressed in a civilian business suit complete with fedora. Thanks to the office's already dim lighting, the sergeant's helmet and the brim of the civilian's hat cast shadows across the upper portions of their faces. Stepping into the room, the sergeant snapped to attention and offered Wainwright a salute.

"Good evening, sir," he said, his tone clipped and formal.

Wainwright, still standing behind his desk, returned the salute. "At ease, Sergeant. What can I do for you?"

"Sorry to bother you this late, sir," the airman replied, "but this gentleman arrived at the front gate asking to see you." Pausing, he glanced over his shoulder at his charge. "He says it's important, sir."

Frowning at this unusual turn of events, Wainwright exchanged glances with Marshall before directing his attention to the mysterious man, who had said nothing since entering the room. "I don't understand."

The civilian lifted his head just enough that Wainwright could see his eyes before saying, "Please forgive the odd nature of my arrival, Major, but if I am correct, then you and Sergeant Marshall are the two people who would be most interested in certain information I have in my possession." His eyes narrowed as he fixed on Wainwright. "It pertains to a set of investigations you have conducted, particularly in Yuma, Arizona, and Carbon Creek, Pennsylvania."

Wainwright forced himself not to respond to the surprising statement. Instead, he cleared his throat and nodded to the airman. "Thank you, Sergeant. We'll take it from here. I'll be sure to call if I need anything."

"Yes, sir," the sergeant replied, saluting before taking his leave. He pulled the door closed behind him as he exited the room, leaving Wainwright and Marshall alone with their unexpected visitor.

"Thank you for agreeing to meet with me, Major," said the visitor, before directing his gaze for a moment to Marshall. "And to you, Sergeant."

Stepping around his desk, Wainwright said, "Well, you've certainly got our attention, sir, and you seem to know who we are well enough, so who might you be?"

Instead of replying, the new arrival turned and reached for the switch on the wall next to the door and flipped it, and the office overhead lighting flickered on and chased away the shadows. With the improved illumination, Wainwright now was able to see that the man's complexion was pale, possessing a tinge that made him think the man might be suffering from jaundice or some other similar condition. His face was long and thin, with sharp, pale eyes regarding Wainwright from beneath dark, upswept eyebrows.

"My name is Mestral," the man said, "and I have come to offer my assistance in your quest to understand the activities of those who have come from the stars to visit your world."

He removed his fedora to reveal his black hair, cut in an odd bowl style that in some respects reminded Wainwright of Moe from *The Three Stooges,* but all of that was forgotten as his eyes fixed on the man's pointed ears.

So, is this what alien mind control feels like?

The thought echoed in Wainwright's mind as he regarded Mestral across the small, round table occupying one corner of the apartment's main room. The room itself was a functional affair, with sparse furnishings that gave Wainwright the impression its occupant had only recently moved in, or perhaps did not plan on staying for any great length of time. Marshall sat to his left, and he noted her worried expression. He offered what he hoped was a reassuring smile.

"It's okay," he said. "To be honest, I haven't felt this well-rested in years."

"You are welcome," said Mestral. "The mind meld can be a

taxing experience, particularly for someone lacking their own nascent telepathic abilities, but the initiating party can mitigate those effects if they possess the proper training. If you do experience any lingering discomfort, I hope you will alert me."

Aside from an odd thirst he did not recall before subjecting himself to Mestral's touch, Wainwright was obliged to admit that there appeared to be no untoward effects to what had just transpired. For his part, Mestral seemed to have anticipated this one consequence and had provided a glass of water, which Wainwright drank in rapid fashion. Forcing a smile, he asked, "Is this all part of the brainwashing?"

Mestral's right eyebrow arched. "I am unfamiliar with that term, Major, but if you are worried that I may somehow have manipulated your mind for my own personal gain, I can only offer you my assurances to the contrary, along with the evidence I already have presented to you."

"What was it like, Jim?" Marshall asked, her tone conveying her persistent concern for him. "Can you describe it?"

Reaching up to rub his temples, Wainwright replied, "Like a very intense dream, though even more vivid than that. It's like I was . . ." He stopped, studying Mestral's face. "Like standing in a foggy room, where every sound echoes, and in front of you is a giant movie screen. It felt real and yet not real, at the same time. Does that even make sense?"

"It does," Mestral said. "Mind melds often produce a sensation of viewing an event from a sort of detached reality. Participants have described the experience as being separated from their corporeal form, feeling as though they are nothing more than an unfettered consciousness."

Marshall placed her hand on Wainwright's arm. "For what it's worth, you didn't seem to be in any pain, and he didn't do or say anything I found off." Her words made

Wainwright glance to the Colt .45 pistol resting in her lap, which she had kept with her throughout the entire "thought exchange." Though Wainwright himself had been willing to subject himself to the procedure, Marshall remained the voice of reason and caution. He smiled at her, placing his other hand atop hers and giving it a reassuring squeeze.

"I'm fine," he said, "really." Redirecting his attention to Mestral, he added, "Calling it eye-opening's a damned understatement, that's for sure." The revelation of Mestral's true identity and reasons for being here sounded like something out of one of those science fiction stories Wainwright had read as a teenager. The devices he had offered for examination certainly appeared to be far more advanced than anything possible from modern human science, and there could be no mistaking the differences in his physiology. First there were his ears, of course, but he also had submitted to an impromptu examination that had revealed his green blood—which had helped to explain his skin's odd hue—and the fact that his heart was located not in the center of his chest but instead along his left flank, beneath his arm, and beat much faster than a human's even at what Mestral called a resting rate. As startling as Mestral's own disclosures had been, it was what else he had offered that now troubled Wainwright.

Leaning toward the table, Wainwright turned to the small stack of photographs Mestral had provided as evidence of his encounter with another alien. "You say he called himself a 'Certoss,' right?" The figure in the pictures—Jaecz, according to Mestral—was lying in what appeared to be a state of unconsciousness, and the Vulcan had captured it from several angles offering full-body shots and close-ups of the alien's face.

"It's the same thing we ran into in Yuma," Marshall said, sliding one of the pictures closer to her and tapping it with one fingernail. "Same general skull shape and facial features, same clothing, and this harness he's wearing is identical."

Wainwright nodded. "The alien we killed in Yuma was a female. If the information you took from this one is accurate, then there are still three of them, running around out there somewhere and doing who knows what." He noticed that Mestral seemed to stiffen a bit in reaction to his words. "Something wrong?"

Clearing his throat, Mestral replied, "Your use of the term 'took' with respect to my mind meld with the Certoss agent. Though your description is essentially correct, the act itself is one in which I do not take pride. My people consider an involuntary mind meld to be a violation of the highest order. We are taught that it is acceptable only in the most extreme of circumstances. While my encounter with Jaecz certainly fit within those parameters, I find that I still am troubled by the entire affair."

"They don't seem to have any problems messing with our heads," Marshall said. "It's the only explanation for why we can't remember what happened in Carbon Creek, right?" She paused, her eyes lowering to look at the table for a moment. "Well, now you can remember it, I guess."

"I guess," Wainwright repeated. Though Marshall had not yet partaken of Mestral's offer to undergo the process, the Vulcan's mind meld with him had helped uncover what the alien described as "suppressed memories" of his and Marshall's visit to the small Pennsylvania mining community the previous November. Wainwright now recalled with vivid clarity the crashed space vessel they had seen that night, where it had come to rest in the mountains outside the town.

"These Certoss," he said, his eyes fixed on one of the photographs depicting the alien's face, "could they have . . . *mind melded* . . . with us to make us forget what happened?"

"I found no evidence that Jaecz possessed such telepathic ability," Mestral replied, "though he was unconscious at the time of our meld and my contact with him was brief. None of the devices I took from him seem designed for that purpose, but this does not preclude some other technology to which I had no access."

"If they can do that," Marshall said, "along with those devices that let them change their appearance? They could be anyone, anywhere, covering their tracks wherever they go. For all we know, we've run into them a dozen times over the years." She pulled back from the table, crossing her arms as though a sudden chill had gripped her. "That's scary just to think about."

Wainwright tapped the photo. "What do we do about it? I don't think we can take this to the higher-ups; at least, not yet. Even with you to tell them, it's still a tough story to swallow. Time-traveling aliens out to destroy us before we're able to get out into space and destroy them? You have to admit it sounds pretty crazy."

Marshall frowned. "You're probably right. Even if we could convince Captain Gregory, what would he do? We definitely need more information, more proof."

"Agreed," Mestral said.

"It's not Gregory I'm worried about," Wainwright countered. "It's the establishment above him." Blue Book's current commanding officer, Captain George Gregory, had no real interest in finding the truth so far as UFOs and alien activity were concerned, which suited his superiors. The bureaucracy surrounding the project and Majestic 12 along with all of their ancillary activities had become so compartmentalized and convoluted that it often was difficult if not impossible to determine how or even if information was being shared. Gregory had no direct knowledge of the truth behind the Roswell affair, nor did he know the full details of incidents involving certain case officers, such as Wainwright and Marshall's adventure in Yuma. Indeed, many of those assignments were carried out at the direction of MJ-12 rather than Gregory. Wainwright long ago had been forced to concede that Blue Book was little more than a façade designed to mollify the public while at the same time feeding it disinformation about the ongoing investigations of extraterrestrial activity. Meanwhile, Wainwright and Marshall and a few other select teams of senior investigators continued their investigations in relative isolation.

"We know Professor Carlson will believe us, but getting the Pentagon involved will be impossible unless we have more in the way of direct evidence. We need to show them that the threat is real, and these aliens are working right now to hurt us." Wainwright looked to Mestral. "You've come this far, and taken a huge risk exposing yourself to us. Are you willing to take it the whole way, and help us?"

Mestral replied, "Regardless of how I came to be here, Earth is now my home, and I do not wish to see it or its people harmed. I will do whatever I can to assist you."

"Good," Wainwright said, feeling a sudden bolt of conviction welling up within him. After years of being marginalized while pursuing the truth, the time at last had come for him, Marshall, and the entire Blue Book project to carry out their primary mission and validate the resources and faith entrusted to them. Wainwright took a small measure of satisfaction in knowing that the naysayers who had obstructed and ostracized the entire effort from its inception now were due for a very rude awakening.

NINETEEN

U.S.S. Enterprise
Earth Year 2268

It required effort for Kirk to keep from staring at the conference table's tri-sided viewer and the small chronometer displayed in the screen's lower left corner, which served as a reminder of how many minutes remained until the arrival of the Tandaran vessel. Every department had checked in with Spock, assuring the first officer of their readiness should events take a turn for the worse. At Scott's suggestion, Kirk had ordered the Certoss vessel brought onto the *Enterprise*'s shuttlecraft deck, rather than having the starship trying to protect the smaller craft by extending its shields should a tactical situation develop with the Tandarans. The *Balatir* fit within the space, though getting it through the hangar bay doors had proven somewhat tricky even with the aid of tractor beams and computer guidance. With that final item addressed, there was nothing else for Kirk to do on that front but wait, and that was an activity he loathed.

Turning his chair so that he could ignore the monitor, he focused his attention on Roberta Lincoln sitting next to him at the table. "These Tandarans have access to at least some of the same information you do regarding the Temporal Cold War. How is that possible?"

Lincoln, sitting with her arms crossed, replied, "They

were smart. At some point during their involvement in the conflict, a cadre of their leading scientific minds realized that time itself was being used as a weapon, altering the pasts of target worlds in order to influence the war's outcome on several fronts. They figured the only way to know if their own planet had been messed with was to create a protected archive that could preserve information for historical review while insulating it against changes in the timeline."

"A form of temporal stasis?" Spock asked.

Nodding, Lincoln smiled. "I think that's the right term. We're talking about a time capsule in the purest sense, here; a container inside which time—for all intents and purposes—has no meaning. You know about the Slavers and their stasis boxes, right?"

Spock replied, "I am familiar with such artifacts, yes."

"Same thing here. Though changes in our timeline would affect us all, anything held within the confines of such an archive would be shielded."

"It sounds like something that could cause its own flavor of problems," Kirk said, admiring yet again how much Roberta Lincoln seemed to have grown in the week—the *year*—that for her had passed in alliance with Gary Seven. "How is someone finding such an archive and discovering its contents any different than the situation the Certoss are facing?"

"In the case of the Tandarans and a handful of other groups possessing similar technology," Lincoln replied, "only highly trained specialists are even allowed to know of the existence of such data, and for the very reasons you bring up. Still, despite whatever organizations or other safeguards are put in place to protect against abuse of such knowledge, that's always a risk."

Spock said, "And this is what the Tandarans fear."

"You got it." Unfolding her arms, Lincoln turned her chair and leaned in the first officer's direction. "They know the real history of their involvement in the war. What I don't know is if they know how history plays out for them from this point forward in the timeline where the Certoss destroyed their planet. I suspect they don't, but I'm learning that you just never know when it comes to this kind of thing."

"So, what do we do about it?" Kirk asked. "We know how easy it is to disrupt history even through the most innocent acts, but we're talking about a deliberate, maybe even targeted, alteration of the time stream." He could not help recalling how, in another reality, McCoy's inadvertent traveling back through time to Earth had altered his planet's future, forcing Kirk and Spock to take drastic action in order to restore the time stream to its proper place. Regardless of how he tried, Kirk could not keep his thoughts from turning to the one person upon whom the conflicting versions of history had converged: Edith Keeler.

Don't. She's dead. It had to be. She would understand. Let her rest in the peace she deserves.

Lincoln, oblivious to his internal battle, said, "What's crazy about a conflict involving time travel is that there's no real way to know if it's really over, everywhere. We're sitting here talking about the war in the past tense, because so far as we can tell, it's been over for at least a century, or three centuries if you go with subjective time, but what about a century from now? Anything is possible."

"Perhaps the Tandarans believe Gejalik represents a faction of the Certoss people that still exists in some parallel timeline," Spock said, "with the ability to travel to our timeline. In that reality, the same one in which the Certoss people view Earth as a threat, the Tandarans would be considered their adversaries, as well."

Lincoln released a long sigh. "I really, *really* hate temporal mechanics."

"Just the fact that she's from a future that knows of the war makes her a concern for the Tandarans," Kirk said. "How far will they go to keep this information from becoming public, or at least being used or misused by someone else?"

The answer to that question was not forthcoming, as the conversation was interrupted by the briefing room's doors opening to admit Ensign Minecci and Minister Ocherab, whom the security officer had escorted from the *Balatir* on the hangar deck. Rising from his chair, Kirk made his way around the table until he stood before the older Certoss female.

"Minister, thank you for joining us," he said, before directing her to a seat at the table. "I trust your crew is being made comfortable?"

Ocherab nodded. "Indeed they are, Captain. I know about Federation starships, of course. Another vessel like this, the *Endeavour,* even visited our homeworld not all that long ago, but we only saw the images as distributed by our information broadcasts. It is a work of beauty."

"My chief engineer will enjoy hearing you tell him that," Kirk said, smiling. "I only wish you could be here under more pleasant circumstances, and I apologize for the abruptness of our greeting when you and your ship were brought aboard. I thought time might better be spent with giving you as much information as possible before the Tandarans arrive."

Now it was Ocherab's turn to smile. "I thank you for everything you have done on our behalf, Captain. It has been a rather enlightening experience, to say the least."

Kirk at first had wanted to keep Ocherab and her crew aboard the *Balatir* insulated from the "truth" of the Certoss people's involvement in the Temporal Cold War, but Spock and Lincoln had convinced him that doing so would only delay the inevitable. Colonel Abrenn would show no such reluctance if and when he was given the opportunity to confront Ocherab with respect to the message he believed her ship had sent to her homeworld. With that in mind, Lincoln spent the next several moments providing a succinct explanation of the war and the role of the Certoss people in that time-spanning conflict, as well as the activities of Gejalik and her fellow operatives sent four centuries back through time to Earth. It was a lot to take in, Kirk knew, but Ocherab seemed to be handling the process with aplomb.

"I can only imagine how difficult this must be for you to absorb, Minister," he said, "but rest assured we're prepared to help you in any way we can."

"Thank you, Captain." Before Ocherab could say anything else, the briefing room doors opened again, this time to allow Ensign Hawthorne and her own charge, Gejalik. The security guard directed the Certoss agent to a chair at the table opposite Kirk's, but instead of taking her seat Gejalik stood behind it, her attention transfixed by Ocherab.

"Gejalik," said the elder Certoss, rising from her chair and clasping her hands before her in what Kirk assumed was a gesture of welcome, "I am Minister Ocherab, of the Unified Envoy Vessel *Balatir*, and I bring you greetings from all the people of our world."

Mimicking the gesture, Gejalik offered a formal nod to the minister. "Thank you." To Kirk, she seemed nervous, as reflected in the way her gaze moved from Ocherab to Kirk and Spock and even Lincoln.

"Is there something wrong, Gejalik?" Ocherab asked, no doubt having perceived her unease.

Her eyes lowering to fix on the conference table, the Certoss replied, "I apologize, Minister. Given the amount of time I spent on Earth, and after learning what has happened, I was unsure how I would feel upon meeting someone from my homeworld. Perhaps this sounds odd, but in some ways I feel as though I now am alien even to my own people."

Would Edith Keeler have felt the same way, three centuries in the future from the world she had known? It was a question Kirk had asked himself countless times in the year that had passed since he, Spock, and McCoy had returned through the Guardian of Forever from Earth. Would it have made a difference to whisk her away from her fate, removing her from danger at the moment of her death so that she might live out her days seeing the universe she had dared to dream might exist one day in the distant future?

Stop it.

"It sounds like a perfectly natural reaction to me," Ocherab said, moving from her chair and walking around the table to Gejalik. "I am still in the process of accepting what Captain Kirk and his people have told me. They say that you are able to provide a unique perspective on our shared, if very disparate, history." The minister took Gejalik's hands in her own, and the Certoss exchanged a long look without saying anything. After a moment, Gejalik turned to Kirk. "How does one react to the knowledge that their entire existence may as well be an illusion? Which of the realities that we represent is the correct one?"

"This one," Lincoln said, her voice firm. "All available information tells us that the Certoss always have been a people of peace. Your past was altered by another civilization so that you could be their ally at a future point in history." She sighed. "Unfortunately, I don't know which of the factions fighting the war was responsible. Perhaps it's for the best that we don't know."

"And you're able to corroborate what Miss Lincoln has told me?" the minister asked Gejalik, who nodded.

"Yes," the Certoss agent replied. "Where I come from, our people, at one time, were at war with the Tandarans; however, by the time I came of age, the conflict between our two planets had ended." Once more she paused before directing her gaze to Kirk. "We destroyed the Tandaran homeworld by subjecting it to an unrelenting orbital bombardment that ultimately led to the entire planet becoming incapable of sustaining life. A fraction of the population was able to evacuate, but the vast majority of the Tandaran people perished at our hands. At the time I left, Tandaran Prime was still projected to remain uninhabitable for centuries."

Kirk asked, "When would this have taken place?"

"Approximately eighty of your years prior to my departure from Certoss Ajahlan to twentieth-century Earth," Gejalik replied.

Lincoln added, "About ninety years from now. In a different timeline, of course."

"Though Colonel Abrenn's concerns are somewhat extreme," Spock said, "they at least are understandable. The Tandarans obviously believe that some sequence of events might be enabled that could, in theory, restore the timeline where they and the Certoss once again are enemies and a threat to Tandaran Prime."

Kirk reached up to rub the bridge of his nose, feeling the onset of another headache. He was thankful for heeding Spock's advice to leave Mestral out of this meeting, which already had broached several topics of future history far ahead of the era he called home. "Just listening to all of that is exhausting."

Lincoln, with a hint of amusement in her eyes, replied, "How do you think I feel? This isn't exactly just another day at the office for me, either, and *that's* saying something."

"What am I to report to my leadership?" Ocherab asked after a moment, and Kirk could see that she was wrestling with her own feelings as well as the staggering revelations she had endured. "How does one tell her entire species that everything we know—everything we represent and have accomplished—might well be the result of someone else's machinations, or their whims? Are we nothing more than playthings for another's amusement?" For the first time, the minister seemed overwhelmed by what she had been told, and she took a seat at the conference table. Gejalik sat next to her, continuing to hold Ocherab's hand.

"Minister," she said, "believe me when I tell you I understand what you must be feeling. After all, I was trained and sent to inflict the same sort of tampering on another world and its people." She looked to Kirk, Spock, and Lincoln. "I do not ask forgiveness for that. I was a soldier, carrying out my duty during a time of conflict. It is obvious that our efforts to disrupt your society's development were a failure, and the evidence before me suggests that this was a good thing, particularly if what Miss Lincoln has said is true, and our people only were acting in response to influences leveled upon us." Returning her gaze to Ocherab, she added, "And you say our world is one of peace and prosperity? How could I not want that for our people? If the worst thing to come from all of this is that I am displaced from a reality in which war was a way of life, then it seems but a small price to pay. Perhaps it is best that no one else ever knows that truth."

Ocherab once more gripped Gejalik's hands in both of hers. "It seems as though fate has seen fit to give you an opportunity for a new life, in a world you may not recognize but which still is your own."

"Thank you, Minister," Gejalik said, and Kirk was certain he detected the Certoss equivalent of an expression of gratitude and even relief gracing her features.

"I don't think it's your own people you have to worry about," he said. "The Tandarans, on the other hand, are going to be harder to convince. They're obviously worried not just about you, but what you represent. The knowledge you possess about future history, particularly theirs, is something they want. They're terrified that you might just be the first of an invading army from a future that, so far as we know, can't exist in this timeline."

"Let's say for the sake of argument that the Tandarans know, suspect, or are in a position where they might find out what eventually happens to them in the other timeline," Lincoln said. "You, Gejalik, are everything they fought against in a war remembered by no one on your planet or theirs. They want that reality to stay buried, and there may be no limit to how far they're willing to go to make sure that happens."

If it was Lincoln's intention to frighten Gejalik, the Certoss agent's body language and expression told Kirk that her efforts were succeeding. After a moment, she seemed to collect herself, the soldier and her training once more coming to the fore. "I suppose I should be able to understand and even appreciate that," she said, her voice taking on a harder tone. "The world I left *destroyed* the Tandarans. We did it because they were working to do the same thing to us. It was *war*, and we were fighting for our very survival. We eliminated a threat."

She looked to Kirk. "Just as I was fighting your people, who also were a threat, or would be a threat, or however you want to describe it. I was willing to annihilate your entire civilization at a point centuries before they ever could do anything to harm us, in effect waging battle against people who would be dead long before our two planets ever became aware of each other. I have no justification for feeling anything toward the Tandarans except understanding. If surrendering me to them is what's required for the Certoss people to continue to enjoy the peace they have known for uncounted generations, then I willingly offer myself to that cause."

"A noble gesture, Gejalik," Spock said, "though one I fear may be insufficient. It is reasonable to assume that Colonel Abrenn will suspect we now possess knowledge of the other timeline and the very different reality experienced both by the Certoss and the Tandarans, to say nothing of our own history with respect to the Temporal Cold War."

Kirk had been considering that very possibility. Would Abrenn risk war with the Federation by attacking the *Enterprise,* believing such radical action was justified in order to protect his people? Kirk had to ask himself how he might react, given similar circumstances.

"*Bridge to Captain Kirk,*" said the voice of Lieutenant Sulu piped through the ship's intercom.

Reaching for the comm switch set into the table before him, Kirk activated the connection. "Go ahead, Mister Sulu."

"*Sir, you asked to be notified when the Tandaran vessel was ten minutes from intercept. They're maintaining course and speed, and their weapons and shields are still active. They've commenced a full sensor sweep of us, including the Certoss vessel.*"

"Have they tried hailing us?" Kirk asked, already knowing the answer.

"*Negative, sir. They've not initiated any communication, and they're not responding to our hails, though Lieutenant Uhura confirms they're receiving.*"

Kirk grunted in irritation. "Maintain alert status. I'm on my way up now." He severed the link and rose from his chair, gesturing for his first officer to follow him. "Mister Spock, it's time to go and greet our new guests. Let's hope they're a bit more cordial than they've been up to this point."

"I find that unlikely, Captain," the Vulcan replied as he moved to follow Kirk from the briefing room.

Sighing, Kirk shook his head. "Yeah, me too."

TWENTY

Wright-Patterson Air Force Base, Dayton, Ohio
September 26, 1963

Crouching in the shadows afforded by the trees lining the access road, Adlar and Gejalik watched the Air Force sentry walking his post around the warehouse across the narrow street. Warehouse 13B was a two-story metal structure, one of half a dozen located in this area of the base at the far edge of the flight line. A careful inspection of the adjacent buildings showed no signs of exterior activity, though lights were on in several windows, testifying to the work being carried out even at this late hour, but only this warehouse seemed to have its own security detail. The guard was one of two on duty, each walking in opposite directions as they circled the building, and they nodded to each other as they passed, continuing on with their prescribed patrol routes. Having observed the sentries make this same circuit four previous times, Adlar now had a sense of how long the guards took to walk their routes. Both men wore helmets and carried what Adlar recognized as M2 carbine rifles slung over their shoulders, and he also noted the holstered pistols on their hips.

"Just the two," Gejalik said, keeping her voice low. In her hand she carried a small scanner, the illumination of its display muted so as to avoid detection by the guards or another random passerby. "However, there are several life-forms inside the structure. Most of them do not appear to be in proximity to the probe. I suspect that it is currently under guard. We'll have to be careful."

Notification of the probe's recovery had come in the form of a cryptic message delivered via phone from Jaecz, ostensibly from the undisclosed location where he was working in the northeastern United States. Following his encounter with the Vulcan, Jaecz had increased his own shroud of security, moving at frequent intervals and maintaining a low profile in the hopes of thwarting any attempts the Vulcan might make to trace his movements. The message Jaecz had sent was short and lacking in detail, but still enough to bring Adlar and Gejalik to Wright-Patterson, where the Air Force had brought the unmanned survey probe they had recovered from a crash site in rural Ohio. At this point nothing about the device was known except that its construction suggested a Vulcan origin. Had the probe been sent to search for Mestral, the wayward scientist who had elected to remain on Earth rather than being rescued the previous year? Adlar doubted that. According to Jaecz, Mestral was believed dead, so the probe likely was part of an ongoing program of covert surveillance intended to monitor humanity's continued societal and technological advancement.

Manned or automated, the device might still prove useful, in that it almost certainly contained components and other materials that could be utilized in helping them make contact with someone—anyone—on Certoss Ajahlan. Though the likelihood of receiving any sort of message or assistance across time to the future from whence they had been dispatched seemed to fade with every passing year, neither Adlar nor Gejalik had surrendered all hope on that front. As always and until ordered otherwise, both they and Jaecz had pledged to continue exhausting all efforts at making contact as well as continuing their mission here.

Still, Adlar mused, *it would be nice to receive some sign that we've not been forgotten, or discarded.*

"If they follow their established protocols," Gejalik said, her attention divided between the warehouse and her scanner, "the device will be moved to the area they're preparing at their permanent facility inside Hangar 18."

Once that happened, Adlar knew that his and Gejalik's ability to access the probe would be hampered if not made outright impossible. The American military groups charged with safeguarding items of this sort had become quite adept at carrying out such tasks. Monitoring their movements and activities consumed a great deal of time and resources, despite the obvious technological advantages they possessed. The humans' approach to security—maintaining information within a small, compartmentalized sphere of control—thwarted most efforts at scrutiny.

Most, but not all. Adlar and Gejalik had been somewhat successful at tracking the movements of certain individuals. Doing so had become a bit easier in recent years now that military and civilian agencies were partnering to further the American government's goal of completing a successful manned landing on Earth's lone natural satellite. Two years earlier, John F. Kennedy, the President of the United States, had laid out his bold vision of seeing such a landing take place within ten years as a means of solidifying the country's superiority over its Cold War rival, the Soviet Union, so far as space exploration was concerned. Advances were being made and the United States was beginning to close the gap. Project Mercury, comprising the first serious attempts to match the Russian achievements, had completed its final flight earlier in the year. The next phase of Kennedy's goal, Project Gemini, would launch test flights within the next two years, and a massive industrial and technological effort now was under way to bring about the eventual goal of landing crafts and pilots on the moon.

Even as the civilian agency spearheaded the lunar program, other firms operating under military oversight were continuing to develop and construct weapons of increasing capability. The United States' nuclear arsenal was growing at an alarming rate, staying apace with that of the Soviet Union. Both powers now possessed far more firepower than ever would be needed in the event an exchange of such weapons ever took place. While sophisticated protocols had been enacted to prevent the use of such weapons unless either side viewed it as the only remaining option, the specter of nuclear annihilation had been a constant presence for years. Such scenarios had been a staple of films and stories depicting the consequences and aftermath of nuclear holocaust for more than a decade, equaled only by the number of fantastic tales showing all manner of invasions by malevolent alien conquerors. Away from those fictions was reality, including one short intense period the previous year that had seen the United States and Russia come to within moments of waging atomic war on each other. Though catastrophe had been avoided on that occasion, how easy would it be to exploit either side's paranoia and fear in order to bring about such an event?

We shall soon see, Adlar thought.

"Are you ready?" Adlar asked, opening the control panel of his shroud harness. Like Gejalik, he already had programmed the device for the human form he planned to assume for their infiltration of the warehouse.

Gejalik deactivated her scanner and returned it to one of the compartments of the belt she wore over her bodysuit. "Yes," she said, activating her own harness. Her outward appearance shifted so that she now was a human female dressed in an Air Force lieutenant's uniform. All traces of her Certoss physiology, clothing, and equipment once again were hidden, the human disguise flawless to detection by anything save scanning equipment far more advanced than what was possible by current human technology.

His own disguise now consistent with Gejalik's as he had taken on the outward appearance of a male captain, Adlar reached into the standard military-issue briefcase he had brought with them and extracted a pair of .45 caliber pistols along with a purse designed for use by female Air Force officers. Gejalik took one of the pistols and, after verifying that it was loaded and its safety engaged, placed the weapon inside the purse.

They waited until both guards had moved out of sight before making their way to Warehouse 13B's front entrance. Managing the door lock was a simple enough exercise thanks to the electromagnetic driver Adlar produced from his briefcase. Once inside, they made their way through the building's front section, which consisted of office and meeting space. Turning a corner in the narrow corridor, they saw a set of large metal double doors leading to what Gejalik already had determined was the warehouse's main floor. Before the entry stood two more Air Force guards, each holding an M2 rifle. Unlike the sentries outside, these two men were dressed in green fatigue uniforms with matching caps pulled low over their eyes. Both men straightened their postures at Adlar and Gejalik's approach, coming to attention and offering proper salutes with their rifles.

"Good evening, sir. Ma'am," said the higher ranked of the pair, a staff sergeant, and when he spoke Adlar detected an accent to his voice indicating the man was from one of the United States' southern regions. "May we help you?"

Affecting a calm demeanor suggesting he and Gejalik had every right to be there, Adlar returned the salute before waving past the sergeant toward the door. "We're actually very late to a pretty important meeting, Sergeant. I'm sure at least somebody in there with more stuff on his collar than all of us is wondering where we are."

The sergeant appeared unimpressed with the fabricated plight. "I'll need to see your identification and authorization, sir. Major Fellini's orders."

Adlar never had the chance to say anything before a thin beam of green energy shot from behind him to hit the sergeant in the chest. The sergeant's eyes rolled back in his head and he fell against the door, only just beginning to slide to the floor before the same fate befell his companion. Adlar caught the guard's rifle, preventing a possible accidental firing as the second man dropped into an unconscious heap. It had taken mere seconds for Gejalik to incapacitate both men.

"You're really rather effective with that," Adlar said, turning to see Gejalik wielding one of their compact stun devices.

Gejalik nodded. "Thank you." She gestured with the weapon before returning it to her waistband and straightening her jacket. "Remind me to thank Jaecz for it the next time we're able to communicate." Constructed by Jaecz, the devices were concealed with minimal effort, and also were preferable nonlethal alternatives to the .45 pistols they carried. Though Adlar had little concern over killing if circumstances required it, doing so when it could be avoided was a practice he had favored despite the endless drills and lectures to the contrary instilled by his various training instructors. Of course, he knew how odd his personal predilections were in the face of his mission, which if successful would see to the obliteration of most if not all of the human species.

Yes, it's contrary, but I do not care. Regardless of the mission and what was required of him, he wanted to retain at least some small measure of dignity and honor. He knew it was a semantic argument he likely would lose if faced with a debate, but for now the minor, even irrelevant distinction would have to be sufficient.

As Adlar verified that they were out of commission, Gejalik retrieved the portable scanner from her purse. Activating the unit, she touched a control and studied its display.

"It's in the chamber beyond these doors. I'm scanning two other life-forms, one male and one female." She frowned, tapping another control. "Interesting. The scanner's detecting unusual power sources. It's small, but there, and inconsistent with present human technology."

"Something from the probe?" Adlar asked.

"I don't know." Keeping the scanner activated, Gejalik reached with her free hand to retrieve the .45 pistol from her purse. "Ready?"

Pulling out his own sidearm, Adlar said nothing as he used the driver to unlock the door before pushing it open. The entrance led to another short, dimly lit corridor that ended ten meters ahead of them at a heavy black curtain. Adlar held up a hand and motioned for Gejalik to listen, and she nodded as she confirmed what he thought he had heard: Someone beyond the curtain was talking. To Adlar the voice sounded female. Gesturing for Gejalik to follow, he peered through the curtain, but saw nothing in his immediate line of sight. With as little movement as possible, he pushed through the curtain.

The room beyond was large and open, rising two stories above the floor to the warehouse's vaulted metal ceiling. Rows of metal shelving dominated the chamber's back half, connected by catwalks and ladders. The forward area had been converted to an open workspace that reminded Adlar of the building in Yuma where they had found the spacecraft being tested by the humans. In the center of the open area, surrounded by work lights mounted on tripods, was a metal object, its shell almost black in color. The probe was not quite a cylinder, its squat height making each end appear ovular in shape. Smaller cylinders mounted to either side suggested to Adlar a form of faster-than-light propulsion. He also recognized one of the written Vulcan languages from collections of symbols scattered across its surface. Standing before the probe was a human male with short blond hair and wearing green fatigues, talking in a low voice though no one else seemed to be nearby. It took Adlar an extra moment to realize that the man appeared to be talking into something he held in his hand, a slim, silver object.

Who is this?

That was all Adlar had time to consider before something moved to his left, and he saw a dark figure aiming something at him.

Cynthia Foster was sure she had hit the intruder with her servo, the compact weapon's stun beam in theory being more than sufficient to pacify a target from this distance. The new arrival's reaction—firing a pistol in her direction—told her otherwise.

"Ian! Look out!" she shouted, diving for cover behind a row of wooden cargo crates as more shots rang out in the warehouse. Who were the man and woman who had come through the curtain? It was unlikely that they were ordinary Air Force officers, not if the small device the woman held was any indication. It had emitted an energy reading unlike anything to which any normal human should have access. Moving to the row's far end, Cynthia maneuvered herself so that she could peer over the top of the crate she now found herself behind, orienting herself to face back toward the curtain and the entrance through which the intruders had come. No sooner was she able to get a look than the woman fired her own pistol in Cynthia's direction.

The guns are conventional enough, she chided herself. *Move your ass, Agent 6.*

Recalling the warehouse's interior, she adjusted her servo's settings before taking off at a run back the way she had come. As she moved, she looked up over the top of the cargo crates and aimed the servo at the large, single-bulb floodlights hanging from the ceiling nearest the entrance and fired. The bulb exploded from the force of the servo's sonic beam, sending shattered glass cascading to the floor. She saw the two figures running away from the curtain, seeking cover, and she repeated the action on another of the lights. The two intruders moved behind another large wooden crate and Cynthia destroyed a third light, plunging the forward half of the room into near darkness.

"Ian," she murmured. Ian Pendleton, standing exposed next to the Vulcan probe at the time of the intruders' arrival, obviously had sought cover once gunfire erupted. *Where was he?* Cynthia forced herself not to worry about her fellow agent and concentrate instead on the two assailants. *Who are they?* It was likely that they had come for the probe, but how did they even know it was here? The device was supposed to be a closely guarded secret, known only to a handful of

American military and civilian officials. She and Ian knew about the probe only because they had tracked its movements as it had assumed orbit over Earth and began its clandestine surveillance of the planet. The mission given to her and her fellow agent was supposed to be simple: Retrieve the probe and safeguard it from further study by the American military or anyone else.

Cynthia dove across an open space between two crates, hearing the whine of a pistol shot skipping off the concrete behind her. Then she heard the sound of Ian's servo followed by shattering glass, and another section of the warehouse fell into darkness. Agent 42 was mimicking her actions from wherever he had ended up in the large room, and now she heard the sounds of footsteps running across the warehouse floor. She saw a lone, shadowy figure sprinting toward the rows of storage shelves at the back of the room and recognized Ian's distinctive running stride. More bullets followed after the agent, a few of them chewing into the crates he passed as he lunged once more for protection. With their attackers distracted, Cynthia rose from her crouch and fired her servo, but the weapon's stun beam again had no effect save to alert the intruders to her position.

"Halt!"

The shouted voice was coming from the other end of the warehouse, and Cynthia looked around the crate to see three men running into the chamber, each brandishing M2 carbine rifles. One of the guards, a senior airman judging from his rank chevrons, was the group's apparent leader and he already was raising his rifle to point it at the pair of intruders. Now that they were standing near one of the lights that had not yet been destroyed, Cynthia could see that they both were wearing Air Force officer uniforms.

"Hold it right there!" he yelled. "Drop those weapons right now!"

Neither of the intruders hesitated before turning their pistols on the new arrivals and firing. Cynthia flinched as the men were cut down in seconds, only one of them able even to call out in surprise and pain before all three dropped to the floor.

No!

"Cynthia!"

Ian's shout made her look over the crate to see that her partner had scrambled to the second-level catwalk bordering one aisle of shelves. He had found a weapon of his own, another M2, and was aiming it at another section of the warehouse floor.

"They're to your right!" he called out, gesturing with the rifle's muzzle. Bullets ricocheted off the metal framework around him and he ducked, returning fire with his own weapon. Cynthia knew Ian was not attempting to hurt or kill their opponents, but instead was laying down covering fire for her. Dashing for a collection of larger cargo crates near the base of the shelves, she saw the other woman aiming her pistol and firing. A pair of bullets whipped past the back of her head and Cynthia heard them tear into the wall to her left before she jumped behind the nearest crate. She landed in awkward fashion on the unyielding concrete floor, wincing at the stab of pain in her ribs.

More gunfire echoed across the warehouse, and Cynthia saw Ian sag against the railing, crying out in pain. The rifle fell from his grip as Ian flailed for something to hold before his body rolled over the handrail and tumbled to the floor.

"Ian!" Disregarding her own safety and the pain in her side, Cynthia bolted from her hiding place, rushing across the open floor to where Ian now lay strewn on the concrete. He was on his back, his left leg bent at an unnatural angle, and she saw at least three bloody holes in his chest. Ignoring the approaching footsteps behind her, she dropped to her knees next to Ian, reaching for his face but freezing at the sight of his open, unseeing eyes.

"No," she whispered, tears clouding her vision. There was nothing she could do for him, but her body refused to heed the warnings her mind sent, screaming for her to remain focused on the dangerous situation still unfolding before her. Then a hand on her shoulder snapped her out of her shock and Cynthia whirled around, lashing out with her right fist. The punch caught the male intruder across his temple with enough force to make him stagger back, his service cap falling from his head and giving Cynthia the opening she needed to regain her feet. She saw the man's female companion coming up behind him but ignored her as she pressed her attack.

"You *bastard*!" she hissed between gritted teeth, landing a kick to the center of his chest. He released a grunt of pain and surprise that was accompanied by an electronic snapping sound, followed by the bizarre sight of the man's entire body wavering and stretching before his appearance underwent an abrupt, startling change.

He was an alien.

Dressed in a black bodysuit and wearing a metallic harness across his chest, the figure now possessed dark, unfamiliar humanoid features. Cynthia could not even begin to place the being's species.

"Leave her!" shouted the alien's companion, still appearing as a human female.

The alien did not heed her, instead setting himself to lunge at Cynthia, but she and both intruders cringed at the abrupt flash of light illuminating the entire warehouse an instant before the explosion.

Holy . . .

Instinct made Cynthia throw herself behind a nearby cargo crate, wincing again at the pain from her ribs as the shockwave rolled past them. Shrapnel and whatever else peppered the walls, shelves, and other crates. Waiting for the storm of debris to subside, Cynthia peered out from her momentary place of safety. The alien and his companion were gone. Their bodies were not lying anywhere on the warehouse floor, leading Cynthia to believe they somehow had escaped the blast. When she looked toward the center of the open work area, she saw only scattered pieces of smoldering metal where the Vulcan probe once had been. The worktables and lights positioned around it also had been destroyed, littering the floor with scorched debris. What could have caused that?

The sirens were very loud outside the building now, and Cynthia also heard frantic voices beyond the warehouse's metal walls. She had to make her escape, but she also could not leave Ian to be discovered or taken into custody. Though the almost perfect product of selective breeding that was Ian Pendleton's human physiology likely would astound whatever doctor was tasked with conducting an autopsy, the devices he carried would attract unwanted attention. Cynthia would have to carry him out of here, with help from the translocator in their office back in Washington. Wiping away new tears, she reached into her pocket for her servo in order to contact the Beta 4 for exfiltration, but the device was not there. She patted her pockets but found nothing.

Damn it! A frantic search around her did not produce the servo, but she felt Ian's in one of his trouser pockets. She tore at the clothing, trying to retrieve the tool when a shadow fell across Ian's body, and she jerked around to see not either of the intruders but instead a man, dressed in a black business suit. He looked to be in his thirties and despite his civilian attire there was a definite military air about him. Another figure stood nearby, wearing a similar suit but also a fedora that cloaked his face in shadow. When the man extended his right hand, Cynthia saw that he was holding her servo.

"You'll need this," he said, tapping one of the controls hidden in the servo's pocket clip. The device emitted a string of high-pitched beeps before Cynthia heard a familiar, almost musical warbling sound from behind her. She turned to see the familiar blue-black mist forming behind the nearest row of cargo crates.

Dumfounded at her bizarre turn of good fortune, Cynthia turned back to her mysterious savior. "Who are you?" she asked, her voice shaking.

"There's no time," he replied. "You have to go, *now*. Come on, I'll help you." Thanks to her enhanced strength, Cynthia did not require assistance to lift Ian's body and lay it across her shoulders, but she still accepted the offer. That done, the man regarded her with a saddened expression. "I'm sorry about Agent 42. I know you were close."

"You're one of us?" Cynthia asked, just before gunfire echoed from the front door leading to the warehouse's main floor. Someone must be shooting off a lock, she reasoned. Only seconds remained until she was discovered.

"Yes and no," said the man. "It's a long story. Maybe later. Now *go*!"

Cynthia glanced to the dark blue cloud, her escape hatch, before thinking to ask the men to come with her, but when she turned back, her benefactors were gone.

"Where . . . ?"

"Secure every door!" a new voice barked. The order had come from someone Cynthia could not see. "I want this whole place locked down!" She caught sight of an Air Force officer, a major, pointing at various airmen and other personnel, deploying them around the warehouse, and she knew it was time to go. With a final look at the room's center to verify that the Vulcan probe had been destroyed, Agent 6 turned and, holding the body of her lover tight across her shoulders, plunged into the blue fog.

TWENTY-ONE

Wright-Patterson Air Force Base, Dayton, Ohio
September 27, 1963

More than four years had passed since James Wainwright last had seen Jeffrey Carlson, but in that brief period the professor seemed to have aged a decade. His black hair had long since been replaced with gray, the same color as the full beard he now sported which, along with the wire-rimmed glasses and their circular lenses, made the man a dead ringer for Santa Claus. The only real distinction was his weight, in that Carlson seemed to have lost a great deal of his. He was stoop-shouldered as he paced a circuit around the meeting room's conference table, which, like the chairs and other furniture, was metal and painted the same shade of standard, military-issue flat gray. The obvious visual evidence suggested the professor was much older than his fifty-five years.

What the hell are they doing to you out there in Nevada?

Carlson walked in circles around the room, his hands buried in the pockets of a worn, beige cardigan button-down sweater that to Wainwright looked as though it had seen better days. In fact, he was sure he remembered the professor wearing it during one of their infrequent meetings at least ten years earlier.

Don't they ever let you out once in a while, at least to buy some new clothes?

"And the device was completely destroyed?" Carlson asked, his voice soft and possessing a raspy quality.

From where he stood at one end of the table, Major Lucas Fellini replied, "That's right, Professor. There's not much left, but it's been collected and sealed in a packing container per your instructions and ready to ship out when you are." Fellini was a tall, broad-chested man, with what Wainwright considered "classical tough guy" looks—square jaw, thin nose, and piercing eyes that seemed to take in everyone and everything in a room in cold, calculating fashion. The major wore his Air Force officer's uniform in a manner as close to picture-perfect as Wainwright had seen on anyone, himself included. Every button, every device above the pocket of his uniform jacket, was precisely positioned and polished to a high luster that reflected the room's lighting. His jacket and trousers seemed tailored with mathematical exactitude to his muscled frame, and his shoes were like mirrors. Even the handgrips of the service pistol holstered at his waist, a revolver from what Wainwright could see, were a glossy bone white. Fellini wore his officer's cap cocked slightly to the left, and while that was a bit outside of accepted regulations, it gave the major a confident, almost arrogant air that seemed to fit him. By all accounts, he was a capable, by-the-book officer who took with all seriousness his assignment as one of Wright-Patterson's three security division commanders. Wainwright already knew that the events of the previous evening which had taken place while Fellini was on duty were—at the moment—nothing short of a sore spot with the major.

Carlson, continuing to pace around the room, paused as he came abreast of Fellini. "And you still have no indications as to what happened?"

Shaking his head, the major looked to the floor for a

moment, as though embarrassed by his answer. "No, Professor. Our first guess is that the satellite had a time-delay explosive planted inside it, or some other self-destruct mechanism that might even have been damaged when it crashed. We were lucky that warehouse wasn't filled with brass or other VIPs trying to get a good look at it before it went off."

"Yes, that would've been most unfortunate," Carlson said, nodding in agreement.

Casting a knowing glance at the professor, Wainwright asked, "Major, do you still think this thing was a Russian spy satellite?"

"That's the most likely explanation, Mister Wainwright," Fellini answered, seeming to regain at least a bit of the confidence Wainwright had seen him exhibit on other occasions. "What else could it be? It's definitely not one of ours. We've already had people calling the space agency and the Pentagon, and neither of them has reported losing anything."

Even though he had not been an active Air Force officer for nearly a year, Wainwright still felt odd whenever another service member addressed him as "Mister." His and Allison Marshall's continued involvement in Project Blue Book—and Majestic 12, to a somewhat lesser, discreet degree—had begun to have detrimental effects on their prospects for advancement. Neither he nor Marshall had any desire to leave the program, so Wainwright had accepted official retirement from the Air Force while Marshall was allowed to transfer to the Air Force Reserves. Both now worked as civilian employees for the Department of Defense. Whereas Marshall still had the option to return to active service, Wainwright decided he had spent enough time in uniform. His son, Michael, was coming up on his seventeenth birthday and already was talking about joining the Air Force and carrying on the family service tradition. The boy's mother had not been happy with this news, judging from the last terse phone conversation with her Wainwright had endured.

She'll get over it, he mused. *Maybe.*

"And what about the intruders?" Carlson asked, keeping his attention on the major as he resumed his pacing. "Are you of the belief that they were Russian spies?"

Fellini replied, "That, or someone they recruited to do their dirty work for them. According to the sentries they got past, it was a man and a woman dressed in Air Force officer's uniforms. The guards don't remember anything after that."

"What about the guards?" Wainwright asked. "How are they doing?"

For the first time, the major reached up to remove his officer's cap. "This is the part where things start to get confusing, Mister Wainwright. These two spies, or whatever they were, incapacitated two sentries outside Warehouse 13B and two more inside. We don't know how, but we think it could've been some kind of tranquilizer. The men are being given the once-over to check for signs of injection or gas exposure. Three more men inside the building were shot. Two are dead, and the other one's in critical condition. The doctors don't have a prognosis for him yet."

"I hope he pulls through, Major," Marshall said, "and I'm sorry about what happened to your other men."

Offering her an appreciative nod, Fellini replied, "Thank you, Miss Marshall." He frowned, his expression growing hard, with a touch of anger. "What I don't understand is why they'd go to the trouble of knocking out four guards without killing them, but then turn around and shoot three others. Seems like they could've easily killed the other men, so why didn't they?"

"Maybe they were trying to keep things quiet," Wainwright said, "but the guards inside the warehouse spooked them while they were working to do . . . whatever it was they were trying to do with the satellite." He had at least as many questions as Fellini, but for very different reasons. The security cordon surrounding the downed satellite had been tight, with fewer than a dozen people even knowing the object had been retrieved from the crash site outside Lima, Ohio. No one else should even have known of its existence.

The folder beneath his hand told Wainwright a different story. He had only been able to examine its contents for a moment prior to the start of the meeting, but even that cursory review had been enough to seize his attention, and he wanted—he *needed*—to let Marshall and Professor Carlson see it for themselves.

"And we don't know how the intruders got away?" Carlson asked.

An expression of obvious embarrassment clouded Fellini's features. "No, Professor. We had the building surrounded, and all vehicles in and around the warehouse area were accounted for. No reports of unauthorized vehicles or personnel leaving the base. Either they're still hiding somewhere, or they got past us. We cordoned off that entire section of the base, and my men are conducting a thorough search of the entire area. If they're still here, we'll find them."

Wainwright exchanged knowing glances with Marshall. The intruders, he knew, were long gone, or else their methods of concealment would trump whatever search methods Fellini and his men might employ.

Removing his hands from his sweater pockets, Carlson now held a pack of cigarettes and a silver lighter. "I appreciate your efforts, Major. Please keep me informed of your progress."

"Thank you, Professor." Fellini cast glances to Wainwright and Marshall before adding, "If you'll excuse me, I should get back to the search area."

Once the major departed and the door closed behind him, Wainwright said, "There was no way he or his men could've known what they'd be up against."

"I agree," Carlson said. "I think we may need to invest more time and resources into enhancing the training of our security forces, if we're going to ask them to be ready for events like this one."

The door at the room's opposite end opened to admit Mestral. He wore a suit similar to Wainwright's, dark gray jacket and trousers with matching tie over a white shirt, with a fedora completing the ensemble. After Marshall had verified that the room's primary entrance was locked, Mestral removed his hat, his hair now mussed just enough to expose the tips of his pointed ears.

"Good morning, Professor," Mestral offered as he took a seat at the table. "It is good to see you again."

Smiling, Carlson replied, "Same to you, son. Jim tells me he sent you to have a look at whatever's left of the probe. What did you figure out?"

"There was very little worth examining," Mestral said, clasping his hands before him, "and nothing with identifying markings remains, but the materials used in its construction are definitely of Vulcan origin. My people sent the probe."

Marshall asked, "An unmanned version, this time?"

"Yes," Mestral replied. "It is reasonable to theorize that my people have altered their surveillance methods in response to the incident involving my vessel in Carbon Creek,

Pennsylvania. They may have determined that the risk of discovery should such another ship be lost in similar fashion is too great. Based on my scans of the remaining debris, I believe the probe carried sufficient sensors and other recording devices that would have allowed it to transmit a comprehensive package of data back to my home planet for study by the Vulcan Science Academy."

"If only everybody who's sending ships and probes to study us were as nice about it as the Vulcans have been," Wainwright said. Since its inception in the fall of 1947, Majestic 12—with the occasional assistance of Project Blue Book and its predecessors—had encountered no less than a dozen such vessels or unmanned craft, their construction and materials suggesting only a few of them had the same points of origin. A great deal of curiosity seemed to be aimed from the cosmos toward Earth, but only the Vulcans, in the form of Mestral, had been up front about their motives.

"Was it Vulcans who came looking for it?" Carlson asked between puffs of his dwindling cigarette.

"No," Wainwright said, before Mestral could respond, and held up the folder he had been safeguarding. "It definitely wasn't Vulcans." As his three companions moved closer, he opened the folder and arranged on the table six color photographs, each of them taken as though the person holding the camera had been perched somewhere high above a floor, aiming downward at an angle. The first image depicted what Wainwright now knew was the Vulcan probe, in its former resting place inside Warehouse 13B, with an unidentified man in Air Force fatigues standing before it. Another picture showed two Air Force officers wearing standard duty uniforms, both brandishing .45 caliber pistols, and a third photo showed the two running in different directions. The next set of three pictures showed the male officer fighting with another woman, this one also dressed in green fatigues, with the woman kicking the man in the chest, and the man suddenly gone, replaced by a dark figure. This was the picture Wainwright wanted everyone to see. "Does this guy look familiar?" he asked, tapping the dark figure shown in the photo.

"A Certoss," Mestral said.

"Give the man from outer space a prize," Wainwright replied. "Looks like our friends are back." Moving aside that picture, Wainwright slid back the one with the other, unidentified woman. "Whoever she is, she was fighting the Certoss, which likely means she's not one of them. If that's the case, then who the *hell* is she?"

Carlson, leaning over Marshall's shoulder, shook his head as he reached past her to stub out his cigarette in a nearby ashtray. "She's not part of the project. I don't recognize her."

"Could she be part of another group?" Marshall asked. "Separate from ours?"

"No," Carlson answered. "There are no separate groups outside the ones we've established. You may not be familiar with everyone connected to the project, Allison, but I certainly am."

Wainwright moved the photograph closer to him. "So, who's she working for?" He tapped the woman's image. "She's going toe to toe with this Certoss. Does that mean she's not really human, either?"

"A plausible hypothesis," Mestral said, "but it is impossible to arrive at such a conclusion with the available evidence."

"Where did these pictures come from, anyway?" Marshall asked.

Sighing, Wainwright began gathering the photos. "Here's

the part that's going to stick in your craws." From the folder, he produced a slip of paper containing a short, handwritten note. Holding it up with a bit of dramatic flair, he read aloud, "Mister Wainwright: I think I can help you, if you'll let me. Name the time and place." He looked up from the paper and frowned. "And it's signed Cal Sutherland."

"Sutherland?" Marshall repeated, her expression one of shock. "That tabloid reporter? Are you kidding?"

Wainwright nodded. "One and the same." For Carlson's benefit, he added, "You remember this guy, right? Writes for that UFO magazine we talked about a few years ago. He's got fans all over the country, and a lot of his stuff is pretty good. He manages to get interviews out of people even after we've visited them and asked them to keep things quiet, and some of the photos he runs are as good as if not better than ones we've gotten ourselves."

"We think he has somebody inside the project," Marshall said, "feeding him information. We've tried to smoke out his contacts, but we've never had any luck. Whoever's talking to him is pretty good at covering their tracks."

Carlson smiled. "I should think so. It's me."

The simple, blunt statement took a few extra seconds to register, but when it did, Wainwright found himself stumbling over whatever he was about to say, which now was forgotten. "What?" he managed to stammer out. "*You're* his inside man?"

Marshall leaned forward in her chair, her face a mask of disbelief. "Holy hell."

"Intriguing," Mestral offered.

Carlson's smile widened. "I have to say, giving him such salacious information has improved his magazine by leaps and bounds over the years."

Wainwright closed his eyes and shook his head, as though the action might force away what had to be a delusion he was suffering. When he opened his eyes and Carlson still stood before him, he scowled. "Why in God's name would you . . . ?"

"Because even though he's a civilian," Carlson said, "Sutherland's a natural for this kind of work. Do you know how many leads you've followed that resulted from something he stumbled across? You didn't know that, of course, because that information was withheld from you, but I've had my eye on him for several years now."

"We know!" Marshall said. "You sent us out to California to throw him off our scent, remember? To see if he had anything that might be damaging."

"I had to make it look like we were trying to deal with him the same way we deal with anyone who gets too close to our activities," Carlson replied. "If I treated him any differently, other MJ-12 committee members would've gotten suspicious."

"He almost shot me!" Wainwright snapped.

Carlson held out his hands. "All right, I'll admit *that* part was unexpected. Look, Sutherland can go places we can't go and do things we can't do without getting all tangled up in yet another knot of red tape. Blue Book doesn't have the backing in Congress it once did. They want to shut the whole thing down. The project's public face is a laughingstock. Unless that turns around, we'll have to let it fade away and continue our work in secret, and that will be harder to do if we don't have a legitimate investigation effort that people can see."

"It'd be nice to get a little support from the brass," Wainwright said, "instead of playing this game where we look like idiots." The initial efforts by Project Blue Book's previous director, Major Friend, to revitalize its serious investigative activities had enjoyed some success, but he had been hampered by a lack of funding and support. Meanwhile, Majestic 12 and its ancillary units continued their work without interruption, often taking from Blue Book the responsibility for checking out reports of sightings and other odd activities around the country where there was a high probability of making a legitimate discovery and recovery. Several of the officers and other support personnel originally assigned to Blue Book, Wainwright and Marshall in particular, also had been absorbed into the Majestic 12 hierarchy. On paper, Blue Book numbered fewer than a dozen personnel, and its mandate was to debunk as many sightings as possible. This tended to leave Friend and the project with little more than witnesses and reports that were refuted with little difficulty, and in turn this had brought about a growing cynicism that most if not all UFO sightings were hoaxes.

Having grown disgusted with the entire affair, Friend had requested reassignment and was replaced the previous month by a new officer, Major Hector Quintanilla. By all accounts, Blue Book's new director seemed content not to disrupt the project's current status quo, a situation that chafed Wainwright. In his eyes, it was a mistake to discount Blue Book's usefulness. Political backing was waning, and with that went any sort of true commitment to funding or resources. Beyond the people in this room, Wainwright could count the number of supporters for the entire effort on his hands, with fingers to spare.

Marshall asked, "We're just supposed to let this guy do his thing? You're going to keep feeding him intel?"

"For now, yes," Carlson replied, pulling another cigarette from the pack in his pocket and lighting it. "He may prove useful, one day. We certainly haven't been able to find the Certoss agents. Given what's at stake, we need all the help we can get."

Mestral added, "There is logic to the professor's actions. Cultivating an asset of Sutherland's apparent talent could prove beneficial."

Nodding, Wainwright was forced to offer grudging agreement. Despite a hunt that had lasted more than five years, they still were no closer to finding and apprehending the Certoss aliens, let alone preventing them from carrying out their plan to destroy Earth at some future point. There was no way to know how they might accomplish such a goal, but both Mestral and Carlson seemed convinced that it would entail the United States and Russia somehow being duped into another war—a conflict that almost certainly would involve nuclear weapons. Was that possible? Wainwright's mind boggled at the horrific possibilities. Were the Certoss capable of pulling off such a spectacular, disastrous ploy?

Not a theory I want to see tested.

TWENTY-TWO

U.S.S. Enterprise
Earth Year 2268

"Colonel Abrenn, surely there must be some way to resolve this situation peacefully to everyone's satisfaction."

Sitting in the command chair, Kirk stared at the image of the Tandaran ship commander on the *Enterprise* bridge's main viewscreen, noting the colonel's tight-lipped expression. That same expression was mirrored on the faces of those subordinates who happened to be captured on-screen.

Fun at parties, I'm guessing.

"*Captain Kirk,*" Abrenn said, his voice low and controlled, "*we now are close enough for our scanners to register the presence of the Certoss vessel in your docking bay. We also detect ten Certoss life-forms aboard your ship. The class of craft you have taken into your custody supports a maximum of nine persons, so I must now ask you to explain this mysterious tenth individual.*"

At the science station, Spock turned his chair in Kirk's direction. "Interesting, that they are so familiar with the operational parameters of Certoss vessels."

"*It's not a matter of interest, Captain,*" Abrenn countered. "*It is the duty of the Tandaran Defense Directorate to be versed in the capabilities of all potential enemies.*"

Kirk rose from his chair, moving to stand before the helm

and navigation console. "Colonel, we've been over this. The Certoss pose no threat to Tandar Prime, and you and I both know why that's the case. Minister Ocherab and her crew haven't shown the slightest indication that they're anything but what they say they are: a peaceful people." He strode closer to the screen, his gaze hardening as he focused on Abrenn. "In another *time,* that might not have been true, but rest assured you have nothing to fear in the *here and now.*"

Abrenn scowled, his eyes locking on Kirk as though trying to bore through him. "*It seems you do possess some understanding of our concerns. Then perhaps you can explain to me why one of the Certoss exhibits a temporal phase variation that suggests she has traveled here from another time period. A similar disparity appears to exist in two other life-forms aboard your ship, Captain: a human and a Vulcan. I find that interesting, to say the least.*"

"I have no idea what you're talking about, Colonel," Kirk said, though he cast a glance in Spock's direction only to see that his first officer already had returned to his console, no doubt performing some kind of information retrieval from the ship's computer memory banks. "Perhaps you could explain what you mean?"

Abrenn said nothing for several seconds, to the point that the silence was becoming awkward, before replying, "*I have neither the time nor the inclination to play such games, Captain. Suffice it to say that we are well aware you are harboring three time travelers. Surrender them, and the crew of the Certoss vessel.*"

"I'm afraid I can't do that," Kirk replied. "At least, not until I have some idea of your intentions toward them. Besides, as I've already explained to you, you're in Federation space, so you're not really in a position to make any demands."

For the first time, actual anger laced Abrenn's words. "*Please do not test my patience, Captain. I seek merely to protect the security of my people.*"

"And it's my duty to protect innocents from oppression or harassment," Kirk responded. "Your actions and intentions toward the Certoss appear hostile with no justification. Unless you stand down, I won't have much choice as to how to proceed."

Abrenn's expression went flat, his eyes never wavering. "*Neither will I, Captain.*" His image vanished from the screen, replaced by a field of stars. No sooner was the communications link severed than red alert klaxons began wailing across the bridge.

"The Tandaran vessel is accelerating," Spock called out from where he bent over the science station's hooded sensor viewer, "and they appear to be routing power from nonessential systems to propulsion as well as their weapons and shields. At their new rate of speed, they will overtake us in three minutes, twelve seconds."

Moving toward his chair, Kirk ordered, "Turn off that alarm. Take us to Warp 8, Mister Sulu. Maintain course, but stand by for evasive maneuvers." He had not wanted to get into an exchange of fire with the Tandaran ship, but Abrenn was removing options in rapid fashion. Reaching his chair, Kirk tapped the control on its arm to open an intraship communications frequency. "Bridge to engineering. Scotty, it's looking like I'm going to need more speed."

"*Aye, sir,*" replied the voice of the chief engineer. "*We'll do our best.*"

"It will not be sufficient, Captain," Spock said, and Kirk turned to see his first officer standing at his station, facing him while resting one hand on his sensor viewer. "At its current speed, the Tandaran vessel will almost certainly overtake us."

Kirk sighed. "There doesn't seem to be any getting around it, is there? What can you tell me about their weapons?"

"Very little," the Vulcan replied. "Those areas of the vessel are shielded against sensors, though the readings I can obtain suggest armaments on par with our own. Similar shielding surrounds what I believe to be areas devoted to the ship's engineering and computer systems. Our scans are not able to penetrate those sections."

The sound of the turbolift doors opening made Kirk turn to see Roberta Lincoln emerging from the car. Her expression was one of concern as she glanced toward the viewscreen before directing her attention to him.

"I apologize for intruding, Captain," she said, "but I was monitoring your communications with Abrenn. Don't believe for a second that he's bluffing. He'll attack to get what he wants."

Gesturing toward the viewscreen, Kirk asked, "He said he detected different 'temporal phase variations.' What does that mean?"

"When someone travels through time, they're out of place with respect to the rest of the timeline, and that manifests itself in a measurable phase fluctuation. You have to know what you're looking for, and even then you can't detect it without the right equipment." Lincoln shook her head. "I'm sorry I don't have any more information. What I just told you was thanks to a crash course I gave myself before coming here from 1969." She sighed. "Have I mentioned how much I hate time travel?"

Spock said, "I am unfamiliar with the phenomenon you describe, and neither did I find any mention of it or anything similar in the memory banks."

"You wouldn't," Lincoln said. "At least, not yet. For one thing, your current experience with time travel is pretty limited. Only a handful of races know what to look for. Unfortunately for you, the Tandarans are one of them."

Kirk said, "We'll have to worry about that later. Do you know anything about their weapons capabilities?"

"Not really. It wasn't something I read up on before coming here." Lincoln appeared embarrassed at the perceived lapse. "I'm sorry, Captain."

The alert indicator positioned along the forward edge of the helm and navigation console began flashing harsh crimson, emitting its own distinctive tone. In response to the new signal, both Sulu and Chekov leaned over their respective consoles before turning to look over their shoulders toward Kirk.

"Sir, the Tandaran vessel is trying to maneuver in behind us. Their speed is still faster than ours."

Chekov added, "They're also trying to lock onto us with their forward batteries."

"Increase speed to maximum. Stand by aft weapons." Glancing over his shoulder toward Uhura, Kirk said, "Notify all hands to brace for incoming enemy fire."

Already turning to that task, Uhura replied, "Aye, sir."

"Let's see them," Kirk said. "Reverse angle on main viewer."

The image on the viewscreen shifted to show the Tandaran vessel, its dark, low profile little more than an opaque spot blotting out stars behind it. To Kirk, the ship's distinct lack of exterior illumination or anything else that might draw the naked eye was, in a word, ominous.

"That is one ugly ship," Lincoln said from where she still stood at the railing in front of the engineering station at the rear of the bridge.

"They've locked weapons on us, sir," Chekov reported, and Kirk heard the tension in the ensign's voice.

"Target their weapons and stand by to fire," he said, his gaze fixed on the approaching Tandaran vessel's black silhouette. No sooner did the words leave his mouth than two globes of harsh green energy spat forth from the vessel's bow, roiling and pulsing as they leaped from the ship's weapons port. Seconds later a yellow-orange maelstrom flashed across the viewscreen as the projectiles—whatever they were—slammed into the starship's aft deflector shields. Having prepared himself for the impact, Kirk was surprised when the ship did not tremble around him, although the overhead lighting as well as the bridge's various display screens and consoles all flickered in haphazard fashion.

"Captain!" Chekov called out. "Our shields! They're down twenty-eight percent!"

"Return fire!" Kirk ordered, and Sulu stabbed at his console's firing controls. On the viewscreen, a single blue-white phaser beam lanced across space to strike the Tandaran vessel's forward shields.

Sulu now was peering into his console's tactical scanner. "No real damage to their shields, Captain. Whatever they lost, it's been replaced or augmented with power from somewhere else."

"Fire again," Kirk said, watching the follow-up salvo hit the enemy ship's shields.

Sulu shook his head. "No effect." Two more spheres of green energy launched from the Tandaran ship to hammer at the *Enterprise* shields, again with no discernible signs of impact despite the light show on the screen.

"Our shields have now dropped sixty-four percent," Chekov offered.

"What the hell are they shooting at us?" Kirk asked, releasing his grip on the arm of his chair and moving to the curved rail separating him from Spock.

"Not a conventional particle beam weapon or physical torpedo," Spock replied. "Sensors indicate a form of high-energy plasma similar to what we've seen utilized by Romulan vessels. Though they appear to be somewhat less powerful, it seems their purpose is not to inflict damage on the ship itself, but instead to dampen or disrupt our deflector shield generators."

"Another shot or two like that," Lincoln said, "and we'll be sitting ducks."

Turning from the rail, Kirk snapped, "Return fire." He considered and discarded various tactical scenarios in the short interval it took for Sulu to let loose another phaser barrage on the Tandaran ship, before arriving at one unconventional course of action. "Drop us out of warp, now," he said, moving back to his chair.

Sulu looked up from the helm. "Sir?"

"All the way to sub light. *Do it!*"

Though the inertial dampers compensated for the worst effects of the ship's abrupt shift from subspace, Kirk still felt an unmistakable pull forward as a result of the transition from warp speed. The hull itself seemed to protest the rude action, and he imagined he could hear Montgomery Scott shouting from the bowels of the ship, lamenting the abuse being inflicted upon his beloved engines.

Sorry, Scotty.

"The Tandaran vessel has overshot us," said Spock, his attention still on his instruments. "They are altering their course to resume their pursuit."

"Come about," Kirk said, eyeing the astrogator situated

at the base of the console between Sulu and Chekov. "Course two nine nine mark zero five." He dropped his fist down on his chair's intercom switch. "Engineering. Scotty, I need everything you can give me if this is going to work."

"*Aye, sir. We're doing what we can down here,*" replied the chief engineer, "*but it'd be easier if you weren't snapping us around like a bloody rubber band!*"

Kirk canceled the connection, ignoring Scott's objection. Instead, he asked, "Shield status?"

"Aft shields are back up to forty-nine percent, sir," Chekov responded. "They're firming up, but slowly."

"Route remaining power to forward shields." Feeling someone's eyes on him, Kirk turned in his chair to see Roberta Lincoln studying him, her features a mask of confusion. "Miss Lincoln?"'

The younger woman frowned. "I don't understand. You're going after them?"

"I'm tired of being shot at."

"Closing on them, sir," Sulu reported. "They're coming at us."

Studying the data being fed to his sensor viewer, Spock said, "I'm detecting a noticeable lack of power to nontactical systems. It would appear they're channeling all available energy to their propulsion and weapons."

"Fire all weapons," Kirk ordered, "and keep after them."

Sulu unleashed the full fury of the *Enterprise*'s arsenal and the viewscreen was filed with phaser beams and a barrage of photon torpedoes. The salvo struck the Tandaran ship's forward shields, all but concealing the other vessel beneath a frenzy of hellish energy.

"Their forward shields have overloaded," Spock called out.

"Again, Sulu," Kirk snapped. "Target their weapons ports."

At the instant he gave the command, he saw a new

barrage of weapons fire leave the Tandaran ship. Sulu had just dispatched his next round of return fire when he jerked his head from his tactical scanner and shouted a warning. Not one but two pairs of surging jade energy advanced across the void between the two ships, untouched by any of the *Enterprise*'s own weapons.

"Brace for impact!" Kirk shouted, sensing that this attack would be worse than its predecessors. He had just enough time to grasp the arms of his chair before the first two energy bolts struck the shields, and alert indicators flashed across the bridge as a hell storm erupted on the main viewscreen.

"Our shields are failing!" was all Chekov could yell before the second round lunged forward, and this time the entire ship shuddered under the force of the assault. The primary lighting flickered and some of the emitters failed, casting portions of the bridge into shadow.

Kirk saw something blue flash in the corner of his eye, where Roberta Lincoln had been standing mere moments earlier, but when he turned in that direction all he saw were the turbolift doors closing. Lincoln was gone.

What the hell?

"Fire at will!" Kirk ordered, forgetting Lincoln. "Full spread!"

When the barrage of fire crossed space this time, there were no deflector shields to soften the blow, and the twin phaser beams and quartet of torpedoes slammed into the Tandaran ship's forward hull. There was no mistaking the sight of hull plates buckling and atmosphere escaping from new gaps in the ship's outer skin. The entire vessel seemed to lurch, though it did not break off its attack to take evasive maneuvers.

Tough little bastard.

"Captain," Spock said, turning from his station. "Their main propulsion unit appears on the verge of failure, but I am picking up a new power reading."

Kirk glanced to the first officer. "Another weapon?"

"Unknown." Spock's reply was punctuated by the sound of a new Red Alert siren bellowing across the bridge, loud enough to make Kirk wince but not so loud that it drowned out the frantic voice of the *Enterprise*'s chief of security, Lieutenant Commander Barry Giotto.

"*Intruder alert! Intruder alert! Enemy boarding party on the hangar deck!*"

TWENTY-THREE

McKinley Rocket Base, Cocoa Beach, Florida
March 16, 1966

Though he was not human, Adlar long ago had learned to decipher and understand the vast array of human emotional states. The range of responses he now witnessed was easy to identify. Tension and fear was evident on the faces of everyone in the Mission Control center. From where he stood at the bay windows of the small, detached room overlooking the center's main operations floor, Adlar was able to observe the reactions of technicians and engineers as the current situation continued to unfold. They hunched over consoles or talked on phones or into headsets or scurried about, focused on whatever task commanded their attention. Noting his own reflection in the window's glass, itself that of "Allen Shull," the human male he had crafted as the disguise generated by his mobile camouflage emitter, Adlar made sure that his expression was similar to those of his colleagues. Even after the years he had spent among humans, some responses still did not come to him without conscious effort.

"*The spacecraft-Agena combination took off,*" said a voice filtered through the Mission Control intercom system. The speaker's voice was tiny and hollow, and laced with the hiss and crackle of radio static. That was not surprising, given that the person talking was at this moment one of two men ensconced within the tiny, fragile spacecraft orbiting hundreds of miles above the Earth. "*Yaw and roll, and we had ACS off and affirmative seven hours.*"

Hundreds of people at this moment were fixated on the spacecraft, which along with its associated mission carried the official designation of "Gemini 8." The mission under way was the sixth manned flight of the NASA's Project Gemini program, a series of missions designed to develop, refine, and test equipment and techniques that would—if all proceeded according to plan—result in a manned landing on the surface of the moon within the next three years.

At present, that goal was not on anyone's minds. Instead, everyone's thoughts were consumed by the emergency unfolding in the void above the Earth.

Another voice replied, "*Okay, I copy. Can you . . . do you have visual sighting of the Agena right now?*"

"*No,*" replied a third speaker, whom Adlar recognized as the spacecraft's second astronaut. "*We haven't seen the Agena since we undocked a little while ago.*"

This was not distressing to Adlar. Turning from the window, he returned to his own workstation, a conglomeration of status indicators and dials, compact digital readouts, and rows of switches surrounding a pair of television screens as well as a telephone, all of it set into a bulky, metal frame. It was one of a half dozen positioned around the room, each overseen by a different engineer. One of the console's status indicators told him that telemetry still was being transmitted from the Agena target vehicle, including the signal from a transponder installed aboard the unmanned test craft, which relayed its information on a frequency undetectable except by equipment developed by the Department of Defense just for this purpose. Packed almost to overflowing with a variety of equipment and recording devices, the Agena was designed to provide astronauts with an interactive test subject for practicing orbital rendezvous and docking maneuvers as well as other tasks while connected to the unmanned, remotely guided craft. The test vehicle, along with its top-secret DoD payload known only to a privileged cadre of military and civilian personnel, had been sent into orbit earlier in the day and prior to the launching of the Titan II rocket carrying the Gemini 8 spacecraft and its two-man crew, astronauts Neil Armstrong and David Scott.

"Shull, what's the status of the target vehicle?"

Adlar looked up at the sound of the gruff, apprehensive voice to see the older human male staring at him from across the room. Colonel Samuel Thorpe, dressed in an Air Force blue duty uniform, was the officer overseeing the Agena vehicle's launch and operations. He was a dour-looking man, with narrow eyes beneath a heavy brow and a long, thin nose that gave his features a predatory air. His head was devoid of hair, which only served to accent his intimidating stature. In Adlar's experience, Thorpe was a cold, stern officer, possessing no discernible sense of humor. He did not engage in any form of casual conversation, so his interactions with civilian engineers or other military members tended to be blunt and succinct.

"It's likely tumbling," Adlar said, remaining seated at his console. "Since it's been determined that the problem is with the Gemini capsule, we should be able to bring the Agena back under control with its own thrusters."

"Yeah," said another engineer, a younger man named James Cushman. "Thank God Scott was able to transfer control of it back to us before they separated. They're already working up a procedure to get it back under control." Though his hair was combed back from his face, a lock had fallen down across Cushman's forehead and his left eye, and he reached up to swipe it up and out of his way. "We got lucky on that."

"So, what happened?" Thorpe asked, his expression wavering not the slightest bit as he resumed his slow, measured pacing around the room.

Cushman replied, "About forty-five minutes after the capsule linked up with the Agena, Scott reported that they were tumbling end over end and had undocked. At first they thought the Agena was responsible, but it's looking more like one of the capsule's maneuvering thrusters was stuck open somehow. They'll probably run checks to verify that once things settle down up there."

Thorpe frowned. "And we're sure there's nothing wrong with the Agena's thrusters?"

"So far, everything looks nominal," Adlar said. The entire sequence of events had lasted less than thirty minutes, with the Gemini 8 astronauts reporting their violent banking and tumbling after disconnecting their spacecraft from the target vehicle. It then had taken Armstrong several minutes to regain control of the wayward ship, using the capsule's reentry control system thrusters to force the spacecraft out of its uncontrolled rolling. During those frantic few moments, they had been forced to concentrate on their own situation, disregarding the Agena vehicle. Throughout that brief period, Adlar had maintained a close eye on the telemetry being transmitted from the unmanned ship.

"What about our package?" Thorpe asked. "Any sign of damage or other problems after all this?"

Adlar shook his head. "Everything's showing normal. Targeting and maneuvering systems are all active and transmitting data."

"Good," Thorpe said, offering an approving nod. "As soon as they regain control, I want a full rundown of everything. Thanks to those astronauts and their quick thinking, we might still be able to meet our mission objectives. Get me that status report on all systems as soon as possible."

As he watched the colonel depart the room, Adlar said, more to himself than anyone else, "He certainly is difficult to please."

"Brother, you don't know the half of it." Cushman shook his head, releasing a sigh. "I'll be happy when this is over, so I can move on to something else. This sort of thing isn't why I joined this company, anyway. I want to be on one of the teams designing stuff we're going to be sending to the moon, not babysitting the military's new pet project."

Intrigued by his colleague's rebellious comments, which the other man had not expressed before today, Adlar asked, "You don't believe what we're doing is important?"

Cushman snorted. "Figuring out how to put a bunch of nukes in orbit just so they can rain down on us is just about the last thing this world needs right now, Allen."

The United States was moving with haste in this regard, attempting to keep pace with the Soviet Union as both countries raced to be the first to place a working nuclear weapons platform into orbit. According to Gejalik, Russia was preparing to launch into orbit its own version of such a package. She had seen to it that information on the American initiative found its way into the hands of Russian spies, who in turn saw to it that the data was delivered to the proper authorities and put to use by their own cadre of scientists and engineers. While Jaecz continued in his role as a technician working for NASA in Houston, Gejalik for the past year had been working undercover in Star City, Russia, also masquerading as a civilian engineer. The assignment, though necessary to monitor Soviet progress, also precluded any form of frequent communication given the severe security restrictions blanketing the entire city. Gejalik's last contact with Adlar had been via a brief article inserted into a recent edition of the Communist-controlled Russian newspaper *Pravda*, copies of which were translated and distributed among the American intelligence community, with information relevant to Soviet aerospace efforts also provided to NASA for its review. It was an imperfect line of communication, and only worked one-way, but it was enough to let Adlar know that his companion was alive and well, and working at the center of the Russian space and military weapons programs.

"Allen?"

Blinking, Adlar realized he had allowed his thoughts to consume him to the point that he had all but ignored his surroundings. He turned in his seat to see Cushman staring at him, concern evident in his features. How long had the human been trying to gain his attention? Had Adlar said or done something that might raise suspicion or cast doubt on his identity?

"Yes?" He made a show of clearing his throat and shifting in his seat. "I'm sorry. I guess I'm just tired."

Cushman nodded. "I know. Long day, right?" He pointed at his workstation. "I'm just about ready to upload the diagnostic program to the targeting system. You want to see what it has to say?"

"Let's take a look," Adlar replied, rising from his chair and moving to join his colleague. "Hopefully, there's no damage."

"Keep your fingers crossed," Cushman said, punctuating his comment with a whistle. "Otherwise, it'll be at least three months before we get another shot, and that's assuming they don't send everything back to the drawing board to figure out what went wrong up there today."

It was a point of valid concern, Adlar conceded. The next American manned spaceflight, Gemini 9, was at present scheduled to launch in two months. That now hinged on whatever determinations were made after a thorough investigation of the Gemini 8 capsule following its recovery later today. No doubt American government and military leaders—well aware that their Soviet counterparts also were working at a feverish pace—would be pushing for resolution of the issues plaguing NASA, all while urging for the finalization of the weapons technology. Even with the current issues, Adlar predicted that at the present rate of progress by both powers, the successful deployment of a fully armed and operational platform would occur within the coming year.

Who would be the first to achieve this feat? For the moment, that remained a mystery. Adlar had no preference as to the victor of this particular competition. After all, one advantage held by weapons of mass destruction was that they could be used to eradicate their creators and their targets with the same brutal efficiency.

Soon, he reminded himself. Soon.

TWENTY-FOUR

Wright-Patterson Air Force Base, Dayton, Ohio
July 17, 1967

"What do you mean, 'it's gone'? Where the hell did it go?"

James Wainwright looked up from yet another in the unending series of reports that had come to dominate his very existence in recent years, eyeing Colonel Stephen Olson with what he hoped was not an expression of disdain. Conversations like this one were becoming more common, it seemed, and Wainwright's tolerance for them decreased with each new occurrence. Standing before him with his customary expression of irritation, the colonel already was getting on his nerves despite being here less than two minutes.

"When I say 'it's gone,' Colonel, I mean it's no longer there. It may have been there at one time, but it wasn't by the time we got there. The eleven witnesses we interviewed all gave us the same story. They thought they saw a shooting star crashing in the forest in the High Sierras on the night of June eleventh. However, none of them described anything like a fire trail you might see when we're talking about a meteorite or other natural object coming down through the atmosphere, or even one of our own space capsules on re-entry."

From where she sat behind her own desk, Allison Marshall added, "Five witnesses also said they thought the object was moving in a straight line across the sky before it fell to the ground. That's definitely inconsistent with any meteorite. All eleven said they saw it crash in the mountains, but their reports varied as to probable location, which is why it took us so long to pinpoint the crash site."

"But there was a crash site," Olson said. It was not a question. "You found where it came down, but it was gone when you got there."

Wainwright replied, "We found it, all right. Definite signs of something coming down, but no evidence of a meteorite, at least according to the forensics team we sent to sweep the area. They did find a few small metallic fragments. We're having them analyzed now, but so far everything points to an aircraft or spacecraft of some kind." Pursing his lips, he added, "Whatever it was, it was moved. Whether by whoever or whatever was flying it, or somebody else getting the jump on us, we don't know."

"Maybe if your teams had moved more quickly," Olson offered.

"It took our people four days on foot to find the site," Marshall replied. "And that was after we received the first reports of the sighting, which came almost a full week after it supposedly happened."

Olson frowned. "Why did it take you so long to get up there?"

This man is a moron. As one of the senior case officers working within the Majestic 12 organization, Colonel Stephen Olson had become something of a de facto liaison between that group and Project Blue Book. His position saw to it that he exerted authority over those officers still conducting UFO sighting investigations, including the project's current director, Major Hector Quintanilla. Wainwright and Marshall, being civilian agents working within the MJ-12 envelope, were not answerable to Olson, a situation the colonel found frustrating and one in which Wainwright took no end of delight. The only problem was that his duties still required him to speak with the son of a bitch.

Forcing himself not to give voice to such thoughts, Wainwright cleared his throat. "Have you ever been to the High Sierras, Colonel? It's not like taking a stroll around the base golf course, after all. It's pretty rugged country. Cars can't get up there. Come to think of it, golf carts can't get up there, either." Though he did not smile, Wainwright still was able to take some pleasure in watching Olson's jaw clench.

"Fine," the colonel said, his voice tight. "Then where is the craft?"

Wainwright shrugged. "It didn't leave a forwarding address."

"I don't appreciate your attitude, *Mister* Wainwright," Olson snapped. Placing his hands on the front of Wainwright's desk, he leaned forward, closing the distance between the two men. It was an intimidation tactic that likely worked for most of the people with whom the colonel interacted, but all it did was annoy Wainwright, who made a point to stand up in such a way that it forced Olson to pull back and straighten his posture.

"I get that a lot," Wainwright said, affecting a relaxed stance even though his gaze never left Olson's. "And yet, they keep me around here for some reason."

The colonel sneered. "I might be able to do something about that."

"If you could, you'd have done it by now," Wainwright countered, "so let's quit pretending you've got power you don't have, all right?" That was enough to make the colonel bristle, but Wainwright pretended not to notice. "As for where the craft is, to be honest, Colonel, I was hoping you could tell us. After all, this smells a lot like the kind of thing you'd have your hands in."

Olson's vexed reaction appeared genuine, and Wainwright saw real anger flash in the other man's eyes. "Are you suggesting a cover-up?"

"Suggesting?" Wainwright shook his head. "No, that's a waste of time. You and I both know that sort of thing's happened before, with Magestic leaving Blue Book holding the bag and looking like idiots. There've been at least, what, three incidents where you swept in and took the legs out of a Blue Book investigation, making off with the evidence they'd found and forcing the case officers to dismiss the initial sighting or other report? I know Carlson would never screw us like this, but you? Yeah, I can see that, easy."

With a grunt suggesting he was growing irate at the discussion's turn, Olson glanced over his shoulder at Marshall before returning his gaze to Wainwright. "Perhaps you and I might continue this conversation in private."

"Miss Marshall has full clearance," Wainwright countered. "So whatever you're going to say, you might as well say it now."

As though sensing an opening to get in his own jab, Olson turned to Wainwright. "Yes, I've heard those . . ." He stopped when Wainwright held up a hand.

"Whatever you're thinking might be a smart thing to say next? Rethink it, Colonel." He let a hint of menace lace the words. "Those birds on your shoulders or the fact that I'm old enough to be your father won't stop me from knocking you on your ass, right here and right now." Though he and Marshall had endured gossip over the years regarding their personal relationship, this was the first time anyone had seen fit to confront them about it in such a direct manner.

"I'd have you arrested," Olson snapped.

Wainwright nodded. "Sure. After they let you out of the hospital."

"Gentlemen," Marshall said, her exasperated tone giving them pause. "With all due respect, I'd like to go home at a decent hour tonight, so can we please get on with this?" She crossed her arms, offering an expression conveying restrained annoyance. "You can fight over my honor after I've gone."

Drawing a breath as though to calm himself, Olson placed his hands in his trouser pockets. "Fine. What else can you tell me about the crash site?"

"The damaged area wasn't that large," Wainwright replied. "No felled trees, no signs of fire, though there was some disrupted dirt and rock from where it touched down. That suggests a controlled landing, to some degree. We also don't think the object was very big, probably the same size as a single-seat fighter jet, more or less."

Olson said, "We can assume it wasn't a Russian rocket or missile, and China's only just sticking their toe into the water so far as that's concerned." A month prior, China had detonated its first hydrogen bomb, and now joined the U.S., Russia, and Great Britain in the fraternity of countries possessing the ability to construct nuclear weapons.

Another day, another headache.

"If it was some kind of craft," Marshall said, "and it didn't just fly back out of there under its own power, then we're thinking something that small could be disassembled and removed from the crash site. There've been no further reports of unidentified craft in that area—or meteor activity, for that matter—since the initial sighting. Of course, that sort of thing suggests a group like us."

"Or just someone with time and resources," Olson countered, "which is alarming on a number of levels."

Wainwright said, "We've thought about ways to look into that. For example, if it's a private group, then maybe one of the UFO organizations or clubs out there might come across some information. We're going to be paying more attention to things like the newsletters and magazines these groups publish, checking for hints of someone bragging about a great find in the California mountains, that sort of thing." Indeed, Wainwright already had dispatched Mestral to Los Angeles to speak with Cal Sutherland, who still was publishing his *Watch the Skies* magazine. If anyone was going to come across juicy information about somebody claiming ownership of a flying saucer, it would be Sutherland. Olson, of course, did not know about Sutherland, thanks to the efforts of Professor Jeffrey Carlson, who had cultivated the tabloid journalist as a resource.

What he doesn't know won't hurt us.

Appearing to mull over this notion for a moment, Olson nodded. "It can't hurt, but we definitely need to explore other avenues. This is the kind of thing that poses a threat to our operational security and as a consequence, there are going to be some changes with respect to other activities."

Uh-oh, Wainwright thought. *Here it comes.*

"What do you mean?" Marshall asked.

Olson removed his hands from his pockets. "For one thing, it's been decided that we've collected more than enough credible evidence proving aliens have been here and they're curious about us. We need to guard that information, to say nothing about the other . . . artifacts . . . we've obtained, not just from outsiders but even those in our own government." He turned so that he could look at Wainwright. "You as much as anyone knows we've been doing this long enough that we have military and civilian leaders overseeing our work who've never actually *seen* what we've done. Most of those people either don't believe, or else they're living in denial."

Nodding, Wainwright sighed as he realized this was one of the few things on which he and Olson agreed. "You can say that again." The simple truth about Blue Book, and even more so with Majestic 12, was that the compartmentalization of the information gathered by both groups over the past twenty years had become so labyrinthine that only a select few individuals even had knowledge, let alone access to everything.

"MJ-12's efforts going forward will be focused on better understanding the information we already have," Olson said, "and following leads that support our defense against specific threats for which we have solid evidence."

"What about us?" Wainwright asked, already knowing the answer.

"You'll keep to your current role, but the priority is finding connections to these threats," Olson said, lifting himself from Wainwright's desk. "Meanwhile, Blue Book will continue its downplaying and discrediting of other UFO sightings and witnesses as appropriate."

For the first time, Wainwright considered mentioning to Olson the Certoss aliens he and Marshall had been tracking with the clandestine aid of Mestral and with the support of Professor Carlson. It was a secret the four of them had kept to themselves for a decade, believing that the fewer people who knew of their effort, the better the chances of being able to hunt for the mysterious aliens from the future without attracting their attention. To that end, Mestral had been working on constructing what he called a "sensor device," which would allow him to scan for and locate indications of advanced or otherwise "non-terrestrial" activity—communications signals or other energy readings not achievable by current human technology, for example. The Vulcan had been experimenting with such devices for some time now, limited as he was to equipment and other materials available to him.

No, Wainwright decided. *Olson doesn't need to know. Not yet.*

"That sounds like a misuse of our resources," he said, eyeing the colonel. "We know the threats are real, so why can't we get the support we need?"

Olson sighed. "Look, I might not like you, Wainwright, but I can't argue that you and Marshall haven't produced results. Carlson and the rest of the MJ-12 committee know the real deal, but the truth is that right now the United States has bigger, more immediate problems. We're upping our commitment of resources to Vietnam, and that means more money needed to fund it. Now, if we could brief Congress on what we know, I'm guessing we could get a blank check, but until such time as the president gives us the green light, we make do with what we have."

"And what if the Ferengi or somebody else comes knocking?" Marshall asked. "What then?"

Turning to head for the door, Olson replied, "Then I imagine the meetings with Congress will go a hell of a lot quicker." He reached the door, but instead of leaving the room, he looked back at Wainwright and Marshall. "Unless, of course, you can find something concrete before that happens." Without waiting for a response, the colonel exited the room, the door closing behind him.

"Idiot," Marshall said, shaking her head.

"But he's not wrong," Wainwright said. "Until we can wave something irrefutable in front of Congress, we're never going to get full support."

"What more do they need?" Marshall asked, rising from her chair and moving around her desk. "Some Ferengi or Certoss to come down here and stick a probe up his butt? Maybe we could get Mestral to demonstrate that to Olson. You know, to help him dislodge his head."

Chuckling, Wainwright smiled. "You've been reading too many of Cal Sutherland's magazines." Some accounts of "abduction" carried with them varying degrees of legitimacy, such as the case involving a New Hampshire couple who claimed to have been studied by aliens aboard their ship in 1961. Their story even was turned into a book published just last year, and many government officials believed it was the book that had launched a spate of similar claims, with witnesses or "victims" being subjected to all manner of obscene medical examinations and other procedures after being taken aboard spaceships. Such accounts were an interesting contrast to the plethora of books Wainwright had read over the years from more "trustworthy" sources, such as Morris Jessup, an astronomer who had made something of a name for himself in the UFO enthusiast community after writing a handful of books detailing stories and theories regarding extraterrestrial activity. Though Jessup enjoyed no mainstream recognition for his efforts, his books all were required reading within the MJ-12 and Blue Book organizations, and Wainwright and Marshall even had followed up on accounts recorded in a few of the books.

There was a knock on the door, and they looked at each other in confusion for a moment before Wainwright called out, "Come in." When the door opened, it was to admit two men he did not recognize. Both wore dark, conservative suits, though the taller of the pair also wore a fedora pulled low over his eyes.

"Good evening, Mister Wainwright," his companion said, before turning to Marshall. "Miss Marshall. We apologize for calling on you unannounced, but we have some information we think you'll find important." He looked to be in his mid-thirties, with brown hair and bright hazel eyes, and carried himself with a self-confidence—perhaps even arrogance—that only natural leaders tended to exude.

"Who are you?" Wainwright asked, scowling. He felt his hand twitch, wanting to reach for the pistol in its holster beneath his left arm, but he forced himself to remain still. "How the hell did you even get in here?"

"That's not really important," he replied, "though to make it easy for all of us, you can call me Agent 937." He indicated his companion. "This is Agent 176. I hope you'll understand that we need to protect our identities, but it's the information we have for you that's of true importance. It's also very sensitive, which is why I need to insist that you not share it with anyone; not even your Vulcan friend, Mestral."

Despite himself, Wainwright could not help his mouth opening in shock at the unexpected demand. He exchanged confused glances with Marshall before asking, "How do you . . . ?"

The man held up his hand. "Hopefully, now, you understand that this isn't a joke. Our information pertains to the Certoss, and how we can help you find them." He paused, offering a small, humorless smile. "Interested?"

Okay, Wainwright conceded. *That's one way to get my attention.*

TWENTY-FIVE

U.S.S. Enterprise
Earth Year 2268

Phaser in hand and followed by a pair of security guards, Kirk lunged from the turbolift the instant the doors opened and sprinted down the narrow observation deck overlooking the starboard side of the *Enterprise*'s shuttlecraft hangar bay. Standing near one of the viewing ports was Lieutenant Commander Barry Giotto, along with two more guards. The security chief, also wielding a phaser, gestured with his weapon toward the window.

"Six of them, sir," he said by way of greeting. "We've sealed off the bay, and I've got teams at every exit. The only way they're getting out of there is the same way they got in."

Kirk nodded, getting his first look at the odd situation unfolding on the hangar deck. "Scotty's working on that." The chief engineer already had reestablished the ship's deflector shields. Though they were not yet at full strength, they still were more than the Tandaran ship could boast. For now, the *Enterprise* had the tactical advantage so far as ship-to-ship combat was concerned, though that was not the issue at the moment.

While Giotto dispatched the four security guards to join teams he had positioned at different exits, Kirk peered down through the viewing port at the *Balatir* sitting in the center of the bay. The Certoss vessel took up much more space than a shuttlecraft sitting in that same position. Two shuttles, the *Galileo* and the *Copernicus,* were positioned before the bay's rear bulkhead, and the enormous clamshell doors to Kirk's left of course were closed, providing the only barrier separating this part of the ship from the harsh, unforgiving vacuum of space. Six figures, all dressed in what Kirk figured to be some kind of tactical assault uniform consisting of torso armor with a molded neck and a helmet with a wide face shield, milled about the *Balatir*, each of them brandishing a formidable-looking rifle. None of the intruders was attempting to gain entry to the craft. "Nice work reacting to the threat, Commander."

"I tried communicating with them through the intercom, but they're not answering. Any idea what's going on?"

Shaking his head, Kirk said, "Obviously some kind of last-ditch play to grab the Certoss." The *Enterprise*'s final phaser and torpedo barrage had succeeded in incapacitating the Tandaran ship, forcing it to fall from warp speed but not before Colonel Abrenn had executed a daring, if inexplicable plan: deploying a boarding party. The move was as bold as it was unexpected, but Giotto and his team seemed to have reacted in fine fashion, and now that the Tandarans were here, Kirk could not see the upside to the strategy. "But why not simply beam them off the *Enterprise*?"

"I might have the answer to that," Giotto replied, examining his tricorder. "They must've figured they could snatch the Certoss and get away before we were able to react, but the Certoss vessel activated her own deflector shields. The boarding party can't get past them to board the ship, and now we've cut them off from beaming away."

"Are all the Certoss on their ship?" Kirk asked.

Giotto nodded. "They're even heavy a few bodies. Another Certoss, a Vulcan, and a human."

Kirk frowned. "You're sure?"

"Yes, sir. Checked it twice. Our friendly stowaways pulled a fast one on the Tandarans. Pretty smart thinking."

That explains where Miss Lincoln went. She must have used whatever technology and abilities she possessed to move from the bridge to the hangar deck during those final hellish moments of the skirmish with the Tandaran ship. It appeared she also had gathered Gejalik and Mestral, anticipating some kind of action either to beam them from the *Enterprise,* or a raid to capture them. Kirk was certain Lincoln had to be the one responsible for getting Minister Ocherab to raise her vessel's shields, thereby thwarting any attempt to have her crew spirited away by Tandaran transporters, forcing Colonel Abrenn into this far more rash course of action. *Well done, Miss Lincoln, but can we take advantage of it?*

His communicator beeped, interrupting his train of thought. Retrieving the unit from where it rested at the small of his back, he flipped it open. "Kirk here."

"*Spock here, Captain,*" his first officer replied over the secure link, for which Kirk had opted in order to avoid the Tandarans from eavesdropping in the event they were able to access the intraship communications system. "*The Tandaran vessel's main engines and most of its weapons remain offline, but they have managed to restore their deflector shields.*"

That was certain to complicate the current situation, Kirk decided. "With both ships' shields up, nobody's transporting anywhere. As for the boarding party, they're all wearing some kind of armor that looks like it might double as an environment suit. I'm going to guess that flooding the deck with anesthezine gas won't work."

"We could depressurize the bay," Giotto said. When Kirk eyed him with skepticism, the commander added, "Just a thought, sir."

Kirk asked, "Spock, is the Tandaran party in contact with its ship?"

"*Negative. We are presently jamming their communications.*"

"What about their ship? Any hints they may be gearing up for another fight?"

"*None that we can detect. They may be holding back from any further attacks now that they have people over here.*"

Giotto said, "I wouldn't count on that lasting, sir. They might decide the boarding party's expendable, particularly if they can't get through to them thanks to our jamming."

"Agreed," Kirk replied. "Spock, hail the Tandaran vessel and tell them that we're not looking to harm their people, but we'll take action if they try anything. And if you think they're about to pull something, you hit them first. Aim to incapacitate, but do whatever you think's necessary to keep them from taking out our shields again."

The first officer said, "*Acknowledged.*"

"Keep me apprised of the boarding party's movements and activities, and open a channel to the hangar deck from this location. I want to try talking to them."

"*Lieutenant Uhura has established the link, sir.*"

"Let me know if there's any change in the Tandaran ship's condition or actions. Kirk out." Closing his communicator, he stared down at the hangar deck once more. The six Tandarans were watching him from where they stood at various positions around the *Balatir,* holding their rifles in a manner that would allow them to bring the weapons to bear in rapid fashion. Studying each of their faces, it took Kirk a moment to realize that one of the boarding party members looked to be Colonel Abrenn himself. Keeping his eyes on the Tandaran leader, he moved to the comm panel mounted to the section of bulkhead separating two viewing ports and pressed the unit's activation switch.

"Colonel Abrenn, this is Captain Kirk. By now you've realized that you can't get to the Certoss, and you can't contact your ship. The hangar deck has been sealed off from the rest of the ship, so there's nowhere for you to go. Surrender now, and I promise that you won't be harmed."

"*Captain,*" replied the Tandaran leader, moving toward the hangar deck's center so that he could see Kirk, "*you know I cannot leave without the Certoss. Allow me to do so, and we can end this without further harm to either of our vessels or crews.*"

"And you know I can't just let you take them," Kirk replied. "You realize that your boarding my ship will be seen as an act of aggression against the Federation? Is that really your intention? Surely we can find a way to settle this. Whatever your concerns, I promise you they'll get a fair hearing. Let me *help* you, Colonel."

Abrenn's statement was as flat as the expression with which he regarded Kirk. "*You can help me by surrendering the Certoss.*"

Shaking his head in irritation, Kirk said, "All right, let's look at this another way. Your current tactical situation is—shall we say—precarious. Nobody's getting in or out of there unless I say so. My people have sealed off every point of entry to the hangar deck. There's only one way out, and I've got my finger on the button for that." To emphasize his point, he gestured with his phaser toward the enormous hangar doors. "I don't know if those suits of yours work in vacuum, and I'd prefer not to test them."

"Suffice it to say that we are capable of fighting in any number of hostile environments, Captain. We may be trapped here, but I assure you we are not without options." Abrenn raised his rifle to aim at the viewing port and fired. Pulling away from the window, Kirk and Giotto dropped to the deck the instant before a bolt of red-white energy punched through the transparasteel barrier. Both men covered their heads with their arms as shrapnel fragments exploded into the corridor. Additional shots impacted against the other viewing ports, inflicting more damage and hurling still more debris into the passageway. Pushing himself to his hands and knees, Kirk scurried to the bulkhead beneath one of the ruined windows, angling for a position that would allow him to peer into the hangar bay without exposing himself to fire, when his communicator chirped. "Kirk here," he snapped after retrieving the unit and flipping open its cover.

"Captain," Spock said, *"I'm detecting a new energy reading emanating from the hangar deck. It is not being generated by any of our systems or the Certoss vessel. It definitely has a self-contained power source, but I cannot determine whether it might be an explosive device of some kind. It appears the device also is jamming the* Balatir's *communications, as I am unable to contact Minister Ocherab."*

"If it's some kind of bomb," Giotto said, "we can't let them set it off down there."

Another tone sounded across the open channel, indicating another party trying to contact him, and Kirk switched his communicator's frequency. "Kirk here."

"Ensign Minecci, sir. We've got eyes on the intruders. They're setting up something on the deck next to the Certoss ship. Can't tell what it is from here, but the way they're moving around down there . . ." The ensign was cut off as a barrage

of Tandaran weapons fire was aimed in his direction and he dropped out of sight. Kirk's eyes widened in horror, and he wondered if he had just seen the man killed right in front of him. A moment later the young officer's bald dome poked up above the destroyed viewing port's frame, and he waved. "*Still here, sir,*" he said over his communicator as more fire assaulted his position.

Giotto said, "It doesn't make sense that they'd detonate an explosive with no place to take any real cover."

"No, it doesn't," Kirk replied as he switched his communicator back to its primary frequency. "Spock, the device you're scanning. Is its power reading anything like the weapons they used to take out our shields?"

There was a pause before the first officer said, "*There is a definite similarity, Captain. It is possible the device is meant to overload the Certoss vessel's shields in the same manner as was done to ours.*"

"Damn it," Kirk hissed. If Abrenn managed to force his way aboard the *Balatir,* he would gain the leverage of a hostage situation. Kirk needed something to turn things in his favor.

There was, he decided, one option.

"Spock, initiate procedures for depressurizing the hangar deck."

The time for talking was over.

TWENTY-SIX

Los Angeles, California
February 23, 1968

Cal Sutherland caught the faint scent of developer solution as he held the photographs, a consequence of him removing them from the darkroom after his return from the bank and before they had been given sufficient time to dry. On any other day he would have exercised the proper restraint and allowed the copies to complete their development process, but everything about them demanded he move with judicious haste. He would have to let them finish drying before readying them for the mail. Was it his imagination, or could he feel an energy radiating from the pictures, some intangible quality linking these images to the actual subjects that had been captured on film?

"And you say you trust this guy, this informant of yours?" asked James Wainwright from the other end of a long-distance connection between Sutherland's office and whatever Dayton-based phone booth Wainwright had selected as his clandestine point of contact. The line was bad enough that Sutherland had to strain to hear over the sound of afternoon downtown traffic coming through his closed office window, and Wainwright already was talking in a raised voice.

"Yeah, he's solid. He's one of my most loyal readers. Had a subscription from the start; the whole smash. Don't get me wrong, I treat anything that comes my way with a grain of salt, but just wait until you get a load of these pictures, Jim. They'll blow your mind." His eyes traced over every feature of the dark figure displayed prominently in the photo's center. Unlike countless other photographs submitted to *Watch the Skies* or rival magazines or even to Blue Book case officers like Jim Wainwright, this was no indistinct, blurry shadow challenging all attempts at identification. Instead, the subject of this photo was depicted in stark focus, leaving little to the imagination.

It's a damned alien.

"You're sure it's what we've been looking for?" Wainwright asked, and Sutherland noted the other man's habitual guarded approach to speaking on the phone. While it was certain that the Blue Book case officer revealed far less information than he possessed on the topic, Wainwright was not a doubter or debunker. He was aware of what was happening all around the planet and right under the noses of nearly everyone, and he wanted nothing more than solid, indisputable evidence to substantiate what he already knew to be true.

"It's just like you described." Though the figure in the picture at first looked human, there could be no mistaking the odd, ruddy tint to its skin or the total lack of hair on its head, to say nothing of having no real ears. Only a pair of small holes above its mouth suggested a nose, but it was the hands that commanded Sutherland's attention, each possessing what looked to be two thumbs flanking three long, thin fingers. Its eyes and mouth were dark and ominous, a feeling accented by the thing's dark, skintight bodysuit and the harness worn across its chest. "I've never had a picture this good, of *anything*."

"I'm amazed your contact was able to get it," Wainwright

said. "From everything we know about these . . . people, they're usually a lot better at covering their tracks."

"According to him, it was a freak accident. I don't have all the details, and I won't have a chance to ask him for at least a month or so."

Wainwright asked, "But you know how to reach him? Where he's working?"

"Yeah, but I don't know his schedule. They send him on a lot of trips." In truth, Sutherland knew his contact's full identity and that he was employed by NASA at McKinley Rocket Base in Florida, working on some top-secret collaborative venture between the civilian space agency and the military. He saw no need to share that information with Wainwright, just as he kept to himself his network of supporters and sources from around the country. Though he figured Wainwright, with the full backing of the United States government, could find anyone and anything given sufficient time and effort, Sutherland felt no compelling need to make that task any easier for him.

"I guess that part's not really important," Wainwright said, "at least for now, though there may come a time when I need to speak to him. Still, I need to know everything about the . . . the person in the photograph. You know he's good at . . . *disguises*, right? Finding him in the middle of thousands of people on that base won't be easy."

"I hear you, brother." Sutherland had seen firsthand the Certoss's abilities to change their appearances to conceal their alien identities, using the odd harness strapped across their chests. He could not even begin to comprehend how such a device might work, but he had to admit it would come in handy, like something a bad guy might use in one of those James Bond movies. "What are you thinking?"

Wainwright replied, "We'll take it from here, Cal. Just get those pictures and the rest of the information from your friend to me as quick as possible."

"Getting ready to put it in the mail right now," Sutherland said, eyeing the brown envelope into which he would be inserting the photographs along with a copy of the note his source had included with the film. The original note along with the negatives and a full set of prints already were tucked away in one of Sutherland's usual safe places. "It'll go out tonight. Same address?" As part of their clandestine dealings, Wainwright had established a post office box well away from Wright-Patterson, in the rural town of Wapakoneta, Ohio, north of Dayton. Prior to the first time he had mailed a parcel there, Sutherland never had even heard of the place. It was the primary delivery point, but Wainwright also had set up others, each in another of Ohio's numerous small communities.

"Use the first alternate address I gave you. I think someone might be watching the other one."

"Okay, you got it. You're going to go after these guys again, aren't you?"

"Eventually," Wainwright replied. "I already know what you're going to ask, and yes: I'll try to make sure you're around to take the pictures."

Chuckling, Sutherland reached for the pack of cigarettes lying atop his desk. "I'll make it the cover story! Talk to you in a week or so."

"Sounds good," Wainwright said. "Thanks."

There was a click and the line went dead, and Sutherland returned the phone receiver to its cradle. To no one, he said, "You're okay, Wainwright." Despite the man's reluctance to offer up any real details regarding the various Blue Book cases he had worked, let alone something like this one, Sutherland on rare occasions had still been able to glean some information from the veteran investigator. He often got the sense that Wainwright was becoming disenchanted with the "establishment" that gave him his orders and might be looking elsewhere for support and assistance. Was that the reason he and Marshall had sought him out five years ago and provided him with real, hard data on the existence of the Certoss and how the aliens were working in secret?

With the photographs and the notes from his source bundled within the parcel and a cigarette stuck between his lips, Sutherland rose from his desk and reached for his jacket and hat. Glancing at the clock, he reasoned there still was time to get down to the mail room before it closed before heading over to Mabel's for an early dinner.

"Peach cobbler for dessert?" he asked himself. "Count me in." It would be a nice treat to round out what had been a busy workweek.

He thought his heart might burst from his chest as he opened the door to find a man standing before the entry.

Not a man, Sutherland realized, his mouth opening and letting the cigarette fall out. It was the thing from the pictures.

The apartment was a cluster of forgotten papers, books, and magazines along with overflowing trash receptacles and dilapidated furniture. Bottles containing varying amounts of liquor were arranged in haphazard fashion on the counter of the small kitchen, and the square table pushed into one corner by the main room's largest window supported a typewriter along with stacks of paper, handwritten notes, photographs, and newspaper clippings. Everything was imbued with the stench of cigarette smoke, old coffee, and sweat. Elizabeth Anderson wrinkled her nose, eager to be out of there.

"I'm not finding anything," she said, pulling herself to her feet from where she had been kneeling in order to examine the contents of a quartet of file boxes stashed beneath her table. Sighing, she wiped a lock of her auburn hair from where it had fallen across her eyes and took another look around the apartment that—until tonight—had been the residence of Cal Sutherland, editor in chief, senior writer, and, by all accounts, the only employee of *Watch the Skies* magazine.

Emerging from the apartment's bedroom dressed in a gray business suit and carrying a portable scanner, her partner, Ryan Vitali, replied, "Nothing in here, either. It seems as though the safe deposit boxes were his big contingency plan. Anything else he might've known?" He shrugged. "Those secrets died with him."

"That, or our mysterious friends managed to get here first, too." Elizabeth and Ryan had been acting on information that an associate of Sutherland's had obtained and shared with the tabloid journalist photographic proof of at least one of the Certoss aliens working in disguise at McKinley Rocket Base and other NASA and military installations. With the identity of Sutherland's source a mystery, Elizabeth had hoped to learn the photographer's name in order to track down and question him. Such a task might prove daunting for the most skilled and resourceful detectives, and she and Ryan had experienced no small amount of difficulty even with the tools at their disposal. Their search had taken them to Sutherland's office at *Watch the Skies* magazine, only to find the journalist dead, and no sign of any information pertaining to the Certoss he may have held there. A scan of

Sutherland's office revealed residual traces of an energy discharge consistent with a particle beam weapon, suggesting that the reporter had been killed by one of the aliens.

"At least the Beta 5 was right about the deposit boxes," Ryan said, patting the leather satchel he wore slung over his left shoulder. An examination of Sutherland's background had yielded the secret safe deposit boxes, which Elizabeth and Ryan had investigated prior to visiting Sutherland's office. Given the recent turn of events, that choice may well have proven invaluable. Returning his scanner to the satchel, he said, "With what we recovered, we should be able to find Sutherland's contact in Florida."

"If he's even still alive," Elizabeth replied, reaching beneath her blue jacket to retrieve her servo from where she kept it along her left hip, inside the waistband of her slacks. The device, a match for the one Ryan carried in his pocket and looking like an expensive silver fountain pen, emitted a short, high-pitched beep as she adjusted its setting and held it close to her mouth. "Beta 5."

"*Computer on. Recognize Agent 201,*" replied the stilted though feminine voice of the supercomputer hidden behind a false wall in the office Elizabeth and Ryan shared in New York.

"I wonder if it misses us," Ryan mused.

Ignoring the comment, Elizabeth said, "Request data search. Collect all available information on a man named Joshua Langsford. All we know is that he's probably a resident of Florida and works for NASA in some capacity."

"*Despite the lack of useful information, I will endeavor to compile a comprehensive dossier.*"

Ryan smirked. "Now, *that's* the Beta 5 I know and love."

"Don't let it hear you," Elizabeth said. "You know how

moody it can get." While the Beta 5 was an invaluable tool, it could at times be damned irritating. Elizabeth had become familiar with this model of computer during her final training stages just prior to the Aegis sending her and Ryan to Earth as replacements for Agent 6, Cynthia Foster. The artificial intelligence algorithms inhabiting the machine seemed at times possessed of an insufferable ego. Whether that was an unintended side effect of its programming or a deliberate choice by those who had created it, Elizabeth did not know.

As for Elizabeth and Ryan's predecessor, Foster had asked to be relieved of her duties after spending several years here, even after the death of her partner, Ian Pendleton, working undercover in pursuit of the Aegis initiative to monitor and influence events in order to keep humanity on the path to eventual technological and sociological enlightenment. Elizabeth and Ryan, possessing the same degree of genetic enhancements as any other human raised and trained by the Aegis over the course of millennia and already in preparation to be sent to Earth as replacements in a year's time, had seen their transition activities accelerated in order to accommodate the changeover. The agents had only been on planet and settling into their new roles for three months upon learning of Cal Sutherland's proof of Certoss activities in Florida.

"*Agent 201,*" said the voice of the Beta 5. "*Preliminary information on Joshua Langsford: civilian employee for the Department of Defense, currently assigned to special projects division at McKinley Rocket Base in Florida. Report submitted by his supervisor two days ago indicates Langsford has not reported for work. Current whereabouts are unknown.*"

Ryan grunted. "That doesn't sound good." He stepped closer to Elizabeth in order to speak into her servo. "Beta 5, have you checked with local law enforcement agencies as well as any hospitals in the area for reports of suspects in custody or patients matching his description?"

"*I am familiar with the proper procedures for conducting a missing persons search, Agent 347.*"

"That's not a yes," Ryan pressed.

The Beta 5 sounded almost chagrined as it replied, "*Search procedures are under way. Stand by.*"

"It's not going to find anything," Elizabeth said. "If he's missing, then we both know what happened to him." Common sense told her that Joshua Langsford, like Cal Sutherland, had fallen victim to the Certoss's need to keep their existence hidden until such time as they could finish their mission.

The debriefing she and Ryan had received from Agent 6 during their transition period had been eye-opening, to say the least. Their predecessor, thanks to several covert infiltrations of Wright-Patterson Air Force Base and the headquarters of the top-secret Majestic 12 committee and Project Blue Book, had learned about those organizations' knowledge of the Certoss and their goal of disrupting humanity's technological development at whatever cost to the planet and its inhabitants. The hard evidence the groups held was lean, but still informative, in that while they were aware of the Certoss and their activities—at least to a point—their efforts at tracking the renegade aliens had been far from successful. Only with the help of unlikely benefactors, namely Cal Sutherland and even a Vulcan, Mestral, who had been living on Earth in secret for more than a decade, had they achieved even fleeting, infrequent success. The Certoss seemed able to frustrate every effort at locating them. As for Mestral, he also had managed to elude detection even from Aegis agents, only coming to their notice after he began collaborating with one of the Air Force officers assigned to Project Blue

Book. A message dispatched to their superiors on the Aegis homeworld had been answered with strict instructions not to interfere with Mestral's activities, and to render whatever anonymous assistance might be required to preserve his true identity. She had no idea what the situation was with the Vulcan, but her directives on the subject were clear: Leave Mestral alone.

"*Agent 347,*" said the Beta 5, "*I find no record of arrest or hospital admittance for anyone matching Joshua Langsford's description.*"

Ryan frowned. "It was a long shot, anyway."

"Agreed," Elizabeth said, sighing. She cast another look around Sutherland's apartment, willing some clue to present itself.

What did surprise her was the figure standing outside the window over the kitchen table, pointing some kind of weapon at her.

"Down!" Instinct took over and she threw herself to the floor, rolling to one side an instant before the ear-splitting whine of an energy pulse filled the room and something punched through the window's single glass pane. To her left she saw Ryan diving for cover behind the slumping couch in the middle of the room, just beating the second salvo that ripped through the furniture's fabric covering. The stench of burned foam rubber and cloth assailed Elizabeth's nostrils and she rolled farther out of the line of fire. Adjusting the servo in her right hand with practiced ease, she brought up the multipurpose tool and aimed it at the shattered window. A burst of blue energy spat from the compact weapon, just missing their attacker. The figure vanished from sight as Ryan aimed his own servo at the window and fired a second shot, hitting nothing.

"Come on!" Elizabeth yelled, bounding to her feet and running for the apartment's back door. She yanked it open and lunged out onto the narrow catwalk running the length of the apartment building's second floor. Aiming her servo ahead of her, she looked for any sign of their assailant but saw nothing. Darkness had fallen, with dim light bulbs set into fixtures at regular intervals along the catwalk's ceiling providing the only illumination.

"He couldn't have gotten away that fast," Ryan said, coming up behind her.

Movement below them caught Elizabeth's eye and she pointed at a shadowy figure running across the apartment building's parking lot. The runner avoided the street lamps casting light across sections of the lot, and he was putting distance between himself and the building, fast.

"Let's go," Elizabeth said, thanking herself for remembering to wear flat shoes instead of heels as she placed her free hand on the catwalk's wrought iron railing and vaulted herself over the waist-high barrier. She dropped the dozen or so feet from the second floor to the asphalt, her genetically augmented muscles absorbing the impact with ease. No sooner did Ryan drop from the catwalk than they set off at a sprint, ignoring the curious stares of other residents looking through windows or poking their heads out of doorways in response to the odd, raucous sounds coming from Sutherland's apartment. Their assailant rounded the corner of another building up the street, having already put more than fifty meters between them.

"Split up!" she snapped, waving for Ryan to proceed down the building's near side as she continued the pursuit. Hoping to catch the fugitive between them, she drove her feet into the pavement and pumped her arms, increasing her speed, which already was beyond that achievable even by the fastest human runner. She turned the corner of the building in seconds, seeing nothing ahead of her but empty street. A few cars were parked along the curb, but she detected no activity within any of them. Keeping her servo out and aimed ahead of her, Elizabeth searched for any signs of movement.

Nothing.

Damn it!

She flinched at the sight of a figure coming around the building's far end, relaxing only when she recognized Ryan jogging toward her. He once more held his portable scanner, and as he drew closer she heard the device's characteristic low warbling whistle. Like her, the brief exertion had not even affected his breathing.

"I'm not picking up anyone running from this location. It's like he just vanished."

"Certoss," Elizabeth said, biting on the word. "It's that harness, cloaking shield or whatever the hell it is." She let her gaze travel over every car on the street before checking each doorway and window within view. "The bastard could be standing right in front of us and we'd never know it."

Ryan deactivated his scanner and returned it to his satchel. "If he was here, then he may have searched Sutherland's apartment and come up empty like we did. Or, maybe we showed up and we spooked him before he could finish picking over the place."

"If he heard us talking," Elizabeth said, "then he might know we're on to him. He probably also knows we're not just anybody, either."

"Yeah, but we have one thing going for us," Ryan replied, patting his satchel. "We know he's been undercover at McKinley. He and his friends might be looking to make their move soon. An upcoming launch or something. Whatever it is, it's worth killing people to keep their plans secret."

Elizabeth nodded, considering the information they had retrieved from Sutherland's cache, and how it likely had cost the reporter and his source, Joshua Langsford, their lives. "If so, then we might be running out of time."

Of course, if that truly were the case, she reminded herself, then everyone on Earth might well be running out of time.

TWENTY-SEVEN

U.S.S. Enterprise
Earth Year 2268

On the *Balatir*'s cramped flight deck, Roberta Lincoln watched the activities unfolding in the *Enterprise*'s hangar bay with growing dread. On the small circular viewing screen dominating the helm operator's console, she saw two figures—both dressed in formidable-looking dark body armor and helmets—working to set up some sort of device on the bay's deck plating, close to the outer boundary of the *Balatir*'s shields.

"What is that?" asked Minister Ocherab from where she stood next to Roberta.

"I don't know." Turning to Mestral and Gejalik, Roberta asked, "Any ideas?"

Mestral replied, "Perhaps an explosive of some kind."

"No," Gejalik countered. "They wouldn't use something like that in a contained space. I don't recognize the exact design, but it looks similar to a device Tandaran ground forces employed against installations to disable their power systems."

"Like our shields?" Roberta asked.

Gejalik nodded. "Exactly. Communications, as well."

"That explains why we can't contact Captain Kirk or his people. Wonderful." Though she had thought gathering Gejalik, Mestral, and the rest of the Certoss crew aboard their ship to be little more than a stalling tactic—something to buy time until Kirk could devise a strategy for dealing with the Tandaran landing party—it was becoming obvious that her off-the-cuff plan was not long for this world. If the Tandarans managed to breach the *Balatir*'s deflector shields, there would be nothing to stop them from using their weapons or a real bomb to penetrate the Certoss vessel's hull. The device they had set up outside the ship, in addition to disrupting the *Balatir*'s communications, also seemed to be interfering with her servo. Roberta could not use it to contact the *Enterprise*, nor could she even utilize its emergency recall function to the Beta 5 for transport back to her own time.

Nice job, Roberta.

"I suppose it's too much to hope that you have any weapons aboard this ship?"

Ocherab seemed not the least bit embarrassed as she replied, "No, Miss Lincoln. We possess no weapons of any kind."

"A laudable stance," Gejalik said, "though of little use at the moment."

Mestral added, "Indeed. I do not believe the Tandarans will be impressed."

"Minister Ocherab," Roberta said, "are you able to show me the rest of the hangar bay?"

By way of reply, the elder Certoss gestured to one of her two subordinates occupying stations along the cramped control room's forward bulkhead. The other Certoss, a young male, moved his hands across the console without making actual contact with the station's smooth black surface, and beneath his fingers a series of soft-lit indicators glowed in varying colors, each accompanied by an almost musical tone Roberta might have found soothing on any other occasion. On the display screen the image shifted to show the

Enterprise hangar deck from different angles based on what she guessed to be sensors positioned around the *Balatir*'s exterior. In addition to the pair of Tandaran intruders working on the device, Roberta counted four others, each of them wielding nasty-looking rifles and acting as though they were on the lookout for potential threats.

"Look!" Gejalik said, pointing to the screen as its image changed again to show the two Tandarans and their mysterious equipment. "They're running away. I think . . ."

Her words were cut off as a tremendous flash of light erupted on the screen, washing across the entire picture at the same instant the very hull of the *Balatir* itself shuddered around them. Every light and console on the flight deck flickered and Roberta heard a warble in the ship's engines, as though they now were fighting not to lose power.

"Minister," the helm operator said, "our shields are down!"

"Can you reestablish them?" Ocherab asked, and Roberta heard the controlled tension in the elder's voice.

His fingers moving across his console in rapid fashion, the subordinate shook his head. "No, Minister! The shield generator has overloaded. The engineer is already attempting to effect repairs."

"I do not believe we will have sufficient time," Mestral said, gesturing to the screen where the image now depicted the pair of Tandarans returning across the hangar bay. One of the intruders was brandishing a rectangular-shaped object in one hand, which Roberta could not identify before he disappeared from view, now unfettered by the *Balatir*'s deflector shields.

"I don't like the looks of that," she said. "Something to override the door's magnetic lock?"

Gejalik said, "It's an explosive charge."

Roberta felt her pulse quickening, as much from fright

as anticipation. Even if the Tandarans captured the Certoss, which was looking more likely by the second, they still were trapped on the *Enterprise*. How far was Abrenn willing to take this? Would he kill Ocherab and her crew if he felt he had no other options?

If you're going to pull off one of your miracles, Kirk, now would be a good time.

"*Captain, the Tandarans have activated their dampening device. The Certoss vessel's shields are down.*"

With Lieutenant Commander Giotto following him, Kirk cursed at Spock's report while sprinting the final dozen meters to the reinforced pressure hatch leading onto the *Enterprise* hangar deck. "What are they doing now?"

"*From what we're able to see, they're now moving on the* Balatir, *and have placed something on the vessel's exterior access hatch. Sensors have determined that it's a form of explosive.*"

"We're out of time," Kirk said. After checking to verify that his phaser was set to its maximum non-lethal setting just as he had ordered for Giotto and the others, he looked to the security chief, who offered a reassuring nod. "Let's do this, Spock."

"*Acknowledged.*"

A moment later, alarm klaxons began wailing in the narrow corridor, followed by the stilted, feminine voice of the *Enterprise*'s main computer. "*Warning, hangar doors will open in thirty seconds. Safety overrides have been disabled. No depressurization cycle will occur. Move immediately to the nearest exit.*"

"Come on," Kirk said, gesturing for Giotto to follow him as he hit the switch to open the pressure hatch. The alarms grew louder as the heavy doors parted to reveal the hangar deck, enough that the sirens were hurting his ears, and all of it accompanied by the chaotic flashing of the alert indicators positioned around the bay. Kirk ran into the cavernous chamber and crouched near the bulkhead. To his left, he saw Giotto mimic his movements, the security chief taking up a defensive position in order to guard his captain's blind side. On the far side of the bay, Kirk saw another hatch open and a trio of Giotto's security detail run onto the hangar deck, two of them carrying phaser rifles. They were led by Ensign Minecci, who gestured with his phaser pistol for the other two men to follow him.

"*Warning, hangar doors will open in twenty seconds. Safety overrides have been disabled. No depressurization cycle will occur. Move immediately to the nearest exit.*"

"I hope the computer knows what it's doing!" Giotto shouted over the sound of the alarms. "Not that I don't trust you or Mister Spock, sir, but still . . ." When Kirk glanced over his shoulder, it was to see the commander shrugging. Despite the present situation, Kirk could not help a small grin.

Though he believed the Tandarans' helmets and armor likely would protect them from any loss of atmosphere, Kirk was counting on Abrenn and his people not wanting to be in the bay should the massive clamshell doors begin to open. The effects of abrupt depressurization would send every unsecured item and piece of equipment careening for the bay doors, carried on the invisible wave of escaping oxygen and turning the entire room into a hazardous gallery of flying debris.

At the center of the bay sat the *Balatir*, and Kirk caught sight of the first Tandarans moving about the hangar deck. As he expected, the intruders were moving away from the rear of the bay, trying to distance themselves from the hangar doors and get behind the various equipment, storage crates, and other items taking up space in the chamber. He counted four figures running for the front of the massive chamber, moving toward Minecci and his men and appearing to focus more on getting to safety than anything else. As they passed another access hatch, that portal opened to admit still more *Enterprise* security personnel.

"*Warning,*" the computer droned, "*hangar doors will open in ten seconds. Move immediately to the nearest exit.*"

Into his communicator, Kirk barked, "Minecci! Take them!" With Giotto on his heels, he rose from his crouch and headed across the bay, angling for the *Balatir* and where he suspected the two remaining Tandarans still lurked. Weapons fire caught Kirk's attention, and he turned to see Ensign Minecci and his people engaging the other intruders. Phaser beams flashed across that section of the hangar deck as the *Enterprise* personnel caught the Tandarans in a crossfire, the maximum stunning force of the security team's weapons penetrating even the intruders' tactical armor. Within seconds, the quartet of Tandarans had fallen unconscious to the hangar deck.

"*Warning, hangar doors are opening.*"

Kirk grunted in resignation. "So much for our big bluff." He of course had no intention of subjecting the hangar bay to sudden decompression with his own people exposed to danger, but he had been hoping the perceived peril might force the Tandarans into dropping their guard and making mistakes. Now that the computer's countdown had concluded and the hangar doors remained closed, Abrenn would know for certain that it all had been a ruse.

Stepping around the *Balatir*'s forward section, Kirk caught movement above and to his right, and he looked up to see a dark figure leaping at him from atop the Certoss vessel. He had time only to brace himself for the impact before the attacker crashed into him, sending them both tumbling to the deck. Kirk's phaser fell from his hand and he heard it sliding away, but he ignored it as he rolled to his feet, bringing himself into a defensive stance. Backpedaling to give himself maneuvering room, he saw Abrenn staring at him through the faceplate of his protective helmet.

"Captain!" he heard Giotto shout from somewhere behind him before another weapon report echoed in the bay and the security chief was forced to seek cover. More shots followed him as he dashed around the front of the *Balatir*, leaving Kirk alone with Abrenn.

"My compliments, Captain," said the Tandaran, his voice muffled by the small speaker grille at the base of his helmet. "You employ deception and diversion with great skill, but I did not think you would risk exposing your crew and ship to unnecessary danger. However, I have no such reservations. Ranzareq! Now!"

In response to the colonel's barked command, a small explosion rumbled through the bay and Kirk felt the shockwave in his chest just as he stepped around the *Balatir*'s forward section. He ducked, throwing up his arms to protect himself, but then realized it had to have been the device Abrenn or his companion had affixed to the Certoss vessel's access hatch. The charge was shaped to cause only the amount of damage necessary to force open the door, and the echo of its detonation still was ringing throughout the hangar bay as Kirk saw another Tandaran—Abrenn's companion, Ranzareq—running toward the hatch. He applied some new device to the hull and activated it, resulting in the ship's outer hatch cycling open.

"No!" Kirk shouted, moving forward despite Abrenn standing in his way, but the Tandaran closed the distance between them. As the colonel reached for him, Kirk grabbed him by the shoulder and drove his knee into Abrenn's gut, just below the chest plate of his armor. He had no expectations of inflicting any real pain but the blow still was enough to catch the Tandaran off guard, giving Kirk the seconds he needed to grip Abrenn's arm and lever his opponent over his hip, dropping him to the deck. The Tandaran fell on his back and Kirk heard his grunt of surprise.

Not giving Abrenn any chance to recover, Kirk drove his boot onto the colonel's helmet faceplate, feeling the transparent material yield beneath his heel. A hairline crack appeared across the protective screen, enough to make Abrenn's eyes widen in concern as he rolled away. He swept his leg to catch Kirk behind his knees, taking his feet out from under him. Kirk, his balance gone, crashed to the deck. Training and experience prepared him for the fall and he was able to absorb most of the impact, already coming up onto one knee and pushing himself back to his feet when an energy blast shrieked past him. It was Abrenn's companion, standing at the *Balatir*'s open hatch. The Tandaran was adjusting his aim to fire again when Kirk heard the familiar whine of a phaser beam. It passed him and struck the Tandaran in his chest, pushing him against the Certoss vessel's hull, where he then slid unconscious to the deck.

"Abrenn!" Kirk shouted as he saw the colonel regaining his own footing. "It's over!" Hearing footsteps behind him, he glanced over to see Giotto stepping into view, his phaser aimed at the Tandaran. "Your people are in custody and there's nowhere for you to go. There's no need for *any* of this!"

For the first time, he saw Abrenn display genuine emotion, his anger evident on his features as he glared at Kirk through his helmet's damaged faceplate. "I'm acting to protect my people!"

"Your people are safe!" Kirk snapped. "You're responding to a threat that doesn't exist! How can you not see that?"

Abrenn sneered. "You have no comprehension of the dangers I see, Captain. The threat is real, lurking beyond your ability to see or understand. That was the reality of the war we fought—will fight, and *lose*—if we do not act against that possibility." He gestured toward the *Balatir*. "*That* is what you're protecting. There's no way to know what chaos that fugitive represents, or can bring down upon us all."

"She's just one person," Kirk said. "Cut off from everything and everyone she's ever known. Even if there was a way to send her forward to her own time, her own planet—its history and culture—is unrecognizable to her."

Sighing, Abrenn shook his head. "You simply have no idea, Kirk." Reaching up, he pressed a control embedded into his suit's chest plate. "And you give me no choice."

"Wait!" Kirk snapped, holding out his hand. Not waiting for an order, Giotto fired his phaser, catching Abrenn in the torso and knocking the Tandaran unconscious. He fell, but Giotto was able to catch him and lower him gently to the deck. "What did he do?"

The security chief shook his head. "I don't know, sir." Reaching for his tricorder, he activated it and waved it over Abrenn's chest armor. "It's some kind of burst transmitter. A distress beacon, maybe?"

Alarm klaxons wailed once more across the hangar bay, followed by the harried voice of Lieutenant Sulu booming through the intercom system. "*All hands, brace for impact! The Tandaran vessel is on a collision course!*"

TWENTY-EIGHT

Cocoa Beach, Florida
March 29, 1968

With dawn peeking over the horizon and stretching across the Atlantic Ocean, the giant Saturn rocket gleamed in the distance at nearby McKinley Rocket Base, just visible over the treetops with the first rays of the sun. It was, James Wainwright conceded, magnificent; a triumph of modern technology and resolve. Soon, rockets like the one now towering into the morning sky would carry men to the moon, in keeping with the bold challenge thrown down by President John Kennedy just seven years earlier. While the president himself was gone, struck down in a moment of horror by an assassin's bullet, his dream persisted, willed into reality by the hundreds of thousands of men and women and billions of dollars committed to the effort.

"It's really quite something, isn't it?" asked Allison Marshall, standing behind him and leaning against the fender of their government-issued blue Ford sedan.

Standing with his hands in his pockets, he looked over his shoulder at her and smiled. "I used to dream about stuff like this when I was a kid, reading all those stories and watching those movies. I wanted to be Flash Gordon, or Buck Rogers, or Captain Proton. Hell, I wanted to be Alan Shepard or John Glenn. I still do." It was a notion that made him smile.

Approaching his fifty-first birthday, he still enjoyed reading the fictional exploits of space adventurers, and he had followed the various missions of the Mercury and Gemini space programs and their progress toward meeting Kennedy's goal by the end of the decade. Still, much of that had lost its allure in the face of the truth about space travel as presented to him by his own job. Despite his best efforts, Wainwright had failed to separate his work from other aspects of his life, and as a consequence the fantasies—and fun—of his youth were forever lost.

What the hell are you doing? Get back to work.

Drawing a deep breath, Wainwright blew it out before returning his focus to the matter at hand. "Okay, let's get to it." He turned back to the car and the briefcase Marshall already had placed on its hood. "You take the scanner this time. Damned thing gave me fits yesterday." Eyeing the clipboard-sized device given to them by Mestral, he shook his head as he recalled his troubles while attempting to master its functions, which he knew were quite simple in keeping with their Vulcan friend's intentions. As designed, the scanner would be able to detect the presence of any non-human. After studying the odd harness belonging to the Certoss killed by Wainwright and Marshall in Yuma fifteen years earlier, Mestral had been able to key the scanner so that it should work even when the target was using such a harness to appear human.

At least, I hope so.

"Let's go," he said, eyeing the apartment complex's parking lot that still was near capacity even at this early hour. "People are going to be heading to work soon." A background check on the apartment village revealed that, like the three such complexes they had investigated the previous day, a significant number of tenants worked for NASA or one of the government agencies or civilian firms attached to the various efforts under way at McKinley as well as Cape Canaveral just a few miles farther up the Florida coast. The day would be one filled with all manner of final preparations for the launch scheduled to take place later that afternoon. Wainwright and Marshall had passed several trucks outside the McKinley gates, with reporters and camera operators from the various radio and television news bureaus, and he had seen a satellite parking lot for journalists and other members of the media already filled to overflowing. While there could be no hiding the fact that a rocket was launching today, Wainwright knew that only a fraction of the people on the base were aware of what really was taking place, and the truth of the rocket's classified payload. The question, of course, was which of those people were not native to this planet.

"Ready?" Marshall asked.

Wainwright nodded. "As ready as ever, I guess." After years of attempting to track the Certoss agents' movements, along with the occasional fragment of information provided by Cal Sutherland's various contacts within the NASA community, he and Marshall—with help from Mestral—had spent weeks putting together a plan for hunting the aliens. Their strategy hinged on the assumption that the operatives, wanting to avoid undue attention while working on the nuclear weapons platform project, would have found roles and jobs that would keep them from anything resembling a "spotlight." Mestral had suggested that an engineering or other technical role, something offering access to the rockets' hardware and computer support systems, was the ideal cover identity. It was a sensible notion, though it only narrowed the field of potential targets to several hundred suspects just here in the Cocoa Beach area.

So, we should probably get started.

The scanner in Marshall's hand went off within the first five minutes.

"Really?" Wainwright asked, his eyes widening as he regarded his partner.

Nodding, Marshall held up the scanner for him to see. The needle on the unit's display—a gauge repurposed from an old Geiger counter so that the numbers on its face now represented distance from their target—had pegged out at the scanner's maximum detection range. "He's within one hundred feet."

"That could be anywhere around here," Wainwright said, lamenting the scanner's one obvious detriment of being unable to determine the direction of their target. Like the Geiger counters from which most of its parts had been taken, only sweeping the device so that its forward sensing component could focus on the object of their search provided any hint as to the correct bearing. Sighing, Wainwright studied the catwalk on which they stood, which encircled the apartment building's third floor. A dozen closed doors lay ahead of them. The Certoss agents could be in any of the first half of those or in a corresponding apartment on either of the neighboring floors.

Marshall shrugged. "Let's keep moving and see what happens."

As they walked, Wainwright glanced at the scanner, eyeing the moving gauge needle as it indicated a decrease in distance between them and their target. That they might have stumbled across at least one of their quarry with so little difficulty already had him feeling suspicious, and this only furthered his worry. Without his thinking about it, his right hand moved up to reach beneath his jacket for the snap holding the pistol in its holster beneath his arm.

At the far end of the catwalk, less than fifty feet from them, one of the apartment doors opened and a man stepped out. He looked to be in his forties, balding and with a thick midsection barely contained by his short-sleeved white dress shirt. His tie, thin and black, was too short, as were the cuffs of his black trousers. To Wainwright he could have been any of the hundreds of employees on NASA's payroll.

When he turned in their direction, Marshall was the first to react to the gun in the man's hand.

"Look out!"

The man's right hand rose toward them and Wainwright saw the pistol's muzzle the instant before it flashed and the gunshot echoed off the concrete walls. Then Marshall cried out in pain. He saw her falling backward but he kept his attention on the other man, drawing his .45 and firing a quick shot down the catwalk. The round went wide but the man ducked anyway, giving Wainwright the chance he needed to better his aim. His next shot struck the man's right arm, pushing him off balance and throwing him sideways against the wall near the catwalk's far end. Wainwright caught sight of something dark spattering the painted concrete; too dark to be human blood.

"Stop right there!" Wainwright shouted, firing again as the man turned a corner and disappeared. His first instinct was to give chase, but then his mind snapped back into gear. *Allison!*

He knelt beside Marshall where she had fallen to the ground, clasping her right hand at the point where her left arm met her shoulder. Blood seeped between her fingers, and her expression was a mask of pain.

"Hold on," Wainwright said, pulling the handkerchief from his breast pocket and pressing it to her wound. Marshall laid her bloody hand atop his, squeezing shut her eyes and gritting her teeth. There was blood beneath her body, and a quick check revealed the exit wound on the back of her shoulder. He pulled back his free hand to see his fingers stained red. "It went through. We need to get you to a hospital."

Doors had opened behind him and he looked up to see a young woman peering out at him from her own apartment. "Call an ambulance!"

"Who the hell are you?" the woman asked.

"I'm with the Air Force. Someone just shot my partner. Now call me a damned ambulance!"

The woman disappeared back into her apartment, but another man now was running the length of the catwalk behind him. Wainwright looked up to see that it was an army captain, his uniform shirt unbuttoned and untucked. He likely lived here and had come running in response to the shots.

"What happened?" he asked as he came closer. "Who shot her?"

"A spy," Marshall replied. It was close enough to the truth. She nodded toward the catwalk's far end. "He went that way."

Instead of running off, the captain instead took off his uniform shirt, leaving him in a white undershirt as he folded the other garment into a square. Kneeling next to Marshall, he applied his makeshift bandage to the wound on her back. "This'll hold her until the ambulance gets here."

Looking up at Wainwright from where she lay on the floor, Marshall whispered, "Jim, you need to go after him."

Her eyes were glazed and heavy, and he heard the slur in her words. She was going into shock.

"I'm not going anywhere," Wainwright said. "Besides, he's already long gone. I'll never find him."

She reached up to grip his arm. "McKinley. He's got to be going there." Hesitating, she glanced at the captain before adding, "You know why."

"He could hide anywhere." A sense of dread and failure was beginning to grip him. Was this encounter enough to send the Certoss running for cover? What if they already had done whatever task was required to put into motion their plans for the nuclear platform stored aboard the rocket? Perhaps everything, including Marshall's being shot, had all been for nothing, and it already was too late. "I'll never find them."

"We may be able to help with that."

Startled, Wainwright looked up to see two men, and his mouth dropped open. "You?" Agent 937, the thirty-something brown-haired man with the intense hazel eyes, and his stoic companion in the fedora, Agent 176, now stood before him. Where the hell had they come from? Both men wore dark gray suits of similar cut, and it took Wainwright a moment to realize that they looked almost exactly the same as the last time he had seen them. How long ago had that been? A year? "What the hell are you doing here?"

"Believe it or not," replied Agent 937, "we're here for the same reason you are."

TWENTY-NINE

Highway 949, Cocoa Beach, Florida
March 29, 1968

Her hands tight on the steering wheel, Elizabeth Anderson kept her foot on the sedan's gas pedal, rounding the last turn and leaving behind the surface street as she accelerated their car, following the white station wagon onto the freeway.

"Where did you learn to drive?" asked Ryan Vitali from the passenger seat, his hands pressed against the dashboard. "Daytona?"

"Monaco," Elizabeth replied, keeping her eyes and attention on the road. Most of the traffic was heading in the opposite direction along the divided highway, and within moments there were but a few cars in the lanes ahead of her. Only one vehicle commanded her attention: the one driven by the fleeing Certoss.

So close. So damned close!

The thought echoed over and over in her mind. After their encounter with the renegade alien operative at Cal Sutherland's apartment last month and following weeks of the Beta 5 sifting through information combed from numerous sources regarding the thousands of people employed by NASA and other government agencies, Elizabeth and Ryan believed at least two of the Certoss operatives were here, having infiltrated McKinley Rocket Base while posing as civilian engineers supporting the military's top-secret weapons project. It was the Beta 5's opinion that the aliens would use their positions to influence or even hijack the platform set to be launched into space later today. Their investigation had given them half a dozen employees to check out, though the first two they had visited had ended up being dead ends. It was upon visiting the residence of one Dennis Thompson that they realized they had found at least one of the Certoss. Their plan to capture the alien and sabotage the rocket so that it would be destroyed shortly after liftoff—thereby preventing the deployment of its nuclear payload—was scuttled by the untimely interference of the two Air Force investigators from the military's Blue Book project.

"We should've found a way to get them to back off," Ryan said, referring to Wainwright and Marshall. "They were in over their heads. We should've stepped in, somehow."

"Maybe," Elizabeth replied, keeping her eyes on the road. "But when you boil away all the nonsense, we're all on the same side. We could've done more to help them, too, if for no other reason than to avoid what happened back there." They had arrived too late to prevent Allison Marshall from being shot, and neither could they risk losing their chance to apprehend the Certoss agent, so they had set off in pursuit when the alien, still in human disguise, bolted from the apartment complex. Elizabeth and Ryan had only just been able to keep tabs on the operative's car as it fled.

Ahead of them, the station wagon was speeding in the left of the dual lanes heading north. The highway's southbound lanes were hidden from view by thickets of cabbage palmettos, pines, and sickly oaks that seemed to be the only trees allowed to grow in Florida. Any chance of sneaking up on their quarry now was gone, thanks to the veritable absence of almost any other cars on this stretch of road. Elizabeth's foot was pressing the gas pedal to the floorboard, coaxing every bit of speed out of the rental sedan. The steering wheel vibrated in her hands, a sign that she was pushing the car beyond its limits.

Rolling down the passenger door's window, Ryan repositioned himself so that he could lean out of the car. Elizabeth glanced over to see him brandishing his servo.

"What the hell are you doing?"

Ryan was resting his right arm atop the side-view mirror on his door. "Maybe I can disable the engine."

"Too dangerous," Elizabeth replied. She did not want to kill the Certoss if it could be avoided, even knowing that the alien would not show her and Ryan the same courtesy.

"So what do we do?" Ryan asked. "You going to try running him off the road?"

The station wagon now was less than ten car lengths ahead of them, close enough for Elizabeth to see the back of the driver's head. As the car entered a curve on the highway, she guided the sedan toward the inside lane, using the opportunity to pick up some precious distance. By the time the lanes straightened out she had cut the distance between them in half. She was preparing to close it even further on the next curve when the white car's brake lights flashed crimson and its nose dropped as the vehicle decelerated. Elizabeth jerked the wheel to the left to avoid crashing into the station wagon's rear end, and as they began coming abreast of the other car she saw an arm extend from the open driver's-side window.

"Look out!" she yelled, lifting her foot from the gas pedal, but by then she already was hearing the crack of the pistol in the Certoss agent's hand. Elizabeth flinched, anticipating the bullet ripping into her own body or the spraying of blood as

Ryan was hit, but instead she felt the sedan jerk to the right and the steering wheel buck in her hand.

"Tire!" Ryan yelled. "He got the tire!"

Elizabeth stomped on the brakes, feeling the car throw off speed as she wrestled to regain control. The sedan skidded over the hot asphalt, crossing both lanes before she felt the car lurching as it left the road and hit the gravel shoulder. The ground fell away from beneath the right front tire and then the entire sedan was heaving in that direction, and Elizabeth felt her stomach lurch as the car began tumbling. The passenger side and the roof spun across gravel, dirt, and grass and she heard Ryan crying out over the cacophony of metal groaning, protesting, and wrenching all around them. White-hot light exploded in her vision as her face slammed into something flat and unyielding, and there was a sharp stab in her rib cage.

The roll was slowing, and Elizabeth was aware of the car settling on whatever remained of its wheels on the grass at the edge of the forest lining the highway, settling against one of the thicker oaks competing for space among the other trees. Light and blurred color danced in her vision and she could not feel her left arm. Her face was wet and throbbing, and she tasted something bitter and metallic. Something was ringing in her ears, screaming for her to move, to get out of the car *right now*.

It took two tries to push open the driver's-side door, and she all but fell out of the car onto the grass. That impact only sent her head spinning all over again, though she still was aware of the grass and dirt beneath her hands and the Florida sun beating down on her. "Ryan!" she called out, her own voice sounding dull and distant in her buzzing ears. Gripping the edge of the door, Elizabeth tried pulling herself to her feet, but dizziness washed over her and she dropped once more to her knees. Now facing the car, she was able to see Ryan, unmoving in the passenger seat and hanging out of the passenger-side window. Blood was everywhere.

Get up!

Her left arm hanging limp and useless at her side, Elizabeth gritted her teeth, biting back pain as she forced herself to her feet. She needed help. Ryan needed help. How to get that?

Servo. Beta 5. The thoughts mashed together in her muddled mind. She could contact the computer back in New York and have it dispatch police and an ambulance. Her right hand fumbled into her jacket, looking for her servo, but her fingers seemed numb and unresponsive to her conscious control. What the hell was wrong with her? Shock, she knew. It already was impairing her. There was something else. What was she forgetting?

Propping herself against the car, Elizabeth willed her eyes to focus and her hand to grasp the servo in her pocket. She pulled her hand free, seeing the sunlight reflect off the device's silver finish. It shook in her grip and she clenched her fist, fighting for control. Something moved in her jumbled peripheral vision and she looked up to see the middle-aged man in a short-sleeved white shirt and black tie, pointing something at her.

"Wainwright!"

Ignoring Agent 937's warning cry as he guided his car around a curve, Wainwright saw the man standing before the wrecked sedan on the side of the highway, aiming what only could be a pistol at the injured, bloodied woman leaning against the car.

The pursuit had been fast, assisted by Agents 937 and 176. After appearing at the apartment complex as though from thin air, the agents had told Wainwright they needed to work together if they were going to apprehend the Certoss agent. Leaving Allison Marshall at her insistence in the care of the army captain before the ambulance arrived, Wainwright had set off with the two mysterious men in pursuit of the rogue alien.

He stomped the gas pedal, driving it to the floorboard as the car shot forward. His hands gripping the steering wheel so that his fingers hurt, Wainwright guided the car off the highway's asphalt surface and into the grass. The man holding the gun turned before he could fire his weapon, and he saw the sedan bearing down on him, his eyes widening in surprise. Just before the car would have plowed into him, the man jumped to avoid being hit, all but escaping from danger save for the glancing blow to his leg by the sedan's front corner as it drove past.

"Shit!" Wainwright snarled, his foot mashing the brake pedal and bringing the car to a halt. The vehicle shuddered in protest at the sudden deceleration, and he felt the hand of the other agent, 176, pressing down against the top of the car's couch-like front seat as the man braced himself against being thrown forward. Wainwright was already taking the car out of gear, his left hand grasping the door handle and yanking it up.

"Wainwright," 937 said, and Wainwright felt the man's hand on his arm. "Wait. It's not safe."

"Forget it," Wainwright hissed. "He's not getting away this time." Fueled by anger, with visions of Allison perhaps bleeding to death taunting him, he jerked his arm free and pushed himself from the driver's seat, his right hand already closing around the grip of his pistol and yanking it from his shoulder holster. With one single, practiced move, he raised the weapon and cocked its trigger, turning to where the Certoss agent should be.

He still was not fast enough.

The single shot rang out a heartbeat before white-hot fire tore through his stomach and Wainwright gasped. His legs gave out and he stumbled, falling against the open car door. Fighting to retain his grip on the pistol as the first wave of pain washed over him, he clamped his left hand to his gut where blood already was staining his white shirt. Movement ahead and to his right made him look up to see the Certoss, its human façade now gone, pulling itself from where it had been kneeling in the grass. Wainwright realized that hitting the alien with the car must have damaged the harness it wore to present its human appearance. The Certoss seemed unsteady as it rose to its feet, though its arm did not waver as it raised its pistol in Wainwright's direction. This time, and despite his own injury, Wainwright was faster, the .45 bucking in his hand as he fired his first shot. It hit the Certoss in its torso and it stumbled backward, almost falling but somehow managing to keep its balance. It was holding its free hand against its midsection as it continued forward.

Tough son of a bitch.

"Captain! No!"

The sudden cry from somewhere behind him was squelched by the sound of a shrill whine as a blue beam crossed the open space between the car and the Certoss. It struck the alien in the chest and this time it fell, crashing backward to the grass. Agent 937 appeared around the rear of the car, dividing his attention between Wainwright and the fallen Certoss. "Damn it," he said as he got his first look at Wainwright's injury, then looked over the top of the car. "Spock, get over here. He's hurt."

From around the driver's-side door appeared Agent 176—or "Spock," as 937, or "Captain," had just called him—moving to crouch next to Wainwright. "He requires immediate medical attention." Removing his suit jacket, the agent rolled it and pressed it against Wainwright's abdomen.

"What about the other two agents?" The question sounded tiny and distant in Wainwright's ears.

Agent 176 shook his head. "Both dead, Captain, as a consequence of their injuries. We do not have much time."

Much time? Time for what?

"Who are you?" he asked, pushing each word past his clenched jaw. While he was somewhat certain that the one man, 937, was human, seeing his partner in the daylight for the first time only strengthened his belief that Agent 176 was a Vulcan like Mestral. The fedora concealed the top of the agent's ears, but Wainwright was betting they were pointed.

His tongue felt swollen and his gut throbbed, a new pulse of agony accompanying every heartbeat. A haze seemed to have fallen across his vision, blurring everything.

Shock.

Leaning close, Agent 937 said, "We're friends, Mister Wainwright. We're going to get you medical treatment as quickly as possible."

Whatever reply Wainwright might have offered dissolved in his mind as saw something moving behind the other man. The Certoss once more was on his feet, aiming his pistol in their direction.

"No!" Wainwright said, pushing at 937 with his free arm and raising the pistol in his other hand. His shot struck the

Certoss in its chest, forcing it back a step, and Wainwright kept firing until the .45's magazine was empty and the pistol's slide locked to the rear. At least a couple of the rounds had hit the alien, including one in its face. The Certoss stopped its advance as its arms and legs went limp, its body falling forward to land with a heavy thump in the dirt.

Leaning against the car, one hand over his ears, 937 turned to look over his shoulder. He stared at the body of the now dead Certoss for a moment before saying, "You saved my life. Thank you."

"Just returning the favor," Wainwright said, dropping the pistol to the ground before his knees as the man's partner helped him to rest against the side of the car. Was it his imagination, or did he hear sirens somewhere in the distance?

"Captain," said Agent 176, and Wainwright heard the man's urgency. "They will be here momentarily."

"Don't worry," said another voice, a woman's. *Allison?*

Agent 937 stood. "Miss Lincoln? What are you . . . ?"

"There's an ambulance that'll be here any minute," the woman said, "along with some people from Wainwright's group. They'll take care of the . . . well, you know."

Struggling to keep his eyes open, Wainwright saw 937 gesture toward the other car, the wrecked one. "What about Agents 201 and 347?"

"That's taken care of," said the woman, and Wainwright thought he detected a note of sadness in her voice. "But we need to get you two out of here right now." She moved into his line of sight and Wainwright saw that she was very young—early twenties, he guessed—with bright blond hair. Kneeling next to him, she reached for him and then he felt her putting something into his inside jacket pocket. "Someone will be coming for those, Mister Wainwright. We can't thank you enough for what you've done here today. You likely helped to avert a nuclear war."

What? Her words were making less sense with each passing moment. He was falling deeper into shock, he knew. It was a fight just to keep from closing his eyes.

"I don't." He coughed. "I don't understand." His vision was narrowing, and her voice sounded hollow, growing more and more faint.

The woman smiled, reaching out to stroke his face. "That's all right," she said as Wainwright allowed his eyes to close. "When you wake up, you won't remember any of this, anyway."

THIRTY

McKinley Rocket Base, Cocoa Beach, Florida
March 30, 1968

The hospital was small, occupying a single-story structure near the base's rear gate, far from the mission control center and its associated buildings and related activities. On any other day, security would be light if nonexistent, but even the single military police sergeant on duty outside the pair of rooms at the end of one hallway would not present much of a problem.

Wearing a doctor's white lab coat and carrying a clip-board—both of which he had found in a linen closet at the other end of the building—Gary Seven rounded a turn in the hallway, the heels of his loafers echoing as he walked across the white linoleum tiles. As he approached, doing his best to look as though he belonged in the hospital at this early hour well before dawn, the sergeant nodded at him.

"Good morning, sir. May I help you?"

His servo already in his hand, Seven said nothing but instead triggered the device and it emitted a small electronic snap. The sergeant's eyes widened in surprise and his body stiffened, and Seven took his arm to make sure he did not fall.

"Sergeant, you're going to come with me, and I'm going to let you have a seat in the room. All right?" The man's only response was a nod, and Seven escorted his charge into the first of the two hospital patient rooms that were his target. Already inside the room and waiting for him beneath the open window was Isis, his cat. Her black hair made her almost invisible in the dark room, which was illuminated only by light from the moon filtering through the thin curtains hanging before the windows. Upon seeing Seven, Isis emitted a soft meow, perking her head up.

"Yes, I'm sorry I kept you waiting," Seven offered. "Some of us still have to sneak into places the old-fashioned way." He directed the guard to the chair situated in the room's far corner. "Have a seat, Sergeant. You look tired. Take a nap." Isis reacted to that, and he realized it was the second time that day he had issued such directions. Earlier, it had been the security police sergeant near the mission control area of the base. That minor event, and everything else that had filled his first day here on Earth, already seemed like distant memories.

Saving the world certainly makes for a busy day, Supervisor 194.

The level of difficulty he had encountered had been unexpected, to say the least. First, there had been that business of his transporter beam being intercepted by the Earth ship from the future, interrupting his transit to and from the Aegis homeworld. It had been a minor yet costly delay, in that by the time he had escaped the *Enterprise,* it only was to find out that Agents 201 and 347 had been killed in an automobile accident in Florida. He had been aware of their mission to sabotage the rocket launch at McKinley Base and prevent the orbiting of a nuclear weapons platform by the United States. His knowledge of that operation had allowed him to step in and complete their mission in their stead, despite additional complications introduced by James Kirk, the captain of the ship from the future, and his crew.

What Seven's own superiors had kept from him was the agents' other mission of tracking and attempting to capture alien operatives living and working in secret on Earth for more than twenty years. Only after a review of the secret, protected records stored within the Beta 5's memory banks had that aspect of 201 and 347's work become clear. Indeed, tracking the movements of the Certoss had been a task handed down from the agents' predecessors, dating back to the 1950s. Not for the first time, Gary Seven pondered the wisdom of his benefactors and their penchant for withholding what others might consider key information. The deaths of Agents 201 and 347, at first perplexing to Seven, now at least made sense. They had been killed while in pursuit of one of the Certoss agents, who also had died during the incident, thanks to the bravery of the man now occupying the hospital bed before him.

"So, this is our hero of the day," Seven mused, eliciting a loud purr from Isis. James Wainwright lay in deep sleep—assisted by a combination of pharmaceuticals prescribed by his doctor—recovering from the injuries he had suffered the previous day. A review of other Beta 5 records told Seven that Wainwright, along with his partner in the adjoining hospital room, Allison Marshall, also had been tracking the movements of the Certoss for more than a decade as part of their involvement with the Air Force's ongoing investigations into extraterrestrial activity. As a consequence, they had experienced their own encounters with the mysterious aliens from the future. Their efforts had taken them to McKinley Rocket Base where, for reasons Seven did not yet understand, fate had seen fit to have them cross paths with Agents 201 and 347.

"Let's get this over with," Seven said, "and leave Mister Wainwright to his recuperation." Opening the room's small closet revealed to Seven what remained of Wainwright's clothing and personal effects. The suit he had been wearing was gone, of course, having been cut from his body when he was brought here for treatment. Among the items he had carried—wallet, keys, identification—was a pair of what looked to be identical silver fountain pens; the servos belonging to Agents 201 and 347.

"There we are," Seven said, retrieving the devices and inspecting them for damage. Both units appeared functional, and he deactivated the homing signals that had allowed him to track them. Seven could only surmise that his subordinate agents had entrusted the servos to Wainwright in order to avoid having them confiscated by local authorities, but that would indicate either 201 or 347 had given the devices to him prior to the accident that had taken their lives. It did not make sense, but Seven was at a loss to offer any reasonable alternative theories.

As for any other secrets the Aegis agents might reveal even in death, Seven already had dealt with that possibility. Infiltrating the morgue at the medical examiner's office on the base had allowed him access to their bodies. Their Earth identities would withstand any background checks and other attempts at information retrieval by base authorities and other law enforcement agencies, and Seven already had put into motion the necessary arrangements to have their bodies returned via normal channels to New York, where he would see to it that they were returned to the Aegis homeworld for proper interment. A check of their clothing and personal effects verified that neither agent had been carrying other items or equipment that might arouse suspicion.

When Isis meowed again, Seven held up the servos and eyed the cat with a raised eyebrow. "I know, but I don't have time to look over all the information they recorded." From his jacket pocket he retrieved a small scanner device, into which he inserted one of the servos. The scanner's display activated, telling Seven that the servo had belonged to Agent 201, and a quick review of the data stored within its compact memory cell told him that both agents had kept notes about their mission with respect to sabotaging the rocket launch as well as their pursuit of the Certoss. There also were references to Wainwright, Marshall, and Project Blue Book. It appeared that some form of cooperative action had taken place, though Seven did not yet know what information Wainwright and Marshall possessed about the Aegis agents' true identities and purpose here on Earth. Seven made a mental note to cross-check that information with the Beta 5 upon his return to New York. For now, though, he had everything he needed.

Isis offered another quizzical meow as Seven deactivated the scanner and returned it along with the two servos to his jacket pocket. "Yes, of course I remembered to bring it," he said, retrieving from another pocket another device. It was the same approximate size as his scanner, and while its function also was similar, this unit was not designed for accessing data recorded on physical storage mediums. Extracting a small probe from the side of the neuroscanner, he affixed it to Wainwright's right temple. Wanting a better view of the proceedings, Isis leapt onto the bed and rested herself atop the sleeping man's chest, after which she released a contented purr.

"You should stay there," Seven said as he adjusted the neuroscanner. "It'd be very therapeutic for him, you know." Isis's reply was to lick her left paw and wipe it across the back of her ear.

It took only moments for the neuroscanner to perform

its work, manipulating Wainwright's memories of Agents 201 and 347 to remove any possible references to their true identities. So far as he would recall—Marshall, too, once Seven performed this procedure on her—the agents were members of some other clandestine government organization. This might prove useful, should Seven or some other Aegis agent ever have some future need to make contact with either officer.

"That should do it, I think," Seven said after the neuroscanner emitted a beep indicating it had finished its work. Pocketing the device, he collected Isis from Wainwright's chest, then rested his hand on the sleeping man's arm. "Thank you for your service, Mister Wainwright. Others may not ever appreciate your sacrifices, but we will."

With Isis purring in approval, he reached up to stroke the cat's neck. "All right, Isis. Let's see to Miss Marshall." Once they were finished here, Seven knew that he and his new associate, Roberta Lincoln, still had one more meeting with James Kirk before the captain took his starship back to the future from whence they had traveled. Despite Seven's initial misgivings about possible interference by Kirk and the *Enterprise* as he attempted to accomplish his mission, it seemed history had intended for the captain and his crew to play some minor role in the previous day's events. That said, Seven would be relieved to see the ship return to its own time, if only to minimize the risk of accidental tampering with Earth history. Indeed, there was something about this entire affair that felt unresolved. What that might be, Seven could not identify. Perhaps his uncertainty stemmed from the odd elements—the Certoss, the *Enterprise,* and Wainwright and Marshall being chief among them—that had all converged at this point in time.

Perhaps.

Only time, Gary Seven suspected, would tell.

THIRTY-ONE

New York City
April 3, 1968

Despite the early hour, Gejalik took her time ensuring that the apartment was free of occupants. From what she had been able to determine, the suite of rooms was leased for use as a business office for some form of data collection effort. Learning anything more would require accessing the apartment itself, which Gejalik had refrained from doing until she learned the routines of the people who worked here. To that end, she spent the past week watching it, noting the arrivals and departures of the three people who came here each workday. Thanks to that surveillance, she felt comfortable making her infiltration well before any of the office's employees arrived.

With her harness giving her the outward appearance of a human female dressed in conservative business attire, Gejalik entered the office building and, along with several other people, rode the elevator from its ground floor. Thankfully, she was the only one to get off on the twelfth floor, allowing her the freedom to work at gaining entry to Apartment 12B. It was an easy task to defeat the door's simple lock, and within seconds she was inside the suite's front room, which resembled the reception area of any other business office with a desk, chairs, and couch, along with file cabinets and a typewriter on its own stand. With her portable scanner, Gejalik inspected the room's two other doors, finding a closet and the entry to another, larger office. As with the reception area, this part of the suite also appeared normal.

But appearances are deceiving, are they not?

Though the office furnishings, ornate as they were, held no interest for her, Gejalik turned her attention to the set of shelves along the rear wall, which held a selection of glassware. The scanner indicated an energy source coming from behind that wall that was inconsistent with current human technology. Data and power connections also ran behind the wall the length of the office to a large bookcase set into the wall near the door. A brief scan of that area was enough to tell Gejalik that the bookcase acted as a panel to conceal something behind it. She adjusted the scanner and the unit emitted a series of melodic tones. In response, the bookcase swung outward, revealing not a doorway or tunnel but instead what could only be an advanced computer interface. As the workstation slid into place, its large black panel began flashing a series of multicolored lights Gejalik could not decipher, and a circular display screen activated.

"*Computer on,*" intoned a stilted, feminine voice. "*Unidentified intruder. Unauthorized access.*" The entire workstation deactivated itself, but Gejalik was ready for that and pressed another control on her scanner, after which the black panel resumed its activity. "*Standing by,*" it said.

"Remarkable," Gejalik said, nodding in appreciation at the level of obvious effort Jaecz had devoted to his study of this equipment. According to what he had told her and Adlar, he had stumbled upon the advanced computer's presence almost by accident several years earlier, while conducting scans with the equipment he had constructed at his base of operations in Trenton, New Jersey. After determining its location in New York, Jaecz spent considerable time studying the computer and its operating software via his own scanning equipment, looking for a way to breach its security protocols without alerting its owners to his activities. The process was slow, taking years, during which he almost had revealed himself to the mysterious humans overseeing the computer. The humans also possessed matter teleportation and scanning technology, setting them far apart from the rest of Earth's inhabitants.

Careful probing actions of the computer's vast information library had given Jaecz little insight into the identities of its users. His original intention had been for the three of them to infiltrate the office and access the device in order to gain more information, but Jaecz's timetable had been disrupted by the acceleration of the nuclear weapons platform development and testing at the rocket base in Florida. Then, his own scanning equipment had detected the spacecraft in orbit above Earth five days earlier, as well as this computer's own scans of the vessel, and Jaecz realized an opportunity to escape this planet might well have presented itself.

Jaecz, however, was dead. At least, that's what Gejalik now believed. In a rare breaking of security protocol, Adlar had contacted her via phone from Florida the evening after the launch from the McKinley base and the subsequent explosion of the rocket in low Earth orbit. Using coded phrases they all had devised over the years, Adlar informed her of Jaecz's discovery by the human agents, the ensuing chase, and the resulting confrontation that presumably had resulted in all their deaths. At the very least, Jaecz now was in the custody of the American military. The mysterious space vessel had disappeared from orbit, and Adlar had instructed

Gejalik to travel from Trenton to New York and see what she might learn about the incident from the human agents' own records.

Gejalik adjusted the scanner once more as Jaecz had instructed her during their training sessions, after which the unit emitted another series of tones that elicited another sequence of flashing lights from the computer's flat black panel. "*Computer,*" she said, addressing the workstation, though unsure about how to proceed, "*identify yourself.*"

"*I am a Beta 5 computer,*" replied the mechanism in the same formal, feminine tones. "*I am an advanced artificial intelligence capable of examining information and rendering independent analytical decisions. My purpose is to assist agents assigned to this planet in the accomplishment of their mission.*"

"And what mission is that?"

"*Earth technology and science have developed at a rate exceeding current political and social advancement. Agents assigned to this planet are to secretly observe progress of human civilization and take appropriate clandestine action to prevent premature annihilation.*"

It was an interesting notion, Gejalik conceded, one at total odds with her reasons for being on Earth. *Was it possible that the work of these agents might one day lead to a human civilization that did not view her people as a threat?* Her superiors had never discussed activities of this type taking place in this time period. Was it a secret to them, as well, or had such agents simply not been present in whatever timeline had brought about Earth's aggression against Certoss Ajahlan? Gejalik's mind swam with the possibilities.

Deactivating her shroud harness so that her human façade vanished and left her with her natural form, she said,

"Computer, are you able to scan me and make a physiological determination?"

"*Scans indicate you are a humanoid; not native to this planet. Notations in my record banks support preliminary findings that you are a member of the Certoss race.*"

Gejalik nodded even though there was no one to see her gesture. "Do your records have any other information regarding other members of my species?"

There was a pause as the Beta 5 processed the query, then it said, "*There are notations in files recorded by Agents 6, 201, and 347 regarding humanoids matching your physiology. Notations supported by numerous classified United States government agency reports.*"

"Are any members of my species in the custody of the United States government?"

"*Affirmative. One specimen collected in Yuma, Arizona, in 1952. No other specimens are indicated.*"

So, either the American military did not have Jaecz in their custody, or else that information had not yet been entered into any file or record to which this computer might have access. Deciding to change her line of inquiry, Gejalik asked, "What can you tell me about the spacecraft that was in orbit five days ago?"

"U.S.S. Enterprise," the computer replied. "*Traveled back in time from the year 2268 to observe activities on present-day Earth.*"

Three hundred years in the future? Not so far as from where she had come, but Gejalik still was impressed. There had been no discussions with her superiors of humans sending ships or teams through time to Earth's own past for study. "Has the ship returned to its own time?"

"*Affirmative.*"

Frowning, Gejalik asked, "How do you know this?"

"*I am able to lock onto their present location in space and time, in accordance with instructions provided by Supervisor 194.*"

Lacking the necessary technical skills, Gejalik had no idea how such a feat might be possible. She also was uncertain as to the identity of the "supervisor" mentioned by the computer, but she assumed it was the older human male she had seen entering and exiting the apartment during her reconnaissance. "So, you're able to link to the ship?"

"*Affirmative.*"

"What about other locations and periods in time?"

"*Yes, but new coordinates can only be entered with direct supervisor authorization and security protocols.*"

Gejalik hissed in frustration. To be so close to home and have it remain just out of her reach? Though she and her companions had long ago consigned themselves to the probability of never returning to their own world, the discovery of these mysterious humans and their incongruous technology had—she was forced to admit—given her new hope. With time, Jaecz might well have devised a way to override the computer's security procedures, but she did not possess his technical expertise.

"What about communications?" she asked, more to herself than the computer. Jaecz's scanner had given her access to the computer's communications system, so perhaps she could send a message, if not to the Certoss Ajahlan of her own time, then whoever might be listening. It took her several moments to compose what she thought might be a message that would not be dismissed out of hand by whomever received it. She did not even know if receiving a return message was possible. With limited time at her disposal before the office's true occupants returned, Gejalik knew she would have to work fast.

"*Message transmitted*," the Beta 5 reported a moment later. From behind her, Gejalik heard a low mechanical hum. She turned to see the glassware shelves parting to reveal what at first appeared to be a large bank vault. The wheel at the vault door's center spun of its own accord before the door itself swung open to reveal the interior chamber, from which emitted an odd high-pitched whine. A check of the scanner revealed that the vault in actuality was the matter transmission device about which Jaecz had informed her.

"This is amazing," she said, at first not realizing that she was talking aloud, and therefore was surprised when she received a reply, but not from the computer.

"Indeed, it is."

Mestral had but a moment to study the advanced computer interface that was the office's most interesting feature, aside from the Certoss herself, who now regarded him with an expression of shock. She stood still, hands away from her body as she caught sight of the particle beam weapon in his hand.

"Gejalik, I presume?" Though he never had met her, the memories from his mind meld with Jaecz provided him with the identities of the Certoss agent's companions, and Gejalik was the only surviving female member of their group.

It had taken some time to locate her, working from the incomplete information given to him, James Wainwright, and Allison Marshall from the reporter, Cal Sutherland, about possible alien activity at NASA facilities in Florida and Texas. Mestral spent months studying the activities, comings, and goings of hundreds of employees matching vague descriptions offered by Sutherland's contact, before he determined the identities of the disguised Certoss. Still more patience and time was required before one of the agents, Gejalik, led him to the loft building in Trenton, New Jersey, where he had found the eclectic assemblage of cannibalized and repurposed equipment. Mestral had been impressed with the setup, and acquainting himself with its functions had been a challenge. In contrast, following Gejalik here to New York had been a simple task.

Her brow furrowing, she said, "You are the Vulcan, Mestral. Jaecz told us about you; the observer, content to watch humanity and their fitful progression from primitive society to interstellar tyrants. You're working with the humans, trying to stop us."

Mestral nodded. "Yes. Your actions cannot go unchallenged. I am aware of the 'temporal war' in which your people fought, and how you believe that your mission is a just one, protecting your planet from potential future harm, but such action no longer is required. That conflict does not exist in this timeline. In the future to come, this planet and yours will be allies."

"How can you know that?" Gejalik asked, making no effort to mask her skepticism. "Are you from this future?"

"No," Mestral conceded, "but Vulcan was a party to the war in the timeline from which you came. That is not the case in the reality we inhabit. My people are peaceful explorers, studying emerging cultures like this one. If you are allowed to carry out your mission, Gejalik, you will not be acting in defense of your people, but instead be committing global genocide."

"I'm supposed to just trust you, Vulcan?" For the first time, the Certoss moved, lowering her hands a small degree.

Mestral raised the particle beam weapon and she again stopped.

"I have no desire to harm you or your companions, but I cannot allow you to proceed. You already have lost two of your friends, and your attempt to trigger a nuclear war has failed. No such further attempts will be permitted. You must know that."

Gejalik scowled. "I know only that I have my mission."

She was fast. Moving before Mestral even could register what was happening, she vaulted over one of the office's stuffed chairs and dropped to one knee behind it. Mestral saw her hand reaching for something at her waist and he fired his weapon. The particle beam whipped past the chair, but Gejalik already was moving again, jumping over the chair toward him. Trying to adjust his aim, he saw the flash of light reflecting off something metallic in her hand.

He raised his free arm in time to block the knife's downward thrust, but Gejalik swept her other arm to knock the particle weapon from his hand. Mestral heard it fall to the carpet behind him but he ignored it, concentrating instead on the immediate threat. The knife pulled back before again coming at him and he dodged, lashing out with his left foot and catching Gejalik in her stomach. She grunted, stumbling to one side and giving him an attack opening. Lunging forward, he ducked beneath her knife and swung with the edge of his left hand, trying to dislodge the weapon from her grip. Gejalik anticipated the move and retreated, scrambling backward to give herself room. Her eyes fell on the particle beam weapon and she snatched it from the carpet. Before she could turn the weapon on him, Mestral sprinted across the carpet to close the distance, crashing into her and carrying them both into the vault.

"Wait!" Gejalik cried as they both fell to the floor, but by then it was too late. Mestral felt an odd tingling sensation playing across his exposed skin as a blue-black mist settled around them. They both scrambled to their feet and Mestral turned to look where the vault's entry should be, but saw nothing. The fog obscured everything.

What was happening?

THIRTY-TWO

Wright-Patterson Air Force Base, Dayton, Ohio
April 22, 1968

Welcome back. —JC

The short missive was lying at the center of his desk. It was written on a small note card bearing no header or other identifying mark, but James Wainwright recognized Professor Jeffrey Carlson's impeccable handwriting. While others might think the greeting lacked flair, Wainwright knew better, and he smiled at his friend's simple yet thoughtful gesture.

"What's it take for a girl to get some flowers sent her way?" asked Allison Marshall from where she stood behind her own desk. Her left arm was supported by a sling in order to keep from aggravating her wounded shoulder, but she showed no other signs of the injury she had sustained. In her free hand was a card similar to the one Wainwright held, and she gestured toward his note. "You, too?"

Wainwright nodded, realizing that he had been resting his free hand on his stomach, his fingers tracing the scar beneath his shirt that ran across his abdomen. It still itched, though he tried to ignore it. "He probably took heat from somebody up top just for offering this much." Given the current climate surrounding Majestic 12 and Project Blue Book, Carlson might be damaging his own standing within both organizations by choosing not to distance himself from Wainwright and, to a lesser extent, Marshall. Since the McKinley incident and throughout his recovery these past few weeks, Wainwright was able to discern the shift in thinking with respect to his and Marshall's status within the project. It manifested in various ways, from the pointed lack of official visitors while they both convalesced at the base hospital to the lack of response as—from his apartment while on restricted duty as part of his recuperation—he attempted to catch up on the backlog of paperwork waiting for him at his office. Now that he and Marshall had returned to their official duties, or whatever remained of them, it was obvious to see that other "adjustments" were being made. Several of the filing cabinets that once had dominated their office's rear wall were gone, as were many of the files and other boxes of documents that had filled floor and shelf space around the room. Change was in the air, Wainwright knew. What remained to be seen was its scope, and its ultimate impact on him and Marshall.

"Do they have UFO sightings in Alaska?" Marshall asked. "Something tells me we've got a good chance of finding out."

Chuckling at her gallows humor despite his darkening mood, Wainwright replied, "I don't think you have too much to worry about. You weren't involved in the worst of it. They'll probably go easy on you, but me?" He frowned, shaking his head. "Maybe I should buy a parka."

"You shouldn't beat yourself up so much," Marshall said. "It's not healthy, Mister Wainwright." She stepped around her desk and he mirrored her movements so that they met in the center of the office. He began reaching with his right hand but stopped himself when he realized he was about to touch her injured shoulder and changed hands. "Everything will work out. You'll see." She raised her free hand to touch the side of his face. "Besides, we've still got each other, right?"

Wainwright grinned, reaching up to squeeze her hand. "Maybe we should retire, find someplace warm and sunny, with lots of beach to walk on, and lots of drinks with rum and little umbrellas in them. Forget all about this, and go enjoy life for a change."

Her eyes brightening along with her smile, Marshall cast a glance toward the window, which revealed the start of another gray day. "I'm liking the sound of that."

A knock on the door interrupted their quiet moment, and they released each other's hands before Wainwright called out, "Come in." The door opened to admit Jeffrey Carlson, the professor carrying a well-worn brown leather briefcase. Now close to sixty years of age, he appeared older still, his thin hair and full beard having gone from gray to white. There were heavy bags under his eyes, and he wore a pair of narrow-lens glasses perched on his nose. He was thinner than the last time Wainwright had seen him, though he moved with a confidence and strength that belied his appearance. Wainwright was not even aware that the elder man was in Ohio, figuring him to be ensconced within the confines of the super-secret Air Force base in the middle of the Nevada desert where he had been consumed with all manner of classified shenanigans.

"Jim, my old friend! Welcome back," Carlson said, entering the office and extending his hand. As they shook, the older man gestured toward Wainwright's stomach. "I trust you're healing rather nicely?" Turning, he embraced Marshall while minding her injured shoulder. "Allison, the years are powerless against your beauty. You're as radiant as ever." Stepping back, he offered them both a warm smile. "It's so good to see you."

"I'm pretty sure you're the only one who feels that way," Wainwright countered.

Carlson offered a derisive snort as he set his briefcase atop Marshall's desk. "Not at all." He waved in a dismissive gesture. "Oh, don't get me wrong; there are quite a few people who are none too happy with what transpired down in Florida." Lowering his voice, the professor added, "But there are those of us who know at least some of the truth regarding your activities, and are therefore among your group of loyal supporters."

Marshall smiled. "Of course. Figures they'd bring you back for that."

"Regardless of what you may think, my friends, your accomplishments have not gone unnoticed." Carlson shrugged. "On the other hand, they do raise as many questions as answers, such as how you were able to track the Certoss agents' movements to the McKinley base and other locations."

Clearing his throat, Wainwright said, "You can thank Mestral for that." After discussing it, he and Marshall had elected to keep to themselves the assistance provided by the two mysterious men, the human and his Vulcan companion who had referred to themselves by their code designations, Agents 937 and 176.

"We're still the only three who know about Mestral, right?" Marshall asked.

Carlson nodded. "So far as I know. Have you heard from him?"

"No," Wainwright replied. "The last time we were together, he was on his way to New York. He thought he'd figured out where the Certoss might've had a base of operations, either there or maybe New Jersey."

"He was going to contact us when he had something

concrete," Marshall added, "but that was before we left for McKinley."

Moving to one of the chairs positioned before Marshall's desk, Carlson took a seat. "So, he's presumably still out there, somewhere, along with two more Certoss aliens who've become experts at keeping a low profile after living among us for almost twenty-five years. For all we know, their life spans are such that they could go another twenty-five years, and simply outlive us."

"Speak for yourself," Marshall retorted, before reaching out and patting the older man's shoulder.

"Where does that leave us?" Wainwright asked.

Carlson settled into the chair. "That's a very good question, my friend. The short-term answer is that very little will happen. For the time being, Project Blue Book's profile is to be curtailed; drastically, in some respects."

Feeling his heart sink, Wainwright scowled. "They're shutting us down?"

Marshall leaned against her desk. "But, we've more than proven that other alien species are out there, studying us, and a few of them don't seem to like us all that much. What about those?"

"As always, my dear, MJ-12 will continue to take the lead in those matters, but this business of investigating every civilian UFO sighting or report of 'alien abduction' has done more to harm our efforts than anything else. It's the debunked reports that give pause to those in Congress who control our funding, and they have other priorities, to say nothing of little time or patience for unrealized threats when there are plenty of real ones plaguing our world right now."

"For years, we've straddled the fence between Majestic 12 and Blue Book," Wainwright said, eyeing Carlson. "So, what about now? Are you finally pulling us over to your side of the fence?"

The professor smiled. "That's certainly my intention, but these things do take time. In the interim, you and Allison will be attending to various close-down activities for Blue Book. Once that's completed, and if I get my way, you'll be working directly for me. No more of this liaison nonsense. You've been watching from the sidelines and staring through the windows for far too long, and I need people I can trust." Reaching for his briefcase, he laid it across his lap before opening it. "And on that subject, I have something I'd like you to see." From the case, he removed a manila file folder, which he handed to Wainwright, whose eyes narrowed as he read the label adorning its front: "TOP SECRET/MAJIC EYES ONLY." He had seen such warnings only on rare occasions over the years, and always as a consequence of Carlson sharing with him information Wainwright likely was not supposed to see.

"Uh-oh," he said. "Won't we get in trouble for looking at this?"

"You mean, more trouble than you're in now?" Carlson asked.

Wainwright considered that response. "Whatever you say." With Marshall standing next to him, he opened the folder, which contained but a single photograph of what could only be a spaceship. A large saucer was the craft's dominating feature, along with a single, blunt cylindrical projection beneath the saucer, and two thinner, longer protuberances sweeping back from it. "Oh, my God," he whispered, showing the picture to Marshall as he looked to Carlson. "Is this real?"

"It was taken by a military reconnaissance satellite," Carlson said. "The object, which remains unidentified, was photographed in orbit on the morning of March 29, 1968. It disappeared later that day without a trace. One minute it was there, and the next? Nothing. We've never seen anything like it, and nothing matching its description has ever been reported in any UFO sighting."

Her tone one of worry, Marshall asked, "Any ideas on whose it might be?"

Carlson sighed. "None. Could be the Ferengi, or it could be the Certoss. On the other hand, it could be someone else entirely." He reached up to tap the photo. "Estimates are that thing is a thousand feet long, so whoever it belongs to? They seem to mean business."

The craft was huge; that much was obvious from the picture. Though the quality of the image was far from perfect, it still was clear enough for Wainwright to get an idea of its construction, which was unlike anything he had encountered in the twenty years he had been with this project. No obvious cannons or missile tubes were visible, so what sort of weapons might it carry? Did it even have weapons at all? "This thing is incredible."

"That's an understatement if I've ever heard one," Marshall said.

"Amen to that," added Carlson. "As you can see, when it comes to preparing for possible alien invasion? We still have quite a bit of work to do."

Turning to Marshall, Wainwright sighed and offered a knowing smile. "That we do." She returned his gaze, nodding in agreement.

The beach, they knew, still would be there.

THIRTY-THREE

U.S.S. Enterprise
Earth Year 2268

Kirk barked into his communicator, "Spock! Tractor beam! Keep that ship where it is!"

His voice filtered through the unit's speaker grille, the first officer replied, "*Tractor beam activated. We are holding the Tandaran vessel at maximum range, but it is attempting to overpower the beam's effects.*"

"Contact them and tell them we'll open fire if they don't stand down." Even taking into account the Tandarans' evident concerns and Colonel Abrenn's apparent paranoia, this entire situation had gone well past bizarre and into the realm of the utterly ridiculous. Studying the stunned Abrenn, who remained unconscious where Giotto had placed him on the hangar deck, Kirk shook his head in disbelief. "I'll give him this: He's committed."

"Should *be* committed, if you ask me." Giotto was completing the process of removing from Abrenn his weapons, helmet, and other equipment, and handing those items to one of his people. Ensign Minecci and other members of the security staff already had performed the same actions on the other five Tandarans in the colonel's boarding party, who now were being escorted under guard to the *Enterprise* brig.

"*Captain,*" said Spock over Kirk's communicator, "*the Tandaran ship's engines are beginning to overheat.*"

"Stand by, Spock," replied the captain, closing his communicator as he saw Doctor McCoy stepping around Minecci, his medical kit in his hand.

"Is he all right?" asked the doctor, gesturing toward Abrenn.

Kirk nodded. "Just stunned. Can you revive him?"

"Yeah. Give me a minute." Kneeling next to his new patient, McCoy removed a hypospray from his kit and eyed its contents for a moment before applying the injector to the side of Abrenn's neck. The hissing sound of the drug being administered was followed a moment later by the Tandaran's eyes fluttering open.

"Colonel," Kirk said, trying to get a fast handle on the situation. "It's all right. You have my word you won't be harmed." Having returned his phaser to his waist, he held out both hands to show he carried only his communicator.

Clearing his throat before attempting to push himself to a sitting position, Abrenn said, "All evidence to the contrary, of course."

"You're talking, aren't you?" McCoy asked, having stepped back from the Tandaran. "You're welcome, by the way."

Abrenn ignored the physician's verbal jab, eyeing Giotto who once again stood with phaser in hand, covering the colonel as he rose to his feet.

"*Bridge to Captain Kirk,*" echoed Spock's voice from the hangar bay. "*The Tandaran vessel's engines have failed. Our sensors are detecting complete primary power loss. Life-support systems are functional, but on reserve power only.*"

Watching Abrenn while listening to his first officer's report, Kirk saw the slight shift in the Tandaran's expression—disappointment or defeat—before he was able to school his features. "It's over, Colonel. This needs to stop."

"You seem to be in control, Captain," Abrenn replied. "What will you do now?"

Instead of answering him, Kirk opened his communicator. "Kirk to bridge. Spock, contact the Tandaran ship and tell them we're standing by to help with repairs. If they have any wounded, they can be treated here on the *Enterprise*. Notify Mister Scott to have a damage repair team ready to beam over."

"*Acknowledged.*"

To Abrenn, Kirk said, "What about it, Colonel? Can I safely send my people over to help your ship and crew, or will the fighting continue over there?"

Sighing, the Tandaran replied, "It does not matter, Captain. I may not have succeeded in my mission, but that does not mean the mission is over. My superiors will simply send someone else, either to your Federation or to Certoss Ajahlan or both. So long as we believe a threat exists to our people, we will not stop."

"I will go with you."

Kirk looked over his shoulder at the sound of the new voice to see Gejalik, accompanied by Minister Ocherab, Roberta Lincoln, and Mestral, standing at the entrance to the *Balatir*.

Turning to face her, Abrenn said, "I beg your pardon?"

"I said I will go with you," Gejalik repeated, stepping down the ramp leading from the *Balatir*'s entry hatch and walking across the hangar deck. Ocherab walked alongside her, with Lincoln and Mestral staying behind them. "I am the one you want. I represent the threat that concerns you. Minister Ocherab and her crew, as well as the rest of my planet, have nothing to do with any of this. Leave them in peace, and I will go with you. I will answer whatever questions you have to the best of my ability."

Moving to stand beside her, Mestral said, "And with your permission, I will accompany her."

Abrenn frowned. "Why would you do that?"

"I will be able to corroborate some elements of what she will tell you," the Vulcan replied. "I was in contact with one of her companions during our joint time on Earth, and I mind-melded with him. Therefore, I know everything he did about their mission, at least up to that point in time."

Looking to Lincoln, Kirk asked, "What's your take on this?"

The young woman shrugged. "This was all her idea."

"Well, I don't like it," McCoy said. When Abrenn turned to regard him, the doctor added, "What's to say they don't just throw her in a prison cell once they've got their hands on her? Or worse?"

"You know nothing about my people, Doctor," Abrenn said.

McCoy grunted, unimpressed. "Then you need to work on your first impressions."

"Enough," Kirk snapped before turning to Gejalik. "You don't have to do this."

Releasing a small sigh, the Certoss replied, "I believe I do, Captain. Almost everything I did during the time I lived on your world was in defense of mine. At least, that is what I believed. It is obvious that whatever alterations have occurred to the time stream, the mission I was given is no longer relevant, and I am all that remains of a world that no longer exists. However, if going with Colonel Abrenn can allay any fears he feels I represent to his world, then I am still acting to protect the Certoss people. I am still fulfilling my duty." She paused, glancing to Minister Ocherab, who smiled and nodded. "Please allow me that privilege."

Ocherab said, "Gejalik's courage inspires us all. It would be my privilege to escort her wherever the colonel wishes her to go."

Nodding, Abrenn drew himself to his full height, and when he spoke, his voice was more subdued. "I believe that will be satisfactory." He turned to Kirk. "Captain, I accept your offer of assistance with repairing my ship. If you will allow me to contact my second-in-command, I will see to it that you are extended every cooperation."

"My people will help you any way they can," Kirk replied. "As for this situation, what about a compromise? Everything can be done here aboard the *Enterprise*. I'm willing to act as an intermediary. We all can work through this problem together."

Abrenn eyed him with wariness. "You would do that, after all that has transpired?"

"Yes," Kirk said. "As for your actions against my ship, they'll certainly raise some eyebrows back at Starfleet Command, but if you agree to what I've proposed, I'd offer mitigating testimony on your behalf."

Casting his eyes toward the hangar deck, Abrenn for the first time seemed uncertain. "I do not know what to say."

"Say yes," McCoy offered.

After a moment, the Tandaran nodded. "Very well. I agree to your terms, Captain."

"Excellent," Kirk said, smiling.

After issuing orders to Spock for the repair teams to continue with their preparations to beam over to the Tandaran vessel, to McCoy to prepare for any medical situations that might need his attention, and for Commander Giotto to escort Abrenn to guest quarters—under guard, for the moment—Kirk turned his attention to Gejalik. "That was a very brave thing you volunteered to do."

"I appreciate your support, Captain," replied the Certoss.

Minister Ocherab added, "As do I."

"Well, we're not done yet, but I think we're off to a good start." Kirk looked to Lincoln. "Miss Lincoln, I can't thank you enough for your help. You provided a rather *unique* perspective on this issue."

Sticking out her lower lip, Lincoln blew out her breath so that it lifted her blond bangs from her forehead. "It was looking crazy there for a while, but you pulled it off."

"We couldn't have done it without you," Kirk said. It would take him a week to write up a report detailing the day's events, and at this point he had no idea what he might say.

"What will happen now?" Mestral asked.

Kirk shrugged. "I have no idea." To Lincoln, he asked, "Any thoughts on that?"

"Believe it or not," she replied, "there are still some loose ends that need tying up. Back in my own time, I mean."

Trying to envision the effort necessary to track an alien working in secret, and hiding anywhere on Earth, boggled Kirk's mind. "I don't know how you do something like that."

Lincoln smirked. "Well, I was hoping you might do me a small favor. Or, three."

FULL CIRCLE

THIRTY-FOUR

New York City
July 10, 1969

The bath would be luxurious, Roberta Lincoln decided as she watched the tub fill. After a long day spent entrenched in the latest modules of study mandated for her by Gary Seven as part of her ongoing apprenticeship, her mind had all but turned to mush. Her back and shoulders ached from hours of sitting at her desk, and her thoughts were awash in the ceaseless stream of facts and figures presented to her in unrelenting, rapid-fire fashion by the Beta 5, the advanced computer system that was the major technological ally to Seven and Roberta as they carried out their work.

As was often the case at the end of days spent in this fashion, she felt it all to be a bit overwhelming for a girl who barely had finished high school. Though she at first had protested the extended coursework Seven had assigned to her, she knew that it was but one part of the rigorous, comprehensive training her mysterious employer felt was necessary if she were to function in able fashion as his partner. And all of this was in addition to the other work she was expected to complete, such as reviewing news broadcasts, intelligence briefings, and other material that was part and parcel of her job.

My job, she mused. *Yeah. Just another day at the office.*

Sitting in her bathrobe on the edge of the tub, Roberta once again chuckled at her own feeble attempts to think of what she did here as just some other vocation; an assignment to be carried out while occupying space in a cramped cubicle in some nondescript office building, proceeding through a set list of tasks while perusing spreadsheets or interoffice memos. After all, saving the world on a more or less regular basis from humanity's own shortsightedness—to say nothing of the occasional alien interloper—was not something that easily boiled down to a handful of sentences on a résumé. Not for the first time, Roberta pondered what her lot in life might have been if she had continued on in her role as the bright-eyed, naïve secretary she had been just a year ago, working for what she believed to be a pair of encyclopedia research consultants?

The road not taken, and all that.

One thing Roberta did not miss was her cramped apartment in the Village. As part of her "employment" with him, Seven had seen to it that she was provided living space here in the same building as their offices; an adjoining apartment with easy, inconspicuous access to the workspace. Her first night here had been an eye-opening experience upon realizing just how damned quiet it was in the soundproof suite twelve stories above the bustling New York street life. With an expansive library in which to immerse herself—and that was before accessing the vast storehouse of information comprising the Beta 5 computer's rather comprehensive database—and with her tea and her rather large bathtub, which was almost done filling, she had almost everything she needed to make the stresses of the day fade away.

Well, she mused, smiling at her own impish thought, *that cute delivery guy they sometimes send over might not be such a bad thing.*

As for Gary Seven—who occupied the apartment on the other side of their joint offices along with Isis, his mysterious shape-changing alien companion who spent a great deal of her time occupying the form of a black cat—presently he was off-world, having been summoned there by his own superiors for reasons he had not shared with her. After a year in his employ, Roberta still knew almost nothing about the Aegis or details of their interest in Earth and its inhabitants. Seven had explained some things to her, promising to continue providing her with more information as circumstances warranted and her training and knowledge level increased. Though she resented the implication that he viewed her as incapable of processing the full truth behind his benefactors and their motives, Roberta had come to realize that Seven in fact was acting in her best interests by keeping some things from her, and thereby minimizing any potential damage she might do—even by accident—as a consequence of the special secrets she and Seven shared.

I still wish he could've taken me along for the ride.

Despite her still being a "rookie," she had accompanied Gary Seven off-world on a couple of occasions, and what eye-opening experiences those had been. As for the work they did here on Earth, their missions had taken them all over the globe, and in recent months Seven had been letting her take the lead, asking her to develop their plans for dealing with this investigation or that intervention. She knew he was testing her, of course, judging her ability to examine a situation from all possible angles and devise the appropriate course of action, or even to determine that the best option was to take no action. A hunch teased her, telling her that Seven was preparing her for her first solo mission. She was not sure if she was ready for such responsibility, but she had learned to trust

Seven's judgment and was confident he would not send her alone on a mission until he was satisfied that she was ready.

"What's the worst that could happen?" she asked no one as she turned off the tub's faucet and stuck her hand in the water to check its temperature. "I blow up the planet?"

Well, hopefully not tonight.

From where it lay on the vanity next to her hairbrushes, Roberta's servo vibrated and emitted a short, lyrical string of electronic tones that she recognized as a communications signal sent from the Beta 5 computer.

"Really?" she asked, eyeing the servo with disdain. Casting a longing glance over her shoulder at the inviting tub, she grunted in irritation as she tightened her bathrobe before swiping the servo from the countertop and padding her way out of the bathroom. The entrance to the office suite from her apartment was concealed at the back of her walk-in closet, and she used the servo to unlock and open the hidden door. A moment later she was stepping into Gary Seven's expansive, tastefully decorated office.

"Computer on," she said, crossing the office toward the set of inlaid bookcases occupying most of the wall in front of Seven's desk. In response to her command, the entire wall swung outward, revealing the sophisticated master control console for the Beta 5 computer. The console activated as it pivoted into view, its central viewing screen flaring to life. "What's going on?"

"*There is an unscheduled activation of communications protocols,*" replied the Beta 5 in its usual haughty, high-pitched voice. "*Program is not a standard component of my software.*"

Roberta scowled at that. "What? Are you saying someone's trying to get into your systems from outside?" So far as she knew, the advanced supercomputer was supposed to be immune from any sort of remote infiltration, with the obvious exception of Gary Seven's Aegis superiors. "Could it be Gary?"

"*Negative. Program initiation occurred within my own framework. I am executing a diagnostic procedure.*" Several moments passed while the computer worked on its own, leaving Roberta to stare at the array of status monitors and other indicators. Finally, it said, "*I have located the program source. It is an encrypted software protocol in an archival directory of my secondary memory core. Program has not been accessed since its installation on June 13, 1968.*"

"Who put it there?" Roberta asked. "Seven?"

"*There is nothing to indicate this program was created or installed by Supervisor 194,*" said the Beta 5. "*Data found in my archives suggests another, possibly unauthorized source. I find no record of this protocol's installation or execution.*" It fell silent for a moment, its inner mechanisms processing as it continued to investigate this apparent breach. "*Additional data recovered from protected archives. On March 29, 1968, my sensors were used to scan a vessel in orbit above Earth. Five days later, two individuals were transported from here to that spacecraft.*"

"Five days?" Roberta frowned. "The *Enterprise* wasn't here five days later. It returned to its own time."

"*Affirmative.*"

"Are you saying someone transported from here to the *Enterprise*, three hundred years in the future? You're talking about Gary and Isis, right?"

"*Negative. Life-forms in question were a Vulcan male and a Certoss female.*"

That made Roberta's eyes widen in surprise. "Certoss? Are you sure?"

"*Affirmative. Sensor and bio-scan readings verified.*"

It had been a year—going back to that same day she and Gary Seven had encountered the *Enterprise*, as a matter of fact—since she last had heard that term. Seven had briefed her on some aspects of the trio of enigmatic Certoss aliens pursued by his predecessors and her former employers, Elizabeth Anderson and Ryan Vitali. They had been killed while pursuing one of the Certoss agents, who also had died during that incident, leaving his two companions missing.

"How did one of those . . . whatever the heck they are . . . get in here and into your systems?" Roberta asked.

"*Unknown. Unauthorized party likely possessed sufficient engineering and computer application knowledge to bypass my security protocols. All record of their activity has been purged from my security oversight files.*" As the Beta 5 spoke, Roberta sensed that the computer seemed almost embarrassed at having to explain its role in this odd situation. "*Review of data management processes shows a subspace message transmitted to the planet Certoss Ajahlan, along with subsequent attempt to delete all evidence of this activity from my protected archives. When that action failed, links from the archives to the main system were severed as part of installed software protocol. I only became aware of the discrepancy due to this program's current execution.*"

"The Certoss contacted its own planet?"

"*No two-way communication; only the single transmission.*"

Roberta shook her head. Trying to comprehend even a small portion of the Beta 5's accounting of what had taken place within its collection of circuits and relays was beginning to make her eyes glaze over. "Okay, okay! So what's this new program you found doing now?"

"*Attempting to contact the vessel that was in Earth orbit,*" replied the computer. "*The craft is no longer there, but scans confirm it was the* U.S.S. Enterprise."

"Wait, what?" Robert asked, frowning. "What the heck was the *Enterprise* doing up there just now? And where did it go?"

"*Unknown. Scanners detected transporter activity between the ship and two targets in the Midwestern United States. No other contact or communications. Transporter activity pinpointed: Offutt Air Force Base in Omaha, Nebraska, and an Air Force fighter aircraft flying over the installation.*"

This was getting weirder by the second. Why had the *Enterprise* returned from the future, a year after its last visit? Were Captain Kirk and his crew conducting another of their historical research missions and trying to see how Earth managed to avoid destroying itself for another year? If so, where had it gone? Had it devised some method of hiding even from the Beta 5's scanners? That made no sense, and why would Kirk not attempt to contact Seven? And what was with the transporter activity to the middle of Nebraska?

"What was transported?"

The Beta 5's status displays blinked and chirped for several seconds before it replied, "*Two human life-forms, one to each location. Identities unknown.*"

Closing her eyes, Roberta took a deep breath and tried to reason through what the Beta 5 was trying to tell her. "All right, let's back this up. One thing at a time. The *Enterprise* shows up in orbit for reasons unknown, beaming people all over the place, and you try to contact it because of some program you fire up from deep in your guts. The program was put there by a Certoss alien a year ago, after the *Enterprise* has gone home, but before that happened this Certoss and a . . . a Vulcan? A Vulcan beam to the future, and now they're on the

Enterprise? And after all of that, someone manages to wipe all the fingerprints off all the tampering his friend did here?"

"*Essentially correct.*"

Wondering what Seven was going to say when he found out about all of this, Roberta reached up to rub her temples as she tried to piece together more of the puzzle. "Did you pick up any transporter beam between here and the *Enterprise* just now?"

"*Negative, though I did detect a burst communications message. The message itself has been purged from my data core, but transmission log is intact. It appears to be an advisory about the* Enterprise."

Now they were on to something. "Where was the message sent?"

"*Trenton, New Jersey.*"

Her heart racing, Roberta said, "Tell me the message is similar to the one sent to Certoss Ajahlan."

"*An astute observation, Miss Lincoln. The same language was used for both messages.*"

"We all get lucky sometimes," Roberta said. Seven had been attempting to track the movements of the two remaining Certoss agents following the death of their companion last year. Despite his best efforts as well as those of the Beta 5, the trail had gone cold. "The other Certoss, the one who didn't escape to the *Enterprise* last year? Maybe he thought he could catch a ride on it or if another ship ever showed up. But, why use you for all of this?" She tapped the console, trying to reason her way through the questions. "Maybe he didn't have access to communications equipment sophisticated enough to make contact with such a ship, and our transporter would certainly make things easier. Wow, the Certoss had you set up to give them a call for a year. Seven's going to love this. We need to contact him." He needed to know everything, from this to the *Enterprise*'s inexplicable reappearance, and however it all might be connected. Roberta paused, realizing that there was one major obstacle standing in the way of her new idea. "Wait, I don't even know how to get in touch with him, but you can do that, right?"

The computer said, "*Affirmative, but I have been ordered not to do so.*"

Roberta blinked several times, sure she had misheard the computer. "What?"

"*New file released from my protected archive, per instructions provided by Supervisor 194. I am directed to assist you with the data it contains and help to prepare you for departing on your next assignment.*"

Next assignment? What the hell was this pile of scrap metal talking about? "Are you kidding me? Gary's sending me out alone? *Tonight?*"

"*Affirmative.*"

This had to be a joke, Lincoln decided. How could Seven spring something like this on her now, when he was not even on the same planet to provide backup? "What if I screw something up?"

"*Supervisor 194 has prepared contingency measures.*"

Shaking her head, Roberta rolled her eyes. "Of course he did. Where am I supposed to be going, anyway?"

Without a moment's hesitation, the Beta 5 replied, "*To the* U.S.S. Enterprise, *in the year 2268.*"

THIRTY-FIVE

Trenton, New Jersey
July 10, 1969

Adlar pounded his fist on the console, grunting in frustration. It did not matter how many times he consulted the array of instruments, rechecked their settings, or initiated scans or attempts at communication. The orbiting space vessel was gone.

"How can you be gone?" he asked no one, alone as he was within the loft. Sitting in a high-backed chair before the console his companion Jaecz had constructed to be the focal point of all the equipment gathered in this place, Adlar shook his head in disbelief. The information provided by the makeshift assemblage of components rigged together by Jaecz over the course of years indicated that the ship—identified by the scanner as being of Federation design, which meant it must have traveled here from the future—had appeared in proximity to Earth for the briefest of intervals before vanishing. The scanning equipment also had detected the vessel's brief use of matter teleportation before its abrupt departure, leaving Adlar still more unanswered questions. *What had brought the ship here, to this point in time? Had it been attempting to track him?* If so, the efforts of the vessel and its crew seemed to have been ineffective, at best, but this was not what angered Adlar. Instead, his rage was fueled by the knowledge that he had missed the opportunity to take advantage of the ship's presence in order to escape what had become an interminable sentence of exile on this planet.

More than a year had passed since Jaecz's death and Gejalik's disappearance. After escaping from McKinley Rocket Base and pursuit by the Air Force personnel and their mysterious helpers, Adlar had found his way here based on the contingency plan devised years earlier. This hideaway had been the center of Jaecz's contributions to their joint mission, in which he had used some of the equipment available to him from their original consignment of supplies as the foundation for a hybrid of Certoss and twentieth-century human technology. The loft he had secured as a workspace and hideaway was crammed to the rafters with all manner of electrical components and their associated wiring. Pieces obtained from large, bulky, and all but useless room-filling computer systems that were the pinnacle of current human information processing machines took up much of the available floor space, with one wall devoted to a bank of magnetic tape drives used for data storage and retrieval.

Despite his familiarity with most of the equipment collected here, it still had taken him weeks to acquaint himself with the functionality of the different components. Jaecz, in typical fashion, had anticipated that eventuality, and Adlar had found his detailed notes. It was due in large part to this set of comprehensive instructions that Adlar had been able to determine that Gejalik had used the scanning system just after his last contact with her. A review of the logs comprising the bulk of Jaecz's data storage library revealed that he had uncovered the existence of humans possessing technology far more advanced than anything that should be present on Earth during this time period. His scanners had pinpointed the location of this unusual equipment in New York City, and

Jaecz even had managed to develop a covert means of infiltrating the other party's computer.

Adlar was stunned to discover these humans also had at their disposal a matter teleportation system, and it was this device that Gejalik had activated and used to send herself—and another party, a Vulcan, according to the data logs—to an unknown location that somehow was linked to the arrival of a Federation starship in Earth orbit during the previous year. The vessel's presence corresponded to the unraveling of the operation Adlar and his companions had been conducting at McKinley and the destruction of the rocket bearing the secret nuclear weapons platform. The data records were unclear as to whether Gejalik had transported to that ship or some other location, and though Jaecz's own equipment was incapable of replicating this feat, Adlar had installed a program in the other, more advanced computer to monitor the other system for signs of the vessel's return. Fearful of having his own activities detected by the odd humans and their unexplained technology, Adlar had left the monitoring process to run undisturbed, trusting in its programmed response to alert him of any changes in its status. He would wait until that ship or one like it was detected, then travel to the humans' headquarters in an attempt to duplicate the steps executed by Gejalik to carry her from this place.

One such opportunity had presented itself today, with the same Federation vessel from a year ago appearing in orbit above Earth, and Adlar had not been ready.

Fool!

Grunting in exasperation as he pushed himself from the console, Adlar once more chastised himself for not being able to act on the ship's appearance. How long might he have to wait for another visit from such a vessel? What if none ever again came? He was tired, not only of the mission that he had come to see as an exercise in futility but also from being forced to live here, trapped centuries from everything and everyone about whom he cared. With Gejalik gone and Jaecz dead, he was alone, with no support system for continuing any efforts at undermining human technological advancement. They had failed here, and there was no way to know if—beyond the gulf of time separating him from home—his planet and its people remained embroiled in endless conflict or had at last found peace.

A bright yellow indicator on one of the control console's banks of monitoring gauges began flashing, accompanied by a sharp pinging tone. It took Adlar a moment to recall what the signal represented, but then he felt anxiety grip him as realization struck.

Someone was attempting to enter the loft.

"This place is incredible."

Standing in the middle of the loft, compact Type I phaser in hand, Kirk could not help being impressed as he beheld the hodgepodge collection of computer and other electronic equipment. He had been in control rooms on remote colony outposts and even a few Starfleet installations that did not boast this much hardware.

Spock, having positioned himself before the U-shaped console that seemed to be the hub of the entire affair, was scanning the setup with his tricorder. "It is a remarkable achievement, particularly given the primitive technology with which the Certoss operatives were forced to work. There are some more advanced components embedded in the larger framework, which appear to act as relay junctions and other oversight mechanisms directing the lesser mechanisms."

"Stone knives and bearskins, Spock?" Kirk asked. Despite their current situation, he was unable to resist the small joke, even if he derived no humor from the attempt. It helped to alleviate the tension he felt as he looked around the room, searching for some sign of Adlar, the remaining Certoss agent.

Spock turned from the console, his right eyebrow raised. "This situation is hardly analogous to the predicament in which you and I found ourselves when we were transported to 1930, Captain. Our arrival in that time period predated the twentieth-century computer age on Earth. Gejalik and her companions benefitted from technological advancements in any number of areas that were still years in the future from our perspective. If our circumstances had brought us to this era, the task I faced would have been far easier to accomplish."

Keeping his attention divided between his first officer and the rest of the expansive loft, Kirk said, "The Certoss certainly managed well enough." With his free hand, he loosened the necktie he wore as part of the contemporary ensemble and unbuttoned the top button of his white dress shirt. Like Spock, he wore a dark suit, though the Vulcan's outfit included a matching fedora to hide his rather nonhuman ears. Gesturing with his phaser to Spock's tricorder, he asked, "Any sign of Adlar?"

The science officer shook his head. "Negative, though with his personal cloaking shield, he could be masking his life signs."

"Miss Lincoln said he'd be here." Kirk did not know how Roberta Lincoln had come to know that Adlar, the fourth and only surviving member of the quartet of Certoss operatives, would be at this precise point and location in time, but given the resources at her disposal, he was inclined to trust her guidance. She was not here, having briefed Kirk and Spock on their role in helping her address two issues occurring almost at the same time on this date in 1969. Lincoln had offered no details about the other situation, while entrusting the *Enterprise* officers to capture Adlar with the goal of reuniting him with Gejalik. Like her, Adlar would be an outcast from his own people in the current timeline, but Minister Ocherab already had pledged to take both wayward soldiers into her charge and see to it that they were given a fair opportunity at assimilating into a culture that would be both familiar and alien to them. Kirk did not envy them the road they would have to travel, but it was better than remaining here, trapped on Earth and centuries removed from anything resembling "home."

It'd be nice not having to worry about the whole "changing our history" bit, too. Indeed, it was not lost on Kirk that today was the same day in Earth history to which the *Enterprise* had accidentally been hurled through time, where they had met Captain John Christopher and very nearly erased their own future. They had been very lucky to have left behind the twentieth century without inflicting any major changes to the timeline. The longer he and Spock continued to traipse around in Earth's past while attempting to help Lincoln straighten out the entire Certoss affair, the more Kirk's concern grew over any possible impacts their presence here might have on history. Neither man needed any reminding of the danger they posed. The slightest action could have unforeseen yet wide-ranging effects on the future, and his anxiety would not ease until they were finished here and returned back to their own time.

"Captain," Spock said, pointing to one of the banks of

control indicators and switches. One of the alert lights was blinking a bright yellow. "According to my scans, this is linked to a series of motion detectors positioned around the building."

Kirk frowned. "An intruder alert system?"

"It would seem so." Spock adjusted one of his tricorder's controls. "Its activation has affected a few of the other components and processes. There is now a form of dampening field in operation around the building, though at present I am uncertain as to its purpose." He paused, then looked to Kirk. "I've also detected the initiation of what I believe to be a countdown protocol."

A knot of unease formed in Kirk's gut. "Countdown?"

Before Spock could respond, movement above them caught Kirk's attention and his instincts told him to move. Lunging for cover, he threw himself over the console as a burst of energy struck the wooden floorboards where he had been standing. Kirk rolled through the dive and came up on one knee, aiming his phaser at where he thought the shooter should be, and saw a dark figure, bald with copper skin and dressed in a black bodysuit, sprinting along a catwalk spanning the length of the loft along its far wall: Adlar.

"Spock! Up there!" Though he leveled his phaser at their retreating opponent, Kirk held his fire.

"Captain," Spock called out, emerging from where he had taken cover near a pair of tape drive units, "we must evacuate this building. I've tracked the countdown timer and it's connected to a series of explosives distributed throughout the loft. The Certoss obviously anticipated being discovered or captured."

It's always something, Kirk groused. "How much time do we have?"

"Two minutes, forty seconds."

"Adlar!" Kirk shouted. "You don't have to do this! We're not here to hurt you!"

He did not see to where the Certoss had run. Where did the catwalk lead? "Spock, how many exits are there out of here?"

"Five," the Vulcan replied, moving from the tape drives, "though none of them are reachable without descending to the main floor."

He has to get past us.

Kirk eyed a set of spiral stairs leading up to the catwalk and ran for them, but he only managed two steps before a shadow moved above him and another energy blast screamed past his left shoulder. Without thinking he raised his phaser and fired, the compact weapon's blue beam streaking into the loft's rafters. The sounds of scampering footsteps echoed from the catwalk at the same time Spock aimed his own phaser and fired at something Kirk could not see.

"Two minutes, twenty seconds," the Vulcan called out as he moved across the open floor toward Kirk.

Trying to peer into the loft's depths, Kirk shouted, "Adlar! We're here to help you! We have Gejalik, and she's safe!"

"Liar!" a voice boomed from the shadows. Kirk saw the Certoss move once more into position to shoot, and he and Spock ducked as another energy bolt came at them and chewed into the floorboards. Kirk flinched as small bits of debris peppered his back and stung his neck.

"Damn it," he hissed, his frustration mounting. "We don't have time for this." To Adlar, he called out, "It doesn't have to be this way! I know you were only carrying out your orders, but they don't mean anything anymore! The temporal war is over, and our two planets are allies. We can take you to

Gejalik, and both of you can return home." At the far end of the loft, he saw the Certoss running across a section of catwalk that crossed the room's width, and without thinking he charged up the stairs in pursuit. Adlar saw him and fired his own weapon, forcing Kirk to crouch for cover on the wrought iron stairs as the energy bolt sailed over his head.

Another shot aimed in his direction passed under his arm, and Kirk flung himself up the remaining stairs and onto the catwalk. Adlar was thirty meters ahead of him and dashing down the walkway, and Kirk realized that if he made it to the stairs at the far end he would be able to get back to the main floor and out the loft's front door. Raising his phaser, Kirk aimed at the Certoss agent's retreating back and fired just as Adlar reached the stairs and began descending. The phaser beam struck a glancing blow across his left shoulder, the partial hit insufficient to incapacitate him but enough to send him stumbling down the stairs to the landing at their halfway point. Still conscious, he already was moving to regain his feet.

"Adlar, wait!" Kirk shouted, running the length of the catwalk. "Please listen to me!" He reached the stairs in seconds only to see the Certoss poised on one knee and raising his weapon, and Kirk realized he had nowhere to hide.

"You won't take me alive, human."

Another phaser beam struck him in the chest.

Grunting more in surprise than pain, Adlar slumped against the wooden railing before collapsing once more to the landing. Footsteps on the stairs preceded Spock moving into view, his phaser trained on the unconscious Certoss.

"Nice timing," Kirk said, descending the stairs toward Adlar.

The Vulcan pocketed his phaser before reaching to pull

the insensate alien to his feet. "Captain, may I remind you that we must depart these premises with all due haste?"

"I know." Kirk reached into his jacket pocket to retrieve the servo Roberta Lincoln had provided him, setting the device to send out the emergency recall signal which would summon the Beta 5 and provide the means for transporting them back to her and Gary Seven's office in New York. The unit only emitted a short, abrupt buzz. Frowning, Kirk repeated the attempt and received the same result. "It's not working."

Shifting Adlar in order to lift him and rest him on his shoulder, Spock said, "The dampening field. It must be hampering our communications."

Why can't these things ever be easy?

"Let's get the hell out of here." Kirk did not even bother asking how much time remained until the activation of whatever protocol their presence had triggered, figuring the answer would be evident all too soon. With Spock carrying Adlar and leading the way, they ran from the loft and down the stairs to the street entrance. Ticking off seconds in his head, Kirk reached thirty-seven before they burst through the doors and into the alley from which they had entered the building.

"This way," he said, pulling on Spock's arm and directing him up the alley. The buildings here were constructed in close proximity, and he did not want to be caught between them when the explosives went off. How much damage would the charges cause? Enough to destroy the equipment cache and anything else stored there, but what else? The entire building? Kirk hoped the Certoss agents had exercised more prudence.

They reached the mouth of the alley at the rear of the buildings when Kirk heard the telltale, muffled thumps of the first detonations. He pushed Spock against the neighboring building's brick wall as he heard glass, brick, and other debris rain down into the alley behind them.

"That was a little too close." Glancing around the corner, he saw smoke and the first signs of fire in the second-floor windows as other, smaller explosions echoed from inside the structure. From what he could tell, the building itself did not look to be in danger of immediate collapse, but fire damage might well exacerbate that situation if left unchecked. He heard a shrill ringing from that direction. An alarm of some sort, warning others of the fire danger? Kirk was grateful that there seemed to be no innocent bystanders caught up in the chaos, though that did not discount the possibility of witnesses in any of the adjacent buildings.

"Captain, we should depart." Spock still carried the unconscious Adlar over his shoulder and showed no signs of exertion. "Emergency responders will be coming in short order."

Nodding, Kirk produced his servo. "Amen to that." He released a sigh, realizing for the first time just how very long this day had been, at least from his and Spock's viewpoint. Darting from New York to Ohio to Florida and finally here to New Jersey, crossing not only space but time as well? When had this whole mess begun in the *Enterprise* cargo bay? Nearly twenty-four hours ago?

And three hundred years.

Looking around to ensure they were not being observed, he activated the device and this time it emitted the expected short, melodic tone before a cloud of blue-black fog appeared at the mouth of the alley. "I just hope Miss Lincoln has an easier time with her part of this crazy plan."

THIRTY-SIX

Offutt Air Force Base, Near Omaha, Nebraska
July 10, 1969

A knock on his office door made James Wainwright look up from the manila folder and the photographs lying atop his desk. Straightening the pictures and returning them to the folder, he called out, "Come in."

The door opened, and a staff sergeant, dressed in the uniform and accoutrements of the base military police, poked his head into the room. "Mister Wainwright? He's awake, sir."

Finally. Wainwright had not counted on the pilot succumbing to illness after returning from his mission. Was it possible his encounter was the cause of whatever had befallen him? That would be yet another question he would have to ask. "Is he okay?"

"A little disoriented," replied the sergeant, "and he says he has a headache. I've already sent for a medic, and they're bringing him some water."

Wainwright rose from his desk, reaching for the suit jacket slung across the back of his chair. He dismissed the guard as he pulled on the jacket, noting that it felt snug across his shoulders, and pushed against the muzzle of the .45 pistol in its holster under his left arm. Had the suit shrunk?

Keep telling yourself that. Though still fit for a man nearing his fifty-second birthday, Wainwright knew that his deskbound lifestyle was beginning to take its toll on him. His thrice-weekly visits to pound the bag at the base gymnasium were only keeping the "middle age spread" at bay. He knew that he needed to increase the frequency and duration of those workouts, but even boxing was losing its ability to provide any respite from his work, which had become little more than an elaborate means of counting off the days until . . .

Until what, exactly?

The previous summer's incident at McKinley Rocket Base had been enough to trigger a drastic curtailing of Blue Book's profile. Though Wainwright and Allison Marshall had been detailed to MJ-12 and acting on their orders, they remained visible members of the project and therefore were not immune to consequences for real or perceived failure. Marshall had opted to transfer from the project, returning to the active service ranks and accepting a new assignment at MacDill Air Force Base in Tampa, Florida. She and Wainwright had been planning marriage prior to her new orders, though Wainwright had suggested waiting until his own retirement was official. The paperwork already was winding its way through the system with little to no resistance from his superiors, who seemed thankful that he had chosen to leave without raising too much fuss. For his part, Wainwright was ready to close this long, odd chapter of his life, but pride prevented him from accepting his fate and waiting for the clock to run out.

And that means doing this one last thing.

For a year, Wainwright had suffered in silence as Offutt's Blue Book liaison officer, filing and following up on investigations conducted by other officers assigned to an organization that was in constant flux, with ever-reduced personnel, resources, and funding. Project Blue Book had become all but a cruel punch line for those who possessed no clue as to the reality that Wainwright, Marshall, and others had faced all these years. With his days numbered, Wainwright knew that his one final chance at convincing his superiors to listen might well rest in the hands of one man: Captain John Christopher.

Retrieving the folder and its photographs from his desk, Wainwright made his way from his office to the elevator that would take him to see his guest. He inserted his key into the lock controlling access to the elevator before riding the car to the building's lowermost level. The doors opened to reveal a long, narrow hallway painted in the same shade of depressing flat gray that was synonymous with the military establishment—a color he had come to loathe, as it seemed a perfect symbol of the plain and uninspired mindset that had gripped his superiors in recent years.

Another key unlocked the door at the end of the hallway, and Wainwright pulled it open to reveal a bare, cinderblock room. A cot served as the room's sole furnishing, with a single bulb suspended within a protective wire cage to provide illumination. For the first time, Wainwright realized the room looked perhaps too much like a prison cell, and regretted the choice to have his guest placed here.

None of that matters. Get on with it.

As for the room's sole occupant, he stood, still dressed in the orange flight suit he had been wearing after leaving the flight line. In his mid-thirties, according to his file, the pilot had black hair and blue, piercing eyes that bored into Wainwright as he closed the door behind him.

"Where the hell am I?" asked Captain John Christopher, wasting no time.

Wainwright replied, "Hello, Captain. I'm told you weren't feeling well when you woke up. Are you better now?"

"Never mind that," Christopher snapped. "Answer my question. I don't recognize this place."

"You're on the base," Wainwright said. "I apologize for the confusion. You passed out before I had a chance to talk to you on the flight line. It was believed you might be suffering from some aftereffects of your last mission, so you were brought here for observation. Where we are really isn't so important as why you were brought here."

His eyes narrowing, Christopher crossed his arms. "Fair enough. That was my next question."

Wainwright paused, swallowing. His throat had gone dry. Why was this so difficult? He had done this countless times before, so what was his problem now? He reached up to wipe at the side of his face and noted the bead of perspiration on his fingers. There also was a slight tremble in his hand, which he stopped by making a fist and holding it at his side.

"My name is Wainwright, Captain. James Wainwright, and you're here because I believe you have information I need."

Christopher frowned. "What kind of information?"

Instead of replying, Wainwright opened the folder he had been carrying and withdrew one of the photographs it contained. It was a grainy, dark image dominated by deep black, with an arcing white line representing the curve of the Earth as seen in pictures captured by satellites and astronauts during manned space missions over the last decade. Watching Christopher, Wainwright saw the precise instant when the pilot recognized the other object depicted in the photo as it floated above Earth, saying nothing as the man's eyes traced over the large saucer shape and its three cylindrical projections just as Christopher had described them from the seat of his plane: two above the saucer and one below it.

"Oh, my God."

Wainwright said, "This photograph was taken last year by a military reconnaissance satellite. The object was discovered in high orbit."

"Last year?" Christopher frowned, his eyes moving between Wainwright and the photograph. "It's the same thing I saw just this morning."

"So I gathered from your cockpit transmissions," Wainwright said, offering Christopher the picture. "Captain, I need to know everything you can tell me about what you saw up there." It was interesting to see how the photograph and questions seemed to make the pilot relax to a degree.

Shrugging as he continued to study the picture, Christopher said, "There's not much to tell, really. Air Defense Command tasked me to intercept an unidentified craft over the base. I got to the designated coordinates and there it was, high in the clouds and climbing away fast. At first I thought it was sunlight reflecting off my canopy. I only saw it for a second or two, and then it was just . . . gone."

Wainwright pointed to the picture in Christopher's hands. "But you're sure what you saw was the object in this picture?"

Though he paused as if considering his answer, when the captain looked up from the photo, it was with a new confidence. "Yes, I'm sure of it," he said without a trace of doubt. "What is it? Some kind of Russian rocket?" Then his eyes widened. "Wait a minute. Are they making a last push for the moon? They're not going to beat us, are they? Not when we're this close?"

"No, Captain. The Russians are nowhere near being ready to launch anything to the moon. Barring anything unexpected, our guys will be on their way by this time next week." As they stood here, the *Apollo 11* astronauts, as well as their ground and support crews at Cape Canaveral, along with thousands more people in Houston, Texas, and at other locations around the world, were in the final stages of preparing for the launch scheduled to take place in six days' time. "Not that it matters." He nodded toward the picture. "We don't believe it's Russian."

Offering the photograph back to Wainwright, Christopher asked, "So what, then?"

"We don't know," Wainwright said. "What we do know is that it's not the first time it's been here. Remember that rocket NASA launched last year? The one that blew up?"

Christopher nodded. "Yes, I remember. It was on the news, and I read about it in a few papers and magazines, including a couple of NASA journals."

"Well, what you don't know is that the rocket was carrying a nuclear weapons platform; the most sophisticated piece of weaponry in our arsenal." Once more, he held up the folder. "We believe this thing, whatever it was, destroyed that rocket and damn near started World War III in the process. And now it's back, just as we're getting ready for the most ambitious manned space flight in our history. Don't you see what's happening?"

For the first time, Christopher took a step back, as though wanting to put some space between himself and Wainwright. "You're with that UFO project. Blue Book, aren't you?"

He paused, studying Christopher's face and seeing the uncertainty in the other man's eyes. No doubt the captain was wondering whether what he was hearing was the product of memory or imagination, and perhaps even was asking himself if he was listening to the deluded ramblings of someone who was in the process of losing his grip on sanity.

"Captain, I believe you saw something up there you can't identify, but you trust your own eyes, don't you?" Wainwright held up the folder and its photographs. "This is what you saw, isn't it?"

"You think an alien spaceship is here to disrupt the moon landing?" Christopher frowned. "What will that accomplish?"

Waving the folder, Wainwright snapped, "Can't you see? They want to slap us down, keep us pinned to our own planet. That way, we're all right here when they come to take us over. They can't wait ten or fifteen years to make their move. By then we'll have space stations and a base on the moon. They're striking now, before we have a chance to learn how to defend ourselves against them." He had no proof of this, of course. All he knew was that the Certoss had pledged to destroy Earth by any means necessary. The mysterious ship photographed in orbit the previous year—the same craft Christopher had described during his intercept mission—could be a Certoss vessel, and if that was the case the world might well have arrived at the eve of invasion.

"This is unbelievable." Christopher looked around the room, and Wainwright saw that the captain's attention was not just on him but also the door leading from the room. Was he contemplating escape?

"You're talking movie stuff," he said. "Martians and mind control and taking over the world. It's ridiculous! There's no such thing as little green men." Then he stopped, as though forgetting his next words. His expression slackened and he blinked several times, as though trying to call forth a memory stubbornly refusing to reveal itself.

"What?" Wainwright asked, stepping closer. "Something's bothering you. I can see it in your eyes. What is it?"

Reaching up to rub his forehead, Christopher grimaced. "No. I . . . I was there," he said, his voice little more than a whisper. "On the ship. They brought me aboard, destroyed my plane." Confusion clouded his face and he shook his head. "But, that's impossible, isn't it? There was no time for that to happen. I only saw it for a second, but I was *there*. I can see a man . . . was it a man? He had weird, pointed ears."

Now it was Wainwright's turn to be surprised. "Pointed ears? Are you sure?"

Christopher nodded. "Yes."

This was unexpected. Had the Vulcans returned? Were they continuing their covert observations of Earth? If that was true, then perhaps the ship in the photograph was not an actual threat. There was no way for Wainwright to know, not without the assistance of someone who could provide the required insight. Mestral might know, but he had not been heard from for more than a year. For all Wainwright knew, the Vulcan was dead.

"You know something about this," Christopher said, his gaze hardening. "I can read faces, too, Mister Wainwright, and I can see that you know something. Who are these people? Where do they come from?" Instead of waiting for an answer, he now started moving about the room as though working to organize his thoughts. "I don't understand why I can't remember everything, but there are still bits and pieces. It's all a jumble." He held up a hand, as though waving away his uncertainty. "I have to report this; tell them what I saw."

Wainwright replied, "Yes. We have to get this information out, warn people that there's an alien ship up there waiting for God knows what."

"My superiors will inform the joint chiefs," Christopher said. "The president will take action, maybe delay the launch until they can figure out what's going on."

"The president?" It took all Wainwright's self-control not to burst out laughing. "Captain, this country is preparing to send three men to the moon. They know about that ship just like we do, but they can't afford to acknowledge it. Putting a man on the moon is a political imperative. There's no way they'll risk screwing that up, even if it costs the lives of three brave men and the work of thousands of other people."

He stepped forward, holding out the folder. "But, we don't have to let that happen. We can take this to the newspeople, get it on television. The government won't have the chance to bury it. They'll have to delay the launch and deal with the problem."

Disbelief clouded Christopher's features. "I can't do that. My superiors already know I saw something. I have a duty to report what I know."

"No!" Wainwright barked, shaking the folder in his hand, and all but waving it under the captain's nose. "All these years we've spent trying to get them to understand, to accept the truth and deal with it, but they've ignored us! Now they're shutting it all down and throwing it away, and me along with it. This could be my last chance to prove to them how wrong they've been. You're not going to take that away from me."

"I've had enough of this," Christopher said, stepping away from him and moving toward the door. "I'm going to go report. Somebody has to be wondering where the hell I am, anyway."

Wainwright drew his pistol and cocked its trigger, which was loud enough in the small room to make the pilot stop in his tracks. "I can't let you do that, Captain."

Eyeing the weapon's muzzle, Christopher said, "Shooting me won't help."

"I don't plan to shoot you unless you force me to," Wainwright countered. He hated that the situation had deteriorated to this point, but the captain was leaving him no choice. Going to his superiors would all but guarantee that both of them would be hushed until after the launch, and by then it could be too late.

Christopher made no attempt to hide his astonishment. "You can't be serious. All this time, you say you've been working to protect us all from supposed alien threats, and now that you've got someone to help corroborate your story, you're going around them just so that you can prove to them how right you've been all these years? Don't you realize how pathetic that sounds? Where's your honor or duty?"

"Gone, along with my marriage and my son and the rest of my life," Wainwright said. The Air Force owed him quite a lot, he had decided, and it was long past time for them to settle their bill. "You'll get to tell your story, Captain, but we're going to do it my way." Using the pistol, he motioned for Christopher to move to the door. "Let's go." The pilot reached the door and opened it just enough to look out into the gray, empty corridor. He paused, and Wainwright placed the muzzle of the pistol between his shoulder blades. "Move, please."

"Fine," Christopher said. Then he yanked the door open, and Wainwright realized he was standing too close. The door's edge caught him across his face and he winced in pain as he reached for his nose. Christopher turned and swung at him, the punch connecting with the side of his head and forcing Wainwright to his knees. His lost his grip on the pistol and he felt it slide from his fingers before it went clattering across the floor. His vision blurred and filled with spots, and he heard Christopher's heavy boots running down the corridor.

Wainwright staggered to his feet and set off in pursuit, lurching into the hallway in time to see Christopher sprinting toward the elevator. "Stop!" he shouted, bringing up the pistol. The first shot echoed in the corridor but Wainwright missed. His aim was better when he fired a second time, watching as Christopher's body jerked before he stumbled and fell to the floor. Blood already was staining the left shoulder of the pilot's orange flight suit. Rolling onto his side, Christopher pressed his right hand to his wounded shoulder, and Wainwright could see the blood seeping through his fingers.

Holding his free hand to his nose and feeling wetness coming from it, Wainwright jogged up the corridor, aiming his pistol at Christopher. "I'm sorry." He had not wanted things to go this way; had not wanted to make the pilot his enemy. Christopher was supposed to be his ally in this. "I didn't want to hurt you."

"Well, good job with that," Christopher said, hissing the words through gritted teeth. "I'm sure the TV stations will love how you shot me so I'd go along with you."

"It doesn't look too serious," Wainwright said, kneeling close enough to inspect Christopher's wound. He extended his hand. "Come on. I'll take you to a medic."

Wincing, the pilot asked, "Before or after I help you?"

Even as Wainwright began to reply, both men turned at the sound of a single bell tone from the elevator just as the doors parted to reveal a young blond woman. At first Wainwright scowled, not recognizing her as anyone who even should have access to the building, then he paused as something triggered in his memory. She seemed familiar, somehow, but from where?

"Who the hell are you?" he snapped.

The woman smiled. "A friend you don't remember."

THIRTY-SEVEN

U.S.S. Enterprise
Earth Year 2268

On the transporter room's viewscreen, Minister Ocherab, flanked by Gejalik and Adlar, clasped her hands in what Kirk now recognized as a Certoss friendship gesture.

"*We are in your debt, Captain. Thank you, for everything.*"

Kirk smiled. "On behalf of my crew, Minister, it was our pleasure. Gejalik and Adlar, I wish you the best of luck. I think you're going to love what your world has become."

Looking first to Adlar, who nodded, Gejalik replied, "*Thank you, Captain. We look forward to seeing it for ourselves. Like Minister Ocherab, we too are in your debt.*"

"Safe travels," Kirk said. "*Enterprise* out." The image on the screen shifted to show the *Balatir* arcing away before it disappeared into subspace.

"Another day, another crisis averted," said McCoy from where he stood in front of the transporter console.

"I quit counting." Kirk looked to where Roberta Lincoln stood with Mestral on the transporter pad, with Spock standing near the steps leading to the raised platform. Mestral once more was dressed in the 1960s-era clothes he had been wearing upon his and Gejalik's arrival aboard the *Enterprise*.

"They're not the only ones in your debt," Lincoln said, smiling. "I'll never be able to thank you enough for everything you did to help me. I'm sorry I even had to ask, but sometimes a girl on her own needs help from people she can trust."

"You and me both, sister," McCoy said, grunting in agreement.

Kirk asked, "So, everything's where it's supposed to be? The Certoss are still a peaceful people, and the Tandarans are satisfied that will remain the case. Earth was never destroyed by an advanced alien race from the future, and neither did it head out to destroy other worlds once it gained the technology to do so."

"Not bad for a day's work, if you ask me," McCoy said.

There still were some issues to smooth over, Kirk knew. The encounter with the Tandarans and their attack on a Federation vessel would keep the diplomatic cadres of both governments working overtime for the next few weeks, but Kirk already planned to submit a report he hoped would offer mitigating explanations on the Tandarans' behalf. It was not hard to understand the situation they believed they were facing, incredible as that scenario might seem.

Great, Kirk mused. *More paperwork.*

"What about Wainwright?" he asked.

Lincoln replied, "I'll keep an eye on him, but I doubt he'll be any trouble. I'd just as soon leave him in peace. He's certainly earned that much."

McCoy asked, "Can you tell us what happened with Project Blue Book and Majestic 12?"

"Blue Book was ended in 1969," Lincoln replied. "Officially, anyway. There were still a few activities that carried into the 1970s, but the United States government never acknowledged that. Some records were declassified and made available to the public as years passed, but it continued to generate controversy and conspiracy theories because of what *wasn't* released."

"Such beliefs persisted well into the twenty-first century," Spock said, "with many people remaining convinced that the government was keeping information about extraterrestrials from the public."

Lincoln shrugged. "They were right, of course. As for Majestic 12, since it was always Blue Book's classified cousin, not much is known about them or their activities. UFO fanatics believed the organization continued in some capacity for decades. I tried to do some digging on this, myself, but they covered their tracks very, very well."

Spock said, "There is almost no documentation about them in the data banks. Either such files were deliberately destroyed by the group to maintain its secrecy, or they simply didn't survive through that period during the twenty-first century when so many records were lost."

"Probably not the worst thing that could happen." Lincoln shrugged. "For my money, the public was better off not knowing how close they came to being destroyed on however many occasions, not just by their own governments but because of interference from outside forces." When she paused, Kirk saw that she seemed lost in thought for a moment. Then, she sighed. "Sometimes I think I'd have been better off not knowing, but what are you going to do? When I think about how I got involved in all of this, it really was my own fault, you know?" That seemed to raise her spirits, and she even laughed a bit. Turning to Mestral, she bobbed her eyebrows. "All right, let's get this show on the road."

"I am grateful to you for allowing me to return to Earth, Miss Lincoln." He nodded to Kirk. "And to you, Captain."

"Earth?" McCoy asked, frowning. "Not Vulcan?"

Mestral replied, "It is my desire to continue my observations of Earth and humanity, Doctor. The time period I left was something of a turning point in your history, and I wish to be on hand to see what happens next."

"What if you're discovered?" McCoy asked. "Won't that affect our history, too?"

Lincoln said, "We'll be keeping tabs on Mister Mestral as well, Doctor. Besides, how do you know his being on Earth doesn't prove beneficial to our history in some way?" She said nothing else, leaving the cryptic question to hang in the air as she retrieved her servo from a pocket. She keyed the device, and a blue-black fog appeared at the rear of the transporter chamber.

"Thank you for your help, Roberta," Kirk said. "And to you, Mestral."

Spock offered a traditional Vulcan salute. "Peace and long life, Mestral."

Returning the gesture, Mestral replied, "Live long and prosper, Spock, and to you and your crew, Captain Kirk. It pleases me to know that our two peoples become friends and allies. I've always believed that it would be our differences—as much as our similarities—that would bring us together."

"That's one way to put it," McCoy said, grinning at Spock, who responded only by lifting his right eyebrow.

Lincoln led Mestral onto the transporter platform before turning back to Kirk and the others. "It was good seeing you again, Captain."

"Same here, Miss Lincoln," Kirk said. "Feel free to drop in the next time you're in the neighborhood."

"I'll see what I can do." After a final wave, she turned and, followed by Mestral, disappeared into the blue fog before the cloud itself dissolved into nothingness. Only the echo of its energy field remained for a few lingering seconds before it also faded.

"Please tell me I'm not the only one who could use a drink after all this?" McCoy asked. "Not that it really matters, but I really hate drinking alone."

"I may have time for one," Kirk said, "but the big question is whether I want it before or after I write my reports for Starfleet Command."

"Before," McCoy answered, crossing his arms. "And after, the more I think about it. Maybe even during."

"I'm probably asking for too much," Kirk said, "but I really hope our next mission isn't quite so . . . *odd*."

His expression unreadable as always, Spock replied, "Past history would suggest that is highly unlikely."

Kirk grinned. "Point taken."

ONE LAST THING

THIRTY-EIGHT

Yountville, California
November 6, 1996

"Dad? Is it okay if I turn it down a little?"

Turning from the television, Michael Wainwright could not help smiling as he looked over to see his father once again dozing in his favorite recliner. That seemed to happen a lot these days, which Michael knew to expect. The doctors had told him that the elder Wainwright's new prescriptions might make him prone to drowsiness, particularly toward the later part of the day and when coupled with his father's propensity for being an early riser. That odd habit had resurrected itself after being absent for many years, but now James Wainwright awoke promptly at five thirty each morning, often without the aid of an alarm clock, and was dressed and sitting in his recliner by the time the nurse came around to dispense the day's first rounds of medications. Michael remembered a similar morning routine from his early childhood, when his father would be up, groomed, and in his Air Force uniform reading the paper by the time he and his mother came down the stairs for breakfast.

His father had eschewed the practice during the early years of his retirement. It was not until he came to live here at the veterans home in Yountville, an hour's drive from Michael's home outside Sacramento, and after the onset of

Alzheimer's disease, that the occasional yet increasing reversion to past habits and memories began to assert itself. The doctors had cautioned Michael that such behavior was normal, and that he should be prepared for references or statements that on their face might make no sense, while still holding meaning for his father. It was not uncommon to hear him call out a name Michael did not recognize, or to make reference to something he had done during the war or some other period of his long military career. Most of the references were cryptic, and later forgotten when his father managed for a while to escape the delusions. It was this aspect of his condition that was the most frustrating, as there were days when he displayed total clarity, with no demonstrable signs of the disease that—although still diagnosed as being in an early stage—was waging slow, inexorable war upon his mind. He and Michael could be having a normal conversation one afternoon, but his father would have no memory of the meeting on Michael's visit the next day. So far, there had been only one occasion that the elder Wainwright failed to recognize his son, an event that had so shaken Michael that he sat in his car for an hour, crying in the home's parking lot.

Pushing aside that unpleasant thought, Michael rose from the couch and reached across his father for the remote control sitting on the recliner's far armrest. He used the unit to reduce the television's volume so that he could only just hear the voice of the late evening news anchor talking over the sound of his father's soft snoring. As Michael suspected, the change in the room's background noise was sufficient to rouse his father, who grunted and twitched before jerking his head upright. His eyes were red-rimmed and heavy, and he looked around the room in a daze for several seconds.

"Mikey?"

"Hey, Dad." One month after his fiftieth birthday, and his father had reverted to calling him "Mikey" as he had years and years earlier. "You okay? If you're tired, I can help you get ready for bed."

Shaking his head, Wainwright replied, "Nah, that's okay. The night nurse always helps me, and she's better-looking than you are."

Michael chuckled at that, heartened to hear a hint of his father's old sense of humor. He seemed to be feeling better after his brief nap. "Are you hungry? Want something to eat or drink? I was thinking I'd run to the cafeteria for a cup of coffee for the road. I need to be heading back." With the drive back to Sacramento, he would not make it to bed until after midnight, and he had to be at work at seven the next morning for a conference call with his company's New York office.

Again, his father declined. "Allison always brings me coffee."

"Allison?" Michael asked, forcing himself not to react any further to the reference. "Don't you mean Stephanie?"

Instead of answering, Wainwright paused, casting his gaze toward the television before looking around the room. After a moment, he said, "Yeah, Stephanie." He sighed. "Allison. I miss her."

"I know, Dad," Michael said, his voice low. "I know."

His father and Allison Marshall had been friends and professional partners during their joint time in the Air Force, becoming lovers at some point after his and Mom's divorce. Allison had remained at his side even during the brief period Wainwright spent in a military hospital while suffering from a form of post-traumatic stress. The condition had been brought about as a consequence of something that had happened during his time in the service, much of which, so far as Michael knew, remained classified. Upon his release from the hospital in 1972 and the final severing of his government ties, he and Allison had married and moved to California in order to be near Michael and his wife, Emily, and their three daughters, where he proceeded to work on being nothing more than a perfect, doting grandfather. It was not until Michael's youngest child, Michelle, had graduated high school that Allison became ill, passing away less than a year later after a brief, harsh battle with cancer. Two years after that, Wainwright began exhibiting early Alzheimer's symptoms. Everything had happened so fast, it seemed, though Michael was thankful for the years his father had been able to enjoy following the long period of his life that remained cloaked in secrecy.

Stifling a yawn, Michael rose from the couch and stretched the muscles in his back. "Okay, Dad, I should get going. Emily doesn't like it when I'm driving late." Though his wife understood his desire to spend time with his father, she often expressed worry that he would fall asleep during the drive home after one of his regular weeknight visits. "Are you sure I can't get you anything before . . ."

Wainwright's attention was fixated on the television. He even had lowered his recliner's footrest and now was leaning forward in the chair as though trying to get closer to the screen, his eyes widening as he stared at the image it displayed. Turning to see what had so riveted his father, Michael caught just a few seconds of what looked to be an airplane flying low—*very* low—over a nighttime city skyline. A red banner stretching across the bottom of the screen highlighted the caption "AMATEUR VIDEO."

"Turn it up," Wainwright said, pointing at the television. "*Turn it up.*"

Michael fumbled for the remote control and aimed it at

the TV to increase its volume as a different news anchor, one he didn't recognize, appeared on the screen before a reduced version of the footage that had just aired, now playing on a repeating loop as the man spoke into the camera.

"*. . . an hour ago by a man using his camcorder to tape a backyard barbecue. The massive unidentifiable object does not appear to be a meteorite, weather balloon, or satellite, and one aviation expert we've spoken to has stated that it's definitely not any kind of U.S. aircraft currently in use. We're awaiting investigation by local authorities, and we'll keep you updated as news develops on this incredible story.*"

"Wow," Michael said, impressed with what he had just seen. "I've never seen anything like that before. What about you?" When his father did not respond, Michael turned and saw that Wainwright no longer was looking at the television but rather seemed to be staring into space.

"Saucer. Three cylindrical projections. It's not Russian. Nothing like it."

Frowning, Michael stepped closer. "Dad? Are you okay?" He considered alerting Stephanie, the nurse on duty tonight in this wing of the home's assisted-living facility, but held off when it appeared his father might once more be settling down. His features seemed to relax, and he leaned back in the recliner. The only vestige of his abrupt change in demeanor was his expression, one of intense concentration as though he was struggling to recall some long-lost memory. After a few more seconds his features softened and he blinked several times before looking up at Michael and offering him a quizzical look.

"Michael? It's getting late. Shouldn't you be heading home?" Wainwright looked around before his gaze settled on the small clock sitting on the table next to his chair. "I should probably get to bed, too," he said, then grinned. "Send Stephanie in here to tuck me in, would you?"

"Sure, Dad," Michael said, chuckling again. "Whatever you say. You sure you're all right?" He gestured toward the television. "You were acting like you'd seen that flying whatever it was before. Was it a UFO?" Though his father discussed his time in the military only on rare occasions, Michael was aware of his work for the Air Force's mysterious Project Blue Book back in the 1960s. The only thing Michael knew about the project was that it was part of a government effort to determine whether flying saucers and beings from other worlds were real. He could not recall his father ever talking about that part of his service career.

Wainwright shook his head, all indications of his earlier agitation now gone. "No. Just in the movies. Those things aren't real," he said, but Michael was certain he still heard a hint of doubt in his father's voice.

"Those things aren't real."

ACKNOWLEDGMENTS

Thanks very much to my editors, for taking a chance on this rather odd book. It's been something of a "passion project" for many years, and I'm grateful that I finally got to get it out of my head.

I'd always wanted to tell a story in a vein similar to what Greg Cox accomplished in *The Eugenics Wars: The Rise and Fall of Khan Noonien Singh,* with its blending of real history and "*Star Trek* history." They are among my very favorite *Star Trek* novels, and I'm grateful that Greg gave me his blessing to try my hand at a story that sort of dovetails with his books.

Thanks also are due to Christopher L. Bennett, for his Department of Temporal Investigations novel *Forgotten History,* as well as Ben Guilfoy for his short story "Mestral," from the *Star Trek: Strange New Worlds 9* anthology. Though I first conceived of this book years ago, I tailored a few aspects of the story so as to remain consistent with what Christopher and Ben subsequently established in their tales. Any mistakes or oversights in this regard are mine alone.

As one might imagine, I conducted a bit of research into the "UFO phenomenon." These three books deserve special mention for the assistance and inspiration they provided: *Flying Saucers: The Startling Evidence of the Invasion From Outer Space,* by Coral E. Lorenzen; *The Case for the UFO,* by M. K. Jessup; and *Project Blue Book,* by Brad Steiger.

Finally, I tip my hat to the following episodes and their writers for their contributions to *Star Trek* lore, as they provided various points of "continuity departure" throughout this novel:

Star Trek "Tomorrow Is Yesterday," written by D. C. Fontana;

Star Trek "Assignment: Earth," teleplay by Art Wallace and story by Gene Roddenberry and Art Wallace;

Star Trek: Deep Space Nine "Little Green Men," teleplay by Ira Steven Behr & Robert Hewitt Wolfe; story by Toni Mayberry & Jack Treviño;

Star Trek: Voyager "Future's End, Parts 1 & 2," written by Brannon Braga & Joe Menosky;

Star Trek: Enterprise "Detained," teleplay by Mike Sussman & Phyllis Strong; story by Rick Berman & Brannon Braga;

Star Trek: Enterprise "Carbon Creek," teleplay by Chris Black; story by Rick Berman & Brannon Braga & Dan O'Shannon.

One last thing: I decided to set "McKinley Rocket Base" in Florida, based on the map we see Gary Seven studying in "Assignment: Earth." Not wanting the base to take the place of Cape Canaveral in "*Star Trek* land," I instead placed it more or less in the vicinity of what in the real world is Patrick Air Force Base, an actual installation in close proximity to the Kennedy Space Center. It's a bit of a hat tip to *I Dream of Jeannie,* which was set in and around Cocoa Beach and the Cape. Patrick was never named in that series, but it's the Air Force base closest to Cocoa Beach. So, there.

ABOUT THE AUTHOR

Dayton Ward has been modified to fit this medium, to write in the space allotted, and has been edited for content. Reader discretion is advised.

Visit Dayton on the web at
www.daytonward.com